DEEP SHADOWS

Center Point
Large Print

Also by Vannetta Chapman and available from Center Point Large Print:

Murder Freshly Baked
Anna's Healing

**This Large Print Book carries the
Seal of Approval of N.A.V.H.**

DEEP SHADOWS

Vannetta Chapman

CENTER POINT LARGE PRINT
THORNDIKE, MAINE

This Center Point Large Print edition is published in the year 2017 by arrangement with Harvest House Publishers.

Copyright © 2016 by Vannetta Chapman.

All rights reserved.

Scripture quotations are taken from
The Holy Bible, New International Version®, NIV®.
Copyright © 1973, 1978, 1984, 2011 by Biblica, Inc.® Used by permission. All rights reserved worldwide.

The ESV® Bible (The Holy Bible, English Standard Version®), copyright © 2001 by Crossway, a publishing ministry of Good News Publishers. Used by permission. All rights reserved.

The text of this Large Print edition is unabridged. In other aspects, this book may vary from the original edition. Printed in the United States of America on permanent paper. Set in 16-point Times New Roman type.

ISBN: 978-1-68324-238-3

Library of Congress Cataloging-in-Publication Data

Names: Chapman, Vannetta, author.
Title: Deep shadows / Vannetta Chapman.
Description: Center Point Large Print edition. | Thorndike, Maine : Center Point Large Print, 2017.
Identifiers: LCCN 2016044917 | ISBN 9781683242383
   (hardcover : alk. paper)
Subjects: LCSH: Large type books. | GSAFD: Christian fiction.
Classification: LCC PS3603.H3744 D44 2017 | DDC 813/.6—dc23
LC record available at https://lccn.loc.gov/2016044917

For Brenda and George

Acknowledgments

This book is dedicated to Brenda and George Lumpkin. Thank you for enduring my think-out-loud process with this story line. Our shared backyard barbecues sustained me through that difficult first draft. You both provided valuable perspective, not to mention good, solid spiritual guidance. The games of 42 were a bonus. Love you guys.

I'd also like to thank the wonderful staff of Harvest House for allowing me to write something outside of my proverbial box. You took a chance on me, and for that I am quite grateful. You are a dream team to work with, and you deserve an acknowledgment page all your own. Also, I want to express gratitude to my agent, Steve Laube, who was invaluable in the negotiation of this contract.

Thanks to my pre-readers, Kristy and Janet, who combed through every word, searching out my errors. Thanks to Connie and Bill Voigt for the use of your names and for answering my questions. Thank you to Dorsey Sparks for the use of your name as well as your spunky personality.

I would like to express my gratitude to the folks in central Texas who not only answered my questions, but also have provided a lovely place to live. You are *salt of the earth* folks, and I'm proud to call you my neighbors.

Last, I would like to thank you, dear reader, for following me down this path of a different genre. My prayer is that this novel will cause you to look at your life, your neighbor, your town, and your faith with fresh eyes. If you've never been to the Texas hill country, come on down and enjoy some of the most beautiful land God created.

And finally . . . always giving thanks to God the Father for everything, in the name of our Lord Jesus Christ (Ephesians 5:20).

So too, at the present time there is
a remnant chosen by grace.

PAUL'S EPISTLE TO THE ROMANS,
CHAPTER 11, VERSE 5

We are living on the brink
of the apocalypse,
but the world is asleep.

JOEL ROSENBERG

Prelude

Abney, Texas
June

Shelby Sparks couldn't breathe.

Max had knocked her to the ground seconds after the explosion. She heard the *swoosh* of a home collapsing and felt the heat of the fire from where she lay in the middle of the street. None of that mattered.

She pulled in a deep breath, coughed on the smoke, and choked on the words she needed to say.

Someone screamed for help.

Another explosion ripped through their neighborhood.

A roaring fire surrounded them.

Shelby was consumed by a single thought—Carter was out there. She had to reach her son. She pushed against Max, pleaded with him to let her up, tried to jab him with her elbows. All the while, she fought the sobs tightening her throat.

"Are you okay?" he shouted.

He'd raised up enough to check on her. She didn't pause to listen to a word he said or answer a single question. A part of her mind registered the wall of flames, the destruction and death. She pushed those thoughts aside, struggled to her feet, and ran toward her son.

One

Shelby stumbled over a tree root, tried to maintain her balance, and ended up bumping into Max, who glanced back at her with a raised eyebrow.

"I'm fine," she snapped.

Hiking was not her idea of fun, especially since she had an almost pathological fear of snakes. Something scurried through the underbrush. She momentarily froze, but all she could hear was the thudding of her heartbeat and the clomp of Max's boots against the rocky trail. Resisting the urge to look behind her, she opted instead to pick up her pace and catch the group. They were heading northeast and climbing steadily up. The nearly setting sun cast her shadow in front of her—elongated and misshapen. She wouldn't have agreed to the afternoon's activities if it weren't for the three friends who insisted she step away from her computer and enjoy the great outdoors.

Max Berkman, Bianca Lopez, and Patrick Goodnight gained the top of the trail a few moments before her. Max was tall and wiry, with black hair beginning to tinge with gray. Bianca

12

was shorter than Shelby—no more than five three, curvy and beautiful. Patrick managed to keep up in spite of his size. He was a big man, with the body shape of the linebacker he had been in high school. He'd retired from the army five years ago. Shelby knew he worked at keeping himself in the same physical condition he'd sported during his years of service.

She literally collided with the group as they stood with their mouths half-opened, staring around them in amazement.

The view was a dramatic one. The Colorado River curved like a serpent, two hundred feet below. The Texas hill country stretched out in the distance, green from recent rains. The state park where they were hiking offered over thirty-five miles of trails, though they'd only covered a small portion of that—from the parking area to the Tie Slide Trail, down to Gorman Falls, and now circling back to where they had started via the River Overlook Trail. Probably less than five miles, but it felt like more. Shelby's heart raced, the muscles in her calves quivered, and sweat trickled down her neck.

She realized, with a start, that she was the only one looking at the view.

Glancing up, she at first thought she must be dreaming—that she would wake to find herself at home, in bed, and safe. She closed her eyes and attempted to calm her heart rate. When she opened them, if anything the scene had become more bizarre. What should have been a dark-blue sky was now streaked with shafts of green, pink, purple, and red. The colors of the rainbow, but more sinister.

The lights of the aurora borealis swirled across the Texas sky.

"Northern lights?" Max pulled off his ball cap and wiped the sweat from his brow. "Here?"

"I've never seen anything like it," Bianca said, her voice filled with awe. She tipped her head back and stared straight up, her mouth partially open in surprise.

Curtains of predominantly red arcs brightened the sky, reflecting off every rock, tree, and cactus. Shelby had asked someone for the time less than a mile back, and Max had said it was eight p.m. The sun had set and the sky was beginning to turn dusky. She'd picked up her pace, wanting to make it back to the truck before complete darkness fell.

But now, the sky was unnaturally bright.

"This shouldn't be visible here," she murmured.

"I've read about it, but I've never seen it." Patrick leaned against a boulder and continued to stare at the sky.

Max watched Shelby.

She glanced at Max and shook her head. "We need to get back. Now."

When he only cocked his head, she said, "I need to check on Carter."

"Can you call him?"

She pulled her cell phone from her pocket and pressed Carter's number under Recent Calls. As she suspected, the call wouldn't go through.

Bianca and Patrick had taken out their phones as well and were using them to take pictures of the northern lights.

Max stepped closer to Shelby. "What's wrong?"

"The call won't go through. I need to get home, Max. I need to be there in case Carter . . . in case he has a problem."

"All right. Let's double-time it."

Bianca had been turning in a circle, photographing the celestial event. She was a freelance graphic designer and sold many of her photos on the web. Finally tearing her gaze from the sky, she asked, "Is this a problem?"

"Yes, it is." Shelby worked to keep the panic from her voice. Maybe she was misremembering her research. Possibly she was overreacting.

The aurora continued to bathe them in its unnatural light, even tinting their skin the color of a red rose. Patrick exchanged a questioning look with Max, who was readjusting the weight of his backpack.

"The lady says we need to hurry. Let's go."

It was a testament to their friendship that everyone held their questions. The group turned back toward the trail, and that was when they heard the whine of a jet engine, followed by a thunderous crash. To the southeast, black smoke rose to meet the swirling light of the borealis.

Bianca gasped, Max and Patrick stood frozen, and Shelby realized that the nightmare she feared was actually happening. Each member of the group instinctively stepped closer together.

"What was that?" Bianca swiped at her hair, and Shelby noticed that her friend's hands were shaking. "Patrick? What was that? Did we . . . did we actually just see a plane crash?"

Before Patrick could respond, they heard the whine of another plane—this one smaller, probably a single engine, and headed south. As they watched, another dot approached, and then the planes collided. They tumbled to the ground as more smoke filled the sky.

"None of those planes were military," Patrick said.

"Those people . . . are they all dead?" Bianca backed up against a tree and slid to the ground. "Are you telling me . . . did an entire plane of people . . . did three *entire* planes of people just die right in front of our eyes?"

"I'm fairly certain the first was a domestic flight, probably headed to the regional airport." Patrick's tone was grim, hardened—the voice of a soldier assessing a situation. "The other two could have been private jets."

Shelby glanced at Max, who had once again pulled out his phone. "Nothing. I can't access

9-1-1, there are no emergency notifications, there's nothing."

She fought the urge to vomit, covered her mouth with her hand, and tried to think clearly. This could not be happening. Not now.

Plane crashes. People burned alive. The borealis.

The thoughts spun and collided in her mind, and beneath those more selfish, more urgent ones rose to take their place.

They weren't ready. Probably they never would have been ready, but Shelby's life had finally begun to resemble something normal. Carter was to leave for college at the end of August.

Please, not now. The words were a prayer coursing through her heart.

Max's expression had settled into a hard, straight line. "We can't help those people. It's farther away than it looks."

"So we just leave them?" Bianca's voice cracked. She stood and swiped at the tears running down her cheeks.

"Yeah. We do." Max repositioned his backpack.

Without another word, the four best friends rushed back down the trail, retracing the path they had covered a few hours earlier. Only now everything was different.

They stayed closer together, though darkness had refused to cloak the hillside. Picking out the trail was no problem. It was eerily bathed in the pulsing light of the borealis. In twenty minutes they covered the distance back to where they'd parked. As they turned the last corner and caught sight of Max's truck, another explosion shattered the evening's silence.

Two

"That sounded different," Shelby said. Her legs trembled, and her right arm had begun to shake.

"Probably a train." Max led the group and Patrick brought up the rear.

Bianca was breathing heavily when they stopped.

The parking area was deserted. There was no sign of park rangers, emergency vehicles, or other hikers.

Patrick stored their packs in the bed of Max's old Ford pickup. When he'd bought the truck, it had been used but in pristine condition. He'd liked it because it didn't have any gizmos— no backup cameras or computers that would require replacing. Now it was twenty years old and showing the wear of travelling down a few too many country roads.

Max pulled out his keys and unlocked the doors, muttering, "Let's hope it starts."

"It would. I mean, it will," said Shelby.

She started to climb into the backseat of the extended cab pickup, but Max nodded toward the front. She hesitated, and then she stepped up on the running board and grasped the grab bar, pulling herself into the passenger seat.

Patrick and Bianca hopped into the back.

They were all buckled by the time Max started the truck. He put it in drive and sped down the caliche, white rock road.

Patrick tapped on the back of the seat. "Someone want to tell me what's going on?"

"Yeah, what is happening? Planes falling out of the sky? A possible train derailment? Are we being attacked?" Bianca attempted to drink from a water bottle, but her hands were shaking too badly. She recapped it and asked, "Can you get anything on the radio?"

Max turned it on and cycled through his preset stations. They heard nothing but static.

"Does this have anything to do with the aurora?" she asked Shelby.

"I think . . . that is, I'm sure the northern lights are caused by a solar flare. Probably the flare disrupted the electrical systems on the planes and the train, and even the radio and phones."

Silence filled the truck, and then everyone started talking at once.

Max accelerated as he turned right onto the blacktop. The back tires of the truck slipped and spun before gripping the road. He held up a hand and said, "Shelby, tell us what you know."

"We're not supposed to see the aurora. It's never been this far south. The fact that we can see it means that this is a solar event of unprecedented proportions."

"Unprecedented?" Max continued staring at the road, gunning the truck, his hands wrapped tightly around the wheel.

"No one knows how . . ." She stopped, closed her eyes, and prayed fervently that she was wrong. "We can't be sure what an event of this magnitude will do."

"The truck started." Max continued driving with his left hand and pulled out his phone with his right. He split his attention between the screen and the road. "Why does my truck work but not the phones? I thought electromagnetic pulses fried anything with a circuit board."

"You're thinking of an EMP. A solar flare is different. It's . . ." She thought again of the notes in her study. Maybe she had the details mixed up. Perhaps this was a nightmare, and she'd wake in a moment. "Some of the effects are similar, but it's not the same. In many ways, it's worse."

"How long will it last?" Max asked.

"Who knows? Twenty-four hours? Thirty-six?"

"Tell me why the truck works."

"Because it's older, would be my guess. The newer ones—anything with an advanced circuit board, keyless ignition, any vehicles with GPS integrated into the system—might not."

"So why does my phone work?" Bianca sat

forward, shoving the phone toward Shelby. "See the pictures? I took them a few minutes ago. Why does it work? Maybe you're wrong. Maybe—"

"I'm not wrong. Solar flares cause power surges. If you'd had your phone plugged in to charge it, then a flare would have fried the circuits. No one actually knows what would happen to automobiles during a major solar flare because it hasn't happened in the last hundred years."

"And the planes?" Patrick asked. "We have had solar flares before."

"Minor ones."

"But we've had them. Air traffic was diverted from the north and south poles, but the flares didn't actually harm any of the navigational systems."

"Because they didn't fly straight through one. With this event—if it's as big as I think it is— there would have been no flying around it."

"The train explosion . . ." Max glanced her way and then back at the road. "Train switches are all electrical. This flare . . . it would have fried those as well?"

"Maybe. I guess so."

"How do you know all this, Shelby?" Patrick was now practically in the front seat, hanging over the space between her and Max.

"I did some research, for a book—"

"You write romance stories."

"Yes, but they're historical. For last year's release, I researched the Carrington Event, the last major CME—"

"CME?" Bianca pushed into Patrick's space, so that both of their heads were comically hanging over the seat back. "I thought you said it was a solar flare."

"A CME is a coronal mass ejection."

"Sounds bad." Patrick sank back against his seat. "God help us if what you're saying is true."

"So it's not a solar flare?" Bianca asked.

"Not all solar flares produce CMEs, and not all CMEs accompany solar flares." She hesitated, and then she added, "That's about all I remember. I need to get home and make sure Carter is all right."

"Why wouldn't he be?" Max asked. He'd been relatively quiet, focusing on the road, but now he turned his attention to her.

"I don't know. I . . . I need to be sure."

Shelby glanced back at her friends.

Patrick stared out the window, his large shoulders tense and his expression unreadable. Whatever they were in for, Patrick would be a port in a storm. Actually, everyone in the truck would be.

Bianca was still trying to make a call.

"It won't work," Shelby said. "Every call is routed through a satellite, and the satellites are almost certainly fried."

Max tugged the bill of his ball cap lower, possibly trying to block out the aurora. As for the catastrophe they faced, he drove as if he could outrun it.

Three

Max knew he couldn't elude what was happening, but the urgency to get his friends back home spurred him to push the old truck. He was an intelligent guy. You didn't make it through four years of college and three years of law school if you were even marginally slow. But what Shelby was suggesting—well, it was difficult to wrap his mind around.

He kept glancing toward her, but she stared resolutely out the window. The cab was oddly quiet, each person lost in images of a world turned upside down. The fear in Shelby's eyes had convinced him of the seriousness of their situation. He'd lived next door to her most of his life, long enough to know that she didn't spook easily. If she thought the aurora was a problem, then he would treat it as such.

His mind shifted to the planes. If all air flight was suspended, it would affect their economy drastically. They'd seen that after September 11. Not to mention the loss of life from those planes caught en route at the time of the flare.

Some would make it, though. Pilots were trained in how to land aircraft without instrumentation. If they could find a safe spot to set down, they would be okay. A field, parking lot, even roadways would work if they were cleared.

The situation was drastic, but they would find a way to deal with it. He didn't for a minute question the validity of what Shelby had described. She might be stubborn and increasingly silent about her feelings, but she wasn't one to overreact.

The truck practically sailed over the last cattle guard, and they flew past the sign that read "You Are Leaving Colorado Bend State Park." He might have sped right past Sad Sam's Bait Shop, but the sheer number of cars caused him to slam on the brakes.

"We're stopping?" Patrick asked.

"Looks like we have to."

The normally vacant store was brimming with people. A few cars were double-parked next to the building, and some even spilled out onto the road. Max slowed to maneuver around a particularly long sedan.

"Maybe we should go in." Patrick rolled down his window. "Might be better to know what we're driving into."

That would be Patrick's military training kicking in. He'd been out five years, but old habits died hard.

"And they might know something about the planes," Bianca said.

Max glanced at Shelby, who shrugged.

"I suppose a few minutes wouldn't hurt," Shelby said. "I'm worried about Carter, but I'd also like to know what these people have heard. As long as we can make it a quick in and out."

As they exited the truck, Max noticed Patrick hanging back. He pulled his pack from the truck bed, unzipped it, and removed his pistol, which he then slipped into a paddle holster.

"Do you really think you're going to need that?"

"Certainly hope not." Patrick's shirt had been tucked into his hiking pants. He pulled it out, then checked to be sure it covered his firearm.

"I think you're overreacting."

"I don't."

"We want to keep this low-key. I'm hoping no one will even notice we're here."

The girls had stopped walking toward the store and turned to watch them. So instead of arguing, Max shrugged and they hurried to catch up.

The four walked together in a tight group, and Max heard Bianca ask Shelby, "Do you think my parents will be okay?"

A year earlier her father had suffered a broken hip and was currently living in their town's only rehabilitation and retirement center, Green Acres. Miguel Lopez had healed from the hip replacement, but other health issues kept him at Green Acres. Currently his main problem seemed to be decreased lung capacity due to years of firefighting in the Houston area.

"*Mamá* is fragile and old, but she doesn't seem to realize it."

"Still rising early every day to bake fresh tortillas?" Shelby asked.

"Yes. When they're ready, she climbs into the old Buick, which she'd never driven before *Papá* was hospitalized, and she takes him breakfast. *Mamá* claims he would waste away to nothing eating the food at the rehab facility."

Max was thinking that it helped to speak of something normal, to calm their nerves so they didn't feel like they were flying apart.

Once they reached the door of the small store, Max glanced at Shelby, who was running her thumbnail back and forth across her bottom lip. Bianca continued to clutch her phone in her right hand. Patrick's eyes scanned left to right and then back again.

"They'll be okay," Patrick assured Bianca. "Your mom will be home by now."

"But *Papá*—"

"Green Acres has a generator." Max reached for the handle of the old screen door. "With any luck, that will be working."

Bianca nodded once, and then they pushed their way through the store's squeaky door. They had stopped there a few times before, always after hiking at the Bend. The place had not been updated since its construction more than a hundred years before. Faded wood siding greeted customers, and the shelves held a surprising variety of goods. Max enjoyed stopping at the old place. For one thing, it wasn't crowded like the large gas stations on the major roads.

Usually.

Tonight the place was packed with people. Every person's attention was trained on the man at the front of the room—Sam Collins, the owner of Sad Sam's.

Max slid along the back wall, just inside the door, and the rest followed.

"Quiet down. Toby's been able to get some news over his ham radio. It's high frequency, so he's heard reports from as far away as Houston."

"He should be able to reach a lot farther than that," someone grumbled.

"Yeah, I should, but I can't." A man with a giant belly extending over his belt and tattoos dancing down his arms stood up. "Y'all know me—Toby Nix. My place is up on the hill to the south of the Pecan Bottoms. Normally I can pick up transmissions from all over the US. What I'm getting since the aurora hit is mainly static."

"So you can't tell us anything." This from a woman who was sitting on top of the ice-cream cooler, a shotgun resting across her legs.

Max surveyed the room. About half the people were openly carrying either shotguns or rifles. Several others were wearing paddle holsters with pistols. Texas had recently become an open carry state, which allowed citizens with a concealed carry license to openly carry handguns as long as they were in a shoulder or belt holster.

"I didn't say that. I've picked up a few transmissions from Abney, Austin, even Houston. The news is all bad."

Four

The room went deathly quiet, and Max questioned the wisdom of their having stopped. This situation could turn ugly very quickly. Too many people, too many weapons, and fear were not a good combination. Shelby stepped closer to Bianca, who clasped her hand. Max and Patrick stood on either side of the women, as if they could protect them from what this man was about to say.

An old man at the back was the first to break the silence. "Tell us about the planes."

"From what I can put together, air traffic control is down completely."

"Everywhere?"

"Seems that way—Houston Hobby, George Bush Intercontinental, DFW, even the regional airports like Killeen. It's mostly chatter. There's been no official word, but when you hear the same thing from several different sources, you can trust it's correct."

Max wasn't sure he agreed with that statement. Lies spread as quickly as truth. But in this case, he was afraid Toby was right.

"So they're crashing? Falling into our fields and highways?"

"I don't know, Mr. Bowman. I realize your son is a pilot. It's possible that he found a safe place to land or that he wasn't in the air at the time."

The old man nodded and stared at the floor.

"That last explosion wasn't a plane." This from a middle-aged woman in the middle of the room. "I heard it all the way from my place on the east side. Folks are saying two of the freight trains collided. What would cause that? And what if those trains were carrying hazardous materials?"

Toby looked to Sam Collins, who stood and cleared his throat.

"I believe it was two trains, and I can't tell you why they crashed into each other. I've owned this shop since I was a twenty-two-year-old pup. Never went to college and sure couldn't fly a plane or drive a train." Sam ran a weathered hand up and down his jaw. "There's going to be a lot of questions about this thing and precious few answers. I can't tell you what was on those trains or why they collided. We're going to have to deal with problems one at a time, as we receive information about them. But if we focus on what we don't know, this thing is going to beat us before the first night has passed."

He sat down, indicating that Toby should continue.

"In some places power is out completely. Other places it fades in and out."

"We've been without power before," someone called out.

"From what I'm hearing—the big transformers are going down, one by one. That has never happened before, and according to the experts it means the power could stay down for some time."

"Because of this?" Another elderly man pointed out the window. Though it was now nearly ten in the evening, the cars were bathed in the red light of the aurora.

"There's all sorts of theories," Toby said. "Solar flares, grid overload, EMP attack . . ."

"Who would attack us?" the woman with the shotgun asked.

From the opposite side of the room, Max heard someone mutter, "Want a list?"

"Could be domestic, could be foreign." Toby hitched up his pants. "I can't tell you, and there are too many theories coming over the ham to make any sense of it."

"Could be the aliens have come to fetch D.J. back to their ship."

This was said by a tall, gangly boy, who was apparently standing next to D.J. The teenager beside him slapped the first on the back of the head, and then they both laughed.

It eased some of the tension in the room, but not much.

Sam stood back up. "I suggest everyone go home and try to get a good night's rest. Tomorrow is apt to be . . . challenging. Keep a watch out for strangers."

"Any strangers appear on my place, and I won't bother with a warning shot." The woman sitting on top of the cooler patted her shotgun. "And don't bother telling me I can't. I know my rights."

"We have a right to defend ourselves," Toby agreed, trying to quiet the group.

But suddenly everyone was talking, and it all sounded reactionary to Max. He glanced at Patrick, who shook his head once, his eyes still scanning the crowd.

"Calm down, folks." Sam raised his voice to be heard over the crowd. "The last thing we need is for everyone to panic and start shooting the first person they see. More than likely that will be one of your neighbors coming to ask to borrow something."

"Best make yourself known before you step on my place." An old man from the back stood and walked to the front of the room. He wore faded dungarees and a soiled ball cap. "I've been warning you all for years, but no one would listen to me. You made fun and talked about my con-spiracy theories."

He paused to spit into a cup. "Mind you, there are those who will take advantage of this situation, and you have a right to protect yourself. That's what the castle law says, and I for one plan to take full advantage of my rights if need be."

"That is not what the castle law says," Max said.

Patrick put a hand on his arm, as if to pull him back.

"And who are you?" The man's tone and expression were far from friendly.

"Max Berkman. We live over in Abney, and I'm a lawyer."

"Is that so?"

"It is, and you should each realize that the castle law is basically a stand-your-ground law. It means you do not have to retreat if you feel threatened in your place of residence."

"Or my truck or my place of work."

Everyone started talking again, but this time Max silenced them by taking another step toward the center of the room.

"You're right about that, Mr.—"

"Jim. That's all you need to know."

"All right, Jim." Max glanced around the room. He'd meant to stay quiet, but he'd never been able to abide people misinterpreting the law.

"You are only authorized to use deadly force if there is imminent danger. That doesn't include someone passing across your field."

"How do I know they're not coming to kill me?"

"Stop stirring the pot, Jim." Toby glanced out the window and then back at the group. "Hasn't even been a couple of hours, and you sound like you're making a second stand at the Alamo."

"Maybe I am, and maybe you need to take this a little more seriously. You know as well as I do that there are folks who wait for situations like this so they can prey on the weak."

"Which we are not," Toby muttered.

"No, but some of us can be gullible." Sam stepped forward, shouldering Jim out of the limelight and throwing a pointed look at the teenagers. "This ain't the zombie apocalypse. It's real and it's happening now. If the electricity comes back on, even for a few minutes, use the time to fill what containers you can find with water—"

"My well has never gone dry," said the woman with the shotgun.

"True, but unless it's hooked up to a windmill, you won't be getting any water out of it. Most of the wells around here are basically small pipes dug deep into the ground and operated by electrical pumps. Without electricity, we're going to have a problem." This caused a smattering of conversations to erupt.

Max could only make out what the people standing closest to them were saying, and they were debating everything from ammunition to water supply to anarchy.

"Go home," Sam said more loudly, his tone silencing everyone in the room. "Watch for strangers, don't trust anyone you don't recognize, and we'll meet back here at six tomorrow evening. By then we should know more."

A few folks had additional questions. One or two on Max's side of the room turned and glanced their way.

Max touched Shelby's arm and motioned with his head toward the door. He didn't want to still be in the building when the impromptu meeting broke up.

"Not exactly a welcoming group," Patrick said. "And I thought we were going to play it low-key."

Max shrugged. "That was the plan."

"Well, someone forgot to follow it."

"I was clarifying the law."

"You could have picked a better time."

The four of them hurried toward the truck, piled in, and pulled back onto the two-lane.

"People need to understand that the law doesn't change simply because there's an emergency." Max pushed the transmission into drive and accelerated as fast as he dared. He'd feel better once they were within the town limits of Abney.

Five

Shelby tried to tamp down her impatience. They'd driven away from the store and turned east, toward Abney. Patrick and Bianca were discussing what they'd learned back at the store.

Max caught her eye and said, "Carter is going to be fine."

"I know he will."

"But you're worried."

"Yes. Of course I am. That's what a mother does. We're bred to worry."

"He hasn't had . . . any episodes in a long time."

"I know that."

"He's a man now."

"Do you think so?"

"I do. He'll be going off to college in a few months—"

"Not now." The realization tore at her heart. "Not now he won't."

"We don't know that. Regardless, he will handle his condition. He's a smart guy."

She was about to argue with him—to point out that insulin was going to be a problem. And balanced meals? Well, that might very well be a thing of the past. But before she could raise her objections, he was braking and pulling over to the side of the road. To their left a sedan had plowed through a fence and was resting against a pecan tree.

"This isn't a good idea, Max," Patrick said.

"So what, we just leave them here? Somebody could be hurt."

Max was out of the car without another word, hurrying toward the driver who had creaked open the door and was tumbling out of the car.

Shelby hesitated. She wanted to be in Abney. She needed to hurry this up. Patrick had gotten out of the truck and followed Max, though she couldn't see him from where she sat. She glanced back at Bianca. "Should we go with them?"

"We might be able to help."

They picked their way across the field, a disorienting maze of darkness and light. She could just hear Max calling out to the driver, "Do you folks need some help?"

"We do. I must have taken my eyes off the road for a minute. My friend, I think he's hurt." The man was in his twenties, with longish brown hair.

Max followed him around to the passenger side of the car, and Shelby noticed the driver step back as Max opened the door.

"Hands up, and I'm going to need your wallet." The driver had pulled a handgun and was pointing it at Max.

Bianca jerked on Shelby's arm, pulling her to the ground.

"We have to help him," whispered Shelby.

Instead of answering, Bianca nodded toward the east, where Patrick was stepping out from behind a tree. He moved without hesitation and was behind the kid in seconds, his own pistol drawn and pointed at the punk's head.

"Drop it."

Even from where they lay, she could hear the calm, cold certainty in Patrick's voice.

The thief—because that was what this was all about, Shelby realized with stunning clarity—dropped his pistol. Patrick kicked it away, and Max scrambled after it.

When Shelby glanced back at the supposed wreck, the driver and the passenger stood with their backs against the car.

"You crashed your car? So you could rob me?" Max held the man's gun down at his side.

The passenger, who was even younger than the driver, shrugged.

"You need to start talking," Patrick barked. He still hadn't lowered his weapon.

"Can't think straight with that pointed at me."

"Well, you should have considered that before you started down this path. Now talk."

"We weren't going to hurt anyone. Just needed a little more cash, what with this . . . this thing happening."

"So you wrecked your own car?"

"It isn't really wrecked. We drove it through the fence so someone would think we'd crashed.

Obviously it worked." The kid sounded almost proud of himself.

Max removed a clip from the semiautomatic. From where they were lying on the ground, Shelby could see Patrick shift his gun to his left hand and hold out his right. He deposited the thief's gun and clip into his pocket.

"You can't keep that, man."

Patrick must have told Max to pat them down. When he indicated they didn't have any other weapons, Patrick barked, "On the ground. Hands behind your back. I don't want to see you so much as twitch."

Patrick nodded to Max, who jogged back toward the truck.

Shelby and Bianca scrambled after him.

Once Max had the truck idling, Patrick leaned down, said something else to the two thieves, and then he jogged back toward the car.

"What did you say to them?" Max asked.

"I told them if they moved or tried to come after us, I was going to come back and put a bullet in their heads." Patrick clipped his seat belt into the buckle, his eyes still on the two men lying in the field.

Instead of reprimanding him, Max said, "You shouldn't have taken their gun. Legally it's their property."

"I was supposed to let them keep it? Let them rob the next car that comes by?"

"I don't know, Patrick, but it wasn't ours to take."

"In case you haven't noticed, we can't exactly call 9-1-1."

"I'll give it to the sheriff when we get back in town."

"I have a feeling the sheriff is going to have his hands full."

"Patrick's right," Bianca said. "They looked like stupid kids, but they could have hurt someone."

"Kids is right," Max muttered.

"The rules have changed." Shelby stared out the window. "In the blink of an eye, everything has changed."

She knew Max didn't agree with her, but he floored the accelerator and focused on getting them back to town.

The second time they stopped was a quarter mile west of Lynch Creek. An older man and woman stood beside what appeared to be a brand-new car. Max pulled to the side of the road when the man stepped out into their lane, waving his hands.

"I can't believe we're doing this again," Patrick said, but everyone tumbled out of Max's truck, each person pausing to stare up at the sky once more.

The car had been purchased the week before and had "just quit," according to Dale Smitty, who introduced himself and his wife with a nod toward the ladies and a handshake for the guys.

"I suspected the newfangled thing was a bad idea. Today's cars have more computers and less reliability. Have you seen the spare? My grandson's bike tire is bigger. I was happy with the Chevy we had, but the wife wanted something new and shiny."

Joyce Smitty didn't bother responding to that. She did turn to Shelby and say, "Our phones don't work either. It's the strangest thing. Happened when we first noticed the lights."

A weathered hand motioned toward the sky.

"We can give you a ride into town," Patrick offered.

"Oh . . . we thought perhaps your cell phone would work. I'd feel better if I could stay with the car until a tow truck arrives." The old man glanced from one member of the group to the other, awareness slowly dawning in his eyes.

"No one's phone is working. We suspect there's a problem with the cell towers." Max stuck his thumbs into the back pockets of his jeans.

Shelby thought it made him look ridiculously like a character from a western. Her mind turned again to Carter, and she had to fight the urge to stomp her foot and tell everyone to get back in the truck.

"We'd be happy to take you into town," Max said.

Dale nodded, and without another word Max transferred the Smittys' baggage to the truck bed. Dale slipped into the backseat, and Bianca slid over into the middle. Shelby moved next to Max to make room for Joyce. Max offered her a reassuring smile, but she only shook her head, willing the truck forward. Until she laid eyes on Carter, until she saw for herself that he was okay, the anxiety clawing at her throat wouldn't recede.

What if he had been driving and the traffic signals had gone out?

What if a transmission line had sparked, causing a fire?

What if he were trapped in the grocery store inside the freezer? It was an absurd thing to worry about. He didn't work in the frozen food section, and even if he did, there was an emergency release handle in the freezer—he'd told her that the first week he was employed at the Market.

Her mind darted over her real concern, shied away, then turned and met it head-on. What if he'd forgotten to check his sugar level and was at that very moment sliding into a diabetic coma? He wouldn't be able to call 9-1-1 with the phones out. How would he get to the hospital?

It had only happened once, but she didn't think she'd ever forget the sight of her son, collapsed on the kitchen floor. She had been unable to wake him.

She glanced over at Max. He smiled, as if he could read her thoughts. Maybe he could. She'd known Max a long time. They'd grown up together and been sweethearts in high school, but then Max Berkman had abandoned her. Her seventeen-year-old self, the girl who had written letter after letter, seemed like a different person entirely.

All water under the bridge. Max had eventually moved back to Abney, and they'd been next-door neighbors since.

Max had heard her shouts the day she'd found Carter lying on the floor. He'd rushed over and sat by her son as she'd dialed the emergency number. Over the years he had been a good friend to them.

"We were vacationing down in the hill country," Dale said. "Headed back toward Dallas this afternoon. So everyone's power is out?"

"Seems so." Max slowed for a deer darting across the road.

"The whole area?"

"The entire state," Patrick said.

Max readjusted his grip on the steering wheel. "Maybe the whole country."

"Were those explosions that we heard?" Joyce asked.

"We think there were at least two plane crashes and one train derailment." Patrick paused and added, "Those are only the ones we know about."

Dale and Joyce Smitty took the news fairly well. Shelby guessed their ages to be at least seventy. No doubt they'd been through many catastrophes in their lives—the aftermath of World War II, the drought of the fifties, the attack on the World Trade Center. Those events and so many more had affected their entire nation, but they had survived. The elderly couple was testament to the fact that their country had faced terrible times before but had always found a way to endure.

Max drove cautiously. Shelby wanted to reach over, push his knee down, and force the truck to accelerate. Instead, she worked some dirt from beneath her thumbnail and tried to pray for Carter.

Why was she so worried?

He was a good boy, nearly a man now. He would know what to do. He'd lived with his condition since he was four. She could trust him to take care of himself.

As they entered the outskirts of Abney, Shelby relaxed. Everything looked exactly as they had left it, except the sky. There was no plane debris scattered across the road, no smoldering fires. The red aurora was now tinged with green and blue. Occasionally starlight pierced through. The sight made her dizzy.

She was suddenly glad that they were crammed into the truck, Max on one side, an old woman she barely knew on the other. She didn't want to be alone during whatever this was, and she didn't want to think about the research in her study.

She shook the idea from her head. They were a child's thoughts, and she was a woman. She didn't have the luxury of being afraid, not now.

Max must have felt her stiffen. "I'm sure he's fine."

She didn't respond. Why bother? It was one of the differences between them. He would never be able to fully understand the strength of the bond between parent and child. He'd never married, never had a kid. He couldn't know that it was akin to having your heart walking around outside your body—out of your supervision, out of your control, vulnerable.

"I'm going to drop Shelby off first, so she can check on Carter. Then I'll take Bianca to check on her parents, and after that I'll drop off the Smittys."

"I can drive my own car to see my parents," Bianca said, "if someone can take me home."

"Sounds like a gig for me," said Patrick. "My car is parked at Shelby's. I'll take you to your place, and if your car doesn't work, I'll drive you over to check on your dad and your mom." He drummed his fingers against the roof of the truck. "If this old rust bucket runs, mine should."

Patrick drove a restored 1965 Ford Mustang. The car was red and fast, and the gas mileage was terrible. Even Patrick admitted it was his midlife crisis car. He claimed everyone needed a diversion from the work of life. Maybe. Shelby couldn't afford such hobbies. She was too busy trying to make ends meet.

She'd made the mistake of voicing that thought, and it was one of the reasons she'd been pressured into their hiking group. It was easier to go than to argue with them about how she didn't have time for such excursions. Once she'd claimed that she had to stay home and do yard work. Bianca, Patrick, and Max had appeared with a trailer full of yard equipment and finished the front yard and backyard in less than an hour.

As he drove closer to their street, Max said, "What do you say we all meet at Shelby's tomorrow morning? We can pool our information."

"Sounds good to me," Patrick said.

"I can't get there before ten. On Saturday mornings I go with *Mamá* to visit *Papá*."

"Ten will be fine," Max assured her.

Shelby leaned forward and craned her neck, trying to see her small home as they turned onto Kaufman Street. Her house was the fourth on the right, and Max's house was the fifth. Mr. Evans was standing in front of the house on the corner, talking with the owner. He raised a hand in greeting, and both Max and Shelby waved back.

They passed houses where the owners were sitting on the porch or out in the yard, gazing up

45

at the sky. A few waved, but most seemed transfixed by the aurora. That would last for a night or two, and then they'd grow tired of it. Shelby didn't want to think about what would happen when these people realized the electricity wasn't coming back on.

If she was right.

She prayed again that she was wrong.

When she spotted her house, white with green trim, the sight calmed her. Max's was a little better maintained—new screens on the windows, a fresh paint job on the exterior, rooms that had been remodeled one at a time—but both houses were the same age and nearly identical in size. Each had two bedrooms and one bath, with a little more than a thousand square feet. For Max, the austere living conditions were a choice. For Shelby, it had been a financial necessity. She had moved into her parents' house after they were killed in a car accident.

It wasn't much, certainly not affluent, but it was their home—and it whispered to her that everything was fine. Yet she was unnerved by the fact that she could see the house so clearly at such a late hour. The aurora continued to brighten and spin in the heavens above them.

As they neared the house, Shelby saw that Carter wasn't at work as he should have been. His Buick was parked in the driveway, and he was sitting on the front porch, hunched over.

Six

Carter glanced up as Max's truck slowed in front of their house. His mom jumped out before it had properly stopped.

"Are you okay? Is everything all right? Weren't you supposed to work late tonight?" The questions tumbled from her as she hurried up the walk.

He stood and stretched, dark hair flopping in his eyes, a smile slowly spreading across his face. He hadn't realized he was worried about her until she was standing in front of him.

"You made it back."

She stopped in front of the small porch and now stood staring up at him.

Patrick waved at them both as he got out of the truck and unlocked his Mustang. Bianca climbed out of the truck and ran over to give Carter a hug. Bianca was cool, so he suffered through the embrace. After ruffling his hair, she ran to catch up with Patrick. The Mustang was a serious ride.

"Stop staring at that car and talk to me. How are . . . things?" His mom was like that when she was worried—vague and ambiguous. As if she didn't want to remind him of his disease.

Like he could forget about it.

"Fine, except that nothing works."

"But you feel . . . you feel okay?"

"Sure." He shrugged, faking nonchalance. "Were those explosions I heard a few hours ago?"

Max leaned out of his truck. "We good here?"

"Yes. Thank you." His mom crossed her arms and tapped her right index finger against her left elbow. It was a nervous tic she had. Not that she was usually nervous. Only when it came to his diabetes. Anything else she handled like a bull rider, full of confidence and spit and fire.

"Back in a few," Max called.

Patrick's Mustang started with a roar. He tapped the horn lightly and waved to them as he drove away.

Carter sank onto the porch steps. "It's a flare, isn't it?"

"Yes."

"Their cars work because they're older."

"That would be my guess." She glanced at the house, as if there was something in there she was dying to get to, but then she sat down next to him.

"And the explosions?"

"Planes. Some planes crashed. And maybe a train."

"This changes everything."

His mom nodded. "What do you know about flares?"

"Not much, but anyone who has ever watched

TV knows what happens if the grid goes down—no phones, no computers, no cars. Soon we'll be foraging through people's houses looking for cans of beans."

"Let's hope things don't deteriorate to that level."

"We studied flares in science, but Jason spent that time throwing spitballs."

"There's a surprise."

"He wasn't coping with being a senior very well." Jason Snyder was Carter's best friend. Some days he thought Jason was his only friend. "But then again, science can be pretty boring."

"I thought you liked Coach Parish."

"Yeah. He's cool. But marine life? Atoms? Stars? All that stuff . . . it's information I don't need to know."

"Huh." That was what she said when she didn't want to start an argument.

"We have Google, Mom. Or we had it. I didn't need to memorize the definition of a black hole."

She didn't agree or disagree. Instead, she leaned forward, casting a worried look toward the power lines. "See how they're starting to sag?"

"Yeah."

"Take a picture with your phone."

"Of the power lines?"

"Yeah. Then we'll take another in an hour."

"Okay." It sounded like a stupid idea to him, but sometimes his mom had good reasons for doing stuff. He took the photo, studied it, and then he clicked his phone off.

"I need to go inside and check my notes."

"Notes?"

"I'll explain in a minute."

He followed his mom inside and stood in the middle of the living room, wondering what he was supposed to do. Finally he called out, "I'm kind of hungry, and the microwave doesn't work."

"Peanut butter sandwich, son. Make us both one while I find my folder."

Carter pulled out the all-natural peanut butter, wheat bread, and natural apple preserves, along with the skim milk. Occasionally he wished he could eat like everyone else, but most days he accepted his life for what it was. As he made the sandwiches, he told his mom about walking to the grocery store, finding it closed, and seeing the note the manager had put on the door.

"Guess I'm out of a job until the power comes back on. *If* it comes back on."

She sat at the table with a large manila folder marked "Carrington Romance."

"Terrible title."

"That was my working title."

There was a time he'd been embarrassed that his mother wrote romance books, but then she'd shown him a royalty check. The stuff paid pretty well, though he knew the job wasn't easy.

He'd seen firsthand how much time she spent at her desk. He could barely crank out a two-page English assignment. The thought of writing four hundred pages made his hands sweat.

"Read this." She passed him a sheet titled "1859 Carrington Event."

He devoured the first of his sandwich as he skimmed the article. Downing his glass of milk, he asked, "You're saying this is happening now?"

His mom passed him another sheet: "Doomsday Fear."

"I'm going to need more milk if you expect me to read all of this." He opened the refrigerator and pulled out the gallon of milk. Thinking of what he'd just read, he held up the gallon and asked, "Should we save it?"

"It won't be cold in the morning. You might as well drink it now."

There was a tap on their front door screen, and then Max stepped inside. Carter liked Max. He liked the fact that someone was looking out for his mom, even though she thought she could handle everything on her own.

"Looks like an aurora feast." Max sank into the chair on the other side of his mom.

"Did you deliver your passengers?"

"I dropped Mr. and Mrs. Smitty off at the police department. Hopefully they can help them with a tow truck."

Carter hadn't noticed anyone else in Max's

truck. Mr. and Mrs. Smitty? Had their car stopped working? He shrugged. There wasn't anything he could do about it if every car in Abney quit. "I can make you a sandwich."

"Thanks, Carter. I'm starved."

Silence pushed against the windows as Carter made the sandwich. No refrigerator hum. No television or radio or phone binging that he had a message. It creeped him out. How did people stand so much quiet in the old days?

He set the sandwich in front of Max. "Mom says the milk won't last. Want a glass?"

"Think I'll stick with water for now." He glanced around the room. "Speaking of water, have you filled your tub or jugs or . . ."

His mom held up a hand, effectively shushing Max. It was obvious that she hadn't been listening. She had been in her this-world-doesn't-exist reading zone. Suddenly she dropped her hand, slapped the folder shut, and stared at Max, then Carter. He knew from the expression on her face that things were even worse than they had first thought.

Seven

"You're sure about this?" Max took another bite of the sandwich, the peanut butter sticking to the roof of his mouth and causing him to reach for the glass of tap water. Something told him they wouldn't have time to eat again before morning.

"I'm not the one who claimed to be sure. NASA wrote that report."

"And there's more . . . more documentation in there."

"Yes. Reports on Carrington as well as the likelihood of a similar event happening in our lifetime." She glanced at Carter and the phone in his hand.

"Still doesn't work," he grumbled. "I mean, I know it won't, but I keep hoping . . ."

"Go take another picture of the power lines. Then I want you to show both of them to Max."

Carter rolled his eyes, but he walked outside and took the photo.

"Why—"

"This report." Shelby thumbed through the contents of the folder again, pulling out a printout titled "Solar Flare or Nuclear EMP."

She pushed the paper toward Max. "This states that a CME can last from a few hours to several days."

"Like Carrington."

"Exactly, except in 1859 we didn't have power lines strung across the country. Telegraph communications around the world failed."

"Explain it to me."

"The voltage from the solar flare is attracted to long, heavy metal lines."

"Power lines." Max didn't have trouble understanding what Shelby was showing him, but he did need time to process it. He finished the glass of water.

Carter came back into the house, screen door banging shut behind him, his phone still in his hand.

Max turned his attention back to the report Shelby had given him. "This says that transmission lines would naturally collect the atmospheric energy."

"And here . . ." She leaned over him and pointed farther down the page. "It says that the wires will heat up, and then they will begin to sag."

They both glanced toward Carter. He moved between them and pushed a button on his phone.

"This is the first one I took."

"About an hour ago," Shelby murmured.

"And this is the one I took just now."

The lines were significantly lower, drooping so that it seemed even the power poles were beginning to tilt.

"We need to go see the mayor." Max stood and began gathering the things he had dropped on the table—keys, wallet, and phone.

"There's nothing Perkins can do."

"She has to know." Max put his plate and cup in the sink. "Carter, you need to fill up any containers you can find with water."

"But the water is still working. I just poured you a glass."

"Just do it, Carter." His mother was picking up all of the papers, stuffing them into her folder.

"Electricity pumps water up to the water tower," Max reminded him. "When you turn on the faucet, the water flows out. But once Abney's water tower is drained, there won't be any way to refill it." As he spoke, Max stared out the window over the sink. He could make out the swing set Carter had played on as a child. It reminded him of everything the boy had been through, but he wasn't a boy anymore. And now? Now he would need to become a man rather quickly.

"Don't you have any good news?"

Max grabbed his ball cap off the table where he'd tossed it. "You can find more containers in my house. You have a key."

Shelby shoved the folder into her shoulder bag. "Stay here, okay?"

"Where would I go? It's past midnight, planes are apparently falling from the sky, and every-thing is closed."

"Promise me you'll stay here." She waited until Carter nodded, and then she added, "We'll be back as fast as we can."

Max was already at the front door when Shelby turned back.

"Carter, if there's a fire, I want you to get out. Don't try to save anything. Get a safe distance away from the house and wait for me."

Instead of arguing, Carter stared down at the pictures on his phone.

"Let's go." Max held the door open, and Shelby walked out in front of him. The neighborhood was quiet, each house dark and all of the residents inside. He could almost forget what he'd seen in Shelby's folder. Other than the glow of the aurora, the street and its row of tidy houses offered a peaceful scene, contradicting the fact that the world as they knew it had already begun to change.

Neither of them spoke as they drove through the streets of town. Abney had recently grown to six thousand residents. It wasn't a large community, but it was a county seat. People would turn to Abney when they needed assistance.

"What about your parents?" Shelby asked.

"They'll be fine, for now."

"But you'll need to check on them."

"Eventually. I'll drive out to High Fields once we know the situation here."

The name High Fields made him smile—it

sounded rather lofty, like something out of a novel. It was indeed on top of a small plateau, affording a nice view of the Texas countryside. If this thing was as bad as Shelby thought, they might consider leaving until it was rectified. He knew they would be safe at High Fields, but first he needed to understand the situation he was leaving behind in Abney.

Shelby leaned forward, peering out the window. "How did you know they'd all be here?"

It was an odd sight—so many cars parked around city hall at midnight on a Friday evening. It confirmed that what they were experiencing wasn't merely a bad dream.

"I drove by when I dropped off Mr. and Mrs. Smitty."

He parked the truck and unfastened his seat belt.

Shelby reached out and touched his arm, "Do you think they'll listen to us?"

"I don't know." He wanted to wipe the worry from her face, but that was something he'd been trying to do for years. Shelby Sparks was not one to accept help easily or often. "All we can do is try."

She nodded once, clutched her large shoulder bag to her chest, and hopped out of the truck. They entered city hall, and Shelby stopped, staring around the room with her mouth open in surprise.

The scene in front of them could best be called controlled chaos.

Emergency lights were working, so their generator was in working order. Officers from the Abney Police Department had congregated in the middle of the room. Max guessed they had come off the eleven p.m. shift but weren't ready to go home until they knew what was happening. All five of the council members were present, but three were staring at their phones. The other two were standing in front of a map of Abney, studying it as if to find answers.

At the front of the room was the mayor, the mayor pro tem, the police chief, and the fire chief. Eugene Stone, the mayor pro tem, was practically shouting at the other three, waving his arms and jabbing a finger in the air to make some point.

The mayor, Nadine Perkins, seemed to be listening to the men standing in front of her, but they were interrupting one another. As Max and Shelby pushed their way through the crowd, he realized the other three were firing questions at Perkins.

The mayor almost looked relieved when she glanced up and caught Max's eye. He motioned toward her office, and she nodded in the affirmative, excusing herself from the group and meeting Max and Shelby at her office door. She ushered them inside.

"Bob Bryant doesn't want to send his officers home until he understands what we're dealing with. Luis has no way to know who might need an ambulance."

"The ambulances work?" Max asked.

"Yes, and so do the police cruisers."

"Probably because they're older," Shelby muttered.

"The problem is that all of the phones are down, and Eugene—" She left the sentence unfinished.

Max could imagine the trouble Eugene Stone was giving her. Stone remained bitter that he had lost in his bid for mayor when Perkins was elected. That he'd lost the position to a woman, and one relatively new to town—she'd moved there ten years ago—had not helped. He had run again in the next election and won the council seat, eventually being appointed mayor pro tem.

"Enough of my problems," Perkins said. "Tell me what you two are doing out at this hour. Tell me I don't already have legal problems from . . ." She gestured toward the window, which was covered with a blind. "This."

Max had filled in a few times when the town needed legal counsel. The job of city attorney officially belonged to Calvin Green, but he'd experienced health issues over the last year.

"I don't know about legal problems, but Shelby has something she needs to show you."

He suspected that Shelby only knew the mayor

because everyone in a small town knew everyone else. She didn't have a lot of reason to involve herself in city business.

The mayor confirmed this when she reached across the desk and shook Shelby's hand. "Sparks, am I right?"

"Good memory."

"I'm a natural politician. Haven't you heard?"

It was another barb that Stone had thrown her way during the last election—that because she had been mayor in one of the Dallas suburbs, she was a "lifelong politician who had never worked a day in her life."

"Have a seat. I've been standing out there since this thing hit at—"

"Eight twenty? We first saw the aurora a few minutes after eight."

Perkins nodded and motioned for her to continue.

It only took ten minutes to lay out what they thought they knew. Shelby presented Perkins with an article for each point she made. By the time she was done, the mayor's desk was littered with nearly a dozen different printouts.

Perkins steepled her fingers and studied them before standing and stacking Shelby's research into a neat pile.

"You're telling me this is widespread—"

"It would have to be for us to see the aurora this far south."

"That our loss of power is permanent."

Shelby and Max nodded.

"And that manufacturing is down as well, meaning our infrastructure will be vulnerable for some time."

"Yes." Shelby's voice was a whisper.

"Best guess, Shelby. How long are we talking about?"

It was something they hadn't yet dared to do, put a number on it. Estimating the breadth of the damage would somehow make it more real and perhaps consign them to a lifetime of hardship.

Shelby glanced at Max, swallowed, and turned back to the mayor. "To rebuild transformers and restring power lines? I don't know, exactly. I'm not a scientist or a city planner, but if I had to guess, I'd say twenty if things go well. And if this is the only solar storm. Some of the experts say it would take more like forty."

"Weeks?"

"No. Not weeks—years. Twenty to forty years."

Eight

Shelby was surprised when Perkins walked around the desk, opened her office door, and started barking orders. What had she expected the woman to do? Argue with her? Throw her out of the office? Weep?

Max was visibly shaken by the time frame that Shelby had suggested, but he didn't correct her. If there was one thing Shelby could count on, it was that Max would tell her if he thought she was wrong.

"Bryant and Castillo—I need you in my office. Stone, find Danny Vail and Calvin Green. Tell them I need to see them now. After that I want you to assemble the council in chambers. They need to be ready to meet in twenty minutes. And someone find me the high school science teacher!"

Stone immediately began arguing with the mayor. "Maybe you don't realize the emergency we have here."

"Eugene—"

"Maybe you can't handle the job during this type of crisis."

"Save it, Eugene, and do what I asked." Perkins slammed the door, took a deep breath, and grabbed a water bottle from her desk, downing the contents in one long drink.

In less than five minutes the group was assembled. There weren't enough chairs, but no one seemed to mind. Bob Bryant and Luis Castillo leaned against the wall. Bryant, the police chief, was roughly Shelby's age and in good physical shape. Castillo, the fire chief, was another matter. In his mid-to-late sixties, Castillo had completely recovered from heart surgery, but the man's skin had an unhealthy pallor. Sweat beaded on his bald head.

Calvin Green took the remaining seat. The oldest in the group, he was probably over seventy. Shelby knew Max had filled in for the man on several occasions—but he looked healthy to her. In fact, he looked much better than Castillo.

As Perkins rounded her desk and took her seat, Danny Vail walked into the room. If their city manager was surprised to see Shelby, he didn't show it, though he did nod her way. Danny was African-American, with a buzz cut and a military bearing. They'd known each other for at least twenty years. Danny was forty-five years old, the same age that Shelby's husband would have been had he lived. In fact, Danny had served with Alex overseas.

They first met back when Shelby was newly married and sure that her husband could master the transition from military to civilian life. Danny had helped them through some difficult situations back then, though she saw little of him now. Perhaps that was her fault. He'd seemed interested in her after Alex died and she'd been left alone to raise Carter, but she'd told him in rather blunt terms that she would not be dating. That had been so long ago, and Danny had dropped off the radar other than the occasional hello at church. She supposed managing a town, even a small one like theirs, was no easy task.

Perkins didn't waste any time. "All of you know Max, and this is Shelby Sparks. She has clarified our situation, and I—"

"How can she possibly know what we're dealing with?" Bob Bryant asked. "Stone's right. This is a crisis situation. I don't think we should be looking to people outside of appointed and elected officials—"

Perkins silenced him with a raised hand. "Shelby was conducting research on an unrelated matter."

"If it's unrelated, why are we wasting our time on it?"

"When she realized it applied to our current situation, she thought to bring it to me. I believe it's valid, and I think you will too."

"It's not valid if it doesn't tell me how to police our streets with no power, no street-lights, and no way for officers to communicate." Bryant was ticking the items off on his fingers.

He'd worked himself into quite a state of agitation. His face was the color of a plum, and he breathed rapidly as if he'd been out jogging. Shelby realized in that moment how quickly things would fall apart if they gave in to panic.

But Mayor Perkins was not panicking. "I want to share Shelby's information with each person in this room before I make an official statement."

Bryant shook his head in disgust, but he stopped talking. There were murmurs of agreement among Castillo, Vail, and Green. Perkins laid out the situation in quick, succinct points, and when she was finished, Bob Bryant was again the first to speak.

"You're ready to accept a massive solar flare is what we're dealing with based on printouts from a romance writer?"

Shelby wanted to ask how he knew what type of books she wrote, but she decided it wasn't the time or place to pick a fight. They had bigger issues to deal with.

"Her research is good."

"Her research is for a fictional book."

"It matches what we're seeing." Perkins nodded toward the window. "I recognized the aurora—had seen it before when I was in Alaska. I didn't realize how it was possible or what it would mean to us. These printouts confirm that we are dealing with a cataclysmic event."

Bob pressed his hands over his eyes, lowered his voice, and said, "This is insane. Eugene Stone is right. You're not qualified to handle this situation."

"Chief Bryant, I will remind you that I'm your mayor and you will follow my orders—"

"Until you're relieved of office."

"That might happen to you faster than me, Bob."

Perhaps it was the use of his personal name. Whatever the reason, Bob Bryant snapped his mouth shut and motioned for them to continue.

Castillo seemed willing to accept Perkins's evaluation. "If what you're saying is true, and I have no reason to believe it isn't, we need to get word out to people to watch the power lines. If they break, there are likely to be explosions."

"What will we do about them?" Max asked.

All eyes turned to him.

"You need to make this decision now," he continued. "Will we use the limited amount of water we have on hand to put out fires?"

Nine

No one in the room spoke for at least a minute, and then everyone started talking at once. Shelby noticed that, as usual, Bob Bryant was the loudest and most argumentative.

Mayor Perkins grabbed a book and slammed it down on her desk. "I will not have this type of behavior in my office!"

Once she had everyone's attention, she turned to the fire chief. "You wanted to ask Max a question?"

"It's preposterous." Castillo turned to Max. "Surely you're not suggesting—"

"That you should let buildings burn?" Max leaned forward and braced his elbows on his knees. "I don't see what choice we have. If I remember correctly, our water tower holds enough supply for a single twenty-four-hour period. At night, when people are sleeping, it refills. But it's not refilling tonight, and if Shelby is right about this knocking out the electrical grid, it won't refill for quite some time."

Castillo didn't argue with his logic. "My concern is that people will panic. If people see the city can't provide fire suppression service, we'll have lost this battle before it's begun."

Perkins cleared her throat. "Castillo, I want a report from you within the hour. Explain how you're going to provide emergency services with limited or no water supply."

She stretched her neck to the left and then right, trying to relieve the tension in her shoulders. Shelby was suddenly glad that this woman was in charge. She wouldn't panic, and she wouldn't allow anyone to run over her with their opinions.

"Power, communication, and transportation," Perkins said. "Those three things are our priorities."

"If what you're saying is true, the only power we have will be provided by the city's emergency generator." Danny shook his head. "When you first hired me as city manager I did a complete inventory and analysis. The three generators we have won't be able to do much good."

"I want you to find out how many of the

67

major businesses have generators. Get me that information."

Vail grabbed a pen from her desk and began taking notes.

"Bryant, how will people communicate their needs to the police department?"

"If the phones don't work . . ." He was still agitated, but now on a familiar playing field. "We might be able to position officers at key positions throughout Abney."

"In addition, I need a way to convey information to the citizens."

"We could tack flyers to prominent places throughout the town," Shelby suggested. "Word will get around once someone reads them."

"And how are we supposed to copy them?" Bryant asked.

"I'll release a concise statement, and we'll handwrite a couple dozen copies." Perkins looked to Vail.

"A few of the secretaries showed up when the power went out. I'll see who else I can wrangle into helping."

"All right. That leaves transportation. For now, some of the cars are working, and I assume they'll continue to do so—right, Shelby?"

"The older models should be fine. No one actually knows what a prolonged solar event can do . . ."

Bob Bryant shook his head in disgust.

"But if they're working now, they'll probably continue to."

"The problem," Max reminded the mayor, "is they'll need gasoline, and the pumps won't work without electricity."

"That's not an issue we have to tackle tonight, but I want someone working on a solution. Maybe we can hook up a generator to one of the gas pumps. Danny, put someone on it."

Calvin Green hadn't spoken, but now he cleared his throat and said, "You are within your purview to declare a state of emergency and martial law. That would allow you to commandeer what supplies are available."

"Martial law will be a last resort, but it might be necessary to declare the state of emergency. Calvin, I want you to draw up the necessary paperwork for both, just in case. Have it on my desk by morning."

"Without a computer?"

"Yes. There are electrical typewriters in the basement if I remember correctly. Find one and get someone who remembers how to use it while our generator is still working. As far as I know, there are no manual ones left, though everyone might be on the lookout for one of those as well. We need to conserve every ounce of energy from our generator."

"I'll make sure everything is in power-save mode," Danny said.

"All right. Now what exactly does our emergency plan suggest?"

Danny held a folder under his arm. He dropped it on her desk. "It's not going to be helpful in this situation."

Perkins opened the folder and studied the top sheet. "This is the county plan?"

"It is."

"Most of this assumes we have communication and can provide basic services, which at this point we can't."

Bob Bryant had been nervously tapping his officer's belt, which held a myriad of equipment. "We need to be sure about this. Maybe we've been attacked, and we don't know it. Maybe this is a national security issue or even a case of domestic terrorism."

Max turned to him and said, "You think a domestic terrorist has caused the aurora borealis to appear in Texas?"

"I don't know." Bryant's face again turned a dark red. "At least I admit I don't know instead of pretending—"

"That's enough," Perkins said.

"I'm asking that you check this out and confirm that what we think has happened, has in fact happened."

Perkins sat back in her chair. "The science teacher should be here any minute. What else would you suggest?"

"Some of the officers have CBs at home. Maybe someone else, someone not in Abney, knows something."

"Good idea. Set up a rotation schedule. Have someone manning them constantly for at least the next forty-eight hours."

"We provide services to the county, not merely the town of Abney." Bryant motioned toward the outer room. "You have to do something for the people out there on the county roads. You have to at least check on them."

Max nodded, surprising Shelby. He actually agreed with Bob Bryant on something?

"We could send scouts out to check on the surrounding towns."

Perkins stood, walked around her desk, and stopped in front of a map of the county. "All of the surrounding communities are within an hour's drive."

"Although I realize we may be dealing with limited fuel . . ." She nodded toward Max. "I believe it's worth it at this point to assess our situation. I don't want anyone going alone. Teams of two—send them here, here, and here." She pointed to communities on the map to their north, east, and south. "West is too far, other than Bend."

"Don't bother," Max said. "We drove back from the Bend earlier tonight. The situation is the same as here."

"All right. We will all convene again at six a.m.

Except for Max and Shelby, who are both free to go."

Shelby should have been relieved, but after seeing the pulse of their town she didn't actually feel comforted. It was an erratic heartbeat at best, prone to flights of panic.

As they walked out of the office, Perkins headed toward the council chambers. Danny pulled Shelby to the side while Max spoke with the fire chief.

"Are you all right?"

"Of course I am."

"Is there anything you need? You or Carter?"

Shelby looked left, right, and finally into the eyes of her friend. "We're good right now. But if this thing unravels the way I think it will, who knows?"

He nodded once, tightly, and said, "Let me know if there's anything I can do." Touching her arm lightly, he turned and hurried off to his office.

Max caught up with her, his eyebrows raised as he nodded his head in Danny's direction.

"It was nothing," she assured him.

As they turned to leave, Bob Bryant stepped in front of them. "You two need to stay out of this," he said.

"Excuse me?" Max tensed, and for a crazy moment Shelby thought he was going to punch their police chief in the jaw.

"No offense, Shelby. My wife loves your books. It's just that . . . well, you write novels."

Which was exactly their problem.

Fictional stories about society's collapse were all well and good. They provided an entertaining read, challenged one's survival instincts, and even taught a few coping techniques. But this? This was real, and it looked to Shelby like they were woefully unprepared to deal with it.

Ten

Instead of taking Shelby home, Max headed out of town on the county road.

"You must be more tired than I am."

"I'm exhausted," he admitted.

"You drove past our street."

"There's one more thing I want to check out."

She groaned, so Max flashed her his warmest smile—what Shelby had once called his endearing cowboy smile. Best he could tell, she hadn't meant it as a compliment.

"Forget it, Berkman. I'm impervious to your charm."

"I've been meaning to talk to you about that."

It felt good to joke about something inconsequential. The aurora continued to twirl and spin, brightening one moment and fading the next. Max was oddly awake and grateful to be out of city hall. He'd never been one to trust local authorities to solve his every need. The truth was, he felt better dealing with things himself, which was exactly what they were about to do.

When he pulled off the pavement and parked in front of the city water tower, Shelby made no move to leave the truck. They both craned their necks to look up at the tall structure, which looked oddly like a large golf ball on top of a tall tee. The words *Abney Argonauts* were written in blue letters on the side of the white tank, alongside a mural of the high school's mascot.

"Want to tell me what we're doing?"

"We're going to climb the tower."

"Climb?"

"Unless you see an elevator, which wouldn't work anyway because there's no electricity."

"Maybe I'll wait here." Shelby pulled her gaze from the tower to study him.

"You're not going to let me go up there alone, are you?"

"And why wouldn't I?"

"Because I heard Perkins say everyone should work in pairs."

"So you want me to go with you?"

"We need a comprehensive view of the area. No one in the mayor's meeting thought about it."

"And what do you expect we'll see?"

"I have no idea, but I do know one thing." He turned off the engine, opened his door, and tugged her hand, pulling her across the seat and out his side of the truck. "We'll see more up there than we can down here."

She shook her head, but she wasn't saying no. Max considered that a victory.

He let her climb first, thinking that if she slipped he could catch her. A more likely scenario was that she'd knock him over on her way down, and they would both suffer broken legs or worse.

He shouldn't have worried. She climbed the ladder like a monkey in a tree.

By the time he reached the top, Shelby was seated with her feet dangling and her arms hooked over the shorter of two rails.

"Great idea, Max."

"I have them occasionally."

He dropped down to sit beside her, trying to process what he was seeing. If the aurora had been startling when viewed from the ground, it was overwhelming from where they sat. Flopping onto his back, he stared up at it. It was now after two in the morning. With all that had happened in the last six hours, he hadn't slowed down enough to consider the thing that was changing their lives. From one hundred and twenty feet up, the sight of the aurora was mesmerizing. The sky resembled a kaleidoscope, and Max felt as if he were caught in a tube somewhere between the array of mirrors on one end and the objects chamber on the other.

"You're looking a little green there, Max. Afraid of heights?" Shelby leaned over him, studying his face. Her impossibly curly black hair fell forward and onto his chest, and her warm brown eyes laughed at him.

He wanted to reach up and touch her face. He longed to pull her to him and forget about this cataclysmic event for a moment. But before he could make a move, Shelby was tugging on his hand, hauling him into a sitting position.

"I know that look," she said. "Carter had the same expression before he upchucked last week."

"He'd bet Jason he could eat three chili cheese dogs."

"It's a good thing he did barf, or his insulin levels would have shot through the roof."

"Boys will be—"

"Yes, I know, but the point is that you have the same look. Deep breaths, please."

He actually did feel better sitting up. "For a moment there, it felt like I was floating."

"A little vertigo is normal if you stare at the aurora too long."

For the first time, Max's gaze sought the horizon toward the west. As far as he could see, in every direction, there was near total darkness punctuated by very few lights. "Amazing, isn't it?"

"It would be beautiful if it didn't spell doom and destruction."

"Do you believe that?"

"I'm not sure what I believe." Her tone had grown serious.

This was the Shelby he knew—contemplative, private, never giving much away. He preferred the one that had leaned over him with the look of amused concern.

"There's only enough water for twenty-four hours?" she asked.

"It might last longer, if people conserve."

"Why don't we have a generator for this water tower?"

"Money. We're a small town and a generator of that size isn't cheap." When she didn't respond, he added, "There's always the water from the springs if it comes to that."

"It's not only a matter of having enough to drink. Think of the sanitary issues if you can't flush a toilet or bathe or wash your dishes." She again slung her arms around the lowest rail and stared down at the ground. "This comes from a lack of imagination. People can't conceive that the world they live in, the society they are used to, can change in a flash."

Instead of arguing, he bumped his shoulder against hers. "I won't let anything happen to you and Carter."

"We're fine." She pushed her hair back out of her face. "I appreciate it. I do. But we're fine."

Max allowed her words to fade into the darkness, and then he said, "Let's check out the other directions."

They followed the platform to the north, east, and south. In each case it was the same, near total darkness broken by the occasional light from a home with a generator.

"We can tell Perkins exactly how widespread this is at tomorrow's meeting," he said.

"A meeting we weren't invited to."

"Most everything is out as far as we can see, which from this vantage is a complete 360. Bryant's men might have driven farther, but they wouldn't have been able to confirm what was happening in every direction."

"How does that help us?"

"We know we're not in this alone." He glanced at Shelby and as usual decided to be brutally honest with her. "With everyone in the same boat, there are going to be some people who try to take what few supplies we have."

"You mean—"

"I mean that we need to start thinking about defense, because I don't see the US government sending in reinforcements anytime soon. Do you?"

They both glanced toward the military base to the east. It was too far away to see, but it was there. Were they also in the dark? Or were they better prepared? And what was their priority—ensuring the safety of the towns around them or protecting their country from outsiders? The dozens of questions Max had held at bay crashed over him in waves. He needed to check on his parents, but first he had to make sure that Shelby and Carter were going to be okay. He wasn't sure when it had happened, but sometime in the last five years he'd decided that he was personally responsible for their welfare. Shelby might insist they were fine alone, but Max wasn't going anywhere until he was sure that was true.

She stared up at him, a question on her lips and concern coloring her expression, when a blast shattered the quiet of the night, followed immediately by the roar and rumbling of fire.

They leaped to their feet, ran around the platform, and stopped on the south side.

"It's near the high school," Shelby whispered.

"There's an electrical substation a quarter mile past the football field."

"There was."

As they watched, an Abney fire truck raced toward the blazing inferno, lights flashing and siren screaming.

"How do I do this?" Her voice was forlorn, and she turned away from him. "How do I protect Carter in a world that no longer makes sense?"

"I don't know. I honestly don't." He reached for her hand and held on even when she tried to pull away. "But I do know you're not in this alone. We'll find a way, Shelby. Together, we will find a way."

Eleven

The sound of Max's truck pulling into the driveway woke Carter from a deep sleep. He was surprised to see sunshine pouring in his window, and then he remembered he'd opened the blinds the night before to better see the aurora.

The aurora.

He grabbed his phone off the nightstand, touched the power button, and waited.

No service.

Of course there wasn't. For a few minutes before falling asleep, he'd allowed himself to pretend that by morning everything would be back to normal. Clearly that wasn't the case. With a groan of frustration, he powered off the phone.

Rolling out of bed, he pulled on a pair of jeans and a T-shirt and then hurried from his room. His mom was still asleep. The sight of her curled into a ball on top of her bed calmed something in Carter's heart. She must have come home late, as she hadn't bothered to change her clothes or pull down the covers. But she was home, which probably meant the world hadn't ended yet. She would never sleep through such an event. She'd probably take notes.

He made a pit stop by the bathroom, wondering if he should use water to flush the toilet or even brush his teeth. He decided no to the first and yes to the second. Glancing out the kitchen window, he saw Max in his backyard fiddling with something on his picnic table. He grabbed a box of whole grain cereal, the last of the milk from the fridge, a spoon, and a bowl.

He stepped outside with his breakfast and walked toward Max. "Hungry?" he asked, opening the chain-link fence that separated Max's yard from theirs.

"Actually, I am." A box of Pop-Tarts sat on the picnic table beside an old camping stove.

"That sweet stuff will kill you." Carter filled his bowl with cereal, sniffed the milk, and poured it up to the rim. He devoured three bites before he looked up. "What?"

"I'm remembering what it was like to be seventeen and starving."

"You joke, but in a week we might all be starving."

Max didn't argue with him, which Carter appreciated. His mom still tended to treat him like a kid, as if she could protect him from bad news. But he wasn't a kid, and the bad news was pretty obvious.

Max filled an old tin pot with water and set it on the stove, but he didn't turn on the flame.

"Bet you're wishing you didn't buy that fancy electric stove now."

"You bring up a good point. Gas is still

working, so you and your mom should be able to cook on yours—at least for now."

"Want to take the coffee inside?"

"Nah. It's cooler out here." Max sat down and tore open a package of the Pop-Tarts. He put half a pastry in his mouth, chewed for a few moments, and then swallowed it down with a swig of orange juice straight from the carton.

"I'd get a lecture for that."

"One of the perks of being a bachelor."

They ate in silence for a few moments. When Carter was done with the cereal, he pulled out his phone and checked it again.

"That's not going to work."

"I know, but it's just—"

"A habit."

"Yeah." Carter frowned, feeling a strong desire to pitch the thing across the yard. He still hoped they were wrong about the flare. As long as there was hope, he'd keep it.

"So what did you and my mom find out last night?"

"Your government is at work doing the best they can."

"Meaning nothing."

Max laughed. "Basically you're right, but I'm not going to encourage your cynicism."

"I learned it from you."

"Probably, and if it prepares you for something like this, I suppose I'm not sorry."

"Why aren't they doing anything?"

"They're trying, but no one has ever dealt with a massive solar flare before. It wasn't one of the scenarios in their handbook."

"But a Russian invasion was?"

"You must have had Mr. Johnstone for government."

"Guilty."

"Yeah. He always did like to pull out the city documents and share them with his class."

"And now I know why. Couldn't they prepare for something logical, like a virus or an IED or a solar flare?"

"Sometimes it takes a while for our emergency plans to catch up with reality."

"We're sunk."

"Not exactly." Max was facing Carter's house, and Carter turned to see who he was waving at. His mom was standing in the kitchen window, waving back at them both. Max stood and picked up a package of matches, lit the burner, adjusted the flame, and centered the pot of water over it.

"Your mom was pretty tired last night."

"I never heard her come in, and for the record, I'm the one who is supposed to be staying out late."

"For the record, thanks for filling all of my containers, sinks, and tub with water."

"No problem." At the time it had seemed like a

lame thing to do, but now he was starting to think it was pretty smart.

His mom wore the same clothes she'd slept in, and her hair had that Medusa look where her curls poked out in all directions. Carter usually teased her about it, but one look told him that they had more important things to talk about.

In that moment, he felt a deep anger well up inside him. He was supposed to go to the Market and work his shift today. He worked fifteen hours a week for minimum wage. The job provided enough money to put a little gas in his car, cruise the burger joint with Jason, and maybe stop to flirt with some girls at the park. It was the summer after senior year, and he was supposed to be enjoying himself before beginning the grueling work of college. Now all of that had been stolen from him. For all he knew, there would be no college by the time September rolled around.

It wasn't fair.

Why did it have to happen to him, to his generation? Why didn't the adults, the people who were supposed to know everything, prepare better?

"Stop frowning. We haven't even told you the bad news yet." His mom leaned her elbows on the picnic table and rested her head in her palms.

Carter shrugged.

Max stood, took the boiling water, and poured

it into a tall glass pitcher with a metal top. Then he added several scoops of coffee.

"Three minutes and we'll have you that important first cup."

"Promise?"

"Yup. That's one promise I'm sure I can keep."

While the coffee brewed, they told Carter the details of the mayor's meeting and how they had seen the substation blow up.

"And you came home and went to sleep? We all could have died in our beds."

"Not likely," Shelby said, stifling a yawn with her hand. "There's a creek between us and the power station."

Max looked from Carter to his mom. "I went to city hall for the six o'clock meeting."

"And?" Shelby and Carter asked at the same time.

"Mayor Perkins already knew about the substation, of course. As far as telling her what we saw from the top of the water tower—"

"You climbed the water tower?" Carter turned to stare at his mother.

Max waved away his concern. "Your mom's still quite athletic."

"Seriously?" Carter turned to Max. "She trips on cracks in the sidewalk. I've seen her do that more than once."

"I'm sitting right here." His mom started to run her hands through her hair, but settled for trying to pat it down into some sort of order.

"As for the mayor, she wasn't surprised, but she was glad to have it confirmed."

"Have what confirmed?" Out of habit, Carter put his hand in his pocket, checking to see if his phone was still there. Already it seemed like a lifeline to a way of life that no longer existed.

"That we're not alone. Every town for as far as we could see was blacked out."

"This is terrible. I can't believe this is happening to me." Carter saw a look pass between his mom and Max, but he didn't care. He didn't even care that he sounded like a child. He wanted to go back to bed, sleep, and wake up to a normal world.

Max had other ideas. "I need to get inside the Market, Carter. Would you mind changing into your work shirt and meeting me back out here in twenty minutes?"

"My shift is cancelled."

"Yeah, I know."

"And the store is closed!"

"Let's deal with that when we get there."

Carter shook his head. He wasn't in the mood for Max's save-the-world ideas. Why couldn't they let him have just one day off, even when the world was ending?

"Fine." He grabbed his bowl and spoon and trudged toward the house. The urge to check his phone again was almost overwhelming, but he knew it was useless. Every time he turned it on, he used up a tiny bit of its power. Soon it wouldn't turn on at all.

He checked his insulin levels, measured a dose from the bottle he was currently using, and injected it into his stomach. Though he barely felt the prick anymore, today the vial of insulin irritated him. It wasn't enough that he had some dread disease. Now he had it in a world that was coming undone.

The phone weighed heavy in his back pocket. As he walked to his room and looked around for a clean work shirt, he realized that his cell phone was about as useful as a rock. All the same, he'd keep it with him. Maybe today something would change for the better.

Twelve

Shelby watched as Max pushed down a plunger and poured her a cup of coffee.

"What is that thing?" She sniffed the coffee suspiciously.

"A French press. It comes in handy when you're camping."

Grimacing, she tentatively took a sip, followed quickly by another. The familiar rich taste of coffee immediately brightened her day. The world might be ending, but at least she would be properly caffeinated for it.

Raising her eyes to Max, she said, "Marry me."

"Right now? Right here?"

"Sure, Berkman. But let me finish my coffee first."

That earned her a smile. Good thing he knew she was kidding, as they were not exactly prime dating material. They had been when they were teenagers, but this wasn't high school anymore. Shelby had learned to be quite happy on her own—or if not always happy, then content. As for Max, what she'd once felt for him was gone. At least mostly gone. On the rare occasions when her feelings for him reared their stubborn little head, she only had to pull out her high school yearbook to remember how he'd broken her heart. It was a wonder they were friends once again, but life was full of such little miracles.

She'd entertained the idea of dating once Carter went off to college. Maybe she could find someone completely different from Max. Someone safe. Someone more her type. She had no idea what her type was, and it seemed now she'd probably never find out.

Social media—gone.

Dating sites—gone.

Anonymous emails from creepy guys she didn't know—gone.

Possibly there would be advantages to being catapulted back to the Stone Age.

"Are you worried about Carter?" Max asked, pouring himself a cup of coffee. "It makes sense for him to be angry."

"Angry? Surly is a better word, and it's his go-to morning mood."

"Possibly. Don't you remember graduating from high school, though? No more boring classes in subjects that didn't interest you, knowing the people you didn't like wouldn't be following you to college . . ."

"This coming from the high school football star."

"The best was around the corner. College and freedom."

"You were going to Baylor. Carter's going to Angelo State. Huge difference."

"No more being under your parent's thumb—"

"Hey!"

Max smiled at her and wiggled his eyebrows. "What I'm trying to say is that the future as he imagined it has changed."

"That's true for all of us."

"But we're adults. We're supposed to be able to handle a crisis."

"Even the end of the world?"

"I doubt it's the end, but things have certainly changed."

Her tone softened. "Tell me what else you learned at the mayor's meeting this morning."

"Eugene Stone wants to invade our neighboring towns, especially Croghan."

Coffee spewed from her mouth. She nearly dropped the cup, but Max caught it.

"Why would he want to do that?"

"He says they have resources we need, and . . ." Max held up two fingers on both hands, making virtual quotation marks. "We'd be doing them a favor."

"Eugene Stone said that?"

"Heard it myself. Apparently, he saw this coming."

"Oh, he did?"

"Unfortunately, no one ever listens to him, which is how we find ourselves in this mess."

Shelby chewed on that for a minute. Finally she asked, "Did he?"

"See this coming? Not that I know of. I try to keep current on city business in case I'm called in when Calvin Green is out sick."

"Looked pretty healthy last night."

"Yeah, Calvin might outlive us all. But Eugene Stone and Bob Bryant could die of stress in the first week if they don't calm down."

"Some people."

"Exactly."

"What other good news do you have?"

"As we saw from the water tower, power is out in surrounding towns as well as here. There's already been looting in Killeen."

"I can't say I'm surprised about that."

"Neither am I." Max hesitated, and then he added, "We're not immune to the same thing."

"Looting?"

"Look, we have a nice small town here. Good neighbors and dedicated leadership—Eugene Stone notwithstanding. But Abney is far from perfect. We'll have our share of crime before this is over."

Shelby didn't have an answer for that. Instead, she focused on refilling her mug.

"I'd hoped there wouldn't be panic for at least forty-eight hours." Max swallowed the rest of his coffee. "Reports over the ham radio are that things are worse in Houston, Austin, and Dallas. So far there's no information from out of state— apparently the aurora is messing with our ability to send or receive radio waves consistently or for any great distance."

Shelby nodded, her heart racing with the scenario he was painting. "And the military base?"

"Locked up tight. The team that went to Killeen had to pass right by Fort Hood's entrance. In fact, they drove up to the gate, but they couldn't get any information and certainly couldn't get in."

Shelby wrapped her hands around her coffee cup to still their trembling. Finally she admitted, "What worries me most is not the water or the electricity. It's Carter's insulin."

"Which is why I want you to go to the pharmacy first thing."

"Do you think they'll be open?"

"Maybe. It's worth a try."

"Bianca and Patrick—they're supposed to be here at ten."

"It's not quite eight." Max glanced at his watch.

Suddenly Shelby regretted that she didn't own a watch. She'd quit wearing one years ago. Who needed them? She could always check her phone for the time. Only now the phones were useless.

"We should both be back before they get here," Max said. "Leave a note on your door in case we're late."

"All right."

"Take what cash you have. Do you need money?"

"No."

"Buy insulin and testing strips—as much as they'll give you."

"I don't think insurance will approve that."

"The pharmacy won't be able to contact the insurance company anyway. It's going to be a giant mess, and I think you'd do well to be the first in line."

Shelby pulled in a deep breath. She reached for one of Max's Pop-Tarts. She was going to need massive amounts of calories and caffeine to handle this day, but one bite of the sweet pastry confirmed she was fooling herself. She dropped it on the table and covered her face with her hands.

She could not eat while her child's health was at risk. She tried to pray, but her mind was numb—overwhelmed by a thousand questions and her darkest fears.

After a moment she peeked between her fingers and asked, "Why are you and Carter going to the grocery store?"

"To talk to Henry Graves."

"About buying food?"

"Yes. How much do you have?"

Shelby stared off across the yard, slowly shaking her head. "There's a little in the freezer—not much."

"What about canned goods?"

She sighed. "I kept putting off doing any grocery shopping. I was under deadline for my next book, and I meant to go on Wednesday . . . but I didn't."

"All right. My pantry's pretty much full. How's the stuff in your freezer holding up?"

"Defrosting. Everything is defrosting."

"You're going to want to cook the frozen stuff soon, before it goes bad."

"On what?"

"Your stove is gas. It will still work. Or if it's too hot in your kitchen, you can use this." He tapped the camping stove.

"So I'm supposed to sit around and cook food while the world is falling apart?"

"We have to do this one step at a time, Shelby. Fortunately, between your research and my customary paranoia, I think we're a little ahead of everyone else."

"I don't understand what you're talking about. I know the people in this town, and so do you. I don't think we'll be fighting over food in the first twenty-four hours."

"I hope you're right." Max stood, walked over to a large pecan tree, and leaned against it, splitting his attention between the street and her. "I also know this town, but in my line of work I tend to see the less-pleasant side of folks."

"Legal wrangling brings out the worst—"

"As do shortages. Food, gas, water, medicine—all of those things are going to be in short supply and high demand."

Max seemed to hesitate, which was unusual for him. He glanced past her, squared his shoulders, and then walked back over. He braced his hands on the picnic table and looked her directly in the eye.

"I need to go home, Shelby."

"Home?"

"To High Fields. I need to check on my parents."

"Oh . . . of course." Her stomach turned and twisted. She hadn't expected him to stay by their side. Why should he? They were neighbors, childhood friends, nothing more. "I hope Georgia and Roy are doing okay."

"My parents are probably fine, but they'll need help." Max paused, and then he added, "I'm not leaving until I'm sure that you and Carter have sufficient food, water, and medicine, plus enough gas to drive wherever you may need to go."

"You don't have to—"

"I do. I do have to do it."

He sat down across from her, and she had the strangest sensation that he was about to reach for her hands. She tucked them in her lap, feeling foolish—feeling afraid.

"I need to do it because I won't sleep unless I'm sure of those things. Remember when Pastor Tony preached on caring for your neighbor?"

"I remember."

"That's what I'm doing. It's what I need to do. Okay?"

"Okay." She squirmed, uncomfortable with the intense look in his eyes.

"But Shelby?"

She finally met his gaze.

"I want you and Carter to think about coming with me."

"Where?"

"To High Fields."

"Why would we do that?"

"Promise me you'll think about it. You don't have to decide now."

She could only shake her head, but Max wasn't listening. He was gathering up the breakfast supplies and carrying them into his house, leaving Shelby sitting at the table alone and wondering what the next twenty-four hours would bring.

Thirteen

Max didn't bother attempting to talk Carter out of his bad mood. It had been a long time since Max had been a teenager, considering he'd turned forty-five a few months before. The number seemed ominous to him. Was it midlife? Did most men live to the age of ninety? He doubted it.

And what had he done with his first forty-five years? His parents were certainly proud of his law degree. He'd always thought it a respectable, solid profession—one he could count on. Now he wasn't so sure. There wouldn't be many people hiring lawyers at the rate things were deteriorating.

No, the wiser choice would have been to be a farmer, like his father and his grandfather. He couldn't go back in time and change his life's path, but he could do everything in his power to live wisely from this point forward. And it was always possible that God had a reason for giving him a love for law and order and the ability to help others through legal quagmires.

So what if they were headed back to the nineteenth century? Lawyers were necessary even then.

"I need your help getting in the store, Carter."

"How am I supposed to do that?"

"I don't know, but we have to find a way. People ought to be able to purchase the supplies that are inside."

Carter tapped his fingers against the truck's window. Finally he said, "I always enter through the main door."

"All right, but I'm going to park in the back."

He slowed down to scope out the storefront. A line of cars was at the gas pumps, probably a half-dozen deep.

"Do the pumps work?" Carter asked.

"No. The mayor's working on rigging up some sort of generator to them."

"Wouldn't want to be around when those people figure out they're waiting in line for nothing."

"Perkins had someone post a sign at each gas station, saying they were working on it."

"So why are they here?"

"I suppose they want to be the first in line if and when the gas becomes available."

A few more people were milling around waiting for the store to open, but it wasn't anywhere near the mob Max had expected. Of course it was early—fifteen minutes after eight o'clock if his watch could be trusted. Folks would be waking, trying to rustle up coffee and food, and attempting to understand what had happened.

A few would start to hear about the mayor's statement, which had been handwritten and posted around town. Though her intentions were good, and though posting information was probably necessary, Max expected the reaction to be panic.

Max and Carter walked to the front door of the store. As he suspected, no one attempted to stop them. They took one look at Carter's green Market shirt and assumed he was reporting to work. Some even looked encouraged, as if the presence of an employee assured them the store would soon open.

Carter walked to the front glass doors and tapped lightly on them. Henry Graves must have been standing just out of sight, because he appeared on the other side of the door and pointed to the sign which said "Closed Until Further Notice."

"I'm here for my shift."

Graves again shook his head.

"I was thinking I could help," Carter insisted.

Graves actually rolled his eyes, but he unlocked the door.

"Go home, Carter. I don't need—"

When he opened the door wider to look directly at Carter, Max shouldered his way inside.

"Hey!"

"We need to talk, Henry."

"I don't need or want to talk to you."

Max had represented Henry's wife when the two divorced. He'd tried to convince them both to go to counseling, or at least agree to a formal separation before the divorce. Although Samantha was willing, Henry had been adamantly set against it. At that point the man's feelings and ego were bruised, and there was no turning back.

Max had seen an ugly, selfish side of Henry Graves—a side he was sure every person had if pushed far enough. His hope was that he'd learned a few things about Henry that would help him deal with the man. If he appealed to his ego, his sense of pride, he might have a chance of changing his mind.

"This town is depending on you. We need to talk about how you can reopen."

Henry shook his head, but he allowed them to stay inside as he closed and relocked the door behind them.

"I can't reopen. The gas generator is running the emergency lights, but not much more."

Henry had placed a lawn chair, cooler, flashlight, and extra batteries together, out of sight of the front door.

"Did you spend the night here?" Max asked.

"You gave my house to my ex-wife."

"I didn't give her anything." Max pulled in a deep breath and tried a different tack. "Why didn't you go to your apartment?"

"Actually I was there when the aurora hit. I was doing my laundry at the little washing room we have." He scowled again at Max. "When the power went out, I knew I needed to get up here and secure the store."

"Which you've done. But if you don't open, people are going to panic."

"That's not my problem. My job is to keep the store secure until it is safe to reopen. It's not safe yet, so the store remains closed."

"We couldn't take credit cards or checks, but we could take cash." Carter was staring at the registers. "It would be faster, and you'd make more money because you wouldn't have to pay the credit card fee or risk taking a bad check."

Henry continued to shake his head, but Max could tell that he was listening.

"Maybe you could allow ten people in at a time," Max suggested. "That way you wouldn't be overrun with customers. You could even limit how many items they could purchase."

"You're making this up as you go." Henry sank into the lawn chair and rubbed both hands up and down his face.

It looked to Max like he'd put on at least twenty pounds since the divorce, probably from too much fast food. His stomach strained against the work shirt, and the emergency lighting gave his skin an unhealthy color.

Now he ran his hand up and over the top of his head, where his receding hairline had left a round bald spot. "Corporate has guidelines. I checked them, and we're not to reopen until the store is deemed safe."

"It looks safe to me, Henry."

"Yeah, well, you're not the one who is going to be sued if someone trips in the low lighting and breaks an ankle."

"Look. Kaitlyn's here." Carter walked over to the door and unlocked it. As he pulled the girl into the store, he spoke to her in a hushed tone. Kaitlyn Lowry was slim with long blond hair, and she also wore her green Market shirt. Max knew that Carter rarely had the courage to talk to her. The boy had actually asked him for advice about girls—as if Max had much to say on that subject. Today, though, Carter and Kaitlyn were chatting like old friends. Everything was different.

Henry stood and stared at them, apparently at a complete loss for how to proceed.

"You have two employees now," Max reasoned. "And you'll probably have more. Let the kids work."

"How am I going to pay them?"

"Pay them out of the cash you bring in." Max

motioned for Henry to follow him toward the business center counter, wanting to put some distance between them and the kids.

He lowered his voice and said, "You get one shot at this, Henry. Those people outside are calm now, but they won't be if you don't open."

"And what happens when I sell out? From what the mayor said, there aren't likely to be any resupply trucks. She wanted my generator! As if I didn't need it."

"No one's going to take your generator."

"That idiot Eugene Stone would. He said as much."

"Eugene isn't in charge. Perkins is."

"The thing can't be moved anyway. It weighs a ton. Even if you had a flatbed big enough, you couldn't load it." His eyes darted left and right, left and right. Finally he looked at Max and said, "Perkins said this might last for years, even longer."

"All the more reason for you to make what profit you can now." Max didn't like the way his words sounded—as if it was already every man for himself—but he needed to persuade Henry to open. Shelby and Carter needed the additional food.

"How is the frozen stuff holding up?"

Instead of answering, Henry led him down the aisle with the frozen cases. "I pulled the night shades as soon as I got here last night."

"And the temperature?"

Instead of answering, Henry pushed his way through a set of double doors, stepped into the cooler, and checked the thermometer.

"Forty-three degrees." He sighed and closed his eyes. "Market policy is to trash anything if the freezers get above forty."

"Market policy . . . aren't there state regulations for this sort of situation?"

"Sure. State law says food must be disposed of if the cooler temperature is above forty-five degrees."

They began walking back toward the front of the store.

"Sell the stuff," Max said. "Sell it now, while you can."

"But Market policy—"

"You have to make this decision on your own, Henry. You may not hear from your corporate headquarters for days or weeks."

"Or ever."

"That's true, but you can sell this now and allow people to take it home. Some of them have generators."

Henry caved when a third employee showed up. When Carter opened the door to let in the middle-aged woman, an elderly man attempted to push his way through.

"Hang on there, Mr. Sims." Henry rushed over to the door and blocked the man's entrance.

"We'll be open in a few minutes. Let me set up things first."

Max nodded at the woman whose name tag said Tina. He hadn't noticed Carter's name tag, but then the boy pulled one out of his pocket and pinned it to his shirt. Carter, Kaitlyn, and Tina stood grinning at each other, apparently relieved that they would have work for the day. Henry relocked the store and set the three employees to writing out several copies of "The Shopping Rules," as he dubbed them. He included all of Max's suggestions and one of his own.

Shopping Rules
1. Only 10 customers in the store at a time.
2. You may purchase no more than 12 items.
3. Cash only.
4. Management reserves the right to refuse service to anyone who doesn't meet the above guidelines.

Carter and Kaitlyn were complaining by the end of the first handwritten copy.

"I have writer's cramp already," he said.

"Too bad we can't text it to everyone." Kaitlyn smiled at Carter, and then she ducked her head.

What passed between them caused an ache to stir deep in Max's heart. He had thought Carter was handling the changes that were coming at them pretty well. So life was changing at the speed of a freight train. That happened, through-out the course of history.

But seeing the embarrassed, somewhat flirty look that passed from Kaitlyn to Carter reminded Max of all that Carter would be denied. Care-free dating. His freshman year at college. The American dream, which had become something they all presumed they would attain. Now life would become a matter of endurance—and only the toughest, the fittest, and the smartest would survive.

Fourteen

Shelby was not the first in line to purchase medicine. She had opted to walk to the pharmacy, though her Volkswagen Beetle did start. She wanted to conserve what little gas they had. Her neighbor, Mr. Evans, had stopped her before she'd even made it out of her yard.

"How are you doing, Shelby?" He walked a mile every day, come rain or shine or—apparently—solar flare.

"I'm okay, Mr. Evans. How about you? Are you doing all right without any air-conditioning?"

Mr. Evans tapped his cane against the sidewalk and offered his customary smile. "It's a small inconvenience considering children are starving in Africa. Never doubt, my dear. God is still in control."

Those words followed her as she made her way to the pharmacy. What if Carter had to go to the hospital? It was a small facility with only twenty-five beds, but it was better than nothing. Was the hospital even still open?

Those questions and many more tumbled through her mind as she walked. They rolled like socks in a dryer. Up, over and around, again and again. She tried to pray, to have confidence that God would care for them, but her fears rose up and threatened to overpower her.

The aurora continued to pulse, but it was less noticeable in the light of day.

The pharmacy was only a few blocks away, so Shelby didn't have too long to stew. Once she was there, her attention was completely captivated by the scene in front of her. The front door was locked, with a sign that said service would only be provided through the drive-up window. That seemed odd, but perhaps they hadn't had enough employees show up to staff both counters. Shelby walked around to the side of the small brick building.

Half a dozen people were in line ahead of her, and she recognized most of them. In a small town, you tended to trip over the same people again and again. But she didn't know their names or their circumstances.

The woman at the front of the line was growing more agitated. She finally hollered something through the window and stomped off to her car—a big Suburban she had left running while she was in the line.

The man in front of Shelby had to be in his eighties. "She tried to drive it through, but they wouldn't let her," he said. His eyes twinkled as he added, "Change is hard for some."

"Do you know if they're filling prescriptions?"

"I haven't been here that long myself. I did see someone in front of the Suburban lady—a middle-aged man. He walked away with a package stapled shut."

"That's a good sign."

"Indeed. I called mine in yesterday. I'm hoping the insurance went through. That way I'll only have to pay the deductible—in cash. ATMs aren't working. My wife always said machines were going to be the end of us."

"There certainly have been plenty of warnings about our overuse of technology."

"Credit card machines, computers, cell phones, even robots." The man cackled as if relieved that life would now resemble some ancient memory he had long held dear. "There was bound to be a massive crash at some point. Now it looks like we outlived the age of technology, if what the mayor says is true."

The old gent nodded toward a handwritten flyer

that had been taped to the side of the building, where announcements about sales or upcoming health checks were usually posted.

Shelby stepped closer and tried to calm her racing heart as she read the words.

At approximately 8:20 yesterday evening we were exposed to a solar flare. From what we've been able to ascertain, this has affected all of the surrounding areas.

We are working to provide backup power and emergency services. Rest assured that fire and EMS personnel are patrolling the area. If you need immediate help, hang a white sheet on your door or send a neighbor to one of the following three emer-gency sites: high school office, mayor's office, library.

There will be a community-wide meeting this evening at 7:00 at the town square. Until that time, I personally encourage you to stay calm and help one another in any way possible.

It was signed by the mayor. There was no new information in it, at least nothing that should have surprised Shelby. But seeing it written and posted gave her a sinking feeling that their reality had changed, and it was never going to be the same.

It took half an hour to work her way to the window. By that time, Shelby had ascertained that indeed they were only taking cash. At least they were open. She tried to console herself with that thought and put on her best smile as the old man in front of her waved goodbye and tottered away with his prescription.

A woman with a beehive hairdo addressed Shelby from the window. "Can I help you?"

Shelby pulled her gaze from the growing crowd and scooted closer to the window.

"Yes, I'd like to pick up insulin and testing strips for my son—Carter Sparks."

"Ms. Sparks, I'd like to help you, but if you didn't call the prescription in yesterday, then I can't run it through the insurance system." Shelby had been visiting this pharmacy since Carter was first diagnosed thirteen years ago. Why had she never learned the woman's name?

"I see. Could I possibly pay cash then?"

The woman frowned and glanced past her at the growing line. "How much do you need?"

"How much can I get?"

"Not more than thirty days' worth. There's no telling when we'll get another supply of medicine, and I need to make sure what we have lasts for the many people who need it. I'm not going to allow anyone to stockpile the stuff."

"Thirty days will be fine."

Shelby had filled the prescription two weeks earlier, so another thirty days would give them six weeks' worth. After that she'd have to think of something else. Or maybe the government would find a way to distribute medicine.

The woman ducked away from the window and returned with a box of long-acting insulin doses as well as a small box of rapid-acting doses. On top of that she placed a box of testing strips. She added up the amount on a receipt pad and didn't even blink when she stated the total.

Shelby pulled a wad of bills from her purse. For more than a year, she'd been doing a savings program where she put a dollar in a jar the first week, two dollars the second week, and so forth. She had hoped that her stash would pay for a nice vacation before Carter went to college, but the price the woman uttered was a major portion of what she'd managed to save.

Shelby didn't even hesitate. She pushed the money through the window and accepted the receipt and supplies.

For the first time, the woman's reserve cracked. "We'll put this through the system, hon. Your insurance will reimburse you as soon as the power is back up and things are working again."

Shelby only nodded, tears stinging her eyes. She walked away quickly, not daring to look back.

The truth was, the power wasn't coming back, and it would be a long time before things were working again. She had six weeks to figure out where and how to buy more insulin. If she couldn't, there was a strong possibility her son would die.

Fifteen

By the time Shelby reached her house, Patrick and Bianca were waiting on the front porch. All three hugged and moved into the living room. The day was already growing warm, and without air-conditioning or even fans, they proceeded to open all of the windows to allow the slight breeze inside. But Shelby doubted she would be able to leave the windows that way. Since the day Carter had been born, she had taken security seriously. Seventeen years of checking the dead bolts on the door, of confirming every window was shut and locked before bedtime. Those habits wouldn't change overnight.

Shelby sat next to Bianca on the couch. "Tell me how your mom is."

"Scared." Bianca's long black hair was pulled away from her face and fastened in the back. She usually dressed carefully, paying meticulous attention to her makeup and hair, and she always wore fashionable earrings. Today she wore no jewelry and hadn't bothered to put on makeup. Her eyes were red, and somehow Shelby doubted she'd had much sleep at all.

"*Mamá* wants to move him home, and I don't blame her."

"At the nursing home he has the medications he needs, and he's surrounded by professionals who know what to do in an emergency." Patrick jiggled his leg, and then he asked, "Is the generator at Green Acres working?"

"It is, but even this morning they were shorthanded on staff. Can you imagine how bad it's going to be if this aurora situation isn't resolved soon? The computers are down, and no one can reach the corporate office. Why should the nurses and aides show up for work if they're not going to be paid? And how are workers supposed to get there without gasoline for their automobiles?"

"We're a small town," Shelby reminded her. "Some people will walk."

Bianca sat forward, her hands between her knees. "What you're both saying is true, but *Mamá* has some valid worries. She is a stubborn woman, and I don't think I can change her mind about this. I'm not even sure I should."

"If that's how you feel, Bianca, then we'll help you." Shelby reached over and squeezed her friend's hand. "When does she want to move him?"

"This afternoon."

"All right," Patrick said. "We'll go and get him after lunch."

"There's one more thing." Bianca sat up straighter, as if she needed to improve her posture to handle the burdens she was carrying. "For the time being, I think it's best if I moved back in with them. With no Internet, I have no work. Who is going to buy pictures during a global crisis? Without work I can't pay my rent."

"I can help," Patrick said.

"No. It's best that I make this decision now. *Mamá* needs me, and it makes sense for me to be there. I won't need to take much with me . . . some clothes and personal items."

"Are you packed?" Shelby asked.

"Yes. I took care of it last night. Everything I need is in two suitcases inside my front door."

"You'll want to take what groceries you have as well." Shelby shared with them Max's concerns about the food supply. "Best not to leave it in your apartment."

"Sounds like we have a busy day ahead of us." Patrick clapped his hands, as if he were coming out of a football huddle. "Oh, I almost forgot. Pastor Tony wants to have a meeting tonight after the mayor's statement."

Shelby exchanged a worried look with Bianca. "Any idea what it's about?"

"Nope. He asked me to spread the word, which

I have now done. Undoubtedly you ladies have a grapevine that you can crank up."

"My grapevine was on my cell phone," Bianca said.

"Same here, but surely between the three of us—four with Max—we can get the word out to a few people."

"Let's start with Max." Patrick had been watching out the front screen door. Now he stood, walked toward the door, and opened it. "About time you got here, bro."

Shelby glanced out the door and saw Max coming up the walk. He raised his hand in greeting.

And the morning's silence was shattered by the sound of gunshots.

For a moment everyone froze. Then Max hollered at Shelby and Bianca to stay inside. He and Patrick sprinted across the street and north toward the intersection of Kaufman and Fourth.

Shelby hurried to the door.

"What happened?" Bianca asked, crowding in beside her.

"I'm not sure."

"We can't see from here."

"I think we should go and find out."

Bianca hesitated, and then she nodded in agreement. "The guys might need help."

Shelby locked the front door and slipped her keys in her pocket. They hurried down the street to where a small crowd was gathering.

As Shelby pushed her way through, she heard a woman say, "He has a gun. You'd all better stay back."

Max was standing in front of Rodney Tull. Nineteen years old with greasy hair and large gauges in his ears, he wore a black T-shirt and dirty jeans.

"Lower the gun, son." Max had his hands raised in a gesture of surrender.

Patrick was on the ground providing first aid to a middle-aged woman. Shelby's mind flashed back to the evening before and the attempted hijacking—Max trying to help the guy and Patrick pointing a gun at his head. It was as if the same scene was playing out in front of her eyes, only this time it was Abney people. Patrick was still helping the woman on the ground, but he wouldn't stay there for long. His gaze kept returning to Rodney.

"Lower the gun," Max repeated.

"Not until he gives me the car keys."

"I won't," Mr. Evans said. "The car is not yours."

"Give me the keys!"

Mr. Evans shook the keys at him. "You think this will fix your life? Grow up, son. Take responsibility—"

Rodney fired three times, and the impact of bullets hitting his chest lifted Mr. Evans off the ground and sent him crashing backward. Those who had been watching began to scream, fighting to put distance between themselves and the desperate kid. Max turned toward the old man and was kneeling down to help him when Rodney scooped up the keys and jumped into the automobile.

Shelby started to run after him, but the car peeled away from the curb.

Patrick's attention remained focused on the woman, who sobbed uncontrollably. Blood seeped through the makeshift bandage on her arm. Max whispered something to the old man, attempting to calm him.

Bianca clung to Shelby's hand, holding her back from danger. But there wasn't anything to fear. Not anymore. Tires squealing, Rodney was already turning toward Main Street. Headed where? What would possess him to kill someone for an automobile?

Shelby made out Mr. Evans's words: "Wasn't his car." When he coughed, she saw blood staining his lips.

"Try to stay quiet." Max glanced up at Patrick. "Two chest wounds."

Max pulled off his shirt, using it to stanch the bleeding. Mr. Evans, whom she had talked to only hours before, lay motionless, staring up at the sky.

"Mr. Evans." She pulled away from Bianca and dropped to the ground beside Max.

"Someone go for help," Bianca cried. She hurried over to a teenager who was gawking at the scene. "Go. Go now!"

"Where?"

"To the library. EMS personnel are stationed there. *Rápidamente*. Go!" She gave the boy a shove.

He turned, stumbled, and then took off running toward the library.

Shelby glanced back down at Mr. Evans. This couldn't be happening. It wasn't possible. People murdered in broad daylight? On her street? By their neighbor?

"Help is on the way." She clasped the old man's hand, her heart slamming against her chest, her mind trying to make sense of the growing puddle of blood beneath him.

Mr. Evans smiled once, a small trembling thing, and then he glanced over her shoulder, sighed, and stopped breathing.

"No. No, no, no, no—"

"He didn't have a chance." Patrick reached up and closed Mr. Evans's eyes. "The kid was standing so close. The bullets literally tore a hole in his chest."

Shelby wanted to argue with Patrick, but she could only cling to her neighbor's hand, silently begging him to open his eyes. Some of the crowd had returned. They clustered together, crying and weeping. The woman who had been injured was groaning—whether from shock or pain, Shelby couldn't tell.

She didn't let go of Mr. Evans's hand until someone brought a bedsheet, and Max helped Patrick cover him.

Max glanced at her and asked in a low voice, "Are you okay?"

She nodded, swiping at her nose with the back of her hand, willing her tears to stop. Everything they'd seen in the last several hours had seemed like television. But the moment that she held Mr. Evans's hand and watched the light ebb from his eyes, she'd known that it was real. This was their new life, whether they were prepared for it or not.

Shelby had always been an adamant believer in the American dream, but in that second, two hundred years of social history was erased. Suddenly she was an immigrant, in a new and dangerous land, and she would need to find a way to protect herself, her friends, and the son who meant everything to her. She would need to find a way to survive.

Sixteen.

Max and Patrick both stood and scanned the crowd.

"Did anyone see how this started?"

"I was sitting on my porch." A young woman with a child on her hip stepped forward. She'd moved to the neighborhood recently, and Shelby couldn't remember her name.

"Mr. Evans came out and said he was going to see if his car would start. When it did, he turned off the ignition and got out. That was when Rodney walked up and pulled a gun."

Mrs. Stinson, elderly and somewhat crippled, hobbled forward, pushing her walker between the onlookers and staring mournfully down at her neighbor.

"Did you see anything?" Max asked her.

She nodded, crossed herself, and said, "You all know I live next door. I heard them speaking, but it happened so quickly. I picked up my phone to dial 9-1-1, but by the time I remembered the phone didn't work . . . by then you were here, trying to talk him out of his mad scheme."

"Why would he do it?" Shelby asked, her voice trembling.

"That boy has been in trouble quite often the last few years. His mother—I don't think she's around much. Haven't seen her at all since the aurora started." Her hand, shaking and spotted with age, waved toward Harold Evans's corpse. "Stubborn old fool. Why didn't he hand over the keys? It was only a car, hardly worth his life."

An ambulance and a police cruiser soon arrived, and Max and Patrick explained all they had seen and learned from the witnesses. Shelby stood next to Bianca, watching the EMS personnel load Harold's body into the ambulance. They also provided triage to the woman who had been injured. The first shot had grazed her arm.

"I'll have someone drive me to the hospital," she assured the paramedic, now calmer, though her hands were still shaking. "You take Mr. Evans."

Shelby and Bianca were talking to the neighbors, well out of earshot when the officer said to Max, "This is the second one today."

"Murder?"

"No. Carjacking. The first was a middle-aged man passing through town. When he ran out of gas and found out he couldn't buy any, he pulled a gun on a woman who had also stopped for fuel. Apparently she had half a tank and was hoping to top it off. The perp left his car, the fuel gauge on *E*."

"Was she hurt?"

"No. She grabbed her purse from the front seat and told him he could have the car." The officer shook his head. "I never thought I'd see the day."

As the officer walked over to the young mother and old woman to take down their statements, Max wondered what the point was. The perpetrators of these crimes were long gone. What was the police department supposed to do? Chase them and use up what little fuel they had? Call ahead and warn the next town? The first would have been foolhardy, and the second impossible.

Together Bianca, Shelby, Max, and Patrick walked back to her house.

"Are you okay, Shelby?" Bianca reached for her hand.

"It's a terrible thing to witness," Patrick said.

Like Max, his hands were stained with blood, but it was Shelby that Max was worried about. Patrick had seen combat—he would mentally and emotionally adjust to what had just happened. Though Bianca seemed shaken, she'd taken the events of the last hour in stride. Perhaps her mind was still on her parents. Shelby, on the other hand, was trying to hide a tremor in her right arm. She kept glancing around as if expecting a killer to jump out of the bushes.

"How did you know what to do?" Bianca asked.

"Medic training when I was in the army. Yesterday I would have told you I couldn't remember a bit of it, but I guess a part of you never forgets."

"Can you give me and Shelby a minute?" Max asked.

Shelby handed her keys to Bianca, who unlocked the front door.

Bianca again hugged her friend, and then she followed Patrick back into the house.

Shelby didn't resist, though sometimes Max wondered if she avoided being alone with him. He knew that she cared for him. They had been best friends since both were old enough to ride a bike. What he didn't know was whether her reticence was due to feelings she didn't want to admit, or whether she actually preferred being alone. The uncertainty kept Max at a distance, but not today, not after what had just happened.

Shelby sat down on the porch step. "Please don't lecture me."

"Why would I do that?" Max sat next to her, shoulder to shoulder. As he glanced out at the street, it seemed to him that if he were patient and looked hard enough, he would see the younger versions of Shelby and himself riding bicycles on a June afternoon. "What would I lecture you about, Shelby?"

"You'll tell me that this is our new life."

"It is."

"And that I need to toughen up." Her voice faltered on a sob. She pulled in a deep breath. "Remind me that ultimately God is in control."

Max did none of those things. He just sat beside her and allowed her to rest, to tune in to the birds that still sang in the bushes and the breeze that rustled the leaves of the red oak tree in the front yard.

"Mr. Evans always brought me a jar full of those small red cherries." Shelby stared at her hands. "He claimed they'd be good with ice cream."

"They were from his backyard. I didn't realize you could even grow cherries in Texas."

"Small and tart."

"Barely worth messing with by the time you removed the seeds."

"But we did it every year—because Mr. Evans always brought a jarful, and he always looked so pleased about them." Then Shelby did something Max couldn't have imagined her doing even twenty-four hours before. She leaned her head on his shoulder.

Max placed an arm around her and again simply waited.

That was one thing Max was good at—waiting.

"Carter's at work?" she asked.

"For his full shift."

"Do you think . . . Is he safe there?"

"I think the Market is probably one of the safest places in town. By the time I left, the mayor had stationed a patrolman out front, and people were queuing up for their turn to shop."

Shelby nodded, again swiped at her nose, and then sat up—straight and tall, shoulders squared, as if to convince Max that she could handle whatever came at them next.

Seventeen

Carter had seen all kinds of crazy before, or at least he thought he had. But as he took his lunch break and let his mind run back over the morning, he decided they had entered a whole new realm of insanity.

People trying to purchase twelve bags of dog food. Henry had added to the list of rules, "Only two of any item," and then he had restocked ten of the bags.

Max buying beans and peanut butter and a large sack of potatoes, even though his pantry was completely full. Carter knew because he'd looked in it when he was filling containers up with water.

An old gentlemen who was nearly toothless dropping ten different packages of candy bars on the conveyor belt at Carter's register. "We can grow taters and corn, but these . . . I believe we're going to miss the sweets."

It had all creeped him out. He still couldn't grasp that this might be it, that possibly they would have to live without the conveniences of modern life.

No Internet?

No phones?

No electricity or toilets?

No, he didn't believe it. How did people survive

without those things? Sure, he'd watched the zombie apocalypse and natural disaster shows, but those were products of an overactive imagination. They were entertaining because they hadn't happened, couldn't happen, and wouldn't happen. His generation was so far ahead of his mom's that it almost embarrassed him. It wasn't that older people were slow at learning certain things, like how to Skype. It was that the entire digital world was foreign to them.

For people Carter's age, computing was natural —more natural than learning to ride a bike. With 3D printers, they could produce prosthetics for missing body parts. He knew a boy at school who had a 3D-printed hand, yet the kid had beaten him at Ping-Pong. They could clone animals and even create hybrid animals. They could grow crops in the desert and design auto-piloted cars. His generation was only limited by what they couldn't imagine.

Which was why he was convinced there was a way around this, or through it. He refused to believe that they were stuck in the Dark Ages.

He was finishing his lunch—low-fat string cheese, a package of nuts, and a bottle of unsweetened tea—when Kaitlyn walked outside to join him at the picnic table.

"Two more checkers arrived." She plopped down next to him and stared at her sack lunch.

"We're going to need them."

"I'll say. Even with only ten customers at a time, it's like they never stop coming."

"Yeah, remember the old days—"

"Yesterday?"

"When we'd have those slow periods and had to straighten the register displays."

"And clean the conveyor belt."

"And check the bathrooms!"

Kaitlyn glanced sideways at Carter and smiled. Then she reached into her sack and pulled out a peanut butter sandwich.

"Thanks, Carter."

"For?"

"For making me feel normal, even if it doesn't last." She took a bite of the sandwich, which must have had too much peanut butter because she seemed to have trouble chewing. After swallowing she placed the sandwich back in her sack.

"You didn't eat much."

"I can't. I keep thinking about that mom with two kids who was in my line."

"Graves explained to her that we were only accepting cash."

"But she didn't have any." Kaitlyn's face puckered up—wrinkles between her eyes, her bottom lip sticking out as if she was pouting. Still, she looked beautiful. "If I'd had any money on me, I would have paid for it—at least for the milk. What are people going to do?"

"I don't know." Carter hesitated, and then he added, "Pastor Tony came through my line. He said there's going to be a meeting later tonight. Maybe he'll have some ideas."

"I hope so."

Carter didn't know that much about Kaitlyn. She had visited their church a few times after she and her mom had moved to Abney at the beginning of June. She was going to be a senior in the fall, her dad wasn't in the picture, and she was the prettiest girl he knew.

She stood and stretched, and then she peeked around the corner of the building at the line of people. "I can't watch many more moms with hungry kids go through my line and walk away empty-handed."

Though she'd barely had any break at all, they walked back into the store together. They made their way through the shipping and receiving area, which was eerily dark and quiet. Next they passed the freezers, which were quickly emptying of food. As they rounded the corner to the front of the store, they heard a man shouting.

A large, burly guy stood in Tina's line. Carter could just make out his profile. He had long hair in need of a cut, a scruffy beard, and tattoos across the side and back of his neck.

Henry stood beside Tina, while the officer at the front door split his attention between the escalating situation inside the store and the crowd outside.

"I have cash," the man said. "You have to sell me stuff if I have the cash."

"No, sir. We don't. The sign on the front of the store says—"

"I don't care what the sign says."

"We're not selling you ten boxes of diapers."

Suddenly the man pulled a gun. As soon as Carter saw the emergency lights reflect off the metal, he pushed Kaitlyn back into one of the side aisles.

"Was that a gun?" she whispered.

He nodded, put a finger to his lips, and peeked back around the corner.

"Sir, I need you to drop the gun and put your hands in the air." The officer had also pulled his weapon and was pointing it straight at the agitated man.

Customers started screaming and dropping to the ground, attempting to make themselves invisible. The burly man stared at the gun in his hand—his expression indicating he didn't understand what it was or how it had ended up there.

"Put the gun down, sir, on the conveyor belt, and take two steps back. I'm sure this is a misunderstanding that we can work out."

Carter thought the man might shoot. A look of stark anger passed over his features, but then a baby cried and the spell was broken. The gun clattered onto the conveyor belt. Tina stood frozen next to the register, but Henry snatched up the gun. "What did you think you were going to do? Shoot somebody? For diapers? If that's your solution now, I don't want to think about what you're going to be desperate enough to do in a month."

Mr. Burly tossed some money onto the belt, and snatched up two of the boxes. The Abney police officer reached for the gun the man had dropped. When he'd secured it, he holstered his own weapon and then grabbed the man by the arm. He gripped his bicep to prevent him from running away, but he didn't cuff him. Together they walked out of the store.

"Everybody get back to work," Henry growled.

Carter turned back to Kaitlyn and nearly knocked her over.

"Crazy," she murmured.

Which was exactly what Carter had been thinking. The question was, how much worse would it get before someone thought of a solution?

Eighteen

Max hurried up the steps of Green Acres—a square brick building on the north side of town. A glance at his watch confirmed it was ten minutes past the time he had agreed to meet Shelby, Bianca, and Patrick to help with Bianca's father.

From the front visitors' room, windows looked out over a pitifully small park area—barely large enough for a few residents to sit around in their wheelchairs and watch birds from the single feeder.

The area was empty of residents *and* birds.

Neither was there anyone at the receptionist's desk. Max took the hall to the right, passing framed photos of the 1965 television sitcom *Green Acres* starring Eddie Albert and Eva Gabor.

The hall was strangely empty, each resident inside their room. He knew the generator was working because he heard the beep of equipment, but windows had been opened, and a shade rattled from the slight breeze passing through.

The temperature was warm but not hot. How would residents survive the hundred-degree temps common in July and August?

Bianca's father was in room 23. Max tapped on the door, and motioned for Shelby to join him in the hall.

"We're really doing this?" he asked.

"Yes."

"And you agree with Bianca, that it's the right thing to do?"

"It doesn't matter what I think, Max. Bianca and her mom want him at home."

"All right. What can I do?"

"I was packing up his personal items. Patrick is carrying things out to his car."

"And Bianca's mom?"

"She's still trying to explain to Mr. Lopez why we're taking him home."

Max pulled back his shoulders and adjusted his cowboy hat. "Where's Bianca?"

"She left a few minutes ago to speak with a nurse about her father's medication schedule."

"Sounds like you girls have it under control. Maybe I'll join the old guy in the rec room for a game of checkers."

Shelby swatted his arm and turned back toward Mr. Lopez's room. She turned around as she pushed the door open and said, "You could find us a wheelchair."

Then she was gone, leaving Max in the empty hall.

He walked toward the nursing station. The place was eerily quiet—deserted almost. Where was everyone? He'd expected the nurses to be overworked. Probably the same shift had been working since the aurora began. He stood at the counter, waiting, glancing left and right, and then he saw a familiar face.

Connie Hartman was sixty, with white hair cut in a straight, low-maintenance style. Her normally pleasant expression was gone, and in its place wrinkles had sprouted between her eyes and around her mouth. Max had known her for years. He was fairly sure that she'd taught a Sunday school class he had attended, and he vaguely remembered her carrying candy in her pocket.

"I haven't seen you since mission night," she said, pulling him into a hug.

"Once a month, come rain or shine, I'm your man to stack food on shelves."

"And we appreciate that. Bill and I need all the help we can get, and our community is going to need those resources now more than ever."

"I'm here to help move Mr. Lopez," Max said. "I hope this is the right thing to do."

"He'll be with his family," Connie said. "In difficult times, that might be the most important thing."

Max had been watching the hall, but now he turned to study her. Connie was unfailingly optimistic, but she was also a by-the-book type of person.

"So you approve of a hasty discharge?"

"Normally I wouldn't."

"But—"

"Everything's changed, Max. You realize that."

"You don't think it could be dangerous? There will only be Bianca and Mrs. Lopez to look after him."

"Officially, I can never recommend a patient discharge against medical advice."

"How is this different?"

"There's no one to ask! I have no way to contact a doctor."

"Mason and Jones?"

"Have their hands full at the hospital."

"So what are you saying, exactly?"

"I'm trying to answer your question—should they take him home? I don't know, but I do know that I'm severely short-staffed. Between you and me, his family can probably give him better care than we can at the moment."

Max ran his hand across the back of his neck where the muscles felt tight and achy. The thought passed through his mind that his migraines often began this way, but he pushed the worry to the back of his mind. Now was not the time for him to be down and out for six hours—which was usually what happened after taking the medicine his doctor had prescribed. He would take deep breaths and stay hydrated, and maybe he would be able to avoid the migraine.

"I'm not sure what we're going to do," she admitted.

"About?"

"All of it. The next shift hasn't shown up."

"Nurses?"

"Well, I'm here, and the state only requires that we have RN coverage eight hours a day. That said, I can hardly leave given the situation we're in."

"So you stayed through the night."

"And my replacement didn't show up this morning."

"Who—"

"Half of my aides didn't report to work this morning, and I haven't heard from the administrator, supervisor, director of nurses, or assistant director of nurses."

"Do you want me to go and knock on doors?"

"Why? They know they're supposed to be here. Either they're unable to come or they're unwilling. In that case, your presence wouldn't change their mind."

She was probably right, but it didn't sit well with Max. People had responsibilities, especially people in the healthcare profession. They couldn't just bail at the first sign of trouble. But even as he had the thought, he knew it wasn't an honest one.

Henry Graves was a grocer, and he was vital to their community. Nearly every position was critical to their community—police officers, emergency personnel, pharmacists, drugstore cashiers, city workers, and store clerks. Teachers were temporarily off the hook since it was summer, but come fall they would still need to educate the town's children. Abney worked because people made sure it did.

They would need every man, woman, and teenager to fulfill their jobs if they were going to see their way through this. Each one was equally important. As far as bailing, wasn't that what he was going to do when he left for High Fields? But what choice did he have? Family came first. Family had to come first, because they were the people that you would sacrifice your life for.

"What about the residents here?" he asked. "Are they safe?"

"We have a generator that operates off natural gas. It provides enough power to keep the equipment working."

"Medication?"

"It's delivered every two weeks. Our last delivery was a week ago."

"So what is your most immediate need, other than workers?"

"Our main problem is food. Two out of six kitchen workers showed up. They're doing the best job they can, but they can't keep up. Many of our patients have special dietary requirements. I don't want to reassign the few employees who are here. They're needed on the floor."

"We're having a city meeting in a few hours, and after that a church meeting. I'll get you some help in the kitchen. I'll also try to find out where your supervisors are. Maybe someone has heard something."

She nodded her thanks, but her gaze kept darting toward a closed door.

"What is it? What else do you need?"

Instead of answering, she pulled him around the corner, glancing furtively right and left as she did so.

"Who are we hiding from?"

"No one, but I'd rather not upset the patients."

"Why would they be upset?"

"Deceased patients are in three of the rooms."

"Deceased?"

"I pronounced the time of death myself and notated it in their charts."

"Do you need a doctor to sign their death certificate?"

"Eventually, yes. The funeral director usually handles that. I sent an aide over to the funeral home, but no one answered the door."

"So they're just lying there? Have you contacted their families?"

"How would we?" Connie straightened her nursing smock, a soft purple color that he supposed was chosen to calm and encourage the patients.

Max rubbed a hand up and down his jawline. It would take more than pastel colors to calm residents once they discovered their neighbors were dropping dead.

"Connie, what did they die of?"

"They were old and worn-out." She shook her head, causing her white hair to sway softly back and forth. "It wasn't Green Acres' fault, if that's what you're asking. For all I know, this aurora or solar flare or whatever we're experiencing, maybe it had some effect on their lungs or hearts or kidneys."

Max thought he'd prepared his mind for the worst. He'd thought, as Shelby sat beside him mourning the death of Mr. Evans, that he understood what they were up against. But he realized in that moment that the mind could only process so much change at once, and they were facing exponential, catastrophic change. He probably wouldn't understand the scope of it for quite some time. As a lawyer, that bothered him more than anything so far. He'd always been good at assessing a situation and seeing the big picture. He no longer trusted his ability to do that.

"You need Hector Smith to collect the deceased, a doctor to sign the death certificates, and someone to contact families."

"Yes, yes, and no. Yes, I need Hector here soon. We can't leave the bodies in their room—it's against health regulations. Yes, he will need a doctor to sign the death certificates. But these residents had families that live out of town, so there's no way to get in touch. Most of our local residents, their family has been by to check on them."

"You can't just bury them without letting some-one know." He had an image of bodies stacked like cordwood, waiting for what? And through the heat of summer? No, it didn't bear thinking of. He needed to focus on the problem at hand.

Connie leaned forward and glanced around before pulling Max farther back into the nursing alcove. "How are we going to dispose of the bodies? Can Hector Smith do what he needs to . . . do?"

"I don't know, but we'll check. I want to make sure that Bianca's father gets home safely, and then I'll go to the mayor's office and find out how she wants to handle the situation here. We will get you some help."

Connie smiled her thanks, patted the pockets of her smock, and pulled out a peppermint. "For you," she said, pressing it into his hand. Before he could say anything, she had turned and walked away.

Nineteen

That afternoon they ate well.

After helping Mr. Lopez, Shelby and Max returned to her house, and Carter made it home from work tired and hungry. Shelby sautéed chicken, fried hamburger meat, and attempted to heat up a frozen pizza on the stove while Max grilled steaks.

Their neighbors had set up chairs and tables in their front yards. And though everyone was frightened, worried about the mayor's speech, and wondering what the next day would bring— they managed to laugh, to enjoy the bounty of food, to share with one another. The scene reminded Shelby of a giant progressive dinner.

But eventually the food was put into refrigerators that were no longer cold, and everyone made their way downtown.

Shelby, Max, and Carter decided to walk to both of the evening meetings.

"Maybe it will wake me up." Max crossed his arms over his head and popped his back as he yawned.

He'd managed a two-hour nap. Shelby was surprised he could sleep after all that had happened, but then he had only slept a couple of hours the night before. She'd had an extra hour or two that afternoon, but she was afraid that if she tried to rest, she would see Mr. Evans's face. She had dealt with the death of church members, other neighbors, even her own parents and husband, but his was so nonsensical.

As they waited for Carter on the front porch, Max told her about finding Hector Smith, the funeral director, walking into town. His car had broken down on a trip back from Austin. Fortunately, he was only twenty miles to the south and had been walking steadily toward Green Acres.

"Any luck finding a supervisor?"

"Tom was at the hospital with angina pain. He kept telling the doctors that he needed to be at work. Finally he checked himself out and walked the three blocks to the rehab center."

"We have some good people in this town," Shelby said.

"That we do."

Once Carter joined them, the three began the mile walk to the downtown square.

"Tell me again why I need to go." Carter's voice wasn't exactly a whine. Neither was it the argumentative teenage tone Shelby had come to expect.

She knew her son had come home exhausted from his shift at the Market. Thankfully, he had taken the time to eat and his insulin levels were good, but Shelby watched him closely. Always at the edge of her mind was the amount of insulin they had left. Would it be enough? What would they do if they ran out? What if someone tried to steal what they had?

She'd been so worried about being robbed that she'd put the insulin and her wallet into her big shoulder bag and placed a shawl on top of it. Any unopened insulin needed to be kept cold, but she couldn't risk it being stolen. She was not letting Carter's medication out of her sight.

"It's your town too, bud." Max also carried a backpack. Shelby happened to know that it held all the money he had in his house, bottles of water, a blanket in case they had to sit on the ground, and a handgun. She'd tried to argue with him when he'd told her about the firearm, but he'd shaken his head and said, "It's nonnegotiable, Shelby. You saw what happened to Mr. Evans. It's not going to happen to us."

Less than twenty-four hours after the solar flare had hit, and they were armed and carrying their possessions like the proverbial turtle.

Bianca had opted to stay home with her parents, but Patrick met them at the corner of First and Crawford streets, as they had prearranged. He proceeded to talk with Carter about some video game they were both involved in—a video game that was now permanently on hold. The conversation seemed to improve her son's attitude.

As they drew closer to the downtown area, the size of the crowd grew. By the time they turned the corner and faced the square, Shelby could see that the place was packed. Some people had brought lawn chairs. Others, like Max, had brought blankets. Many of the teens rode bikes or held skateboards under their arms. But most people appeared to have walked, like they had. On the stage, which usually held the high school band or a local choir or even a country-western duo, were four chairs.

Max found them a place directly in front of the platform, but toward the back on the sidewalk that flanked the small-town businesses, including his one-man law firm. He spread out the blanket for them and settled in for the speech. Carter nodded toward a group of teenagers. In the middle was his best friend, Jason. A smile broke out on her son's face, and he said, "Catch you later, Mom."

She opened her mouth to stop him, but Patrick stayed her with a touch of his hand.

"He needs a little normalcy, Mom. You can watch him from here."

She nodded and tucked her hair behind her ears.

By the time Carter reached Jason, the mayor, fire chief, police chief, and city manager had all climbed the stairs. Eugene Stone stood at the bottom, watching the crowd and scowling. Finally he turned and stomped off in the direction of city hall.

"She wants to see us when they're finished on the podium," Max explained.

Everyone in the crowd fell silent as Perkins stepped in front of a makeshift podium. There was no microphone, but she didn't need one. Mayor Perkins had their attention.

"I have asked the Reverend Polansky to open us with a word of prayer," Perkins said.

A stranger might have thought this call to prayer was owing to the flare, but public prayer was fairly common in their town. At the start of sporting events, during commencement addresses, even before the council opened for session, they had a time of prayer. Some of those prayers were silent. Other times, like tonight, they invited one of the local clergy to voice the prayer. It was one of the many things Shelby liked about their town. They might not be the most devout, but they didn't pretend that God didn't exist.

The reverend's prayer was brief—a petition for strength, wisdom, and faith. When he'd finished, the mayor again stepped forward.

"You all know these men on the podium with me. We understand that you are tired, that you're worried, and that you have questions. Each of these city leaders will give a brief report, and then I'll add an official statement from my office. After that we'll have time for a few questions, but I want everyone out of here early. You will be home before dark, which as of right now happens to be our new curfew."

A groan spread through the crowd, and some of the men at the back attempted to heckle her. Their protests died away when she motioned the police chief to the podium.

"We've had three carjackings today, one of which resulted in a fatality." Chief Bryant didn't continue until he was sure he had everyone's attention. "In none of the instances was the perpetrator caught, and we can assume that they are miles away from Abney by now."

"Where were the police?" someone behind Shelby asked.

Bryant gripped the podium and paused—trying to bring his anger under control. When he did speak, it was a low growl. "We have ten officers on patrol, and each one has shown up for his or her shift regardless of the fact that I have no idea how we're going to pay them."

Shelby noticed glances between folks, but no one spoke.

"Every town has people who are willing, even eager, to break the law. Abney is no different. Our danger is twofold—those who live in Abney and those who are trying to pass through. I have spoken to men and women from each neighborhood in our town, and they are going to be in charge of establishing neighborhood watch groups. The parameters of each group's tasks and legal boundaries—what they can and cannot do—will be explained to you."

Bryant consulted his handwritten notes. "Either tonight or tomorrow, I want you to find the coordinator for your neighborhood. You'll know them because they'll have a red flag on their mailboxes. Be willing to listen and to serve your shift. We must work together to ensure that Abney is a safe place. As the mayor mentioned, there will be a curfew. Anyone not honoring that curfew, anyone outside their place of residence who is not on neighborhood patrol or serving this town in an official capacity, will be arrested. Thank you for your support."

Conversations broke out throughout the crowd, but everyone again grew quiet as the fire chief approached the podium.

Luis Castillo had just returned to his position from a six-month disability leave. The town had rallied around Luis and his wife, Anita, when he'd suffered a heart attack. After four bypasses, rehabilitation, and losing thirty pounds, Luis had been cleared to return to his job.

The fire chief pulled a handkerchief from his pocket and wiped at the sweat beading on his head. The man looked as if he wore the weight of Abney on his shoulders. Shelby noticed that he had no notes to read from, but his expression said that what he was about to share with them was important. When he began to speak, she found herself leaning forward in anticipation.

"This situation," he said, "is a fireman's nightmare."

Twenty

Shelby's mind flashed back to a book she'd written when she'd first become an author. The story was set in San Francisco in April 1906, during the historic earthquake and fire that had destroyed 80 percent of the city and killed approximately three thousand people. The earthquake had been devastating, but it was estimated that 90 percent of the destruction came from the subsequent fires.

Goose bumps pebbled her arms as she remembered the research she'd done for that book. Fires could quickly become infernos. They were a force to be reckoned with, but they had largely been conquered over the last century because of the improved infrastructures of modern cities.

How would they face such dangers now without the resources to fight a fire?

"Most of you heard the explosion last night. The substation south of the high school over-loaded. Fortunately the fire was stopped on the north side by the creek and on the east side by the road. It travelled south and west until it burned itself out, which didn't take too long with the recent rains we've had." Castillo again wiped at the sweat running down his face, pocketed the handkerchief, and continued. "I don't mind telling you that our situation scares me something fierce."

Now the crowd was deathly quiet, watching the man who had served them for over twenty years struggling with his emotions.

"The first place I served as a fireman was in a little one-stoplight town in West Texas. It's a dusty, dry, hot, godforsaken place—at least it was then, and I expect it still is today. Fire was our biggest fear because of the heat, low humidity, and our lack of water. When there were fires, we cut breaks to slow it down, removed any people or animals in its path, and waited for the fire to burn itself out. It's not a good way to fight fires, but for now it's what we'll have to do."

He scanned the crowd, nodding at his wife in the back of the crowd.

Shelby wondered what would that be like—to

know that your husband was on the front lines, standing between the town and obliteration.

"The city manager will explain the water crisis. I want to remind you to keep your generators outside, keep the area around them clear, and only use propane camping stoves outdoors. Candles need to be kept well away from curtains, and besides—you'll want to save those for when the batteries in your flashlights run out. Think safety first, folks."

When he stepped away from the podium, there was utter silence.

"He didn't bother softening the news," Patrick murmured.

"Castillo always tells it like it is," Max said.

Shelby could hardly take it all in. There had been no real surprises so far, but each announcement felt like another nail in their collective coffin. As she looked upward, she noticed the aurora diminishing in strength.

Perkins approached the podium and offered a shaky smile. "I want to thank Chief Bryant and Chief Castillo for their service to our town. While I would never ask for a catastrophe"—she waved toward the sky—"if I have to endure a dramatic change in our society, in the very way we live our lives, I'm proud to do it with the folks on this podium with me, and with citizens like those found in Abney, Texas. Now Danny Vail has a few words to share with you."

Shelby again found herself leaning forward, listening intently to Danny. He'd always been persuasive, exuding confidence and calm. She realized that this was something Abney desperately needed, as much as they needed water and food and gas.

"We have assessed what resources we have within the borders of our town. There's enough food to last us at least a month if we're careful."

"What are we supposed to do in July?" Someone at the back stood up and repeated the question, raising her voice to be heard over the crowd.

"By July you need to have vegetables growing in your front yard." Vail waited for his words to sink in and conversations to cease. "If you live in an apartment building, you'll be assigned a section in one of the parks to farm."

They had decided this in twelve hours? Corn growing in the public parks? Front yards replaced with okra? Shelby had known the danger was real, but she could not fathom how quickly their town officials had made major decisions. It was unprecedented. The wheels of bureaucracy always moved slowly. How had Perkins convinced the others to respond with strong and decisive measures?

Shelby glanced over at Max. Eyebrows raised, he shrugged his shoulders. Yeah, he had the same questions she did. She knew him well enough to read his thoughts, as if there was a digital display on his forehead.

"Use dishwater and bathwater to nourish those crops."

He paused and glanced at several folks in the crowd, older men and women who were nodding their heads in agreement.

Clearing his voice, Vail said, "You know how it was done during the Great War, the war to end all wars. Families did the same during the Second World War. You've heard your grandparents talk about ripping out the flower beds and planting green beans and okra and squash. They called them victory gardens."

"You want me to pull up the sod I spent a thousand dollars putting in?"

Shelby was certain that this question came from one of the Archer Heights residents. It was the wealthiest portion of their town, with McMansion-style houses and professionally manicured lawns.

"If you want to eat, you will." Vail didn't blink. He just waited until the man once again sat down. "We're fighting a different kind of war than that of our grandparents—one against nature instead of man, but it will take the same type of dedication and ingenuity that this country showed in 1914 and again in 1941. It can be done. Am I right?"

Several of the old-timers near Shelby raised their hands as if to testify.

"It can be done. As far as the water, we will not die of thirst in Abney. While we might not have enough water to fight fires, we have enough to drink."

"The springs?"

"Are you kidding?"

"I'm not drinking that water."

Vail held up his hand to ward off the arguments. "Our springs have been open to the public for over one hundred years. The water bubbles straight out of the limestone, and though it's laced with sulfur, it's perfectly fine for drinking and cooking."

"How much water do the springs produce?" someone asked.

"The pool on the north side of town holds three hundred thousand gallons. It bubbles out of the ground at seventy gallons per second. We will use city vehicles to bring that water to your neighborhood. It might not be enough to wash the stink of the day's work away"—he waited for the laughter to subside, and then he continued—"but it will be enough to drink. We are more fortunate than most. Many towns will be depending on their lakes or streams. We have an unlimited abundance of fresh water. Yes, it has a sulfuric smell—"

"Like rotten eggs," someone called out.

"I positively hated that odor growing up." Vail laughed at himself, but grew serious once again.

"The taste might initially be bitter on your tongue, but it will sustain us through this trying time."

He went on to tell them that sewage would be a major issue. Instructions for building out-houses would be disseminated through the neighborhood watch leaders.

"What about my money?" a small woman in the front asked. She had one child on her lap, another in a stroller, and a third standing beside her. "I need to buy diapers and food. I tried to use the ATM machine, but it didn't work."

Vail looked directly at the woman. "Ma'am, I can't guarantee you diapers, but we will be sure you have food. As far as cash on hand, banks are required to keep a reserve of 3 percent for checking accounts. There is no required reserve for savings accounts."

"There's only 3 percent of my money in the bank?" the woman asked.

"No. I'm afraid there is less than that. Not all of a bank's holdings are at each local branch. Our bank's main branch is in Killeen, so one third of their reserves is kept there. I've confirmed with the bank manager that he has on hand 2 percent of checking deposits."

"You're saying there's no money in the bank." This from an African-American rancher standing at the back of the crowd, holding his horse by the reins. He looked weathered by many years of working outdoors.

It wasn't lost on Shelby that he was already using the horse for travel, saving the fuel he had for what? To power his tractor? In case of an emergency?

"There's 2 percent, and that's what you'll be able to withdraw beginning Monday morning."

"So it won't be open tomorrow?"

"No. Monday morning." Vail hesitated, and for the first time an expression of doubt colored his face. He cleared his throat and added, "Folks, you need to realize that for as long as this crisis lasts, money is of limited value. What are you going to purchase with it? Until the federal government steps in with a solution, you need to think of bartering as your primary means of purchasing items."

"Some people have money stuck under the mattress," the woman said. "They're going to buy up all the food and all the medicine."

"No, they're not." Mayor Perkins stepped forward. "We will limit what each family can purchase. No one will be hoarding in this town, not if I can help it."

There was a pause in the meeting as a police cruiser pulled up and Eugene Stone stepped out. The man was as round as he was tall, which Shelby guessed wasn't over five feet seven or eight. He always dressed a bit too nattily for her tastes. His blond hair was professionally cut, and she would swear he had regular manicures.

He'd attended the high school graduation ceremony, and Shelby had found herself standing near him as they made a tunnel with their hands for the seniors to exit through. The man's cologne had been too strong—something she and Max had laughed about later.

But this was nothing to laugh at.

"Eugene Stone is trouble," Patrick muttered.

"Why did he bring the vehicle?" Shelby asked. "City hall is two blocks from here."

"And he didn't come alone." Max nodded toward the officer who had been driving. He stood beside the police cruiser, scanning the crowd.

"Who is that?" Shelby asked.

Max couldn't remember his name, but Patrick leaned forward, lowered his voice, and said, "Stewart Nash—new police recruit. Moved here from south Austin. Word is that Austin PD asked him to resign, but we hired him anyway."

"Gossip," Max cautioned them. "I've heard the same rumors, but they're only that."

"Where there's smoke . . ." Patrick started to say more, but suddenly the crowd grew quiet as the scene up front took yet another turn for the worse.

Twenty-One

Stone thrust an envelope in the mayor's hands. She looked at it but didn't speak.

Max had the sinking feeling that whatever information Stone brought was only going to intensify the severity of their situation. The man delighted in bad news, and he was in his element delivering it in front of a crowd of people.

Shelby scooted closer to Max and glanced toward Carter, who was still standing a few yards from her. Patrick reached over and squeezed her hand.

Max had his attention focused on the podium, but he felt Shelby's shoulder touching his. He felt the same alarm at seeing Stone that she did. Leaning back, he glanced at Patrick, who shook his head.

Perkins had stepped off the podium to confer with her mayor pro tem. Max couldn't make out what was said, but he knew the dynamics of the town's leadership well enough to guess. Stone had no doubt strategically picked his moment to arrive on the scene. In Max's opinion, the man had never recovered from losing the mayor's seat. Bitterness rolled off him like pollen off a tree in the spring.

When Perkins stared down at the letter, her

normally composed expression colored with anger. Though she raised her voice, there were too many other conversations going on around them, and Max couldn't make out a single word. After Stone tried to push his way onto the stage, Perkins took back the letter, read it, and then slowly climbed the steps back up to the podium.

"We have personnel monitoring the radio waves, trying to catch some sort of official word. What we've been able to discern has been spotty and uncorroborated. I will share it with you when I know more." She held up the sheet. "According to Councilman Stone, this letter is from Washington. He insisted that I share its contents with you."

Perkins cleared her throat and began to read. "From the desk of the president of the United States of America . . . On Friday, June 10, at seventeen minutes after nine in the evening Eastern Standard Time, our atmosphere was hit by a massive solar flare that affected nearly every aspect of our infrastructure. Although there are pockets of areas less affected than others, it appears the event was felt worldwide."

She took a deep breath, and Max thought he saw her hand shaking as she glanced up and back down at the letter.

"Be assured that the United States government is at work to protect our country from enemies both foreign and domestic. In addition, we are aggressively seeking a way to restore basic services to affected areas. Until that time, we ask you to remain calm and to assist other people in your area."

The crowd must have thought she was done, because everyone started talking at once.

"Quiet," she barked. "I'm not finished. Quiet, please."

She continued to read. "If you have a job in the area where you find yourself, show up for work. If you don't have a job, ask for one."

"I'm supposed to work for free?" a heavyset man asked. "Not likely."

Perkins kept going. "If you are a praying person, pray that your leaders will find a way through this dark time."

Perkins glanced over at Stone. To Max the man looked almost smug, as if he was enjoying himself.

"Due to the vulnerability of our current situation and recent riots in many of our metropolitan areas, I am hereby declaring a national state of emergency and implementing martial law. Where necessary, I am authorizing the US military to perform law enforcement functions—"

Max never heard the rest. Suddenly, everyone was on their feet. Some people shouted at the mayor, others at Stone, and a few argued with one another.

Mayor Perkins tried to call the crowd to order,

but it was hopeless. Finally, she accepted defeat, walked off the podium, and was swarmed by a dozen people.

Carter rejoined them, asking what martial law meant. Shelby and Patrick had closed ranks, as if they could protect Carter from what lay ahead. But Max was watching Perkins. As people began to loudly debate what was and wasn't addressed in the president's speech, Perkins quietly and quickly slipped through the crowd and made her way toward the city offices.

"I need to talk to her."

"Who?" Shelby asked.

"Perkins. I want to talk to her about Stone. Plus, she needs to know about Green Acres."

"I'm not sure that's the worst of our concerns now, bro." Patrick was scanning the crowd, every muscle in his body on full alert.

"We have fifteen minutes until the church meeting. I'll be there when it starts, but I have a feeling there will be a crowd. Find us a place near the back where we can slip away if we need to."

Max locked eyes with Shelby. That unspoken acknowledgment would have to be enough, even though Max wished he had time to assure her that this thing would not spin out of control. But he didn't have time—and he wasn't sure where they would be when the spinning eventually stopped.

Twenty-Two

Max hurried toward the mayor's office. He made it halfway to the building when he saw that Eugene Stone was standing on top of a bench, speaking to a growing group of men.

"The truck's on the south side of town, and we're going now. We'll split what's there between those who go."

He was immediately swarmed with men eager to volunteer.

"What's he talking about?" Max asked a man standing at the back of the group.

"Supply truck headed to the prison in Croghan."

"What about it?"

"The truck broke down. It's full of food. Stone says he left an officer there to guard it."

"Food meant for the prison?"

The man shrugged. "Don't know who it was meant for, but it's ours now."

"Is it even within the town limits?"

"Don't suppose it matters."

"It does matter. Legally, you can't—"

But the man had already turned away. Stone climbed into the police cruiser, and Nash blipped the siren once and drove south.

Max resumed his way to the mayor's office.

Fortunately, when he arrived, Perkins was alone.

"I suppose everyone is still out there dissecting the president's words."

"Some are." Max sank into a chair across from her desk. "Stone is leading a group of men out to raid a prison supply truck."

Perkins's face turned a darker shade of red. "I told him to leave that alone."

"Well, he's not. I doubt Croghan will be happy when they find out we took it, not to mention the prisoners who need that food."

"We don't know that the prisoners are still there." Perkins reached for a bottle of water and downed half of it.

"Why wouldn't they still be in the prison, Nadine?"

"The guards might not have shown up for work. If there was no one to keep them in the compound—"

"The flare happened at night. Prisoners would have been in their cells."

"It was eight o'clock our time. They're still in the open areas until nine." Perkins tapped a stack of folders. "This is a portion of our emergency plans, and one of them is for the prison because it's in a neighboring town. All of our plans depend on communications and basic emergency services being in place."

Max forced his mind to refocus on the reason he'd come to see her. "What was the argument between you and Stone? When he first approached the stage?"

She seemed to consider whether to share city business, but Max was their backup city attorney. At some point, he would probably need to know whatever she knew anyway. She shrugged and leaned back in her chair.

"We'd been receiving transmissions from the state government, as I said."

"But you couldn't corroborate them. It was smart to hold off on sharing that information."

"I'm convinced they are in fact from the governor. Problem is, they repeat-broadcasted the message until twelve minutes after three this afternoon, when all communication stopped." She rifled through some papers on her desk, pulled one from the stack, and handed it to him. "Take a look at this. It was being broadcast via Morse code over several different frequencies."

"Low-tech. Makes sense."

"One of the old-timers explained to me that it's less sensitive to poor signal conditions than voice communication."

"And you found someone who could translate it?"

"Believe it or not, those guys were still down at the coffee shop this morning—same as any other day." She smiled, and it softened her face, reminding Max that she was only a woman trying her best to do a job that she probably wished she'd never accepted.

"Some things never change," he murmured.

"Yeah, I suppose those gentlemen will keep meeting even after the coffee has long run out. The officer monitoring the airwaves recognized the code immediately, but he couldn't translate it." She leaned forward, crossing her arms on the desk and studying Max. "Our codger club was happy to step in and lend a hand."

He glanced at her once more before focusing on the sheet of paper in his hand.

This is an emergency announcement from the Office of the Governor of the State of Texas. A solar flare experienced on the evening of 06.10 caused catastrophic failure of statewide power grid. All municipalities urged to plan for extensive, long-term outages. Priorities of state agencies will be restoring order to urban centers, providing medical care to entire populace, and protecting borders from enemies both foreign and domestic. Municipal governments should refer to Emergency Plan C, Section 8. This message will repeat.

"That's it?"

"Yeah. It says a lot, but—"

"But it leaves even more unsaid."

Perkins spread her hands in surrender. "Wait until you see Emergency Plan C."

She pulled another sheet from the stack and began to read: "Municipalities shall make every effort to ensure clean water supply. Any and all resources within your municipal borders may be commandeered for the use of the populace."

"That sounds like a bad idea, and one that I— as your lawyer—would not endorse."

"I agree with you, but I'm having a hard time convincing Eugene Stone as much. He's already drawn up a list of things we should commandeer."

Max shouldn't have been surprised. It was all happening too fast. He had the sense of trying to catch up, trying to stop something that was already out of control.

"The recommendations don't stop there. We're to set up a triage area, facilitate the building of latrines—"

"Plant victory gardens?"

"Yeah." Perkins stared out the window. The blinds were cracked an inch, allowing them to see the sun inching toward the horizon. "Someone foresaw this happening."

"Shelby's research showed that NASA has been warning Congress of the possibility for years."

"But no one listened."

"Or no one was willing to spend the money on preparation." Max knew how politicians worked. Why spend money on something that might never happen when defense contracts brought big money to a congressman's district? Lawmakers had focused on the problems at hand without considering the problems of the future. Or maybe they'd simply lacked the imagination to foresee such a nightmare.

"Section 8 goes on to tell me that I may institute martial law if I feel it is necessary in order to control our citizens."

"But the president's letter already did that."

"The president's letter arrived after the state message stopped transmitting."

"How did we even receive the letter?"

"Stone says that a sergeant from Fort Hood drove up in a Humvee, dropped it off, and then left. Apparently they're going to every municipality."

"Do you believe him?"

"I don't know." She picked up a pencil and tapped it against her desktop. "Maybe. But how do I even know that this letter is from the president? It could be from anyone with a computer and a printer that still work."

"This phrase . . . 'enemies both foreign and domestic.' It appears in both."

"It does, which suggests to me that there is a struggle going on."

"I've always heard that we would be vulnerable if the grid went down. But if everyone's grid is down, it seems we're all in the same boat."

"Metaphorically speaking. However, the president's letter says there are pockets of areas less affected than others." Perkins returned the paper to the top of her pile and straightened the stack.

"So now would be a good time to start a war? That doesn't make any sense."

"It doesn't to me, but it might to some people."

Max thought of that, of the countries that had been striving to maintain peace for years, even decades. Anyone not affected by the flare would suddenly have the upper hand. "We're not going to get much help from the military."

"My guess is no, at least not until whatever crisis the president hints at is resolved."

"And the reason that the governor's transmission stopped?"

"I can't say for certain, but it seems to me that there might be a struggle between state and federal agencies as to who is in charge."

It was the worst possible scenario. As if they didn't have enough to deal with, now they had to worry about who ultimately had authority and what they were doing.

"Basically all of this says we're on our own," Max said.

Perkins nodded in agreement. "My fear is that Stone sees this situation as a chance to control the populace."

"Most of the folks in Abney don't need controlling. Left to their own, they'll make the right decisions. Save any extreme measures for those who don't."

"I agree." Perkins stood and moved next to the

window. She stared out at the people walking down the street, headed toward their homes and another night of darkness.

"I needed to talk to you about Green Acres." He explained the situation as succinctly as possible.

Perkins turned toward him, her expression now all business. "I don't know how to get the nurses and aides to show up. Maybe more of them will as they realize they're needed."

She pulled a sheet of paper off a white square tablet and began to write on it. "This man is staying at the hotel."

"You have a list of hotel guests?"

"I asked for one when this first hit. Initially, I'd hoped to be able to facilitate their transportation back to their homes, but that's looking less likely."

"And you think he can help?"

"Maybe. He's a doctor, and he might be willing to fill in some shifts."

"I'll talk to him tonight."

"Where are you headed now?"

"Tony Ramos has called a special assembly at the church."

Perkins nodded, and Max realized he needed to leave if he was going to make the meeting.

"For what it's worth, I think you're doing a good job, Mayor."

"Thanks." She waited until he'd reached the door to add, "While you're at the church, say a prayer for me."

Twenty-Three

"Whoa," Carter said as he followed his mom into the sanctuary of their church.

"Exactly," Patrick agreed. The room was full to overflowing.

"I've never seen this place so packed." His mom led the way to a back corner, where they could see the door Max would come through as well as the front where Pastor Tony stood.

At least they found some room to lean against the wall.

Carter wasn't sure how he felt about church and religion. Occasionally he doubted the value of the whole thing. Some days it felt right to him. Other days he knew it was right, but he simply didn't want to go. Max had assured him that being confused was normal, but it didn't feel very normal. He'd been looking forward to college, where he could find his own way without the expectations of people who had known him all his life weighing down on him.

Based on what the mayor had said, he guessed college wasn't going to happen.

Only a few of the kids from school attended their church. He saw Jason enter with his parents, and they, too, picked a place along the wall. He noticed Kaitlyn sitting up near the front. He was glad she was there, and when she turned to look toward the back, she smiled at him and waved.

Max entered through the back door and squeezed his way through the crowd until he stood next to them.

His mom gave Max the *What?* look, but Max only shrugged.

There wasn't time for her to grill him, because Pastor Tony had moved to the center of the podium and was holding up his hands.

"Can we pray?"

Carter mostly closed his eyes and waited when they were praying. What was he supposed to say? If God was as omnipotent as everyone claimed he was, he'd know Carter had his doubts. There was no fooling God. That was Carter's position. So he kept his head down and waited for the prayer to end.

Pastor Tony thanked them all for coming, and then he got down to business. "I've spoken with the mayor, and most everything will be coordinated through your neighborhood leaders. But there are some things that we, as the church, need to address."

He went on to talk about providing clothes and even lodging for people who had been stranded in their town. Stranded! Carter thought his life had taken a turn for the worse, but at least he wasn't away from home when his car refused to start.

Pastor Tony had a list, and he worked his way down it.

Check on your neighbors.

Share your food.

Be alert and call for help if you see anything suspicious.

Take meals and water to the elderly.

Pretty much it was commonsense stuff. Their pastor seemed like a nice guy, but he was a bit intense in Carter's opinion. Maybe it came from all the praying, or maybe he simply believed what he preached. People began to grow restless, but then Tony hit his stride.

"Lastly, I want to remind you that our God is the god of the universe. I encourage each of you to go home, search your heart, and open your Bible to the book of Job. Read of Job's trials and of how he questioned God." Tony paused, peering left and right, taking in the whole crowd. "Do we question God? When our world is turned upside down, do we trust or doubt? When the heavens themselves seem to bring destruction on our lives, do we cry out *why?*"

Carter heard someone weeping to his right. He stared down at his hands, hoping the service would end soon.

"Job questions God, and God answers. 'Where were you when I laid the earth's foundation? Tell me, if you understand. Who marked off its dimensions?' That is our God. Remember that he was not surprised by the solar flare." Tony motioned out the window, where the day's sun was nearly gone and the aurora continued to spin, brighten, fade, repeat.

"Go home. Read God's entire answer to Job. And tomorrow, when you rise to another day in a world that is confusing to us with its unique dangers and opportunities, go out and be the body of Christ to one another."

That was it?

Those were his words of advice? Read the Bible and help each other?

"We'll have one service here tomorrow morning at ten a.m. Invite your neighbors. It could be that this is the moment they need to hear some good news."

Carter was suddenly weary, and they still had to walk home. He didn't even want to think about walking back in the morning. And in the afternoon, what? Start digging latrines?

Five minutes later, he wished he had such simple worries. As they walked home, Max told them about the governor's message, and that the federal and state governments might be fighting over who was in charge. It was like a debate in his high school government class, only this was real life. The grown-ups were fighting like a bunch of kids.

They reached the corner where Patrick needed to turn off of Main Street, and he promised to see them the next day. He also said he would check on Bianca and her parents. As Patrick turned right, Max said, "I need to go over to the hotel."

"Why?" The word popped out of Carter's mouth before he could snatch it back. It was none of his business where Max was going or why he was going there.

"There's a doctor who was stranded here in town. I'm going to ask him to help at Green Acres."

"Why would he do that?" Carter asked.

"Because it's the right thing to do." Max studied him a moment in the waning light. "Some people will do the right thing during this, Carter. You won't be able to count on everyone, but the good people . . . you'll be able to depend on them."

Carter shrugged. He wasn't so sure about that. At the Market earlier, he'd had a hard time telling who the good people were.

As they continued toward their street, he told his mom about the guy who pulled the gun. Surprisingly, she didn't freak out. She hitched her bag up on her shoulder and glanced around.

"Anything good happen today?" she asked.

"I don't know. I had lunch with Kaitlyn."

"The girl you were watching at church?"

"I wasn't watching her."

"Well, I'm glad you had lunch together."

"Kaitlyn said if she'd had any money she would have given it to the mom who needed milk. I

don't know if I would have done that or not."
When his mom didn't comment, he continued.
"I'd want to, but what if you needed the money?
What if Max did? What if I helped to feed her
kids, but it caused the people I care about to go
hungry?"

They had reached their house. Instead of putting
her key in the lock, his mom sat down on the front
porch step. Carter dropped beside her. It was
probably cooler out here than inside anyway.

"It's not always easy to know what the right
or wrong thing is."

"That's not helpful, Mom."

"Remember when Pastor Tony told us to go
home and read our Bible?"

"Yeah."

"It helps. There's a lot in there about right and
wrong."

"My Bible was on my e-reader." He hadn't
opened the reader in months, but he remembered
how happy his mom had been when she'd bought
it for him. "Now it probably doesn't work."

"That's all right, son. We have the old-
fashioned paper kind in the house."

"Paper?"

His mom put her palms together, flat against
one another, and then she rotated her thumbs out.
"It opens like this."

He laughed at her stupid joke. He couldn't
help it.

The world might twirl into chaos, and his life might take a completely different path than he'd envisioned, but his mom would remain the same. She was one constant he could count on.

Twenty-Four

Max walked toward the lobby of the Star Hotel.

Most towns now had at least one chain hotel, but Abney clung to its heritage. The Star Hotel was part of the town's history. It had been built in the 1870s when people were still visiting Abney for the curative powers of the spring water. The hotel was situated to the east of downtown, across from the stagecoach stop and later the railroad depot. In recent years the small depot had been turned into half a dozen artist shops. Abney was no longer a tourist destination, but people still came to visit family or to use the town as a jumping-off spot for the hill country. The shops and the hotel made a respectable profit.

Max wasn't surprised to see that the Star Hotel's parking lot was half-full. When he glanced upward, he saw the aurora continuing to spin in the night sky, the colors alternately growing bolder before fading.

As he walked toward the front door, weariness threatened to overwhelm him. What was he going to say to Dr. Bhatti? How would he convince a man he didn't know to help the folks of Abney? He couldn't even offer him a salary. He was there because Mayor Perkins had asked him to appeal to the man's sense of moral responsibility. Max knew from his courtroom experience that such an approach often didn't work.

Instead of marching into the hotel and demanding the doctor's room number, he paused under the canopy and read the historical marker on the building's front wall: Texas Historic Landmark. Star Hotel, 1870.

The marker further explained that the building had once housed a famous stagecoach inn. The windows were placed within keystone arches, and native rock had been hauled in by oxen. Originally the site included additional buildings, which were now gone after years of neglect. They had been replaced by the city park, a walking garden, and a fenced dog park. Max turned and studied the darkness. In 1870 this community had thrived, and it had done so without the benefit of electricity. They could flourish again, but steps backward were usually more difficult than steps forward. He prayed that his friends and neighbors would rise to the challenge, that he would have the words to convince Dr. Bhatti to help, and that God would continue to watch over them. Then he pulled in a deep breath and walked into the hotel.

It occurred to him that he was getting older as

he looked at the teenage boy behind the desk. Was he old enough to cover the night watch of the hotel? Nearly six feet tall, the clerk had lanky, blond hair and large owlish glasses. His uniform hung on his slight frame like a garment on a coatrack. According to the tag on his shirt, his name was Skip.

"Can I help you, sir?"

"I'm looking for a Dr. Bhatti."

Skip looked to his computer, and then he seemed to remember that it wasn't going to provide him any information. "I'm sorry, but I can't give out room numbers on guests. I would ring him for you if the phones were working."

"Landlines are down too?"

"Yes, sir, which doesn't make much sense to me." Skip pushed his lanky hair out of his eyes. "I thought that was the only benefit of landlines—that they would work when the electricity went out."

"In most situations that might be true, but this is something we've never dealt with before."

"I heard someone was killed for their car today. It's like we're living in an apocalyptic video game."

Max reached for his wallet and pulled out a business card. He rarely bothered to throw around his credentials, but sometimes it opened doors. In this case, maybe the correct door. "I really need to speak to Dr. Bhatti."

"You're the lawyer with an office on the square?"

"I am."

"You helped my friend with his MIP charge."

"Did your friend stop drinking after his minor in possession?"

"He sure did—for now anyway, until he's old enough. Said he couldn't stand to clean out another kennel."

"Community service sometimes has a lingering influence on what we are and are not willing to do."

"I wish I could help you." Skip glanced toward the windows. "Does this have to do with the aurora thing?"

"The mayor asked me to stop by, and yes. It does have to do with our current situation."

"The thing is, I need this job more than ever now. My dad works in Killeen, and there's no way he can drive back and forth until the gas pumps start working again."

"I understand, Skip. Maybe you could just tell me the last place you saw Dr. Bhatti."

"I suppose I can do that. Courtyard, down at the end. He was sitting outside having a smoke."

"You're a good man." Max turned and started across the lobby.

"Mr. Berkman?" Skip had his elbows propped on the counter, and he was nervously running his fingers up and down his jawline. "Are they going to be able to fix this? Like, we're not all going to die or anything, are we?"

Max thought of the historic marker, of the many people who had walked through the Star Hotel's lobby before him. "This place is pretty old." He glanced at the brick entry and the large plate-glass windows that looked out onto the courtyard. "Folks built it without electricity, and they survived."

Skip nodded thoughtfully, and the barest hint of a smile curved his lips. "True that, Mr. Berkman. Stop by anytime."

Max stepped into the courtyard, which had been decorated with Western patio furniture and native landscaping. He was surprised to see lights shining next to rosemary, Texas sage, and a flowering crepe myrtle. Solar lights. Unlike everything else, they hadn't been fried. He filed that thought under a mental *check out later* folder. Turning left, he walked toward the end of the building, where a man sat smoking a cigarette.

Twenty-Five

"Dr. Bhatti?"

From his name, Max had guessed the man in question might be Pakistani. What he saw as the man stood and put out his cigarette seemed to confirm that. Five feet ten and slight, he had light brown skin and dark hair. His voice, when he responded, was soft and lilting. "I am."

"My name is Max Berkman. The mayor sent me here to speak with you."

"Does she have a way for me to return to Austin?"

"No. I'm afraid not."

Dr. Bhatti sank back into the chair, reached into his shirt pocket, and pulled out a pack of cigarettes. He offered one to Max, who shook his head. As the man lit up, Max sat on a three-foot wall that enclosed a border of landscaping. The exhaustion he'd felt before entering the hotel returned. He didn't trust himself to stand and negotiate.

"I gave up this habit eleven years ago when I turned thirty. It didn't seem proper for a physician to bear the smell of nicotine." He stared at the end of the cigarette. "After the solar flare . . . well, I thought, *Why not?* I walked to your local store and bought one of the last packs."

"Dr. Bhatti—"

"You may call me Farhan."

"Farhan, I'm here because we need your help. We have a small hospital and a nursing home."

"No doubt you also have doctors."

"Yes, we do—several, actually. Two were in town when the flare hit—Dr. Mason and Dr. Jones. They are swapping twelve-hour shifts at the hospital."

"So your hospital is very small and only equipped to do the most basic type of care."

"Twenty-five beds, which are never filled. Any major cases are transferred to Killeen."

"But not now."

"No."

Bhatti paused for a moment, as if considering what Max had said, and then he asked, "Why only two doctors?"

"There are at least half a dozen others. Most live in neighboring towns and commute. The three who live here in town were at a convention when the flare hit."

"So they are stranded elsewhere. As I am stranded here."

"Probably. They will come back. Their families are here, and I know they will find a way to return to them."

"But you are now in the lurch."

"We are. In particular, our nursing home needs—"

"I am not here as a physician. I came here to rest, and because . . . well, I needed some distance from a situation in Austin."

"But you are a doctor."

"Yes. I am an ENT specialist. My office is in Westlake."

"Our situation at our nursing home, Green Acres, is drastic. Some of the patients are deceased, and we need death certificates signed. At the moment, you're the only available doctor."

Bhatti didn't respond. He certainly didn't seem

particularly moved by their situation. Max supposed that doctors grew used to death and sickness, just as the miracle of birth no doubt became everyday to them.

"We need you to sign the death certificates, check on the other patients at Green Acres, and help out at the hospital."

"Is that all?"

"It'll keep you busy, I admit. But you're going to be done with that pack of cigarettes soon. What do you plan to do then?"

"I had thought of perhaps walking back to Austin."

"You're going to walk seventy miles?"

"In Pakistan, many people walk farther distances than that." Bhatti shrugged. "Pakistan is the sixth most populous country in the world, and yet most people do not own vehicles."

"Is that where you're from?"

"No. *Abba* and *Ammi* were, but they moved to the States before I was born."

"I wouldn't recommend walking to Austin. I don't think that would be safe."

"And staying here would be? How long will I stay? What will I eat when there's no food on the store shelves and my wallet is empty? Will I live here in a hotel room? How will I continue to pay for that room?"

"I understand your concerns—"

"But you have no answers." Dr. Farhan Bhatti

stood, crushed out the second cigarette, and stuck his hands in his pockets. "I can't help you."

He started to leave the courtyard, but Max said, "This isn't just about you."

Bhatti paused, but he didn't turn around.

"You took an oath, as I did. My oath was a legal one, to support the Constitution of the United States and of the State of Texas."

"Many doctors no longer take the Hippocratic oath—at least, not the original one."

"Did you?"

"A modified version." Bhatti turned toward him. "I swore to fulfill, to the best of my ability and judgment, a covenant. That doesn't include treating people outside my specialty amid conditions that are . . . less than ideal."

"If you're worried about being sued, I think we're way past that."

"Easy enough for a lawyer to say."

"Dr. Bhatti, I hope and pray that our legal system can withstand this unprecedented collapse of our infrastructure." Max stood, energy surging through him as his anger spiked. "I can assure you that no judge is going to be listening to medical malpractice suits anytime in the near future."

Instead of answering, Bhatti shook his head and again turned away.

"You don't know the people of Abney like I do. They will appreciate any help you can give."

"People seldom appreciate, though they are quick to second-guess and place blame."

Something in the man's tone hinted of past battles, but Max didn't have time to delve into his history.

"What if I can provide you a place to live, as well as food?"

Food supplies the mayor had offered in lieu of payment. A place to live, well—that idea had popped into Max's mind out of desperation.

Bhatti turned and faced him, and for the first time the man didn't seem defeated. "You're offering me a room?"

"Yes. In my home. I have an extra bedroom. The house is small, modest even. Not what you're accustomed to in Westlake, but no one is using it right now. I'll even come over tomorrow with my truck and take you there."

"If I agree to treat the patients in your nursing home and your hospital?"

"If the hospital needs you, yes. And don't forget the death certificates."

"Yes, those need attention."

"We realize it's a lot for one man. Hopefully more of our doctors will find their way back to Abney."

"And you can guarantee that I will have food to eat?"

"As long as there is food to be had, the mayor gives you her word that you will receive supplies.

We're not stupid, Dr. Bhatti. We realize that without additional medical personnel, this situation could quickly slide into a crisis."

"You are already in a crisis, and you don't even know it yet."

"Is that a yes? You'll help us?"

Instead of answering, Bhatti stepped forward and offered that age-old form of agreement—a handshake.

Twenty-Six

Shelby struggled to stay awake until Max got home. She pulled her reading chair and ottoman to the front window and sat there, watching out toward the street. Not that she could see much. Without the streetlamps, only the aurora offered any light, and it came and went.

The night was warm, but she'd insisted on keeping the windows closed. How could she protect Carter if their windows were unlocked? It would be open season for anyone to sneak in, steal what little supplies they had, or even kill them in their sleep.

What would they do for food?

How would they care for the sick and the elderly?

After arriving home from church, she'd dug out an old backpack that she'd used while taking college classes—mostly at night or when her parents could babysit Carter. She'd managed to spread out a four-year degree over more than eight years, but she'd eventually finished. Now she planned to use the backpack for something even more important than learning. Pulling the medical supplies out of her shoulder bag, she'd placed them into the backpack, zipped it up, and set it beside her chair. She vowed to keep it within her sight at all times, and she found herself looking for it, confirming that it was there and that Carter's medicine was safe.

Six weeks' worth of insulin. What would they do when it was gone?

The questions bumped into one another, filling her with anxiety and a horrible feeling of helplessness. She would do anything for her child, but she couldn't manufacture insulin. She couldn't give him hers. She couldn't go out and dig some up from a field. They were dependent on others—corporations, businesses, strangers. She hadn't encountered anyone offering to sell medical supplies, and as far as she knew, all of the corporations and businesses were now out of business.

But hope lingered. What had the president's letter said? *There are pockets of areas less affected than others.* Perhaps some places still had electricity, and all she had to do was find out where. Once there, she would be able to purchase what they needed. She'd find the money, one way or another.

Someone had money.

Someone always did.

Life as a single mom hadn't been easy for Shelby. As a plan began to formulate in her mind, she found herself thanking God that she had grown tough and resilient over the years. She was no longer that young woman who had first faced life as a single mom—terrified and alone and unsure if she could provide and care for a child.

She had and she would.

Her Bible rested on her lap. She'd picked it up when she first pulled the chair over to the window. Now she opened it to the book of Job, flipping through the chapters until she found the verses Pastor Tony had mentioned. When the aurora brightened she could read the words.

Do you know when the mountain goats give birth?

Each time the aurora dimmed, she found herself drifting toward sleep. Her head would bow toward her chest until the aurora brightened. Then she would sit up straighter, look around, and refocus her attention on the page.

Do you give the horse its strength or clothe its neck with a flowing mane?

Slowly, hope filled her heart and a stubborn certainty filled her mind.

Does the hawk take flight by your wisdom?

She stopped staring at the street, searching for Max, and allowed her eyes to drift shut. It would be okay for her to rest for a moment until he returned.

Suddenly Carter was standing in front of her, smiling, dressed in jeans and a new shirt, reminding her they would be late.

The smell of pizza caused her stomach to growl. Plates were stacked on the end of a long table beside a pitcher of soda and another of tea. Glasses filled with ice glittered in the bright light of the restaurant.

She worried about the choice of food—what it would do to Carter's insulin level—but why not allow him this single night of celebration? One piece of pizza wouldn't make that big of a difference, and if his numbers were off—well, that's what the medicine was for.

Suddenly the noise of a band filled the room. Actually, just a drummer. She remembered how Carter had tried the drums during middle school, and how relieved she was when his interest waned and he suggested they sell the set. But this drummer was pretty good, though his rhythm was punctuated by beats of silence.

Bam, bam, bam. Pause. *Bam, bam, bam.* Pause.

She glanced toward the front of the pizza parlor, wondering if perhaps the drummer was distracted. Or was she hearing music too?

Max whispered, "If it's too loud, you're too old," and then he smiled when she turned to swat him.

Bam, bam, bam. Pause. *Bam, bam, bam.* Pause.

The room shifted, and they were home. The beat continued, and she realized someone was trying to break in. She grabbed her phone and dialed 9-1-1, but nobody answered. The call rang and rang until it was picked up by an answering machine instructing her to leave her name and number. Jumping from her bed, she hurried down the hall, but Carter was gone—his window open, the blind tapping in the breeze.

Bam, bam, bam. Pause. *Bam, bam, bam.* Pause.

She turned to run. She had to find Carter, had to make sure he was safe—but as she slipped one leg over the windowsill, an explosion rocked the room, sending her sprawling back inside and onto the floor. Everything went black, quiet, but she could still smell the burning. *Stay low,* she told herself. The first aid class she'd taken had cautioned them to stay close to the floor if ever caught in a fire. Heat rises, so smoke will go up. Crawl out slowly, covering your mouth with something, with anything.

Except now she couldn't breathe. She coughed, choking not on the smoke but on her own tears. Sobbing, she fought to crawl across the room, but she couldn't move. Her arms weighed more than a thousand books, and her legs were pinned to the ground by her desk. When had it collapsed? Why couldn't she wiggle free? Where was Carter? Desperation clawed at her throat as she realized something else was holding her down.

"Stop fighting, Shelby. It's okay. Calm down."

She woke to find Max crouched beside her chair, his arms around her, his voice low and steady in her ear.

"What—" She struggled against him, but he held her securely in his arms.

"It's okay, Shelby. Calm down. You were just having a nightmare. Take a few breaths."

Only it wasn't a dream because she could still smell something burning.

"Where's Carter—"

"The front door was locked. I'm sure he's asleep."

When she continued to struggle, Max said, "I'll go and check on him. Promise me you'll wait here."

She nodded, pulling in a deep breath and exhaling, forcing her mind to quiet.

Max returned a moment later and sat on the ottoman in front of her. "He's fine. He's sound asleep."

"What are you doing here?"

"I came over to tell you about the fire."

"Where—"

"Downtown. I knocked, but you didn't answer. When I heard your shouting, I let myself in with my key."

Max placed his hands on Shelby's shoulders and rubbed them gently. His touch and the look of concern in his eyes were more than she could bear. She'd resisted her feelings for him for years, and she longed to collapse into his arms, to allow him to comfort and calm her.

Instead she pulled away and buried her face in her hands. It had all been so real—her dream, her fear. She could still taste it in her mouth. It was all she could do not to run to Carter's room and watch him breathe.

"Are you okay?"

Instead of answering him, she stood, walked to the front hall, and snatched her house keys off the hall table. "Tell me about the fire."

"The power lines broke. My guess is when they did, it sparked several blazes."

"But the transformer was already out."

Max shrugged. "The one south of town was. There's another smaller substation on the east side. I suppose the flare overloaded it. Or maybe it was the buildup in the lines. Either way, there are several fires burning."

She opened the door and stopped so abruptly that Max bumped into her.

"The aurora—"

"It stopped a few minutes ago."

"There will be pulses. It'll probably come back again."

"It can't do much more damage than it's already done."

"It sets everyone on edge, though." The night air was filled with the acrid smell of her dreams. She pushed away the feelings the dream left behind —of fighting to crawl across the floor, of fearing for Carter's safety. "Downtown . . . it's burning?"

"Some of it, but the fires won't spread past the east side of town. You don't have to worry about that. The blaze would have to jump Main Street."

"Carter is safe." She pushed her fingers against her lips, denying voice to her worries and fears.

"He's safe."

"But there might be others who aren't."

She turned back into the room, snatched up her backpack, and crammed it onto the bare bottom shelf of her refrigerator. Grabbing a pen and scrap of paper from the junk drawer, she scribbled a note telling Carter to stay in the house. A note was not really necessary. She was certain he would sleep through the night, because nothing short of a fire engine in his bedroom could wake him. But she taped the note to the inside of the door anyway, closed the door and locked it, and then she turned to Max, who was still waiting.

She knew he needed to be downtown, helping with the fires. She had slowed him down, and his constant glances toward the horizon—a horizon that glowed with the light of the fires—confirmed that he was anxious to go.

Shelby pushed past him, hurrying down the sidewalk. He jogged to catch up with her.

"You don't have to go. I wanted you to know what was happening. I didn't want you . . ." He pulled her to a stop, looked down at his handon her arm, and quickly stuck his hands into his back pockets. "I didn't want you to be frightened."

"I'm awake now, Max. I'm not frightened, and I am going to help."

Twenty-Seven

Like many small Texas towns, Abney's downtown area was built on a square with the courthouse in the middle. Parking extended around the courthouse, and a paved area was bordered by a two-lane road that many of the teenagers "circled" on Friday nights. Max had done so himself all those years ago, with Shelby by his side. On the outer side of the road was a rim of buildings—a hardware store, a bank, restaurants, a tax office, law practices. The business of Abney took place around *the square*. Five years ago, the top floors of some of these buildings had been converted into apartments. The renovations were part of a downtown rejuvenation grant.

Abney had grown over the years, and much of its expansion—large gas stations, fast-food joints, auto supply stores—happened on the edge of town or on the county road that intersected the town several blocks west of downtown.

But the heartbeat of Abney? It was on the square, and now that square was on fire.

Max told himself that a hundred men would already be there, including all of the Abney fire department. He convinced himself that the ten minutes he'd spent at Shelby's wouldn't matter much. Could one man make any difference amidst a multi-structure blaze?

As they neared downtown, he heard the sound of breaking glass.

"There." Shelby pointed east and across the street. "At the jeweler's."

Two people wearing hoodies had shattered the front window. Max could see one person filling a backpack with items, while another took a hammer to smash in the lock on the front door.

Instinctively, he started toward them.

"Don't!" Shelby jerked him back.

"We can't just let them—"

"We have to, Max." She grabbed his hand, pulling him in the direction of the blaze.

They covered the next two blocks quickly. People hurried toward the courthouse, coming from all directions. Some carried blankets and others had buckets. Max wasn't sure what good either would be. When he and Shelby rounded the corner, they both stopped and stared. The scene before them was like something out of a disaster movie.

The fire had engulfed all of the structures along the north side of the square—the bank, Western wear store, café, and flower shop were a burning mass of lumber and shingles and supplies. He couldn't help glancing in the opposite direction, toward his office. He knew the words *attorney* and *family law* were stenciled on the windows, but he couldn't see them through the smoke. He couldn't see anything on that side of the square. He could only pray those buildings weren't on fire too.

Two fire trucks—one a ladder truck—had parked between the burning structures and the courthouse. A rescue squad stood between the fire trucks and their EMS vehicle, not attempting to enter the building. How could they? Without a fire hose to calm the blaze, it would be suicide.

Flames crackled and poured from the windows at the top of the structures.

Interior walls groaned as they collapsed.

Smoke billowed in every direction.

From where he stood, Max could feel the heat. As the southern portion of the fire found additional fuel, it seemed to explode outward, causing the emergency workers in front of it to take a step back.

"How did it spread so quickly?" he muttered.

The power lines running from one end of the block to the other had snapped in places, their poles leaning toward the flames.

"How are we going to stop it?" Shelby pointed toward the east side, where the fire was beginning to spread. As they watched, a line of grass stretching from the north side of the square to the east caught fire. Just before it hit the wall of the county tax office, a young man in a cowboy hat ran toward it, beat at the flames with a blanket, and succeeded in putting it out.

In the center of the square, Danny Vail appeared to be directing volunteers. His face was covered with soot, his clothes dripping with sweat. As Max and Shelby hurried over to him, Max noticed the temperature around the square had to be ten degrees hotter than around his house.

"Shelby, we need more people on the bucket brigade!" yelled Danny.

"We have water?"

"The springs at the park. You'll have to backtrack a few blocks to get there." Danny pointed in the direction they had come. "Go to the west at least two blocks before you turn back north."

Shelby didn't wait for more instructions. She took off at a jog in the direction he'd indicated.

"Bucket brigade?" Max asked.

"Yeah. Jackson Young had the sense to open up his hardware store when the fire first started.

We're using everything that can hold water."

"I'll go—"

"We need you on the east side."

"But the north side—"

"Is already gone. All we can do now is hope to keep it from spreading." Danny pointed to a stack of blankets, no doubt also from Jackson's hardware store.

Max grabbed one and hurried past the fire trucks. The fire personnel were decked out in full gear—boots, helmets, coats and pants, gloves, and even hoods. Max heard one arguing with the fire chief, but Castillo wasn't budging. "I said no one goes in until we have this blaze under control."

"But Cap—"

"They're already gone." Castillo's voice hardened. "We can't save whoever was in there, but I will not lose more men on a fool's errand."

By the time Max reached the east side, the fire was once again trying to cross the road. He could feel the heat of the pavement through his feet. He joined a line of men that he hadn't been able to see when they had first entered the square, and together they beat at the perimeter of the fire with their blankets, trying to smother the flames that sought new fuel. He didn't notice who stood to his right or left. Time slowed and eventually stopped altogether. Max focused all of his attention on his three feet of pavement, on doing his part to keep the blaze from consuming the heart of their town.

Each time he raised his arms, the blanket grew heavier. Castillo walked down the line, handing out bandanas wet with water from the springs. Max wiped his brow with the bandana, smelling the sulfur on it. He thought of the times he'd swum in the springs, certain that the sulfur water would ward off any mosquito or tick bites. It was something they had told themselves each summer. The water had been crystal clear and always cold—even on the hottest of days.

As he tied the bandana around his nose and mouth, he thanked the Lord for those springs and for the fact that they were situated only a quarter mile away from town.

He didn't realize Patrick had joined him on the line until his friend hollered, "You look like you need a break, Berkman."

"I'm fine."

"Sure about that?"

"I'm sure."

At that moment they both stopped talking and stared at the row of burning buildings. Dense black smoke poured out of the bottom floor where doors and windows had been.

"It's curling," Patrick muttered.

Castillo yelled, "Get back! Everyone back!"

Max heard the words *flashover* and *black fire*.

The firemen who had tried to get closer to the buildings now ran in the opposition direction. Moments later an explosion shattered the night.

Twenty-Eight

A flash of heat enveloped them. Max felt it singe his eyebrows, his arms, even his neck. He instinctively raised his hands to cover his eyes and stumbled backward.

Finding no additional fuel, the fire pulled back as quickly as it had surged forward.

"I need EMS over here!" Castillo shouted as he ran forward and crouched next to one of his firefighters.

There was another swoosh of air, and the roof beams along the entire northern row of buildings collapsed. Everyone in Max's line stepped back even farther as the flames rose—hotter, higher, hungrier.

"Should we go help?" Patrick asked.

"All of the town's EMS workers are helping."

They moved forward and once again began beating the fire back.

"Never thought I'd see a thing like this," Patrick said.

"The bank is a total loss."

"That whole side is."

"If it weren't for these volunteers, we would have lost the entire square."

With every few words, they both raised their blanket and slapped at more flames. It seemed that an endless procession of fire was intent on gaining ground in their direction. Max stopped worrying about Shelby and Carter and the future. In the intensity of the moment, the burden of all the things he couldn't control fell away and it was only him, his friends and neighbors, and the fire.

They worked as one, a fresh recruit taking the place of anyone who backed away. The rhythm uninterrupted, the fire slowly conceding to their efforts.

How long had they been fighting? Max didn't realize they were winning the battle until Castillo brought in a new line of volunteers. "Everyone who has been working, you're relieved. I want you over at the springs cooling off and drinking water. The last thing we need is more injuries due to heat exhaustion or smoke inhalation."

Max handed his blanket to the guy behind him, a twenty-year-old with acne and a bad haircut. "Thanks, man."

Patrick raised his eyebrows, which had been singed in the flashover. His skin was red as if sunburned, and sweat ran in rivulets down his face. "Let's go find Shelby."

The fire appeared to be under control. It was

burning itself out, though hot spots occasionally still emerged. Max saw a paramedic load a firefighter into the ambulance and drive away. Another emergency worker knelt beside an injured woman.

He and Patrick walked in the opposite direction, circling the block and heading toward the park and springs.

Two lines of people stretched a quarter mile, running from the springs at the city park to the northeast corner of the fire and back again. One line passed buckets of water toward the fire. The other line passed empty buckets back toward the springs. Each person stood facing the north, legs spread, arms ready to receive and pass the bucket along.

Max and Patrick stood staring, heads swiveling from the human chain to the fire and back again. "I've never seen a bucket brigade," Patrick said.

"How much water do you think each bucket holds?" Max asked.

"Not much, but their intent isn't to put out the fire." Patrick and Max gazed at the now-smoldering buildings. "With a fire this size and no water pressure, the best they could ever hope to do was contain it. See? Most of the water from the brigade is soaking the area around the fire, not the actual buildings."

As Max watched, the person at the end of the

line threw the bucket of water on the base of a tree. He saw the line slowly inching west, and when it reached the end of the block, everyone turned and made their way back again. This way, they kept the ground around the buildings saturated in spite of the scope and intensity of the flames.

Ten minutes later, Max and Patrick sat next to the creek. The water from the underground springs bubbled up and into a giant cistern made of rock. When it reached 80 percent capacity, it flowed out through openings that deposited the water into Sulfur Creek, which joined the river.

"I wonder how long ago that cistern was built," Patrick said.

"Eighteen hundreds," said Shelby as she collapsed between them.

Her hair had frizzed into a torrent of black curls, and her voice sounded raspy. Max was able to make out her expression from the light of the blaze that continued to leap up occasionally. The only other source of light was from camping lanterns that had been hung from nearby tree limbs.

"My parents said their grandparents worked on it."

"And still it stands." Max handed a jug of water someone had given him to Shelby. She took a long swig and passed it to Patrick.

Max nodded his head toward Shelby. "Remember how she used to refuse a drink from an opened bottle of water?" he asked.

"Yeah. She caught me offering Carter the rest of my Dr Pepper once and nearly came unglued. Something about germs and transmittable diseases."

"Fine. Laugh at me. I'm too tired to care." Shelby flopped back onto the grass and looked skyward. "I can't believe we lost the bank, the Western wear store, and the flower shop tonight."

"Don't think anyone will be buying flowers anyway," Patrick said.

"You know what I mean." Shelby rubbed at the soot on her face, succeeding in spreading it around even further.

"We lost a lot, but we saved three sides of the square and the courthouse." Max glanced around them. In every direction he saw dozens, possibly hundreds, of people—all there to save the town square. His thoughts flashed back to the two thugs he'd seen breaking into the jewelry store, but he pushed that image away.

"This proves we can do it." Shelby sat up and looked around. "We can survive. We're capable of putting our neighbors' needs first."

"Folks are pulling together now," Patrick agreed. "But will it last when they get hungry and desperate? Because if it doesn't, putting out a fire will be the least of our worries."

Twenty-Nine

Shelby felt numb and exhausted. Her muscles hurt, smoke burned her eyes and throat, and she felt dirtier than the time she'd agreed to help Max pull his truck out of the mud when they were in high school.

She was a mess then, and she was a mess now.

At the same time, part of her felt more alive than ever. As she'd stood in the bucket brigade line, she'd felt part of something. Together they had managed to keep the fire from spreading.

They rounded the corner and made their way back toward the downtown square, intending to check in with Castillo. Instead they stopped short, and all Shelby's good feelings evaporated in an instant.

In the middle of the road was an ambulance, and beside it were two stretchers. Each stretcher contained a body, covered from head to toe with a sheet.

Shelby felt the world tilt, and Patrick and Max rushed closer to support her on both sides.

"I'm fine." She shrugged them off. "I'm fine."

Even to her own ears the words rang hollow.

"Who . . . who is it?"

"Mr. and Mrs. Dailey," said a woman who held

a blackened blanket. "Guess they lived upstairs."

"Over the flower store," Patrick said. "Mrs. Dailey always reminded me of the time she'd waited on Matt Damon. She kept a clipping of the newspaper article right beside the register."

And now they were dead?

Shelby heard a ringing in her ears, and the palms of her hands suddenly felt slick with sweat. She pushed her way through the crowd to the curb outside the courthouse and plopped down, putting her head between her knees.

She closed her eyes and tried to shut out the smells and sounds and sights of death and destruction.

"Are you all right?" Max's voice in her ear pulled her back to the present.

She glanced up at him and nodded. Patrick slipped the bandana off his head and handed it to her. It was dirty and smelled of smoke, but she used it to wipe the perspiration off her forehead and across the back of her neck. She did so slowly, stalling, using the time to gather her wits about her.

What wits?

People were dying right and left.

In Abney, Texas.

"I have to get home," she muttered as she jumped to her feet.

As they walked, the wind shifted and carried the smoke away from them. Shelby tried to focus simply on breathing, on pulling in clean gulps of air. She tried to recall the words she'd read in the Bible just a few hours ago—about Job, his losses, and God's plan for his life.

"I'll see you in the morning," said Patrick. He pulled her into a hug and nodded at Max, and then he turned toward his street.

Max didn't speak. He knew her well enough to understand she needed silence. When they turned the corner of their street, something deep inside her gut relaxed.

"He's fine," Max assured her.

And that was all he said until she started up the steps of her house and unlocked the front door. Before she went inside, he put his hand on her arm, and motioned toward the rockers set to the side of the porch.

She wanted to say no. She didn't have the energy to comprehend one more thing. But Max laced his fingers with hers and tugged her toward the chairs. She sank into the one nearest the front door and groaned.

"You'll have even more aches when you wake up," he said, sitting down in the other rocker.

"Fought a lot of fires, Berkman?"

"No. That was my first."

She knew by his tone of voice that a frown was forming lines between his eyes.

"Reminds me of football, though. At first you don't think you can do something, but then you get caught up in it. You tell yourself to keep going. Eventually it's as if you reach a . . ." He paused, glancing out at the street where they could see the silhouettes of others straggling home.

"A rhythm," Shelby said. "You reach a rhythm. It becomes automatic."

"Exactly. But the next morning? You pay the price."

She set the rocker in motion and wondered if she could sleep there, as the slight breeze cooled her skin.

"Take two ibuprofen when you go to bed. I'd tell you to take a hot bath, but I guess those are things of the past."

"I studied it, researched it, even wrote about it. This flare—it shouldn't have come as a surprise to me. The Carrington Brides, that's what I called the series—a name dangerous and hopeful at the same time. They were some of my bestselling books, but I didn't . . . I never understood what I was writing about."

"Studying a thing is not the same as living it."

"Not even close. I had no idea how much it would hurt, inside."

"We're going to make it through this, Shelby."

"You can't know that."

She turned toward him in the dark. She could just make out his profile by the light of the nearly full moon, something she hadn't even noticed until this moment. Max always reminded her to take time for the good things in life, to step away from her computer and writing deadlines and take the time to live.

There had only been one time in her past when he wasn't there, and it was the worst time of her life.

"We are going to make it," he repeated.

"So you're telling me that you know we won't die in a fire like the Daileys."

"That's not what—"

"Or that we won't be killed by someone who wants our car."

"Shelby—"

She was suddenly very tired, and the certainty of what she needed to do came back to her full force. She'd had nothing short of a revelation while sitting by the window and reading Job. It was born of desperation, but it dictated her path nonetheless.

"I can't talk about this right now."

"Look, it's late, and I know that you're exhausted. But there's not going to be a good time to say this. Things are moving quickly now, and they're not likely to slow down."

"So say it." She turned her gaze to him, willing him to voice the fears tapping on her heart.

"Things are going to get worse around here, much worse, before they get better. Folks in Abney are pulling together, something I'm very happy to see. But they're not hungry yet. They're not fighting one another for the last can of beans, shooting the deer that moseys into their front yard, eating their neighbors' pets . . ."

"Why are you telling me this?"

"I want you to come with me to High Fields. Ride this thing out there. My parents will be happy to have you and Carter. There's plenty of room, and if I know my folks—an adequate supply of food."

"I can provide for Carter." Even as she said it, she wondered if it was true.

"At High Fields you won't have to sleep with your windows closed because you're afraid someone's going to break in."

So he'd noticed that. No surprise. Max missed very little.

"Are you finished?"

"No. I'm not." He stood and paced in front of her. Finally he turned, crossed his arms, and studied her. "I want you and Carter with me."

The words were a confession, a plea, a caress.

She pushed herself up and out of the rocker and walked over to where he stood. Standing close enough to catch the scent of sweat and smoke, she also smelled something that was quintessentially Max.

Was there anyone on earth who she understood better than Max Berkman? Even her son puzzled her at times, but Max . . . she could read him like a familiar passage in her favorite book. If she were honest, High Fields sounded like the perfect place to be—a refuge, a place to weather the storm. But the insulin Carter needed was in Austin. Their future lay there.

"Thank you, Max, but no." She placed her hand on his chest, felt his heartbeat pulsing under her palm. "We won't be coming with you."

Without another word, she turned and walked into her house.

Thirty

By the time Max walked into his home, he wanted to fall on top of his bed fully clothed and sleep for twelve hours. Instead, he turned on the battery-operated lantern he'd found among his camping supplies. He walked to his bathroom, dipped a washcloth in the pail of water Carter had filled, and began to clean his face and hands. He glanced once at the bath, thought briefly about how nice a long, hot shower would feel, and then he nearly laughed at himself. They had taken so much for granted.

Hot water? No problem!

Sore muscles? Take some ibuprofen.

Hungry? Go to the pizza parlor.

As he scrubbed away the soot and sweat, he acknowledged to himself that he was much more dependent on modern conveniences than he'd ever realized.

Staring at the filthy cloth, he debated whether he should dip it into the pail again, but he wasn't willing to dirty his limited water supply. Instead he walked to the kitchen, retrieved a cup, and poured clean water over the soiled cloth.

Why hadn't he bought a generator?

Why hadn't he laid in more supplies?

Dropping his grimy clothes into the laundry basket, he wondered how he would ever wash them. That was one problem he could put off for a few days. He donned fresh clothes and walked to the kitchen. His home looked different in the soft light of the lantern, and it was strikingly quiet. He'd never been one to watch a lot of television, but most evenings he enjoyed listening to a ball game on his iPhone or satellite radio. Now he heard only the chirp of crickets outside his window and a dog barking down the road.

He drank a glass of water and made himself a peanut butter sandwich.

A plan was beginning to form in his mind. Shelby's answer had been a definite no, but he wondered if she needed more time to consider the option. He had a few days before he would be ready to head out to High Fields.

He had to convince Shelby and Carter to go with him.

In the meantime, there were things he needed to do—starting with picking up Dr. Bhatti after church the next morning. After that errand was done, he would focus on gathering supplies.

Max went to his desk and pulled out a sheet of paper. Beginning at the top he worked his way down the page, making a list of things he could trade for gasoline. The mayor had worked out a way to hook a generator up to the station pumps, but each customer was limited to two gallons. He thought perhaps he could barter with some of his neighbors for more.

He'd filled up his truck before their hiking trip, but since then he'd made a couple of emergency runs in it. He guessed that he could add another four or five gallons before leaving town. He also owned two gas cans and would like to top those off. It might be his last chance to find any. His dad kept a couple of gas cans full in case they were needed for the tractors, but the supply wouldn't last for long.

Next, he made a list of what supplies he should take with him. *Think long haul,* he reminded himself. *Think worst-case scenario.*

That wasn't too difficult for him to do. As a lawyer he'd been taught to analyze a situation from every possible angle—defense, prosecution, judicial. Nothing was one-dimensional, and he needed to see this situation as completely as possible.

So he drew two lines down the next sheet and headed the first column *One Week,* the second *One Month,* and the third *Indefinitely.* If he had to guess, he figured their problems would last a while—but were they talking a year or five years? Or twenty? He didn't know much about transformers, and he couldn't research it with the Internet down. But he had glanced at Shelby's notes—and the outlook wasn't good.

Of course some things depended on what the president's message had said. He pulled out another sheet of paper and began a list of questions.

How much of the United States has been affected?

Is it a global phenomenon?

What is the current situation in urban centers?

How will the legal and judicial systems continue until the power is restored?

His last question would not be most people's first concern. They would be thinking about food, safety, and income—probably in that order. But Max understood that the legal system was what held their society together. Laws made it work. Without that framework, they would be transported back to the days of outlaws, cowboys, and Indians. And the judicial system supported the legal. Should the court system break down, they would have to resort to local law. That might be okay in a place like Abney, but how would it work in Houston? Or Philadelphia, Los Angeles, or DC?

He pushed aside his questions and pulled the sheet with the three columns toward him. He was halfway through the second column when there was a light knock on his door and Patrick stepped inside.

"I figured you would still be up."

"And I figured you'd be home passed out."

"Nah. Couldn't sleep. Too much adrenaline." Patrick pulled out a chair and sat down across from him. "Most folks are ignoring the curfew, in case you're wondering. After the fire . . . well, you can't exactly lock people up for helping."

Max noticed Patrick had cleaned up somewhere. His face and hands were no longer covered with soot, though his clothes still carried the smell of smoke.

"We've got a problem," Patrick said.

"You don't say. No electricity? Fire downtown? Maybe you're talking about the recent car thefts—"

"Okay, okay. We have several problems, but this is a new one, and I'm pretty sure it's worse than the other things you're worrying about."

Thirty-One

Max groaned and leaned back against his chair. Patrick waited, his arms crossed, the expression on his face grave.

"If it's that bad, I suggest we break into my cookie stash." He found the package of cookies at the back of his cabinet and brought it to the table with two glasses. "Would you like water or . . . water?"

Patrick grunted, but then he reached for one of the cookies.

Max pushed his papers to the side. "Talk," he said. "What's this about?"

"Tonight I saw two of the enlisted guys from our church."

"Brian DeWitt and—"

"Gary Burch."

"Both good guys."

"They are, and they've both been recalled."

"I don't understand." Max wasn't sure why this was relevant to him, but he trusted Patrick. If he said it was important, then it was.

"DeWitt and Burch both had three-day passes. They weren't supposed to report to Fort Hood until Monday morning. Tonight a WO1 shows up—"

"Warrant officer?"

"Correct. This guy shows up at their front doors and tells them they have three hours to get back to base."

"Unusual."

"I suppose drastic times calls for . . . unusual measures." Patrick reached for another cookie. The sugar seemed to be calming him somewhat, though he still looked concerned.

"All right," said Max. "They're needed on base. That's not so hard to imagine, especially given the severity of this situation."

"That was the official message."

"But there was more?" Max crossed his arms on the table and leaned forward to study his friend, sensing they were reaching the real reason that he'd stopped by.

"Unofficially the warrant officer admitted the base is powering up—some big deployment that will happen domestically."

"Maybe they're being sent to help regain control in the urban areas."

"Possibly, but according to disaster plans, martial law should be implemented first by the Texas State Guard followed by the National Guard. The US military only becomes involved as a last resort."

"I don't know what you're getting at. Why is this a problem?"

"Because it shouldn't be the troops who are doing this. Their movement suggests that there is a struggle going on between the feds and the state."

Max sat back, glancing at his list of questions and trying to put the pieces together. Wasn't it enough that they were without power, without additional food sources, and in need of medical supplies? His eyes hit on the page with questions.

How will the legal and judicial systems continue until the power is restored?

"Do you think someone is making a power grab?"

"I don't know."

"Do you think there's a danger of invasion from foreign forces?"

"Maybe."

Max picked up another cookie and took a bite, but the chocolate was suddenly bitter and unpleasant on his tongue. He washed it down with the rest of his water, stood up, and began to pace.

"If it's a power grab, what you're suggesting is that the foundation of our country is crumbling, less than three days after a natural catastrophe."

"Didn't the mayor tell you that she was suspicious of the president's message?"

Max ignored that question. "On the other hand, you're suggesting it's possible we may have been or are in danger of being attacked by a foreign power that is probably struggling with the same issues we have."

"Unless they aren't."

Max rubbed at his forehead as fatigue threatened to overpower him. When had he last slept? What time was it? And behind that, what would they face once the sun came up?

"Either scenario is hard for me to swallow, Patrick."

"Because we're the generation that has never known war—at least nothing that affected us domestically. But think of World War I and World War II. Both brought about a fundamental change stateside—rationing, blackouts, curfews. A domestic scenario is less difficult to imagine if you've actually served in the military. Trust me."

"And you're getting all of this from the fact that two guys we know have been called back to base?"

"They're deploying . . . domestically. That much I've confirmed from three different sources." Patrick ran his hand over the top of his head.

The crew cut reminded Max that his friend was former military. Many of his habits and even his way of thinking had been formed by his twenty years in the service. For the last five years he'd been a consultant to various security firms, so he knew danger when faced with it. If Patrick said there was a problem, there was.

"We've known that there are sleeper cells here," Patrick added. "People who were placed here ten, twenty, even thirty years ago. They've assimilated into the culture."

"And they'll be affected the same as everyone else. They're going to be looking for food and water."

"Maybe. Maybe not. It could be that they were waiting for an opportune moment—"

"A time when our infrastructure fell into chaos."

"And if that's the case, we have more to worry about than whether downtown Abney burns."

Thirty-Two

Shelby opened her eyes to sunlight slanting through the window. Her first thought was of her current manuscript—what did she plan next for her characters? How could she make their lives pure misery before granting them a happy ending? It was Sunday, and she wouldn't actually work today—but she did enjoy the first few minutes of daydream writing. She purposely avoided writing on weekends so she could attack her work with a fresh attitude first thing Monday morning.

Her gaze shifted to the clock.

No time.

No power.

The solar flare, and the fire, and Harold Evans dead because someone wanted his car.

She closed her eyes, longing to push it all from her mind, but that didn't happen. More questions crowded into her thoughts, so she jumped out of bed to keep them from paralyzing her. Stumbling to the bathroom, she remembered that they had no water. Max had shown her how to place a garbage bag in the toilet, but as soon as she opened the lid she wished that she hadn't.

Holding her breath, she took care of her toiletry needs in record time. Once in the kitchen, she grabbed a mug out of habit before remembering she had no way to make coffee. She stared at the coffeepot with longing. Her stove still worked, so she could boil water as Max had done—but she didn't have the same fancy glass pot. What had he called it? A French press? She'd have to add that to her wish list. Peeking out the window, she stared over into Max's yard to see if he had his camper stove going.

His truck was parked under the carport, but he wasn't in the backyard. What time had he gone to bed?

Urgent problems first—she needed caffeine.

Maybe she could boil water and add grounds. Didn't they call it campfire coffee? She tested the burner on her gas stove. One strike of a match, and the flame caught. Next she pulled out a pan and set it in the sink. But when she turned on the faucet, nothing happened. No water.

Carter had filled quite a few containers with

water. They were sitting all over her kitchen counter. But should she use it for coffee?

Weighing the pros and cons, she finally turned off the burner and opened the refrigerator. What was left on her shelves wasn't cold, but neither was it warm. The backpack she'd stuck on the bottom shelf looked ridiculous, but maybe it provided some degree of coolness for the insulin doses. She noted that Carter had finished the milk. She snatched a diet soda from the shelf. It wasn't her breakfast of choice, but it would do.

She was halfway through the soda and rolling an apple back and forth across the table when Carter stumbled into the room.

"You going to eat that?"

"It's all yours," she said.

She tossed the apple to him and almost laughed when he caught it. How could some things feel so normal when the world had fallen apart?

Carter slumped into the chair across from her and bit into the apple. "Why does it smell so smoky in here?"

So she told him about the fire and the bucket brigade, but she didn't mention the Daileys. She wanted to protect him from the harsh truths as long as she could, though that might not be much longer at the rate things were deteriorating.

"Our bathroom is gross," Carter said.

"That it is, and the water is officially out. We're down to what you put into containers. I never realized how important modern plumbing is to a household."

"So what are we going to do? Build an out-house?"

"We'll check with our neighborhood coordinator. There's supposed to be—"

"A red flag on the mailbox. I remember. Why wouldn't they just make Max our neighborhood coordinator? He's the smartest guy on the block."

She suddenly remembered her late-night conversation with Max—the way he'd pleaded with her, the hurt in his eyes when she'd said no. She might be able to shield her son from some things, but he'd notice when Max wasn't around.

So she walked across the room, put her soda can in the recycling bin—would they still be recycling?—and turned back toward Carter. "Max can't be the neighborhood coordinator," she said. "He's going to check on his parents."

"He's leaving?"

"Not forever, just for . . . a while."

Holding the apple core in his hand, Carter stared at her, openmouthed in surprise. He sat up straight and said, "Oh. I guess that makes sense."

"Of course it does."

"We'll be okay without him."

Shelby walked back across the kitchen and sat down next to her son. "We have always been okay, just the two of us."

"He makes killer coffee, though." Carter

reached forward and ruffled her hair, something she would never have tolerated from another person on the planet.

Her son was like that—resilient. She should have known that he'd take the news better than she had. While she'd tried to appear nonchalant the night before, the thought of Max leaving filled her with dread. He'd become a cornerstone in their life, and maybe she should have never let that happen.

"There's a lot I haven't figured out, Carter. I don't even have a watch. I keep fighting the urge to check my smartphone to see what time it is."

"That's an easy enough problem to fix." He sauntered out of the room, his hair sticking straight up, still rubbing sleep from his eyes. When he returned he was holding a watch she had bought him the year before.

"You laughed when I gave you this."

"Yup. I told you that no one needed a watch anymore. I guess I was wrong."

"What are you going to use?"

Carter set another nearly identical watch on the table. "Remember? Usually you and Max coordinate gifts, but last year you apparently didn't."

Shelby did remember. Max had been at a law conference in Austin when he'd picked up the watch with a guitar imprinted beneath the glass. The neck of the guitar acted as the minute hand,

and a star on the body of the guitar pointed toward the hour. Max's gift had been "way cool" according to her son, while hers had been practical. Carter had been late multiple times that year, and both she and Max had come up with the same solution—give the boy a watch.

"What are we going to do about my meds, mom?"

"We're good. I bought a thirty-day supply, and we already had two weeks."

"The insurance approved that?"

"Not exactly."

"So how much did a month's worth cost?"

"Don't worry about it."

"How are we going to keep it refrigerated? What are we going to do when the supply is out? How am I going to eat right if there's barely any food?"

"I don't have the answers to all those questions, but I'm trying to think of something."

Carter buried his head in his arms.

"It's not that bad."

"It is," he mumbled. After a moment he raised his head and forced a smile. "I'm not naive, Mom. All those television shows you hate—they pretty much cover the collapse of society."

"So I may be asking *you* what to do next."

Carter groaned. The sound made Shelby laugh.

"Check your levels, find yourself something more to eat, and I'll go change. We have a neighborhood meeting, followed by church at ten."

"You might want to wash up."

"I did that last night."

"Are you sure?" he asked.

"Okay. I'll do it again."

"And add a ball cap," he called after her.

When she took a good look in the mirror, she understood why he'd suggested a ball cap. Had she actually gone to bed with soot and leaves in her hair? Her face and arms were still charcoal colored, and now that she thought about it, she smelled.

It had been less than forty-eight hours, and already she wanted to trade her right arm for a night at the Hyatt—with power, please.

Since the Hyatt wasn't open, and it wasn't near Abney either, she made do and managed to be ready to go in fifteen minutes.

"Record time," Carter said as she pulled the backpack out of the fridge. "And why are you carrying that with us?"

"There could be thieves."

"Looking for insulin?"

"You never know." She tried to sound flippant, but she was thinking that the supplies in her backpack probably had as much trading power as little bars of gold.

Thirty-Three

Carter stood next to his mom, listening to Frank Kelton explain how to build a latrine. The man was wiry and old, but he seemed to know what he was talking about. Carter definitely wasn't looking forward to digging a three-meter hole in the ground. He wasn't the best at metric conversion, but wasn't that around nine feet? How were they going to dig a hole that deep? With shovels?

He couldn't imagine how long that would take, but anything would be better than the current situation in their bathroom.

Someone at the back hollered out a question the minute Frank paused. "Does everyone need to build one of these?"

"No. Our goal is to build one for every five houses."

There had to be forty people who had shown up for the meeting. Now all of them were talking at once.

"Look, folks. We don't have the supplies—"

"What supplies do we need?"

"Something to sit on when you're using the . . . facility. Lumber to build a frame that provides some sort of privacy. Are you going to be satisfied with a hole in the ground? Or do you want to have something where you can close the door?"

"We could just put up a sheet," said an older woman who sat on a contraption that converted from a walker to a chair. "A sheet works fine, especially in the summer."

"That's a great idea, unless it's raining. We have enough lumber and tarps to make coverings for one latrine for every five houses. Now look, folks, you're free to use whatever supplies you can find, but it's going to take several people per latrine to get this done. Our neighborhood group covers this single block of Kaufman, from Third to Fourth Street. There are ten houses on each side, so we'll put latrines behind the third and eighth houses on each side. I've already spoken with the homeowners—"

"Lucky them," Shelby muttered.

Carter could tell that she'd meant the comment for his ears only, but there had been a pause in Frank's lecture and everyone had heard.

"In one sense, yes they are." Frank scratched at his right eyebrow. "The facilities will be closer to their back door. But look at it another way. Would you want folks traipsing through your backyard in the middle of the night when nature calls?"

Everyone laughed, and the tension in the crowd dissipated. After a few additional instructions, Frank started handing out assignments. Shelby pulled Carter back from the crowd.

"I just thought of a way I might be able to keep this stuff cold." She shrugged her shoulders, indicating the insulin she was carrying around. He knew it was important—in some ways his life depended on it—but his mom was freaking out about this. It wasn't their only problem.

"Hasn't it already been exposed to the heat?"

"No. I wrapped it in ice packs. They're melted now, but they did pretty well the first twenty-four hours."

"So what's your plan?"

"I'll explain later. We have an hour until church. Find out your team assignment and then—"

"Meet you there? Sure. But maybe I should stay and start working on our new bathroom." It came out more sarcastic than he intended. No one had asked for this situation.

"Listen, Carter." His mom pulled off the ball cap and finger-combed her hair away from her face, and then she set the cap back on her head. "There's a lot to do, and for the next few days or weeks, everything is going to be urgent. But if we don't attend to our spiritual needs, if we don't draw strength from our church family, well . . . this thing could roll over us like a bad storm."

Carter reached up and tweaked her cap. "Message received. I'll see you there."

"Meet me at the back of the sanctuary?"

"Sounds good." He watched her disappear around the corner, then turned his attention back to Frank. He was trying to get everyone to listen as he explained about neighborhood patrols.

Apparently Abney wasn't the safe small town it had once been. Patrols would cover a stretch of two blocks with the cross street in the middle open to neighborhood residents only. The folks on patrol would be armed, and anyone sixteen or older was needed.

Carter signed up for a time slot. His mom might not like him standing guard, but they needed able-bodied people. It would only be two hours every afternoon—from four to six. He supposed the later shifts, the more dangerous ones, would be covered by the men in their neighborhood.

Frank pointed him toward a group of folks. "They're building the latrine closest to your home, son."

So he moseyed over to his new group—which consisted of a single mom, someone's grand-mother, and two couples who looked as if they hadn't moved from the couch much in the last few years. Those were all harsh thoughts. He realized it and murmured a low, "Sorry, God," before he joined them.

Thirty minutes later they had a plan, and Carter asked to be excused so he'd have time to meet his mom.

One of the larger women, Rhonda, said, "How nice to see a young man attending church." Her husband, Ed, joked that it might be a good idea for all of them to go.

But no one asked to join him, so Carter figured it was just chatter.

He thought of what his mom had said, about their spiritual needs and drawing strength from their church family. What were spiritual needs? He understood bodily needs—food, shelter, safety. But he wasn't exactly sure what his spiritual needs were. If it made his mom feel better, he'd go, but he had doubts as to whether going to church was practical or a waste of valuable time.

Thirty-Four

Carter walked the mile to the church. The parking lot was noticeably empty, but most folks had walked like he had. He pulled the door open and stepped inside, expecting to see the kind of crowd they'd had the night before. Instead the group was about half the size of what he'd see on a normal Sunday morning.

The smaller crowd made him feel conspicuous, so he stood at the back, scanning the room to see if his mom had arrived. He'd never been in the sanctuary when the lights weren't on. It gave the place an ancient feel, with light piercing through the stained-glass windows. His mom walked in a few minutes later with Max. Following a few steps behind them were Bianca and Patrick.

Carter let out a breath he didn't realize he'd

been holding. He was being overly paranoid. It wasn't as if his mom could have disappeared between their house and the church.

He, his mom, and their friends found a pew halfway toward the front of the sanctuary. "How'd your errand turn out?" he asked.

"Great." She offered him a smile that seemed a little pasted on.

"So where did you go?"

Before she could answer, the youth minister moved to the front of the sanctuary and told them all to stand for an opening prayer.

"I'll tell you later," she assured him.

Sitting there between his mom and Max, listening to Chris pray to God for wisdom and mercy and grace, Carter convinced himself that everything would be fine. Whatever was ahead, they would face it together, and they would be okay. But throughout the prayer and the next two songs— one a praise song, the other a hymn—his mind kept returning to the plans for their latrine. How were they going to dig a hole nine feet deep?

Pastor Tony moved to the front of the pulpit. As usual, he wore a dress shirt and tie. He had to be miserable in those clothes. The room was hotter than normal without air-conditioning or fans. Carter supposed the stained-glass windows looked nice, but they weren't very functional. They couldn't even be opened to allow a breeze inside.

If Pastor Tony noticed the heat, Carter couldn't tell.

Together they read some verses from the Old Testament, more from the New Testament, and finally some words from the Psalms.

"Give thanks to the Lord, for he is good. His love endures forever. Amen?"

People squirmed in their seats. Someone began to fan herself with a pamphlet. Another person checked his watch.

"Amen." A short elderly woman near the front nodded her head, white hair bobbing up and down, up and down.

"The Lord is good and his love endures forever. Amen?"

There were more nods of agreement and a handful of folks murmuring *amen.*

Carter had been to church with a few of his friends, when there was some sort of special youth emphasis. One of those churches was what his mom called charismatic, but the church they attended wasn't. In fact, there wasn't much audience participation at all. He glanced at Max, who had his eyes fixed on Tony. Patrick stared out one of the windows, his arm around Bianca, who was weeping for some reason. Suddenly, Carter felt a giant lump in his own throat, as if someone were squeezing his windpipe.

Was he about to cry too? Here in front of everyone? He blinked his eyes rapidly and tried to slow the thumping of his heart. He'd only felt that way once before—when Max's parents had moved away. He thought he remembered crying when his grandparents had died, but he'd been pretty young then—second grade. He definitely didn't remember his dad or his dad's death. How could he? He'd been a little kid when it happened.

An outsider might have said that everyone in Carter's family had died—but it had never felt that way to him. It had always been him and his mom. She'd made him feel secure, and she had been his entire family. He missed his grandparents terribly, but when Max's parents were living next door, they were willing and ready to fill the void.

When Max's parents moved, Carter felt as if his adopted family were leaving. He'd been about to start fifth grade, but suddenly he wasn't interested in his new teacher or returning to school to see his friends. Max's parents had spoiled him, but he didn't understand it at the time. After they moved, he and his mom were alone again. That time had been very dark. He thought the fabric of the world had ripped in two.

This pressure in his chest reminded him of then.

Pastor Tony was still talking. He held up his Bible and said, "I will sing of the Lord's unfailing love forever!" This time he didn't wait for an amen. He walked out from behind the pulpit, tugged on his shirt collar, hitched up his pants, and sat down on the top step.

"Forever, friends. Not until he grows weary of us. Not until his heart turns toward others who are more faithful. Not until the lights go out, but forever."

Amens popped like kernels in a skillet—to the left and the right, from folks all around Carter.

"Psalm 138:8 says that the Lord has a purpose for me and a purpose for you. He will fulfill that purpose, and his love will endure—forever. Did we lose friends in last night's fire? Yes. Yes, we did."

Carter had been mesmerized by his pastor's intensity, an almost pleading desire for them to understand. But at the mention of lost friends, he turned to his mom. She shook her head once, quickly, and reached for his hand, her eyes still trained on Tony.

"There may be dark days ahead. I suspect there are. God help us, I suspect there are." Tony stood and walked back up the steps to stand behind the pulpit. The armpits and back of his shirt were stained with sweat.

"I only ask that you remember: He is good, and his love will last all of our days. Or in the words of the psalmist, 'The Lord will fulfill his purpose for me; your steadfast love, O Lord, endures forever.'"

Thirty-Five

Shelby realized that she should have told Carter about the deaths the night before. Perhaps protecting him from the truth had been an ill-conceived parental reflex. She couldn't shield him from the harshness of the world that was now their life.

Tony ended his sermon, and before they concluded the service, Chris asked them to exit by way of the fellowship hall. "We have placed sheets of butcher paper around the room. Those on the south side list *needs*. Those on the north list *resources*. If you have anything to add to either list, either for yourself or for someone else, please do."

After they stood to sing the doxology, Carter peppered her with questions. "More people died? Was it anyone we knew? How? And when were you going to tell me?"

"I'll explain it on the way home. I-I should have told you. I'm sorry."

Carter stuck his hands in his pockets and ducked his head. It was an adolescent pose. What did she expect? He was only seventeen, but they both knew he was going to have to grow up faster than either would have wished.

Shelby turned her attention to her best friend. "Are you okay, Bianca?"

"Yes. I'm just . . . I'm emotional is all."

"How is your father?"

Bianca shrugged and rocked her hand back and forth.

"Will you let us know if there's anything we can do?"

"Of course."

They followed Patrick and Max into the fellowship hall, where the light was brighter from skylights in the ceiling. It was also warmer, but someone had propped open both doors to let in a gentle breeze. Shelby wasn't sure what she'd expected, but she was surprised to see the long lists on butcher paper adorning the walls.

"Someone was busy last night," Max said.

"As were we, *amigo*." Patrick led the way to the closest sheet of butcher paper. "As were we."

The list of needs covered everything from food to lodging to diapers. Carter moved over to talk to his friends, while Shelby, Max, Patrick, and Bianca spread out as they read one list after another. The needs far outweighed the resources, but still Shelby was surprised.

Someone had an RV that a family could stay in for as long as needed. Another person had a wheelchair in the garage that hadn't been used in at least a year. If anyone could get it to the hospital, they'd be happy to donate it. Someone else had an extra-large backyard that they couldn't begin to farm themselves. They were offering use of the land in exchange for a portion of the harvest.

People obviously had very little to share, but the fact that they *were* sharing tugged at the strings wrapped around Shelby's heart.

"Kind of surprising," Max said.

She hadn't realized he was standing behind her, and she didn't want to turn around and face him—not while tears were stinging her eyes.

"That there are so many needs?"

"And so many resources. You know, Shelby . . ." His voice dropped so that only she could hear him. "This is a good idea. If you came to High Fields with me—"

"I've already told you my decision."

"Someone could live in your home. We could list it right here." He stepped closer, close enough that he could have wrapped his arms around her, and then he pointed to a blank space at the end of the list. "Imagine it here: 'Available house for family of four.' "

"Four?" She stepped to the side, putting a small amount of distance between them. Though the lists they were studying were quite serious, she couldn't help laughing. "You're going to put four people in my little house?"

"Two bedrooms—mom and dad in one, two kids in the other. It would work. Or maybe Mr. and Mrs. Smitty could stay there."

"I had forgotten all about them."

"Bianca and I saw them as we walked over this morning," Patrick said, catching the tail end of their conversation. "They're staying until things settle down. Mr. Smitty has some angina, which he has medicine for, but he would rather stay put until he's less anxious. Plus, it's a long walk back to Dallas, and they'd have to bum a ride with someone since their car doesn't work."

"Does Mrs. Smitty agree with that decision?" Max asked.

"She says the city will be worse than whatever they have to endure here."

"She's probably right." Shelby crossed her arms and tapped her index finger against her left elbow. She needed to get to work. She hadn't even told anyone she had found a solution to her most immediate problem.

She'd agreed to work at Green Acres in exchange for shelf space in the refrigerator to keep Carter's insulin cold. The nursing home had a massive generator with plenty of gas, and they needed the help. She started to mention it but stopped midsentence when Pastor Tony walked up to them.

"Morning, Pastor." Max shook hands with Tony. It was such a natural action, something she'd seen him do a million times.

"Small group this morning," Bianca said. "I was a little surprised."

"Especially after the crowd last night." Patrick's

expression turned suddenly serious. "You'd think folks would attend this morning, that they'd want to hear your words of encouragement."

"Thank you. Good to know you were listening." Tony cleared his throat. "In times like these, people either fall on their faith—fall on their knees—or they try to handle it on their own. Last night people were scared, bewildered even. They showed up here—the one place they knew would be safe. This morning they decided to stay home when they looked around and saw how much work needed to be done."

"Like building latrines?" Carter had been talking to the youth director, but he scooted over to join them.

"Exactly. Faced with no one to take care of their toilet needs, church will often get pushed to the backseat."

"How's your family?" Shelby asked. She'd seen the pastor's wife during the service. He also had two small children that were running around on the other side of the room, playing as if nothing had changed.

"We're good. Peggy's made of very tough stuff, and both of my boys take after their mother."

They spoke another few moments, and then Patrick, Bianca, and Carter waved goodbye and drifted toward the door. Shelby held back with Max.

"Say, Tony, I'll be headed to the ranch soon."

"I thought you might want to check on your parents."

"It's more than that—I plan on staying as long as this thing lasts. I'm trying to convince Shelby and Carter to go with me."

Tony crossed his arms and smiled. "Hunker down mentality, huh? Can't say I blame you."

"I know you have that little place to the east of town. If you need fuel to get there, I could try and get you enough."

"No need, but thank you, Max."

"You aren't going out there?" Shelby asked.

"No. Peggy and I talked about it, but our place is here—leading the flock."

"If things get bad enough, the flock may turn on you," Max said.

"That's always a possibility, but ministry is what we're called to do."

"If you change your mind . . ."

"I would let you know, but I doubt that will happen. Thank you, Max. I'll pray for safety for both you and your parents." He turned to Shelby. "And I'll pray that you know God's will as far as where you should be with Carter."

Those words echoed in Shelby's mind as she made her way outside and down the sidewalk.

God's will . . .

Had she given any thought to that?

Or had she simply reacted to the events pressing down on them?

Thirty-Six

Max slowed his pace to match Shelby's. They walked toward Carter, Patrick, and Bianca, who were waiting under the large pecan trees that bordered the church's parking area.

Patrick said, "Bianca and I are headed to her parents' house. Seems they were chosen to host a latrine."

"That's a good thing," said Bianca. "*Mamá* would have never agreed to walk into someone else's backyard to use the toilet."

"How are things at your place?" Shelby asked Patrick.

"Okay. There was some construction taking place on the cross streets prior to the flare, so we actually have two porta-potties that someone requisitioned—"

"Requisitioned from whom?" Max asked. He realized belatedly that a lawyerly tone had crept into his voice.

Patrick held up his hands in a gesture of surrender. "Wasn't my idea. I woke up this morning and they'd been moved—one to each end of the apartment buildings."

"Well, I've been assigned digging duty until three," Carter said. He hesitated before adding, "And security patrol from four to six."

"What?" Shelby had been distracted, but now she focused on her son with the precision of a laser beam.

"Anyone sixteen and up is covering two hours," Max explained. "Men and women."

Carter looked pleased at being called a man, but Shelby shook her head and said something about the world collapsing around them.

"Where are you headed, Shelby?" Bianca asked. "Wait—I know that look. You're trying to decide whether or not to tell us."

"Am not."

But Max noticed the blush that reddened her cheeks and said, "Out with it."

"Actually, I have a job—at Green Acres."

"A job?" Patrick teased. "You've decided to join the working class?"

"When will you write?" Carter asked.

"I think that job is over, at least for now."

"Your mom's right, Carter." Max turned back toward Shelby. "Don't you need to be trained to work at the nursing home?"

"Normally, but I took CPR and basic first aid when I was researching that book about frontier nurses."

"You might know some things they haven't thought of yet. It certainly feels like we're living in frontier times." Bianca reached over and gave her a hug.

"Actually, Connie said she'd teach me what I

need to know. I'm not getting paid, but they have a generator which keeps their medication refrigerated."

"You'll have a place to store Carter's insulin." Max wasn't even a little surprised that she'd come up with such a good plan.

"Exactly. And I'll be helping somewhere I'm needed." She hitched up the backpack she'd taken to wearing everywhere. "I don't want to leave Carter's supplies there overnight, though. A nursing home would be a prime spot for thieves, but it will keep the insulin cold during the day, and I can make sure we have our freezer packs for the evenings."

"It's a good plan." Patrick stood with his posture ramrod straight and his hands clasped behind his back.

Max wondered if his friend knew he looked like someone who had left the military last week rather than five years ago.

"I can't believe you want a job at a nursing home," Carter muttered.

"Well, I will see you at Green Acres." Max pulled out his car keys. "I'm driving over to pick up Dr. Bhatti right now."

"You drove?" Carter sounded amazed. "Already that seems like ancient artifacts—wheels and motors. Radical."

Bianca looped her arm through Carter's. "Radical," she agreed.

"Who is Dr. Bhatti?" Shelby asked.

Max told them about the mayor's request, Bhatti's response, and the agreement they'd made.

"So he's going to live with you?" Bianca shook her head. "I don't like it. Why is he here? What's he hiding from? And what type of doctor has to be bribed to help?"

"I don't have answers to any of those questions, but I can promise you that he's better than what we currently have."

Max was headed toward downtown, and though he offered to go out of his way and give the others a ride, they all declined.

"Might as well get used to walking," Carter declared, nudging his mother and daring her to keep up.

Max walked over to his truck, started it up, and backed out of the parking area. He glanced in his rearview mirror as he pulled up to the stop sign. When he saw the group moving down the sidewalk together, he realized they were his family. They'd become more important to him than any distant cousin. It reaffirmed that he needed to do everything he could for them before he left. And the first thing was to see that Green Acres had a doctor.

Bhatti was waiting for him, sitting in the same chair, smoking another cigarette.

"You seem to be enjoying your nicotine relapse."

"Indeed. Though quitting again will be no fun at all."

"Maybe you'll be so busy you won't notice the withdrawal."

Bhatti carried his single suitcase, and raised an eyebrow when he saw the truck.

"It still runs," said Max.

"I envision lawyers driving BMWs and Porsches."

"Practicing law in a small town is somewhat different than in the city."

"As will practicing medicine, I suspect."

Max took him to the house first, showed him the room he'd be staying in, and offered to fix him an early lunch.

"I had breakfast at the hotel—granola bars and coffee."

"Breakfast of champions."

"Might as well take me to your nursing home," said Dr. Bhatti.

"Actually, our first stop needs to be the morgue."

Thirty-Seven

Shelby spent the first two hours of her shift emptying bedpans, fetching cold lunches, and taking out the trash. Fortunately, two more aides had shown up, because she didn't know what she would have done if she'd had to handle that first shift alone. As Shelby threw yet another bag of refuse into the large metal receptacle, Connie walked outside, popped open a warm soda, and rested her back against the wall.

"What are we going to do with all of this?" Shelby nodded toward the nearly full Dumpster.

"The bigger question is, what are we going to do when we're out of supplies? We're already running low on diapers, clean towels, and wash-cloths, not to mention sheets." She took a sip of the warm soda and grimaced. "Soap, Kleenex, oxygen—and then there's the medication that we need."

"So trash is the least of our troubles."

"Well, at some point soon it will have to be addressed. No one will be picking it up, that we know. The mayor sent word that someone would show up to oversee a burn pile."

"That will take care of some of it, but we should probably be separating things into what can be burned and what needs to be buried."

"I'll add it to our list of things to do."

Shelby's feet hurt, and her mind frequently turned to worries about Carter. Was he remembering to check his blood sugar? Was he finding the right things to eat? How was his body responding to physical labor out in the June heat? Was he old enough and mature enough to cover a shift on neighborhood patrol?

She hadn't worried this much about him since the time he'd gone on a sixth grade field trip to Washington, DC. At that point, she'd decided to hand it over to the Lord rather than make herself crazy. As she leaned against the wall next to Connie, she realized that it was time to take her own advice again.

"How long has your son been a diabetic?"

"He was diagnosed when he was four. I knew that something wasn't right, but I'd never had a toddler. I thought perhaps his moods were normal. He couldn't get enough to drink and whined about being hungry when I knew he'd just eaten." Shelby shook her head, the memories cascading over her like a tidal wave. "He started losing weight and sleeping more. One afternoon I went into his room where he was supposed to be playing with Legos, and he was seizing."

"Diabetic shock?"

"Yeah. I didn't recognize it, though. I could tell he was still breathing, but I had no idea what was wrong with my son. I knew enough to turn him on his side and call 9-1-1. I thought my heart would stop beating in my chest. I was terrified of losing him. Sometimes I still am."

"This thing we're going through . . . it's going to be hard on a lot of people with medical conditions."

"I know it will."

"Many of our patients won't make it." Connie sighed and checked her watch. When Shelby had first arrived, Connie had admitted that she'd only had four hours sleep the night before. The long hours and lack of rest were taking a toll. Dark circles rimmed her eyes, and she blinked rapidly behind her large glasses.

"Why do you say that? Because they won't have their medicine?"

"Some, maybe. But mostly . . . mostly I think it will just be the conditions. How will they withstand the heat of July and August? And if we get them through the summer, what will we do when the weather turns cold?"

"Hey. One day at a time."

"AA?"

"Church."

Connie smiled, and then she reached over and hugged Shelby. She smelled of peppermint. Shelby inhaled deeply, thinking of her mother, remembering her smile and her commonsense ways. Even when it was obvious that Shelby had made a major mistake marrying Alex, her mom had reminded her, "But God uses our mistakes to teach us and sometimes to bless us." She'd been holding baby Carter when she'd said that.

As they walked back to the nurses' station, the outer door opened. She looked up to see Max walking toward them. Beside him was a small, slighter Asian man. Or maybe he was Middle Eastern. Whatever his ethnicity, there was no doubt that he was the infamous Dr. Bhatti.

Max made the introductions. "Any sign of Marshall Murphy?"

"None."

"He's the director of this facility," Max explained to Dr. Bhatti.

Connie closed the chart she was writing in and tapped her pen against the desk. "He was headed to a conference in Nashville. It was supposed to last over the weekend."

"We can assume he won't be back anytime soon."

"I need someone to sign this form." Dr. Bhatti placed a sheet of paper in front of her. "If you're in charge—"

"I don't know if I'm in charge." Connie picked up a pen. "But if you'll help us out, I'll sign your form."

Shelby peeked over her shoulder as Connie quickly scanned the sheet of paper and signed her name at the bottom. The sheet gave the doctor full indemnity from any malpractice suits that might result from his working outside his field of specialty. Had Max drawn this up? Would a handwritten agreement stand up in court? And why was Bhatti so worried about being sued?

Bhatti pulled a stethoscope out of the messenger bag he was carrying and set the bag under the nurses' station. He walked over to the sinks, poured clean water into a basin, and thoroughly scrubbed his hands.

Shelby was curious as to what he'd do next.

But Dr. Bhatti seemed satisfied now that any legal quagmires were behind him. He turned, nodded toward Connie, and said, "If you'd be so kind as to assist me."

Without another word they were gone, their shoes echoing down the hall. Shelby and Max were left to man the nurses' station, and she fervently hoped that no one would need them. After all, she'd only learned to empty bedpans and offer cups of water. Any other type of emergency would have to wait.

Thirty-Eight

Carter had worked hard before. Shifts at the Market were no piece of cake. Folks could be rude, and some things—like retrieving carts from the parking lot—were basically manual labor.

None of that compared to digging a latrine.

Though the group took turns, the soil soon revealed white rock, which had to be broken up with a metal pole before digging could resume. It was backbreaking labor. Everyone was careful to stay hydrated, and Carter made sure to go back to his house to check his sugar levels and grab a snack. Fortunately, they still had plenty of food in the house, especially after what Max had brought. But it also wasn't what he was used to— no snack packs, granola bars, or Gatorade. Carter understood the basics of nutrition, having received plenty of training in his last thirteen years. He knew the difference between a healthy complex carbohydrate and junk food—not that his mother kept anything of a "junk" nature in their house.

He ate and used the bathroom, which was more disgusting by the minute. The conditions only fueled his desire to make progress on the latrine. He went back to work, and within two hours they had managed to dig down approximately three feet.

"Look at it this way," said a guy named Ed. "We're one-third finished."

The guy was doing his fair share, so Carter attempted a smile and climbed back into the hole.

An hour later, Carter had to leave for his shift on the neighborhood patrol. He wasn't sure what he expected, but he was surprised when he made it to the end of their two-block section and found two pickup trucks positioned across the middle of the road.

"We have a roadblock?"

"We do now!" An old man he didn't recognized unclipped a radio from his belt at the same time that an older woman showed up.

"My name is Wanda Plumley, but you may call me Mrs. P."

Apparently, she was Carter's shift buddy. He might have doubted her clout as a patrolwoman, but she was carrying a shotgun and looked plenty comfortable with it. Not that he thought they would need a firearm.

Ken Walker introduced himself and explained how the radios worked. "We have one for this end and one for the other. You can talk to each other, and anything you say will also be heard at the home base."

"Frank's house?"

"Yup. We have someone monitoring it at all times. They can be here within two to three minutes if you have any trouble, but you need to call at the first sign that something is up. Don't wait. Also, whoever is manning the home base can contact the local police. Officers are stationed throughout Abney so that someone is relatively close to each neighborhood."

"Isn't this kind of . . . overkill?"

"Ask Mr. Evans."

Mrs. P gave Ken a reproving look.

He held up his hands. "There's no use sugar-coating this, Wanda. In case you haven't noticed, we can't dial 9-1-1 anymore. The folks of Abney need to protect themselves."

And with that grim declaration, he grabbed his water bottle and walked away.

"Don't mind him, young man. Nothing is going to happen today that you, me, Oscar, and the good Lord can't handle."

Carter was almost afraid to ask. "Oscar?"

Mrs. P patted the shotgun. "My husband gave me this 12 gauge Remington for our twenty-fifth anniversary, and he made sure I knew how to use it."

"So it's loaded?"

"Certainly. An unloaded gun wouldn't do us any good."

Carter wasn't sure how to answer that, so he didn't. Maybe Mrs. P wasn't as old as he thought, or maybe old people were tougher than he had imagined. She hopped up onto the bed of the pickup truck and sat down in one of the lawn chairs Ken had positioned there.

Patting the seat next to her, she said, "Join me. I suspect your distance eyesight is a bit better than mine."

Carter shrugged and scrambled up into the truck. From there he could make out what must be the other roadblock at the far end of their two-block perimeter. Was he actually standing guard in the bed of a pickup truck, beside an old woman with a loaded shotgun?

"Why don't you tell me what you've been doing since the sun started to create havoc with our atmosphere?"

Though he hadn't wanted to talk about it, he found that Mrs. P was a good listener. She would stop him occasionally to ask questions—such as, what sort of expression the man who pulled the gun at the grocery store wore.

"Sad, I guess. Kind of . . . defeated."

"You know, Carter . . ." She hesitated, and then she smiled at him. "This thing we're living through, it's a real shock. Some people will respond to it better than others. But your circumstances shouldn't shape your attitudes. Your attitude actually shapes your circumstances."

Carter wasn't exactly sure what she meant, but he liked the sound of it. Maybe the things they were doing and the way they were doing them would make a difference after all.

Their two-hour shift passed quickly and without incident, unless you counted an old tabby cat crossing the intersection. Though they'd seen no one, the team on the other end had called in both times a suspicious car had passed them.

"Casing our neighborhood, no doubt." Mrs. P patted Oscar. "They won't get past us."

It occurred to Carter that if he were a burglar,

he wouldn't want to confront Wanda Plumley. The woman was fearless, or at least that was how she seemed to Carter. Maybe she was old enough to have seen it all already. That is, except for this. It had never happened before. It was what his history teacher would call a historic event.

Mrs. P said she'd see him the next afternoon, and Carter shuffled back home—sore from the hours he'd spent digging, followed by the two hours sitting tensely in the truck bed. He'd need to find a way to relax. The muscles in his shoulders felt as if they'd been poised for a fight all day.

His mom wasn't home yet—probably still working at the nursing home. Carter tried to picture the old folks who lived there.

Were they stuck in their beds, unable to move?

Did they need to be fed?

Who would bathe them, and how?

What would happen when Green Acres ran out of medicine?

And how could his mom help with any of those things?

Thirty-Nine

When he thought of the situation at Green Acres, Carter was glad that his job was as simple as building a latrine and sitting in a truck.

Once he got home, he grabbed a can of tuna,

some crackers, and a vacuum-sealed cheese stick. It was warm, not cold, but surely it hadn't spoiled yet. He took it all to the front porch, where there was at least a faint breeze stirring, and collapsed on the top step. He might have fallen asleep if he hadn't seen Jason riding his skateboard up the walk.

"Dude," said Jason. "You're dirty and you smell bad."

Carter was surprised to see his best friend, especially with his skateboard. Jason stood about his height but had gained a good twenty pounds on him their senior year.

"Didn't know you still had that thing."

"In the back of the closet. Took me a while to remember my best moves."

"Wasn't aware you ever had any," Carter teased.

"We both know I could have made it to the X Games with just a little work."

"Uh-huh."

"The point is, it's a perfectly acceptable form of transportation during the Drop."

"The Drop?"

"Sure. The solar flare dropped down, the electrical grid dropped off the map, and any prospect of a normal life for you and me dropped out of sight." Jason popped up the nose of his skateboard, kicked it into a spin, and landed back on it, smoothly maneuvering across their front walk in one fluid motion.

"You skate better than you drive," Carter said. Then a random thought pulsed through his head. "You know what? I miss cell phones."

"True that." Jason popped the skateboard again, a smile playing across his face. "I wanted to text you earlier when my little sister was driving me batty, but I couldn't. I had to deal with her instead. That's my mom's favorite new saying—*deal with it*."

"Yeah, but . . . I miss video games."

"And music. I have some on my phone, but I'm afraid to use what little juice is left in it."

"Television reruns."

"Air-conditioning."

"Microwave popcorn."

"Cold sodas."

"Facebook."

"Dude. You hate Facebook."

"Yeah, I did." Carter glanced over at his car— something he'd made fun of when his mom wasn't around. He understood it was the best car she could afford for him, and he appreciated it, but . . . well, it was a real joke. A Buick sedan that had been seriously used and abused. The hood was a different color from the body and the air-conditioning didn't work. Still . . .

"I miss driving."

Jason stopped messing around on his skate-board and dropped down beside him.

"Want some tuna?"

"Nah," said Jason. "My mom pushed all the defrosted freezer leftovers on us before they ruined. I'm stuffed. Though I could go for a burger and fries in a major way."

They sat in silence for a few minutes. "Why aren't you helping to dig down to the bedrock of Abney?"

"One person per family—I worked the first few hours, and my pop took over the afternoon shift."

"There has to be a way we can fix this."

"The world?"

Carter shrugged. "Maybe not that, but we're the next generation, the millennials."

"Correct, dude. We're the last of Generation Y."

"That all sounded so stupid when the speaker came to our school." Carter finished his cheese stick and stuck the wrapper in the empty can of tuna. "What was his name?"

"Motivational speaker . . . dude was in a wheelchair . . ." Jason snapped his fingers. "He reminded me of Stephen Hawking."

"His name was Raymond."

"Raymond's World."

"He said that millennials—"

"Which we are."

"Have the ability to adapt better than any generation before it—that we've seen more change in our lifetime than our parents or grandparents combined."

"We certainly have a major change to adapt to now."

"The Drop."

One thing Carter appreciated about Jason was that he allowed a person to randomly think. At the moment something big was whirring inside Carter's brain. "We should be able to think our way past this."

"Got any specific ideas?"

"No. I'm coming up blank."

"How about we start by getting the Brainiacs back together?"

"Let's not do anything drastic." There were things about the Brainiac Club Carter had enjoyed—not that he thought of himself as a brainiac, but he fit in better there than he had with the sports crowd. It had filled a void throughout his freshman and sophomore years. The last two years had been too busy, what with work and college prep. Now the days spent in a lab designing outlandish experiments seemed like a thing from his childhood.

"We swore off that two years ago," Carter reminded Jason.

"Because it was seriously affecting any chances we had with the girls, not to mention that little fire we started in Coach's lab."

"Then Coach Parish missed a semester because his wife got sick."

"And he couldn't sponsor us anymore."

Coach Parish's wife had died not too long after that, but the old guy had looked so sad, so utterly bereaved, that no one had the heart to bring up reconvening the group of geeks. Now, though, he might be ready to see some of his old students. What else was he doing all day? Digging a latrine?

"Might be a good idea," Carter admitted. "I guess it couldn't hurt."

"Let's do it." Jason jumped up and mounted the skateboard again.

"First we need to contact Coach, and then somehow find the other members of the Brainiacs."

"Zane and Quincy live near me."

"Maybe I'll ask Kaitlyn." When Jason gave him a look, Carter shrugged it off. "I'll see her at work tomorrow, not that there's much left at the store to sell."

"Wanna meet at the school at four?"

Carter had latrine digging in the morning, his shift at the Market from ten to two, and patrol at four. He'd thought their new life would be boring . . . he'd even pictured himself lying on his bed and bouncing a tennis ball off the ceiling. At the moment, he was too tired to throw a ball.

"Two thirty works better for me."

"That will work too."

"How do we get in contact with Coach Parish?"

"He lives over by my gran. I saw him once when he was out walking a little dog. I'll stop by and ask."

"Once we're together, maybe we can think outside the grid."

"Ten four." Jason held up his hand for a high five.

Carter slapped his palm against his friend's. It was juvenile—something they'd stopped doing in grade school. As Jason skated off, Carter realized he didn't mind juvenile things so much. Being an adult? It wasn't panning out like he'd hoped.

Forty

Shelby came home to a can of tuna on the front porch, the neighbor's cat licking hungrily at what little was left, and Carter sound asleep in his bed. A little odd for eight in the evening. A few minutes later Bianca came over to talk.

"Carter worked on the digging?" she asked.

"For a few hours, before his stint on the neighborhood watch group—which I'm not happy about."

"We didn't realize we had the perfect life, did we?"

"I don't know how perfect it was, but it certainly was more manageable than this."

They moved to the back porch, which was

barely big enough to hold two lawn chairs. Shelby peeked at the sky, relieved to see no sign of the aurora. She didn't want to sit in the front where she would be forced to watch the street. She didn't want to think of Mr. Evans or the blockades set up at both ends of their block. She wanted to pretend, if just for a few moments, that life was as it used to be.

"Tell me about your shift at Green Acres."

Shelby paused, wondering if she should share all that she had seen. But this was Bianca—her closest friend besides Max. The four of them, when you included Patrick, made up the ragged support network that had seen her through the last fourteen years, ever since Alex had died and she'd become a single mom.

In a way, Shelby had already been a single mom even before Alex's death. His drug addiction had destroyed any semblance of a normal life. While her parents had been alive, they had been incredibly supportive. After Alex died, her dad was always bringing up the names of eligible bachelors—hinting that she should give love a try one more time.

Shelby wasn't interested in going through that particular type of heartache again.

Their church had also provided help— prayer, meals when she had her appendix removed, and guidance when she didn't know how to navigate the waters of single parenthood.

But now they were all floundering, trying to get their feet back beneath them.

"We transferred the patients who had died over to the morgue, but we have no way to contact their families. Food is limited, and there aren't many people there to fix meals anyway. Although they have a big generator to power the medical equipment, they're going to run out of medication. Everyone there is doing the best they can, but I'm not sure it will be enough."

"Do they need more volunteers?"

Shelby shrugged. "Employees are beginning to trickle back to work. At least three showed up while I was there today—a nurse and two aides. They could only stay a few hours, as they had their own emergencies to tend to. But they cared enough to stop by."

"What did you do all day?"

"Cleaned bedpans, offered sips of water, and occasionally took a temperature with the fancy thermometer that you wave over their forehead."

"At least bedpans, cups, and thermometers still work."

"Some of the residents understand what has happened, and others don't. One old guy kept calling us to his room because he couldn't get his television to come on. When we explained that the power is out, he seemed to understand, but twenty minutes later he'd call for help with it again."

"*Papá* is a little bit like that, and maybe it's a blessing. Maybe if he completely understood the scope of the mess we're in, it would frighten him too much."

"I think of your dad as a very capable man."

"He was. However, this illness has left him more childlike. Now he looks to *Mamá* for everything."

"How's she holding up?"

"Are you kidding? My mother is tougher than a solar flare. She's in supercharged mode, which is why I'm here. She basically insisted that I leave for an hour."

"Well, I'm glad she did. It's nice to be able to decompress with someone."

Shelby slipped inside to find them both a bottle of water. Max had purchased a case somewhere and left it in her kitchen. Did she take him for granted? Soon he'd be gone, and then she would be searching for her own water. But she could handle it. She and Carter weren't helpless. She was turning to go back outside when she saw movement on her front porch. Her heart rate accelerated and she almost screamed, but suddenly she recognized Danny Vail, the city manager.

Opening the front door, she motioned him inside. Once he entered she locked the door behind them.

"Just stopping by to see how you're doing."

Shelby somehow doubted that. How long had it been since he'd been to her house? Before and after Alex died, but certainly not since Carter started school—so 12 years at least. There was no way this was a casual visit. But she played along, nodded, and said, "Bianca and I are sitting on the back porch. There's actually a breeze. Would you like a bottle of water?"

"No, but thank you."

Bianca looked surprised when they both walked outside. Shelby's mind flashed back to a month ago, when Bianca had suggested that Danny might be interested in pursuing a relationship with her. He had invited her out to eat after church, but that had been . . . well, that had been Danny being polite and nothing more. In fact, she didn't think he'd been at church lately, or perhaps she just hadn't seen him.

"How are things at city hall?" Bianca asked.

"About what you'd expect."

"I don't think anyone knows what to expect."

"Confusion at first, followed by people dividing into camps." He grimaced at the last word as he sat down on the porch floor and leaned back against a corner post.

It was funny that he seemed at attention even as he sat on her porch. Perhaps that was something military men never lost—a sense of alertness. She'd noticed it in Patrick as well.

"What kind of camps?" Shelby asked.

"Yeah, I don't like the sound of that." Bianca glanced over at Shelby.

"I'm not surprised, though." She shrugged. "There are factions within every group."

"I suppose there usually are." Danny reached a hand up and rubbed the muscles along the back of his neck. "When this thing first hit I thought it would split into young and old—the old having trouble accepting the scope of the problem, and the young going into disaster recovery mode."

"But it hasn't worked out that way." Suddenly her throat was dry, and she wasn't sure she wanted to hear what Danny was about to say. Shelby uncapped her bottle and took a long drink. Why was Danny here? Why was he sharing this information with them?

"Nope. We have people who refuse to react, those who overreact, and then a precious few who are reacting thoughtfully."

"Sounds like a mess. *Como siempre.*"

"It does seem to develop that way. It's worse than I expected, though. Eugene Stone is making moves to force Mayor Perkins's resignation."

"She wouldn't do that." Shelby crossed her arms tightly.

"She wouldn't want to, but it might depend on how much pressure Stone can add to the situation."

"He wants the job," Bianca said.

"He does. In the event of a vacancy, the mayor pro tem immediately assumes office."

"Eugene Stone." Shelby felt sick to her stomach.

"The process to remove her from office is lengthy and difficult, as it should be. Stone wants to be in charge now, and he's not beyond stooping to underhanded, even illegal means to achieve that."

"Like what?" Shelby glanced again at Max's house. Perhaps she should go and get him. He needed to hear this.

"Stealing supplies from Croghan, requisitioning what little the shop owners have, intimidating people to hand over their supplies for the general good—we've had all sorts of complaints. Of course Stone denies it all, and it comes down to their word against his."

The three fell silent as they digested the possible collapse of their local government.

"Why are you here, Danny?" The words popped out before Shelby could corral her thoughts. "I doubt you came by to catch us up on current events. It's nice to see you, but . . ."

"But I haven't been here in a long time, and you're wondering why I bothered to visit tonight." Danny placed his palm against the smooth boards of the porch. "After Alex died, I made a vow to myself that I would do what I could to help."

"We're fine."

Danny grinned ruefully.

"So you have assured me, every time I've tried." He held up a hand to stop her argument.

"I'm not criticizing you. I admire what you've done, and Carter . . . well, he seems to be an upstanding young man."

"Thank you, but even if we weren't okay, you're not responsible—"

"I know I'm not, in one sense. In another, maybe I could have done more to intervene before Alex sped past the point of no return."

"Because you were deployed with him? Were you supposed to anticipate and intervene in his crisis?" Shelby shook her head, suddenly too tired to argue. "Even I didn't fully understand the scope of Alex's problems, and I was living with him. Besides, that's the past."

"The distant past," Bianca agreed.

"And I'd rather leave it there."

"It is, and you're both probably right." He stood, paced the length of the porch, and stared out at the night. When he turned to face them, he said, "We've had contact with Fort Hood."

Forty-One

"You've been in touch with the base?" Somewhere in Shelby's mind bloomed the bright thought of communication restored, which too quickly wilted with Danny's next words.

"Not directly. A few soldiers returned late last night from maneuvers. Took a little detour and just happened to contact one of our patrols."

"Took a detour?" Shelby stared at him in disbelief. "Sounds like they were AWOL."

"No. Not yet. They returned before anyone noticed and claimed it was a mechanical problem." Danny stared out into the evening sky, which was just beginning to darken. "According to them, and these are men I know and trust, there's a power struggle going on between state and federal entities."

"What type of power struggle?" Bianca sat up straighter and appeared more interested in the conversation.

"Texas has an abundance of resources, and the feds want access to them. Every military installation is comprised of troops from all over the country, but a fair number of those stationed at Fort Hood are locals. The powers that be are not going to send those troops into their hometowns with commands to take supplies away from Mom and Pop and the neighbors."

"So there's nothing to worry about." Shelby twisted the bottle cap on and off, on and off. "The soldiers would refuse their orders."

"It isn't that easy. Enlisted men—and women—can't just ignore orders, but they can work to sabotage them, if they're not caught. Anyway, the word going around is that at the moment the military is attempting to deploy troops domestically, and re-forming regiments so that soldiers are sent away from their hometowns."

"And they think that will work?" Bianca asked.

Danny shrugged. "At the same time, state troops are gearing up for a confrontation. There could be trouble."

Shelby stood now, anxiety surging through her. How would she protect Carter from civil anarchy? Did it have to be one emergency after another? How long would things continue to get worse? "What does this have to do with us?"

"I'm not sure it does or will. There's not much in Abney for the feds to requisition, except for our water. At this point there's plenty of that, and there's no need to limit anyone's access. My guess is the military will be more interested in fuel supplies, and assets such as ammunition, grocery warehouses, pharmaceutical supplies, et cetera."

"This is *loco*." Bianca's accent grew stronger as she wound herself up. "Domestic supplies are not under the jurisdiction of the US military. People are barely making it as things stand, and the government should be helping us, not plundering our supplies."

"I agree, but in their minds a strong military will help to defend our country." He cleared his throat, and then he got to the point of his visit. "I have a few friends who own places outside of town. If either of you would rather wait this thing out in a more remote location, I could make it happen."

"And move *Papá*? Again? No. I won't put him

or *Mamá* through it. And I won't be intimidated by someone who thinks they are"—she made quotation marks in the air—"protecting us."

"Max has already offered to take us to his parents' place," Shelby admitted. "But we're staying. Thank you just the same, Danny."

As she spoke, Shelby saw Max and Dr. Bhatti stepping out on his back porch. Max waved and Dr. Bhatti nodded. They both looked around a few moments before going back inside.

"What do you know about him?" Bianca asked, nodding after the doctor. "How can we trust him to provide medical care when we can't confirm where he's from? Who knows what kind of work he actually did, or even whether he was a good doctor or a bad one?"

"I'm afraid I don't have an answer for that." Danny stared at Max's empty porch for a moment, and then he turned his attention back to Shelby. "Did I hear you're working at Green Acres?"

"A few hours a day. Dr. Bhatti showed up to help there. He seems like a nice enough guy, if a bit reserved."

"I don't like it," Bianca said. "I'm glad that *Papá* is home, where he's surrounded by people he knows—not doctors who had to be bribed to pitch in a helping hand."

Danny didn't appear to know how to respond to that, so instead he said, "Guess I should be going. If either of you change your mind, you can find me at city hall whenever I'm not sleeping."

Shelby walked him through the house and thanked him for stopping by. When she'd returned to the back porch, Bianca was preparing to leave.

"That was a little strange," Shelby said.

"I told you he was interested in you, and you know it's true. It's just that you don't want to believe it. You're afraid of relationships, my friend. But now might be a good time for you to change that attitude."

"How did I ever get by without your advice?"

"Badly."

Shelby hooked an arm through Bianca's as they walked to the front porch. The woman was like a sister to her. And whether or not Shelby liked it, Bianca would always describe things exactly as she saw them.

"Are you sure it's a good idea for you to walk home alone?"

"There are patrols everywhere. I couldn't be safer."

"Thank you for coming by. I'll try and stop over to see your parents tomorrow."

Bianca hugged her. "You think about what Danny offered, and Max too."

"Seriously?"

"Yes, seriously."

"But you're staying."

"Only because of my parents. Plus, I have Patrick around if I need help."

They both glanced over at Max's. A lantern still burned in the front room, its light spilling out into the creeping darkness.

Shelby admitted to herself that she felt safe knowing that Max was next door. "I guess we're both pretty lucky—"

"Blessed."

"Blessed," Shelby agreed. "At least we have friends who are looking out for us."

"And now, more than ever, friends and faith will see us through."

It was much later, in the middle of the night, when Shelby woke from where she'd fallen asleep on the couch. She stumbled into the kitchen for a glass of water, which she poured from a gallon jug Max had given them. She stretched a kink that had formed in her back. Why hadn't she just gone to bed? Now she would pay for it with a crick in her neck.

She eyed the Advil but decided to save it for a real emergency. As she placed the glass back on the counter, she happened to look outside. The moon was high in the night sky, casting long shadows. Perhaps that was why she could see Dr. Bhatti, kneeling at the back of Max's property, burying something beneath the boughs of a cedar tree.

Forty-Two

Max startled awake to the sound of someone in his home. He had a disjointed recollection of Dr. Bhatti, their agreement, and the solar flare. His mind worked back through the events that had occurred since Friday evening. Was today only Monday? How could his entire life have changed so drastically in such a short period of time?

He'd wanted to talk to Shelby the night before, after he'd seen Danny on the back porch. What was he doing over there? Had there been news? Surely if there had been, he would have heard. He'd given Bhatti a quick tour of the place, intent on hurrying back outside. But Bhatti had wanted to talk. He'd finished the last of his cigarettes and was antsy, pacing the space between the living room and the kitchen. After an hour, Max had stretched and claimed he was bushed—which was the truth.

When Bhatti finally went to his room, Max had hurried back outside. No sign of Danny, Bianca, or even Shelby—and her home was completely dark.

Now the sunlight was peeking in through the window, which meant it was at least six thirty in the morning. Max dressed quickly and walked into the kitchen, but there was no sign of Bhatti.

Had he left already? Was he suddenly dedicated? Max glanced out the front window and noticed Bhatti sitting on the porch, staring out at the street.

"Still wishing for another smoke?" Max asked, walking out and stretching. His watch said the time was six forty, his normal time to get up. Funny how the body kept to certain rhythms even when circumstances had radically changed.

The day promised to be warm. Which made him wonder—what would be worse? The heat of summer or winter's cold? How could they prepare for either now? Or should they stay focused on medical supplies and food and safety?

"Unfortunately, yes." Bhatti sat forward, his arms propped on his knees. He stared at the ground and then glanced sideways at Max. "Though I enjoyed my brief flirtation with a long-abandoned bad habit, I suppose one pack was enough. I wouldn't want to die of cancer."

"You're an optimist this morning."

"Hardly. You do realize that most of the residents at Green Acres won't make it through the summer?"

"And on that sobering thought, I need coffee."

By the time he had coffee brewing in the French press on the picnic table, Shelby had joined them. She'd already met Bhatti at the nursing home, but he acted as if he barely remembered her. If Max had to put a word on it, he would say the man worked at keeping himself distant from everyone.

It occurred to him that he had a right to know what Bhatti had been escaping from in Austin. After all, the man was living in his house. But the best time to ask would be when they were alone.

Shelby had no such reservations. She'd consumed half a cup of coffee and was clutching the mug as if someone might wrestle it from her hands. Her eyes were alert, and she openly studied Bhatti.

"Max tells us that you used to live in Austin."

"I did."

"And yet you were here when the flare hit."

"I was, and I still am."

"Not too many people pick our town as a vacation destination," she said. "What brought you to Abney?"

"Took a drive on the back roads, ended up here."

"You have a car here?" Max asked.

"I do."

"You didn't tell me that."

"You didn't ask. Did you think I walked from Austin?"

"Must be a newer model if you're not driving it." Shelby sipped from her coffee. "I assume it wouldn't start?"

"You're correct. I can't even get in it since the vehicle boasts a keyless entry and the circuits are fried."

"But we can get into the gas tank." Max pushed the box of Pop-Tarts toward Shelby. She rarely indulged in sugary treats, but occasionally if Carter wasn't around, she could be tempted. She glanced at the box and shook her head.

Bhatti shrugged, as if his car was no longer of any consequence to him.

"Max also said you *needed to get away*."

"Something I told him in confidence."

"And yet it could be pertinent to us, since we are entrusting the care of our elderly to you."

Bhatti reached for the pack of cigarettes in his pocket before realizing that they were gone. "I can assure you it has nothing to do with my practice, though my specialty is not geriatrics. I was an ear, nose, and throat doctor."

"Are you saying that you aren't qualified to treat the residents of Green Acres?"

Bhatti had been answering in a stilted, stand-offish manner, but now he sat forward, crossed his arms on the table, and looked directly into Shelby's eyes. "I am a certified physician, but if you don't want me in your nursing home, just say so."

Shelby frowned, shook her head, and pushed her nearly empty cup toward Max. As he refilled it, she said, "Certainly you can understand our concern."

"I can."

Max reached for another Pop-Tart and poured the last dregs of coffee into his mug.

Shelby finally asked what must have been weighing heavily on her mind. "What do you think their odds are?"

"As I told Max earlier, I doubt many of the patients in your facility will survive the summer."

"And how did you arrive at that assessment after only one shift?"

Max had been content to watch this confrontation play out. He'd learned in the courtroom that if you saw a storm brewing and stepped out of the way, sometimes good things resulted from the fallout. He'd had the same questions about Bhatti, but they were probably better coming from Shelby, who could be written off—at least by the doctor—as a nosy neighbor.

"You have five residents with pulmonary disorders, three who are recovering from recent surgeries, eight who have varying degrees of dementia, and six who have a history of cardiac trouble."

"And?" Shelby abandoned her mug and crossed her arms.

"My point, Ms. Sparks, is that there isn't much we can do for these people. We can't even keep them comfortable, and we certainly can't treat them with the resources we have."

"So you're giving up."

"Actually I'll be reporting to work within the

half hour, but I'm fairly certain there is little I can do." And with that, the doctor turned and shuffled into the house.

Max watched Shelby and shrugged when she turned her gaze to him.

"Real winner you brought us there."

"Easy does it, Shelby. He's only telling us what we would rather not hear."

"Doesn't make it the truth."

"And it doesn't make it a lie." Max waited, but Shelby didn't explain her mood. Finally he asked, "What's bothering you this morning?"

Shelby plopped back down onto the bench of the picnic table. "I saw him last night. I saw him burying something in your backyard."

Forty-Three

"Bhatti?"

"Last night—late."

She scrubbed a hand across her face, which was devoid of makeup. When she was like this, when she wasn't aware that he was watching her, Shelby reminded him of the young girl he'd grown up with. In those moments, it felt like she was the other half of himself, the half he had lost somewhere along the way.

Now she leaned forward, lowered her voice, and reached across to clutch his arm. "He was here in the backyard, near that cedar, burying something."

"You saw this?"

"By the moonlight. I was in the kitchen and happened to look out—" She pointed toward the offending tree. "I just happened to see him."

Max didn't answer right away, hoping she would elaborate. But she didn't.

"He's hiding something. Burying something. And we need to know what."

"So go dig it up," said Max.

"He's still here."

"We could ask him."

"Come on, Max. Someone who buries who-knows-what in the middle of the night is not going to tell the truth when you ask him a hard question."

"So what do we do?"

"You figure it out. You brought him here."

"To Abney? He was already—"

"To our neighborhood."

"Are you suggesting that I've put us in danger?" Max pushed away his cup of coffee.

"I'm not suggesting anything. I'm telling you that it's your mess and you need to clean it up. Find out what's going on."

"And what are you going to do?"

"Finish my breakfast. Get ready for work. Check on Carter."

There were a dozen things Max could have

said to her at that moment, things he wanted and needed to say. But the lawyer in him spoke up before he had a chance. "What was Danny doing at your house last night?"

Instead of answering, she picked up a package of Pop-Tarts, opened it, took a bite, and grimaced. "Tastes like sugar."

"Uh-huh. Now what about Danny? By the time I'd settled Bhatti into his room, all the lights were out in your place."

"So you're watching my house?"

"I'm not spying on you, Shelby. I'm keeping an eye out for trouble—watching your back. That's what we do for each other. Remember?"

With a quick "sorry" for being so prickly, she gave him the quick rendition of what they'd learned.

"Can't say I'm surprised," said Max.

"That the federal government and state governments are locking horns? Already? After only two and a half days?"

"The mayor hinted as much."

"I can't imagine how she's dealing with the pressure."

"A power struggle with Eugene Stone is not what we need right now."

"I knew he was bitter about losing the election, but it's hard to believe he'd put his political aspirations ahead of the good of Abney."

"That's the problem—he thinks they are one and the same."

At the look of concern on her face, he reached across the table and covered her hands with his.

"This isn't going to be easy, but we are a tough people—a country birthed in revolution. God has seen us through the struggles of the past. He'll see us through this."

She pulled her hands away. "Is that why you're leaving?"

"I'm leaving because my folks aren't as young as they once were—and while they'll try their best to outlast this thing, I need to be there to help them."

"You're going to become a farmer?" She raised her eyes to his, tears welling and threatening to spill. She glanced away quickly and shrugged. Max sat back and aimed for a casual posture.

"Think I can't do it?"

Shelby shook her head, turned over his hand, and rubbed the center of his palm. "Lawyer hands. No calluses."

"I suppose it's time that changed." When her mood still didn't lighten, he added, "There won't be any legal work for me to do here."

"You don't know that."

"And besides, I don't like crowds. If the military moves in, I'd rather be somewhere else."

"They're not going to move in to Abney."

"Probably not."

"But it sounds as if they'll take whatever we have that's worth taking."

"If that happens—and I'm not saying it will—there will be trouble."

She stood, tossed what was left of her coffee into his rosebushes, and thanked him.

But he couldn't let her leave, not on that note. He had to try one more time. "That's the real reason Danny came, isn't it? To tell you to leave?"

She was halfway across the yard when she turned around. "Talk to Bhatti, or get a shovel. But figure out what is going on with him and figure it out soon."

Forty-Four

Max cleaned up, putting on a pearl snap shirt, his best jeans, and his good boots. He'd walk to the office instead of taking the truck. Bhatti had already left, as had Shelby, though there was a good twenty minutes between when she hurried off and when Bhatti followed. Max imagined Dr. Bhatti would be avoiding Shelby Sparks today.

He enjoyed the walk to the office, realizing that it could be his last walk through Abney. If things went well, he could leave first thing the next day.

The neighborhood patrols he passed reported no trouble. Maybe things would settle down. Maybe the world would leave Abney alone to recuperate as best as it could. That fantasy lasted until he approached his office on the square. One of the deputies was standing out front waiting for him.

"The mayor wants to see you."

Twenty minutes later he was in an interview room at the jail, sitting across from one Charles Striker, accused of attempted armed robbery. The man was forty-six years old according to his file, and he had the look of a mechanic or factory worker—big muscles but no tan line. Not a farmer. Also not a burglar, if Max were to guess.

The interview room was hot, though it was still early in the morning. Lights powered by the emergency generator buzzed, giving Max the faint beginnings of a headache.

"Would you like to tell me what happened?"

"Can you get me out of here? Do you know how hot it is in those cells? No air-conditioning, no fans, and barely any food. This is a civil suit waiting to happen, man."

"Supposing you're correct, it might be awhile before you have a chance to file that suit."

"Well, I can't just sit in there and rot. You gotta do something."

Max felt his eyebrows rise. At least, the skin above his eyes rose, considering some of his eyebrows had been singed off during the fire blast on the town square. "I don't have to do anything since I'm not technically your lawyer, Mr. Striker. The mayor asked me to check in on you, and I agreed because she is a friend of mine."

"All small towns are the same. Old boy's club—"

"Actually, the mayor is a she. Why don't you tell me what happened."

"I live ten miles outside of town, on the east side."

It was an unincorporated area, which meant there was an odd combination of old mobile homes, RVs, and the occasional prefab house. Not a good neighborhood, and technically not a part of town at all since Abney had decided not to annex it two years earlier. The place was something of a dump, and the mayor hadn't felt optimistic about taking on the problems there— especially with Eugene Stone breathing down her back.

"And?"

"And there are some real lunatics living out there. Came home Friday night, nothing was working, folks sitting around speculating, but no one knew what happened. Then Larry—he's the only one with a CB—he starts talking about riots in Austin, complete road closures in Houston." The man's hands began to shake, so he clasped them together. "And Dallas? Well, apparently it's burning."

Max's heart rate accelerated at the news. The mayor had hinted that the urban situation had taken a turn for the worse, but she hadn't shared any details.

"After that everything turned crazy. Folks

were arming up and going out in pairs—taking whatever they could find in abandoned cars, looting people's houses—and I'm telling you, it was every man for himself."

"So you decided to come and rob houses in Abney?"

"No! That wasn't it at all."

Max opened the file folder the police chief had handed him and spun it around to face Striker. He tapped the part where it listed possessions— a Remington 870 pump shotgun, a switchblade, and a pair of brass knuckles.

"Yeah, okay. That stuff is mine. A man has to be prepared to defend himself."

"Defend yourself?"

"I wasn't about to let anyone get a jump on me."

Maybe he was telling the truth. Maybe he wasn't.

"Tell me what happened when you approached the roadblock."

"I turned around. I tried three different ways to get into town, ended up having to cross through a pasture off Old Mill Road. Nearly bottomed out my truck."

"Where were you headed?"

"A house over on Avenue K."

"I know the area."

"Well, a . . . a friend of mine used to live there, but it appeared to be deserted."

"Go on. You're in the house and—"

"I'm looking around, thinking maybe I'll stay

there. It's plain as day no one was living there. I wasn't going to rob anybody, but if the stuff is just sitting there and no one is using it . . ."

"What happened next?"

"Suddenly a couple of trucks pull up. Guys told me to get out of the house, which I did, and then two guys jumped me from behind."

"According to the officer's statement you exited the home with your rifle raised and said . . ." Max spun the folder back around so he could read the statement word for word. " 'Back away before I shoot something up.' "

"I guess I could have said that. I don't remember." Striker blinked rapidly, his right knee jiggling.

He raised his hands in surrender, which might have been amusing since he was wearing handcuffs. But nothing about this was amusing. Max was suddenly tired, and he hadn't even made it into his office yet.

"Okay. Probably I did. I was desperate, man."

"Which doesn't justify your actions."

"You don't know what it's like out there. You don't know what people are doing." Striker had been staring at the wall, but now he turned his gaze on Max. "Step outside Abney and you'll find out. If you don't have someone watching your back, if you're alone, you don't stand a chance. I didn't have any choice. A man will do what he has to do to survive."

Forty-Five

Max closed the folder and didn't speak until the battery-operated clock on the wall ticked off another three minutes, which in an interview room seems much longer. Sweat was running in rivulets down Striker's face by the time Max cleared his throat.

"It seems to me you have three options." Max ticked the first off on his index finger. "Plead innocent and wait for a trial, which as I stated, could be a while."

Striker gave one short, definitive jerk of his head.

"Second choice." Max touched his middle finger. "Plead guilty and hope the judge, when we find the judge, is lenient and gives you probation."

Again Striker immediately dismissed the idea.

"Or ask the mayor for leniency."

"She could do that?"

"I don't think Mayor Perkins wants you living in our jail any more than you want to be living here."

"I'll do it, though I doubt I'll be treated fairly."

Max's temper exploded. He slapped his palm down on the table and leaned forward, not even bothering to mitigate the anger pounding at his temples. "You came to our town, a town with law-abiding citizens who are trying to pull together and make it through this catastrophe, and you showed a willingness to break and enter—"

"The door was unlocked."

"Take what wasn't yours—"

"I didn't have a chance to take anything!"

"And use a lethal weapon. What is fair, Mr. Striker, is that you be prosecuted to the fullest extent of the law."

He sat back and stared at the man in front of him. Was he an evil man? Maybe. Maybe not. But he was desperate, uneducated, and lacked a proper respect for any type of authority. How many more just like him were circling the edges of Abney?

"You know what? Forget those three options. We don't want you in our jail, and we don't need the responsibility of feeding you. I'm going to suggest that the mayor do one of two things. We can escort you to the border of Abney and let you go—but if you show up here again you will spend at least a month in our jail. I can guarantee that, and I can also promise you that there will be even less food and the cells will be even hotter."

"Is that the only option I got?"

"No. Maybe, just maybe, Mayor Perkins would allow you to work in exchange for a place to stay within the city limits. Provided, of course, that you are willing to relinquish your weapons."

"Why would I do that?"

"Because you have betrayed the civil trust, Mr. Striker."

The man had stopped jiggling his knee, and his defiant look evaporated. "What kind of work?"

"Does it matter?"

"No. No, I suppose it doesn't."

Max stood and walked to the door. He tapped on it to indicate that the officer should let him out, and then Striker spoke up again.

"What am I supposed to eat? While I'm working off this supposed crime?"

"I don't know, Mr. Striker. Whatever you can find? If you're lucky, maybe one of the local churches will take compassion on you and share some of their supplies."

"And if I'm not . . . lucky?"

"Try the next town, I suppose." Max turned to study the man one last time. "If that's what you wind up doing, I suggest you not threaten to shoot them before you ask for help."

He stepped out of the interview room and strode toward the front of the building. The police chief was in, and when he looked up and saw Max, he motioned him into his office.

"Get anything out of him?"

"Enough." Max repeated the story that Charles Striker had told him.

"You believe him?"

"Yeah, I do."

"Are you saying that as a lawyer or as a good citizen of Abney?" Bryant ran his hand over the top of his head, which glistened with perspiration.

The office was hot, though not nearly as hot as the cells would be. At least he had a window that was open, though little breeze actually came through it.

"Both. You know, as I know, that the conditions in those cells are not acceptable."

"What's not acceptable is a man trying to rob another man's dwelling and threatening my officers. If we don't get a handle on this, the scumbags in our county are going to kill us in our sleep. We won't have to worry about starving to death."

"Striker is scared and he's stupid. If that's a crime, you might as well arrest all of us. I'm going to suggest Perkins give him community service and a place to stay."

"We're providing lodging now?"

"Our church has set up a shelter. Let him go there, sleep on a cot, get at least two meals a day. If he makes another mistake, drive him to the city's edge and let him go."

Bryant's face turned a dark shade of red. If the police chief didn't find a way to bring down his temper, he'd stroke out before anyone could kill him in his sleep. But Max knew the anger wasn't directed at him. He and the chief stood and shook hands, and as they were walking toward his office door, Bryant said, "Eugene Stone stopped by here. He wants us to make an example out of Striker. Put the fear of God into the people."

"Sounds like something Stone would suggest."

"I've got enough on my hands without baby-sitting a numbskull from the east side."

"And you're the police chief. In a case like this, with no judge to mitigate, it's within the mayor's authority to make the decision. As long as the plaintiff agrees to the suggestion, it's perfectly legal for you to impose community service."

Bryant nodded, obviously relieved that he had a way out.

"Stone won't like it," he said.

"Well, Stone isn't the mayor, and he certainly isn't the chief of police." Grateful that both of those sentiments were true, Max left the building and returned to the job of closing down his business.

Forty-Six

Shelby fought the urge to scream.

She'd arrived at her bank—the one that had not burned—an hour and a half before it opened. Her timing had been a gross miscalculation. She should have arrived the night before. From the looks of things, some people had slept out on the lawn. The mood was decidedly grim, and she heard several dire predictions from people who thought the bank wouldn't be opening as promised.

But it did, straight up at nine o'clock. The president of First Texas stood there shaking hands with folks, thanking them for coming, and never once letting on that an economic catastrophe had occurred. Shelby assumed that Wall Street was closed. How could it not be? What had happened to pension funds and IRAs? Was this worse than the stock market crash of 1929? And how would common, everyday people—folks like those standing in front of and behind Shelby— survive with only 2 percent of their money?

The line slowly unwound until she found herself waiting in the doorway of the building. At least they were still open. From the door the single line split into two—one for cash, and the other for people who wanted to access their safety deposit boxes. Shelby didn't have a safety deposit box because she didn't have anything of value. The small diamond Alex had bought her all those years ago? It was in the back of her jewelry box. The car titles were in a fire-safe box under her bed. She did, however, need some cash.

She half-expected them to run out of money before she stood in front of one of the three tellers.

"Plenty of signs so we don't forget the rules," the woman in line behind her said.

Indeed there were. Large signs written on white poster board with colored markers. They looked more like high school football posters than banking directions.

> You may withdraw 2 percent from each checking account. The balance of your funds will be available once we have resumed communication with the Federal Reserve bank.

How long had it taken someone to write out those posters? It wasn't exactly a five-word slogan, but then this problem couldn't be easily chiseled down to a catchphrase.

"How do they even know what our balance is?" Shelby asked.

"What I heard is that they're giving everyone the same amount—200 bucks. If you're a customer in good standing."

Shelby turned to study her. The woman's professionally colored hair was teased and sprayed, her makeup was applied to perfection, and her nails glittered with red polish. Shelby tried to remember if she'd pulled a brush through her own hair. Yes, she had. Before she had donned the baseball cap. She told herself that she was simply adjusting more quickly than others to their new situation. It made her feel better about the lack of makeup and hair spray.

"My 2 percent is more than 200 bucks," said an old gentleman in overalls. He raised his voice as he became visibly more agitated. "The sign says 2 percent, and that's what I expect to receive."

The manager of the bank hurried over to them, his eyes nervously darting up and down the line. "Is there a problem?"

"She said we'll only get 200 dollars." The old guy jerked a thumb toward the perfectly made-up woman.

"No, sir. We've done the calculations, and we have enough cash for everyone to receive 2 percent."

"Even if my balance is more than twenty thousand?"

"Yes, sir. Regardless of your balance, you will be allowed to withdraw 2 percent. Of course, if you choose to leave your money in the bank—"

"Humph. You're keeping 98 percent. Think I'm going to give you the other 2?"

"We're not exactly keeping it, sir."

But the old guy wasn't listening. The person in front of him had left the line, so he turned his back on the bank manager and shuffled forward.

Shelby had her own questions for the manager. "How do you know what our balance is? I brought my most recent statement, but—"

"That's not necessary, ma'am. Few people print their statements anymore."

Few people bothered to balance their accounts,

either, but Shelby was old-fashioned about that. Instead of arguing the point, she asked again, "So how do you know our balance?"

"We have a backup generator. Most banks installed them after Hurricane Ike and Hurricane Sandy hit. We learned from those terrible events, so we have backup data here on-site and at a remote location."

"But why wasn't your system knocked out by the flares?"

"Wasn't plugged in."

"You unplug it every night?"

"Yes, though we weren't thinking of a solar flare. Our concern was power surges and the cost of replacing compromised equipment. In this case, it's been a real lifesaver, as we can see exactly what everyone's balance was at the end of the day on Friday."

Shelby had never realized how much disaster planning went into the average business. As a writer, the biggest disaster she had to plan for was a hard drive failure. Not even cloud backup would do her any good now.

Nodding her thanks, she moved forward, surprised to see that she'd actually made it into the bank.

That's when a man pulled his gun. "Everyone down on the ground!" he hollered.

Shelby dropped like a stone, trying to flatten herself against the cold lobby floor.

"Stay calm, now. I'm not after your money, folks. You didn't rob me, but these people? Bankers and their supposed rules? Well, I'm getting what's in my account—all of it."

Scuffed up work boots strode past her, continuing toward a teller. Then she heard the man say, "Open your cash drawer and put all of it in a deposit bag."

She could feel her heart hammering against the ceramic tile, beating in rhythm with her prayer: *Please don't let me die. Please don't let me die here. Please don't let me die.*

"Drop!" someone commanded, and Shelby looked up to see the teller drop to the floor. Bob Bryant had stepped up behind the robber, his service revolver hovering only inches from the man's head. "Set your weapon down on the counter . . . slowly."

The man apparently didn't comply because Bryant added, "You don't have a move here and you know it. Put the weapon down, back up three steps, and kneel. Do anything else, and you will die right here, right now."

The man deflated—Shelby could see the fight drain out of him. He didn't argue, didn't attempt to explain what he'd done. He set down his gun, and Bryant cuffed him and marched him out of the lobby.

The bank manager raised his voice to be heard above the crowd. "It's all right, folks. We anticipated someone might try something today."

A few people left, mumbling that 2 percent wasn't worth being shot over, but Shelby needed her money. If there was any chance of bartering for more insulin, she would need all the cash she could get her hands on. Legs trembling, she stepped up to the teller window.

"I always suspected that guy was a jerk." The teller looked to be about nineteen, but she wasn't intimidated by what had just happened or by the size of the crowd. Shelby gave her bonus points for that. "I just need to see your identification."

Shelby pulled out her driver's license and handed it to the young woman.

"We show your balance was $4,235.68 as of Friday. Does that sound correct, Ms. Sparks?"

"Yes. Yes, it does." She'd received and deposited a royalty check on Thursday. This morning she should have been paying bills online, but that wasn't going to happen.

The teller counted out $84.71 and pushed it through the window. The sum of two hundred dollars had been running through Shelby's mind since the perfectly made-up woman had uttered it. But of course 2 percent of $4,235.68 wasn't that much. It was only $84.71. The cold, inflexible rules of math temporarily stunned her.

Less than one hundred dollars was supposed to see her and Carter through—until when? Until the government reestablished some sort of monetary solution? Shelby shoved the money into her purse, thanked the teller, and hurried out of the bank. She told herself, *I will not cry. I will not.*

But as she made her way toward Green Acres, tears coursed down her cheeks and fear wormed its way into her heart.

Forty-Seven

For Carter, the day had been far from perfect, but it was definitely taking a turn for the better.

His shift at the Market had been a bit depressing. Mr. Graves was sticking to his rules: only ten customers at a time, a limit of twelve items, cash only, and the right to refuse service. None of those rules were a problem. In Carter's opinion, they could have scratched out one and two—there wasn't that much left on the shelves to sell. There was also no line outside the store.

"I guess folks know there isn't much to buy," Kaitlyn said as they stood at their registers and waited for a customer.

"Graves had a shipment of dry goods scheduled to come in Friday night."

"A lot of good that does us."

Graves usually stood at the front, watching

them closely. Carter thought his boss was losing his grip on the situation. He knew for a fact that Graves was sleeping at the store. He'd seen the man's cot near the front door when he'd first arrived. Graves had sent him off on some bogus errand and stored the sleeping bag and fold-up cot before any customers arrived. He'd always been a bit cranky and distant, but over the week-end those personality traits had grown even more prominent. His eyes didn't seem able to focus, he constantly snapped his fingers as if to remind himself of something, and he smelled terrible. Had he even tried to clean up since the Drop?

Carter almost laughed at that thought. Jason's crazy slang had a way of sticking in his head.

Carter moved closer to Kaitlyn's register, pretending to clean a display that was completely empty. "I heard that he hired some guys to go out and find the shipment that was coming from the warehouse—it was supposed to arrive Friday night but never did. Maybe he thinks it was close."

"Seriously?"

"Yup. Promised them 20 percent of whatever they found."

"If they found a truckload of food, why would they bring it back to him? They could keep it and get 100 percent."

"Graves thought of that. He told them that there were at least three trucks headed this way and he knew their route and approximate location. If they came back with the goods from the first, he'd tell them the location of the second."

"How could he know that?"

Carter shrugged. "I worked shipping and receiving a few times. The guys from our regional warehouse have a pretty routine schedule, and we know who was supposed to show up Friday evening."

Graves had appeared at that point and barked, "Back to your register, Sparks. I'm not paying you to chat."

Carter wanted to walk out. There wasn't enough left on the shelves to make it worth being open—some jars of jalapeños, most of the spices, and a display of summer stuff no one had wanted to spend money on. Who needed sunscreen and sandals? Food was the priority.

Carter would rather be home helping with the latrine. He'd stopped by on his way into work, and the digging was going well. Ed said they had hit more dirt, having worked through the layer of rock the day before. Rhonda was already working on the frame, and Frank had brought by a toilet that had been delivered the week before to a house under construction. Not much chance a partially constructed house was going to be finished, so the builder had said they could salvage anything there.

When Mr. Graves ordered him to get back to

work—as if there was any work to get back to—Carter almost took off his name tag and walked away. He thought of that truck of dry goods. If it was true, if the guys Graves hired brought it back, employees would be allowed to purchase three items off the truck first. Graves had said as much. He'd also announced when they'd walked in that he was paying them twenty dollars in cash each day. That was half what Carter made from a normal six-hour shift before, but he'd heard about the lack of cash at the bank. Graves was flush with cash, and Carter knew his mother needed whatever he could earn.

So he didn't quit his job.

He managed to tell Kaitlyn about the Brainiacs, and she'd acted interested in joining him. When their shift was over, they collected their 20 dollars and headed out the back door.

Carter wasn't sure how successful the Brainiacs would be, but nothing could be more depressing than standing in an empty grocery store as people searched for food.

Forty-Eight

In many ways it seemed like a perfect summer day. Carter was walking down Main Street with the prettiest girl in town. How did it get better than that?

"The walk is only about fifteen minutes from here," he said.

"I always aced science at my old school."

"Do you miss it?"

"I guess. Moving here before my senior year was kind of the pits. At least I thought it was when I first got here."

"Moving anytime is tough."

"Now there probably won't even be any school." She laughed and glanced sideways at Carter. "I should be happy about that, but it feels . . . strange."

"Yeah, I was planning on college, but it looks like that isn't going to happen."

"Where were you going?"

"Angelo State."

"I have family in San Angelo—an uncle we go and visit a couple of times a year."

That thought made Carter's stomach flip, which was stupid. He wasn't going to college, so it didn't matter if Kaitlyn might have been able to visit, but his mind hadn't quite caught up with events. It insisted on slipping into what-if scenarios.

Instead of taking her through the front door of the school, which he suspected was locked, Carter walked her around to the back. True to his word, Jason had left the door nearest the science labs propped open.

Coach Parish, Jason, and five other geeks were

waiting. Coach had put on a few pounds since Carter had last seen him, and his red hair was streaked with gray. Other than that, he was the same old Coach Parish, and he didn't waste any time.

"We're dealing with something that has never happened before, so we need to think in a way we have never thought before."

Kaitlyn glanced Carter's way and rolled her eyes. She also seemed excited about being there, so he thought the eye roll was just a nervous gesture.

"Let's start a list of our community's biggest needs. After you work on that, break into small groups and tackle one of the items that sparks your imagination." Coach paused, his eyes sweeping the room and taking in each person there.

They were a ragtag group. Carter would admit that, but they were also a smart group. Every person in the room had done well on the SATs, except for Kaitlyn, who hadn't taken them yet.

Coach's voice took on an even more somber tone. "Fear can destroy imagination. It's worse than quicksand. Give in to fear, and you might as well hang up your cleats and go on home." Coach was big on sports analogies, though as far as Carter knew no one in the room had played sports.

"Banish fear, put on your thinking caps, and find solutions." He waved them toward the board.

"Did he just say put on your thinking caps?" Kaitlyn asked.

"And banish fear," Carter reminded her.

"Seriously?"

"Oh yeah. Coach is linguistically stuck somewhere else." Jason picked up an erasable marker and tossed it at Kaitlyn. "But up here?" Jason tapped his head. "He has it going on."

An hour later, Carter, Jason, and Kaitlyn had drawn up a design for a solar oven. Jason had sauntered off to the supply room with a list of items to find.

"It won't be large," Kaitlyn said. "But it will be big enough to cook a family roast. Not that anyone has any fresh meat left."

"Plenty of deer in the area. Not the right time to shoot one, but I suspect that won't stop some folks." Carter glanced around the room. "Let's go see what everyone else is inventing."

Zane was working with his little sister, who hadn't even been in high school when the club had last met.

"Windmill. Cool."

"It's better than cool," Lila said. "It could charge a small generator, maybe enough to operate a few lamps or a fan. The use of sustainable energy to provide creature comforts is the wave of the future."

Zane nudged his sister. "We all know that. It's why we're here."

"I thought you just wanted to get out of digging a three-meter hole in the backyard."

Instead of answering her, Zane pointed at their design. "The cool aspect of this design is that e can use items people would have in their garage to make the windmill."

"Bicycle parts?" Kaitlyn moved closer. "That is awesome."

Zane grinned and pushed his glasses up his nose.

Quincy was working with Cooper and Annabelle. Carter introduced Kaitlyn, everyone nodded hello, and then they turned their attention to the whiteboard the group had been working on.

"Our idea was to reclaim all possible water," Quincy said.

"But there's water and then there's water." Cooper pointed to the top of the crude house they'd drawn. "Water straight from the roof will be cleaner than water that runs off into a cistern, which is bound to have dirt in it."

"Though water from the roof might still need to be filtered before drinking." Annabelle played with one of her dangly earrings. As long as Carter had known her, ever since elementary school, she'd worn dangly earrings to match every outfit.

"It would depend what the composition of the roof is," Kaitlyn said.

"Exactly." Quincy turned back to his drawing.

"We're trying to create a system that will provide three types of water—for drinking and cooking, personal hygiene, and crops."

"We have the spring water, though." Carter rubbed his thumb against the new callus on his palm. What he wouldn't give for a hot shower.

"The spring water will provide enough drinking water for the community," Cooper admitted. "Our local officials were right about that. But enough to bathe with? Or grow crops? We're going to need to reclaim every ounce we can find."

Coach Parish was standing at the board, adding to the list of needs. Carter and Kaitlyn walked back over to their table where Jason had dumped boxes, foil, black paint, insulation, a piece of glass, and a thermometer.

It was time to get to work.

Forty-Nine

Max spent the afternoon in his office, closing up case files, writing notes for the mayor and the chief of police, and creating a notice for his door saying he was temporarily suspending his practice. He had a secretary, but she only came in on Tuesdays and Thursdays, and he doubted he would see her again since she'd been commuting from the next town. No doubt she was home, planting a victory garden while the men built a latrine.

He decided to skip lunch, opting for peanut butter crackers that he kept in the bottom drawer of his desk. He was tempted to not eat at all, but the hint of a migraine had been dancing just past the corners of his eyes. The last thing he needed was twenty-four hours in a dark room when he should be preparing to leave.

He'd been diagnosed with basilar migraines when he was in law school. He had been studying in the law library one moment and unconscious the next. The symptoms read like those of a dread disease—double vision, slurred speech, even temporary blindness. Regular migraine medica-tions were useless and could even lead to a stroke. He had painkillers, which he'd rather not take as they knocked him out.

More than once he had ended up in the hospital.

That wasn't an option, so he pulled out the crackers and forced himself to eat.

His goal was to close up the office by three. He glanced around, wondering if there was anything he should take with him. Feeling foolish, he pulled his law degree off the wall and stuffed the framed document into the leather messenger bag he'd brought. On the one hand, it seemed ridiculous to carry around his degree when the world had moved on, but on the other hand, he'd worked hard for it. At two thirty, Dr. Jerry Lambert walked in. The man literally filled the frame of the door. Standing six feet four inches and weighing in at a solid 250 pounds, he made Max feel small.

"Jerry. What are you doing here? And how did you get to town?"

"I drove, same as always." Jerry clasped Max's hand in a firm shake before settling into one of the chairs across from his desk.

"Sorry I don't have anything cold to drink, but I can offer you a warm soda or a bottle of water."

"I'll take the water. Thanks."

Max fetched two bottles from his refrigerator, and then he settled in the chair next to Jerry, turning it so they were facing one another. Jerry Lambert was a retired veterinarian, and one of the best farmers that Max had ever had the pleasure of knowing. He was a no-nonsense kind of guy who had made his first million by the time he was forty-five. You wouldn't know it by the type of car he drove or the clothes he wore—today he had on old blue jeans and a faded short-sleeved denim shirt, plus the requisite Stetson that he wore everywhere he went. He removed the Stetson and dropped it on the coffee table next to his chair.

"How are things at High Fields? I was hoping to head that way tomorrow."

"Your folks are fine." Jerry fished in his shirt pocket and pulled out a folded sheet of paper. "Since I was coming to town anyway, they sent along this list. Wanted you to know that it is not a rush—just bring as much of this as you can."

Max quickly scanned the list. A few of the items surprised him, but he could probably scrounge up most of it.

"How up-to-date are you on all that has happened?"

Jerry finished off the bottle of water and tossed it into a nearby trash can. "My foreman keeps a ham radio. He monitored the emergency station until the reports stopped." Jerry spent the next five minutes sharing the information he'd heard.

Max said, "Same things we're hearing around here. Other than . . . did you hear about the president's announcement?"

"Folks have been talking about it, but we didn't hear the actual announcement ourselves. One old boy who lives down the way from your folks, he was in town that night and gave us the gist of it."

"What concerns me most is the president—if that message was indeed from the president—" He paused and waited for Jerry to offer his opinion, but the man motioned for him to continue. "If he did in fact authorize the US military to perform law enforcement functions, I think we might have a bigger problem than the lasting effects of the flare."

As an afterthought he added what Danny Vail had told Shelby the night before.

"Out where we are, folks are arming up. There's a reason your pop put ammunition on his list."

"I hope it doesn't come to that."

"As do we, but we won't sit idly by and allow anyone to seize what few resources we have."

"Even if it means taking on the military?"

"I can't answer that question, Max. We'll know what to do when the time comes. I can guarantee you that if Eugene Stone shows up trying to *requisition supplies,* he'd best be wearing body armor."

Jerry stood and repositioned his Stetson on his head. "I should get on about my business. My plan is to be home well before dark. There's talk of bandits in Adamsville."

"Bandits?" Max thought of Charles Striker and his story about folks looting east of town.

"Haven't seen them myself," Jerry admitted.

"Why are you in town, other than delivering my mail?"

"I still have a few friends who are in the veterinary business. Thought I'd stop by and call in a few favors . . . pick up some salt and mineral licks."

"Do you need them already?"

"No. But we will later in the summer. As well as vaccinations for next year's calves."

Max reached for his water bottle, his throat suddenly dry. He thought he'd accepted that the changes were permanent, but knowing it and having others confirm it were two different things.

Jerry walked to the door, but before he opened it he turned back around. "Be careful, Max. I'm glad you're moving to your parents' place for the duration, just . . . don't wait too long."

He turned and walked out to his truck.

Alone once again, Max pulled out his parents' note and smoothed the sheet with the palm of his hand. Something about his mother's handwriting stirred bittersweet emotions deep in his heart. He had known they were fine, had convinced himself they were. Why wouldn't they be? Both had grown up in the fifties, when technology was just finding its way into most homes. They'd often laughed at the new gadgets he bought them. And now? Well, now they would probably have less trouble adjusting to the new order than Max.

Pop says to tell you there is no rush with this list. We trust you are well and know you will make your way to us as soon as you can. There's plenty of room for Shelby and Carter in Granny's old house.

Ammunition for handguns—
*   S&W, Sig*
Shells for Remington and Browning

Cartridges for Winchester, Ruger,
    and Marlin
Gun cleaning kit
Fishing line
Fishing hooks
Brandy
Aspirin, ibuprofen, or acetaminophen
Wrap bandages
Quick-clot gauze
Disposable gloves
Burn creams
Antibiotic ointment
Matches and/or flint
Tire repair kit
Bleach
Heirloom seeds
Salt

Max reached the bottom of the list and started over at the top. He sat back, tapping his pen against the piece of paper. Everything on the list his parents already had, except maybe the brandy. It wasn't lost on him that the alcohol was listed at the beginning of the medical supplies. He'd always thought that brandy as a cure-all was an old wives' tale, but what did he know? He wasn't a doctor, and his knowledge of first aid was rudimentary at best.

He hoped the ammunition was for hunting.

The last five items on the list seemed a random

assortment. Things they expected to need more of? Worst-case scenario provisions? Supplies for a neighbor?

At the bottom his pop had added the word *chocolate,* but someone had scratched it out—probably his mother. He would have added it for her, and she would have insisted it wasn't a necessity.

Max folded the list and stuck it in his pocket. He stared around the office and wondered what he was doing there. No one's divorce was going to be presented to a judge. Child custody agreements and wills would have to wait. The legal system had halted, and who knew when it would start again?

What he did know, what he could tell from the list, was that his parents were thinking long-term.

Max donned his own Stetson. Yes, he wore one similar to Dr. Lambert, but in Abney every male over twelve wore a cowboy hat. He taped the handmade sign on his door—"Closed Until Further Notice." Max had spent the last seven years building a steady, solid, small-town business. Now he was walking away from it, not knowing or caring if it would still be there when he came back.

One thing he was sure of. His priorities had changed.

Fifty

Max stepped out into a day that had begun its descent, casting long shadows down a nearly deserted Main Street. Should he take a few minutes and walk over to speak with the mayor? Maybe check on the situation with Charles Striker? But there wasn't time for that. He didn't know why he felt things were moving along so quickly. Jerry had been adamant that he didn't need to hurry, as had his mom. Both assurances did little to mitigate his growing sense of alarm. Instead of heading to the mayor's office, Max turned toward home.

His plan was to spend the next few hours collecting, buying, or trading for what he could on his parents' list, and then he needed to talk to Shelby.

He walked home at a quick pace, deliberating the pros and cons of what he planned to do next. The ammunition store was on the north-east side of Abney, and based on what Charles Striker had said, he didn't relish the idea of being on foot in that part of town.

Driving wasn't a decision he arrived at easily. On the one hand, he could easily walk the distance, which was probably three miles. Even though his parents' message through Jerry

Lambert had explicitly told him there was no emergency, Max could hear a clock ticking in his mind. He could take two, three more days at the most, and then he wanted to be on Highway 281 headed north.

He didn't need to look at his watch to know it was past four in the afternoon. The shadows stretching across the deserted roads told him that. If he hurried, he could walk to his truck, drive to Guns & More on the edge of town, and still pick up Shelby from her shift at Green Acres.

The drive to the edge of town was uneventful, but he came to an abrupt stop on the lane leading to the store. Guns & More sat at the top of a hill, little more than a rise off the flat highway heading east. Normally he would turn off the highway onto a caliche road, which led to the store and its gravel parking lot. Not today.

Someone had used a backhoe to the east of the caliche road and on the outside of the fence. Freshly overturned dirt covered a ten-by-twelve-foot area. There had always been a cattle guard leading onto the property—which had once been an old ranch—but he'd never seen the cattle gate closed, and certainly not during business hours. In addition, a wire fence had been stretched across the road, directly up against the cattle gate and extending off into the trees on the right and left. Behind the wire, a teenager sat inside a pickup truck, talking into a CB radio.

When the boy stepped out of the truck, Max saw he was carrying a rifle. He looked comfortable enough handling the weapon. Many kids who grew up in the country had been hunting since they were young, and this kid's grandfather owned the only ammo store in town.

"Howdy, Mr. Berkman. Gramps said you could go on up." Resting the rifle against the fence post, he fetched a key out of his pocket and opened a sturdy padlock that was holding the gate closed.

"Thanks, son." Max slowly drove forward. He wanted to ask the kid what was going on, but he'd have a better chance of getting information from his grandfather.

The name Guns & More sounded like a seedy place, but the store was actually a member of the Abney Chamber of Commerce and known for donating generously to local groups. It was owned by a longtime Abney resident who was a few years older than Max. Stanley Hamilton was a solid guy—retired military, community volunteer, and grandpa of four at last count. Now Stanley's grandson, a talented running back, was playing the role of armed guard.

Max parked his truck in front of the store. No one else appeared to be in the parking lot, and when Max tried the front door, he found it closed and shut up tight. Not a big problem, since Stanley lived in the old home positioned several hundred yards behind the store. Max walked back to the truck and locked it—which was probably ridiculous, since there was an armed patrol at the bottom of the hill. Regardless, he felt better with the old truck locked. Next he hustled over to Stanley's home. He found the man on the east side of the house, in the shade of the building, planting a garden with two of his younger grand-children.

Stanley was an average-sized guy—maybe five feet ten or eleven. He'd managed to stay in shape in spite of being on the north side of fifty. His look had definitely changed since he'd retired from the military. He sported long hair and a full beard. It now reached halfway down his chest and was more gray than black. A red do-rag held his shoulder-length hair back away from his face. He wore jeans, a T-shirt, and a pouch around his waist. He looked like an ad for Harley-Davidson motorcycles. The picture would have been com-plete if he'd sported tattoos down his arms, but he'd once confessed to Max that he had a strong aversion to needles.

"Max." He pulled off a garden glove, and they shook hands. "How are you?"

"All right. Just closed up my place downtown."

"Headed to High Fields?"

"I am. My folks . . ." Max pulled the list from his pocket. "They asked me to pick up a few things."

Stanley studied the list, nodded once, and told his grandchildren to wait inside. "Tell grandma I'm going to the shop for a few minutes."

When he turned toward the kids, Max noticed Stanley was wearing a paddle holster, and it held a Sig Sauer 9mm pistol. In addition, a mobile CB station was set up on a card table under the patio cover, which must have been how he'd answered his grandson at the gate.

The kids ran inside, and Stanley motioned toward his business. "I'm pretty sure I have what you need. Do you have cash?"

"I do."

"Sorry I have to ask."

"Not a problem."

A mockingbird called out from a nearby tree, and the normalcy of that sound hit Max like a punch in the gut. Nothing about their life was normal now. It seemed that everything had changed, and their lives had begun to feel like a doomsday movie.

"I was afraid you might be sold out."

"I've sold a good bit, but I still have about half my stock. Folks don't have much cash. What they do have they're spending on food or seed."

"You're not taking trades?"

"Not yet, but I might—eventually."

"When did you start wearing a paddle holster?"

"Two days ago, when a customer tried to rob me."

"Is that why your grandson is standing guard?"

Instead of answering, Stanley unlocked the back door of the shop. The room was pitch-dark, but he reached for a battery-operated lantern and flipped it on. He handed the list back to Max and pointed toward the workbench, where another lantern waited. Max walked over and turned it on.

Stanley proceeded to walk through the supply room, gathering up shotgun shells, rifle cartridges, and several boxes of handgun ammunition.

"Things went south here pretty quickly." He pulled a gun cleaning kit off a shelf and added it to the stack of supplies.

"We hadn't heard."

"No time to notify the authorities, and I doubt they could or would have done anything if I had."

Max didn't know how to answer that, so he kept quiet, trying to process what Stanley was describing.

"Your parents are doing okay?"

"They are. I received that note from them earlier today. I was a little surprised Pop wanted this stuff. You and I both know he keeps plenty at the ranch."

"He's thinking long-term. Your pop, he isn't one to paint a rosy picture if there are storm clouds on the horizon."

Max thought about that as Stanley walked to the front counter, where the last of the day's light pierced the front windows. Something had happened here. On the one hand, Max wanted to know the details. But on the other hand, he was still a lawyer. He'd dedicated his life to upholding the law.

What Stanley was about to tell him was probably outside the boundaries of the law. If so, Max would have to decide whether to choose the side of the law or support his friend.

Fifty-One

Stanley tallied up his purchases by hand on an old-fashioned receipt book and then circled the total. Max pulled the requisite bills from his wallet. Stanley unzipped the pouch he wore and made change, and then he tucked the money Max had given him into the bag and zipped it shut.

"What's going on, Stanley? Your grandson is standing guard at the road, you've installed a perimeter fence, your shop is locked up, and you're carrying a pistol on your hip and your money in a bag around your waist."

Stanley ran his fingers through his beard and studied Max. Finally he nodded toward the back room. "Let's talk back there. I don't like standing near the windows any longer than I have to."

When they'd reached the back room, Stanley pulled an empty clip from a box and a tray of ammo from a shelf. As he talked he thumbed ammo into the clip.

"Two days ago a skinny, drugged-up kid from the east side tried to rob me. I clipped him on the side of the head and kicked him out of my store. Later that night, he came back—this time with three of his buddies."

Max's mind immediately shifted into lawyer mode. He wanted to stop Stanley, ask questions, get the details, and somehow create a complete picture of what Stanley was describing. But he didn't.

"The store was locked up and darkness had fallen by the time they returned, but I was sitting in the bed of my truck. It was parked to the east side of the building. You know I have a flood-light on the top of that truck."

"For when you go hog hunting. I remember."

"When I spotlighted these fellas, one pulled a handgun and started shooting."

"And you shot back?"

"I did, though I didn't aim to kill him—after all, he was just a kid." Stanley shook his head and reached for another clip. "That was my first mistake. Thinking the old way."

"What do you mean?"

"Come on, Max. We both realize no officer is going to arrive and arrest that kid or his buddies, plus I couldn't even call 9-1-1."

"So you shot one of them. What happened then?"

"These punks had never thought through what

they were doing. I guarantee you not a single one of them had envisioned bullets coming toward them. They scampered out of here the minute the first kid was hurt." Stanley shook his head. "I know better than to make that kind of mistake. The last thing a person needs in this environment is enemies—especially young, stupid ones."

Max pulled out a stool from under the counter and sank onto it. "So they came back?"

"The same four guys, and this time they were sporting rifles, shotguns, and a few handguns." He glanced at Max and shook his head. "Rather ironic that they were willing to use so much ammo in order to steal ammo."

"What did you do?"

"I knew they'd hit that same night. Cowards like those four avoid the light. They think the darkness is their friend." He filled another clip and tossed it into a bin. "This time I was on the roof, wearing my infrareds. They didn't have a chance."

"You killed them? You killed all four of them?"

"I protected my wife and property." In spite of the steel in his voice, Stanley stopped to wipe the sweat rolling down his face. "Next day I put up the fence, insisted my son and daughter-in-law move back here with the grandkids."

"And the people you killed?"

"You mean the robbers who trespassed onto my property armed and intent on doing me bodily harm?" Stanley stopped now and looked Max directly in the eye. "I buried them near the road. Haven't had any trouble since, which doesn't mean I won't."

Stanley nodded toward the back door and they both walked out, each carrying half of the supplies. Max wasn't sure what his responsibility was here. Stanley had just confessed to killing four men and burying their bodies. But if it had happened as he said it had—and Max had no reason to doubt him—it had been a clear case of self-defense. Max worked in family law, but he had friends who had tried plenty of murder cases. What had happened to Stanley would never make it past a grand jury. It would never be tried.

They loaded the supplies behind the backseat and covered them with an old tarp that Max kept there.

"It bothers me, you know." Stanley stared out toward the road. "Don't think it doesn't. A thing like that, killing a man—it's not something to be done lightly."

"I know that." Max climbed into his truck. He tried to say the next words with conviction, but they came out more of a question. "I know that you did what you think you had to do."

"What? You think that I could have talked them down?" There was no malice in the words. Stanley grinned, slammed the door shut, and waited for Max to roll down the window. When he did, Stanley crossed his arms and leaned onto the sill. "You be careful out there, Max. The world? It's changed, and we have to adapt. Adapt or die. It's the oldest law of nature, and maybe of God too. Check your Old Testament."

"Yes, but—"

"Most of us are more comfortable with the Gospels," Stanley admitted, stepping back. "But the world that the Old Testament prophets lived in was a tough place. And the world we live in? Well, it's starting to look the same."

Fifty-Two

The third time she tripped on nothing, Shelby knew she was too tired to keep working.

"Girl, if you drop those supplies, we're going to be in a world of hurt." Elena was one of the aides who had shown up, with the disclaimer that she could only afford to work three hours a day for free.

"Yes, but you need help with—"

"Go on home. We'll take care of this. Connie is coming back in for the night shift."

"She only left at noon."

"I know that, but have you ever tried to talk Connie out of something she sets her mind to? Easier to change the direction of the wind."

Shelby laughed and hugged Elena. It was

surprising how close she'd become to these women in such a short amount of time.

"Go home, be with your kid, and come back tomorrow when you can. We appreciate you." And with that, Elena took the tray of snacks and padded down the hall.

Shelby retrieved Carter's medicine from the refrigerator. Unzipping the pack, she checked the supply of insulin—it was nice and cold. That brought a smile to her face and gave her the extra jolt of energy she needed to walk home.

She nearly passed Max's old truck without recognizing it. He was parked at the corner of the nursing home's property, and when he tapped the horn, she practically jumped out of her skin.

"Want a ride?"

He gave her that slow, easy smile she'd known all of her life. This time it caused her pulse to jump—another indication of how tired she was. Normally she was immune to Max's charm.

"Why are you driving?"

"Long story. Get in and I'll tell it to you."

As they sat there watching the light fade from the sky, Max told her about Charles Striker, the note from his parents, the blockade at Guns & More, and the robbery.

Shelby could only stare at him, her mouth dropping open when he reached the part about Stanley waiting on top of his roof for the robbers to return.

"He shot them?"

"Killed all four and buried their bodies outside his property line—a clear warning to anyone else who might try to rob him."

"Stanley?"

"I know."

"He came to see me after Alex died—tears running down his cheeks."

"Same Stanley."

"Wow."

"My thoughts exactly."

Shelby hesitated, and then she asked, "Should we tell the authorities?"

"I considered that, but it's a clear case of self-defense."

"*If* it happened like he said."

"We have no reason to doubt him, and who is going to investigate? It's not like we can send a forensic team to his place to check the direction of blood splatter, exhume the bodies, and try to re-create what happened."

"No. I guess not."

Neither said anything for the space of a few moments, and then Shelby cornered herself in the truck to study Max.

"Did you talk to Bhatti?"

"Not yet."

"But you will?"

"Yes."

She sighed and stared out the open window.

"It's like . . . it's like we've been dropped into the past, somewhere in the Old West, where it's still each man for himself."

"I suppose it is."

"Carter insisted on taking my dad's old Winchester on patrol this afternoon."

"Always was a good rifle."

"He cleaned it and set it by the door—"

"I'm glad he remembers how. It's been awhile since I took him out to sight it in."

"My son is on patrol, at a roadblock in our neighborhood, carrying a Winchester rifle."

Max nodded and changed the subject. "My parents, they asked me to remind you about Granny's house. It's there if you—"

"We've already been over this."

"I know we have, and I know how stubborn you can be—"

"Do not start with me, Max."

"When you make up your mind about something."

"You think this is mere stubbornness?" Heat crept up Shelby's neck. She could feel her temper rising, and she struggled to tamp it down. She did not have the energy to argue with him now.

"I don't think you realize how bad this situation is or how much worse it could get."

"You know what? I can walk home." She started to open the door, but Max reached across and stayed her hand.

"I care about you, Shelby."

His voice was a soft caress, and for just a moment her barrier of self-righteous indignation fell.

"I know that."

"You're an amazing woman, and I have no doubt you can make it on your own."

"I've been making it on my own for years."

"But . . ." Max rubbed his thumb back and forth over her fingertips. She couldn't focus when he touched her like that.

"If men are willing to kill for ammo, don't you think they'll also kill for medical supplies? You're walking around town carrying Carter's meds on your back, and you're a clear target."

She snatched her hand away. "I can't leave the insulin here or at home. I suppose you have a better suggestion?"

"Come with me."

"No."

"Come to High Fields."

She shook her head. What was she supposed to say? She couldn't explain her plan to him. If he even suspected that she was contemplating going to Austin, he would probably hog-tie her and drag her to High Fields. But she would find a way. There were pharmaceutical distribution centers in Austin, and she would beg or barter. One way or another, she would get more medicine for Carter.

She pulled in a deep breath, smiled, and said, "You can't bully me into changing my mind."

Max's hand was still on the door handle, where hers had been. He was so close that she wondered if he would kiss her—and instantly she was in high school again, surrendering her heart and dreams to him.

But he didn't kiss her.

Instead, he scooted back to his side of the truck and started the engine. "Will you at least think about it? If not for me, then for my mom and pop?"

"Of course." That wasn't a lie. She always considered Max's suggestions, but this time she knew he was wrong and she was right.

He flashed her the cocky smile of his youth and drove toward their street. It was when they had turned the corner and were approaching the roadblock that they saw a jeep hurtling toward them, a police car and SUV in hot pursuit, and then they heard the ring of gunfire.

Fifty-Three

After the officer shot out the jeep's two rear tires, everyone started shouting at once.

Mrs. Plumley had her shotgun raised to her shoulder. She stared through its sight at the jeep that had careened to a stop in front of their roadblock. The shots had come from a police officer's vehicle, and he had stopped, jumped out of the cruiser, aimed at the tires, and hopped back in the vehicle when he saw that he'd incapacitated the jeep. It was possibly the coolest thing Carter had ever seen.

The officer and SUV driver braked suddenly, their vehicles positioned nose to nose across the road to block any possible escape. Both of the drivers jumped out of their vehicles and raised their weapons. To his left, Max drove up—and suddenly Carter's mother was running toward them, screaming for Carter to get down.

Before he could say anything, Max had knocked his mom to the ground, covering her body with his.

The person driving the jeep raised his hands in surrender, and Carter noticed someone slumped over beside him in the vehicle.

"Keep them up high!" The officer slowly approached the vehicle from the left, and the SUV driver approached from the right, his hand-gun raised and aimed at the driver of the jeep.

Max remained on top of Carter's mom, who was squirming and waving, still trying to get him to drop down. But he was on patrol. He didn't think he was supposed to hide behind the cab of the truck. So instead he raised his granddad's old Winchester Model 94 and trained it on the guy driving the jeep.

"Just keep him in your sights, Carter. Finger

next to the trigger but not on it. We don't want anyone shot accidentally." Mrs. Plumley didn't sound at all rattled. Her steadiness helped to calm Carter's nerves, which were jumping like popcorn in a pan.

The officer opened the door of the jeep with his left hand, his right still holding his service revolver, which was pointed at the driver. He pulled the guy out, pushed him to the ground, and then he cuffed his hands behind him. The man was large with a giant belly, and Carter had the random thought that it must have been a tight fit behind the steering wheel. From where he stood, he could also see a string of tattoos reaching from the man's shirtsleeve to his wrist.

Max jumped up and ran to the passenger side of the jeep.

"We need a paramedic over here!" he shouted.

Mrs. Plumley nodded toward Carter, so he put down his rifle and picked up the radio. "We've got . . . uh . . . a situation."

Frank came back over the radio. "Tell me what's going on."

"Some guy just ran through the roadblock in a jeep. The police have the driver on the ground, but the other guy in the jeep—Max says he needs a doctor."

"Paramedics are on their way. Do you need assistance?"

Plumley shook her head, so Carter said, "No.

Everything's under control now." His heart was still hammering. He could feel the sweat slicking his palms, but no one seemed to be in danger.

Carter heard the approach of the ambulance at the same moment his mother made it to the back of the pickup. She jumped up into the bed and ran her hands up and down his arms.

"Are you okay?"

"Mom, I'm fine."

"No one shot you?"

"Mom, stop." He put one hand on each of her shoulders and looked directly into her eyes. "I am fine."

She nodded twice and sank into the bed of the truck. "I think I had a heart attack."

At that point Dr. Bhatti arrived on the scene. Carter had no idea who had called him. Maybe he had just heard the ambulance, which was pulling up. The ambulance cut its sirens and its lights.

A crowd of folks was steadily gathering on the sidewalk, but everyone was silent—stunned and trying to piece together what they were seeing.

Bhatti was halfway inside the jeep, but he popped back out and shook his head.

"GSW. Abdominal cavity. No exit wound."

The paramedics had a gurney next to the jeep. One began to open an emergency medical kit, but Bhatti stopped him. "Save your supplies."

The officer had the driver of the jeep standing

now. He heard Bhatti and began to scream. "It's my brother. You have to help my brother!"

Bhatti didn't even flinch.

The paramedics waited, like frozen statues.

"Sir, I need you to calm down." The officer held the handcuffed man's arm with one hand. His other hand remained close to his gun.

Max emerged from the other side of the jeep and walked toward Dr. Bhatti.

"Is there anything we can do for him?" Max asked.

"No. There isn't."

The paramedics glanced at one another. Carter's mom popped back up, looking over the cab of the truck. She stood next to Carter and clutched his arm as if she was afraid he might jump out of the truck and run to the center of the scene.

The driver began to weep. "You have to help my brother."

"We can at least stabilize him," one of the paramedics said.

"And then what?" Bhatti asked. "If there was an exit wound, I might agree with you, but there isn't."

"Standard procedures are—"

"Do you think we can perform surgery with no electricity? Would you like me to cut the bullet out of him with a pocketknife? Do we have blood ready for a transfusion, because he's going to need one. How do you plan to stop the bleeding and prevent infection?"

"We can't let him die," the other paramedic argued.

Max climbed back into the jeep as Bhatti argued with the paramedics.

"It's a moot point," Max said.

He walked toward the man who had been driving. "I'm sorry. Your brother is dead."

The man's face turned red. Carter thought maybe he was going to have a stroke right there in the middle of the street. Instead, he sank to his knees, hands still handcuffed behind him, and sobbed—a low, gut-wrenching sound that made Carter's hands shake.

Fifty-Four

Mrs. Plumley and Carter remained on patrol for another hour. They had both volunteered to serve an extra shift when their replacements, a man and wife, had taken ill. Probably food poisoning, according to Frank.

"Careful what you eat," he'd cautioned Carter and Mrs. Plumley. "Most of the meat has gone bad now."

It took the paramedics less than ten minutes to load the body and drive off to the morgue.

The police chief arrived, cleared the street, and

moved the driver back toward their roadblock. The man collapsed on the tailgate.

Chief Bryant asked Carter's mom and Max to stay. "Everyone else go home," he said to the crowd. "There's nothing to see here, and if you impede my investigation I will arrest you."

People slowly shuffled off. Carter glanced around to see who remained—the two men who had chased the jeep, Max and his mom, Mrs. Plumley, and the man whose brother had died.

"You can uncuff him," Chief Bryant said. "There's five of us, and he's unarmed."

The officer grunted in agreement and pulled the key from his pocket, warning the man not to try anything.

"Name?"

"Toby Nix."

His mom looked at Max, and Max nodded in agreement to something.

"You know him?" Bryant asked.

Max cleared his throat, and then he explained, "We were hiking at Colorado Bend when the aurora made its first appearance. We stopped in at Sad Sam's to see what was happening. Mr. Nix was there, explaining to the group what he'd heard over his ham radio."

Nix wiped at his eyes. "I don't remember you."

"A lot has happened since then," Shelby said. "And the place was very crowded."

Nix pulled in a deep breath and continued to

brush away the tears streaming down his face. Carter noticed how badly the man's hands were shaking.

"We thought we were prepared."

"We?"

Carter returned his attention to the road in front of them, assuming the same stance as Mrs. Plumley. But he could hear every word between the man and the police chief.

"Folks at Bend."

"So what happened?"

"We'd set up a perimeter at both access points."

Bryant named two county road numbers.

"Yeah."

"Perimeter? So you weren't letting anyone through?"

"They could go around. It's no different from what you have right here."

"It's completely different. We're cutting off access to our neighborhoods, to folks' homes. We're not blocking roads that provide a way through Abney—at least not yet."

This was the first Carter had heard about possible roadblocks on the outskirts of town. He understood the need to protect their homes, but did they want to keep everyone out of Abney? And what about the people inside Abney who wanted to leave? It wasn't as if he had anywhere he needed to go, but the questions swirled in his mind nonetheless.

"We're not a town. We don't have the resources like you folks here in Abney have." When Bryant didn't argue with him, Mr. Nix continued. "Folks had to go around. Those were the rules. The guys who hit us, they'd scoped us out a couple of times—coming close enough to see how many men and what type of weapons we had, but not close enough for us to warn them away."

"When did they hit?"

"Maybe an hour ago, as the light was slanting from the west—makes it difficult to see well. They slammed into our vehicles and started shooting."

"What were they after?" Max asked.

"I couldn't care less, and I guess we'll never know."

"They're dead?"

Carter was still facing forward, but he heard Bryant's voice take on a harder edge. He glanced at Mrs. Plumley, who shrugged.

"Yes, they are."

"You killed them?"

"I didn't, but the men at our roadblock did."

Bryant let out a heavy sigh. "That's murder, Mr. Nix."

"No. It's self-defense."

"Defense of a town is the authorities' responsibility."

"So you only have officers manning your roadblocks?"

"We aren't shooting people."

"But you would." The man stood. When he did, the truck bounced up a little. "If someone came in barrels blazing, you would."

Bryant had no answer for that. Finally, he said, "I'm going to need you to wait in my police car."

"Are you going to arrest me?"

"That will be for the mayor to decide."

Nix walked around their truck. The man who had been driving the SUV guided him to the back of the police cruiser.

Before he ducked in, Nix said, "I'm glad they're dead. If they weren't, I'd go find them and I'd put bullets in their heads myself. They killed my brother, and I'm glad they paid for it with their lives."

No one spoke for a moment, and then Bryant turned toward Carter and asked, "Got any water in that cooler, son?"

Carter fetched him a bottle. They would need to start filling them from the springs soon. He wasn't looking forward to that.

"For what it's worth, I don't recommend you arrest him," Max said.

"How can I *not* arrest him?" Bryant asked.

"First of all, according to Mr. Nix, he wasn't even there at the time of the shooting. Once he'd arrived on scene, the event was over."

"But he knows who did it."

"Maybe. Are you going out to Bend to find

them? Because I can assure you those people are armed to the teeth."

"You should have seen them in Sad Sam's," Carter's mom added. "Nearly everyone was carrying."

"We can't allow thugs to intimidate us, and you both know that."

"True." Max had taken on what Carter thought of as his lawyer voice. It was easy enough to imagine him arguing in front of a judge instead of in the middle of the road. "At this point, though, it's hearsay, which is generally inadmissible."

"I can't believe you're saying this," Bryant grumbled.

"If we were talking about a clear case of murder, I'd agree that you should book him. But it sounds, smells, and looks like self-defense. I'd say we have enough on our hands at the moment."

"And if I book him?" Bryant asked.

"He'll need a lawyer."

It wasn't an outright dare, but it was close enough. Even Carter understood that Max had won round one, and he'd probably win the rest too. He knew the law, and he wasn't afraid to call it like he saw it.

"Take him to Perkins," Max said. "Under martial law, she's authorized to make such decisions."

"For as long as she's mayor," Bryant said.

There was a pause, a beat where all Carter heard was the thump of his heart against his chest.

Max practically growled. "What's that supposed to mean?"

"Stone is gathering support to force her resignation."

"That's not something they can force."

"True, but if he gets enough folks on his side, we both know that Perkins will step down. She doesn't have the stomach for a political fight under these circumstances."

"You'd better do everything in your power to see that doesn't happen, because you do not want Eugene Stone in charge of our town."

Bryant grunted and walked away.

Carter glanced back at his mom. Her expression was one of exhaustion and, well, sadness. She kissed him on the cheek, which was embarrassing to say the least, and then she murmured, "I'll have dinner ready when you get home." That made him smile. Another of her famously balanced meals.

He could always count on his mom to keep the important things front and center, and in her opinion, eating was pretty important. It was something she'd impressed on him since he was a small child—carrying around his fanny pack of glucose testing strips, a compact machine that a five-year-old could operate, and small pieces of candy in case he needed them.

Folks were dying on the streets of Abney, and his mom was still balancing his meals.

Helping her from the truck, Max said good night and they both walked away. The last Carter saw of Toby Nix, Officer Bryant was driving him toward downtown.

Fifty-Five

The mayor called a town meeting for the next evening.

Shelby and Carter worked on their garden during the morning, before he had to leave to help with the latrine. She couldn't help worrying about her son, but she had to admit that he seemed fine both physically and emotionally—even after the tragedy of the night before. She shuddered to think he might have been hurt. When she'd tried to convince him he didn't need to serve on the patrol, he had only patted her head and said, "It'll be okay, Mom."

Shelby covered a four-hour shift at Green Acres before hurrying home to throw together a quick dinner. She was used to meticulously balancing Carter's meals and knew the experts' recommendations by heart.

Moderate your carbohydrate intake.

Make your plate colorful.

Watch your calories.

Remember to include fiber.

Easier said than done when you had limited supplies. What would she do in a month? Or six months? She pushed the worries aside and allowed herself a moment of satisfaction when Carter looked at dinner and said, "Weird, but cool." Their meal included tuna sandwiches for protein, using the last of the bread. She'd added canned green beans for fiber and unsweetened yellow peaches for color.

Who was she kidding? It was a terrible dinner. She needed to do some meal planning, but it would have to wait until after the town meeting.

Max knocked on their door at six p.m. By the time they reached downtown, Patrick and Bianca had joined them. It was good to be together again. Even if things weren't the same, it reminded Shelby that she could always count on the friendship of the people surrounding her.

She spotted Mr. and Mrs. Smitty across the square and waved. They waved in return and gave Shelby a thumbs-up to let her know all was well. She supposed that meant they had found a place to stay. The last she'd heard, Pastor Tony had been working on it. Had it been only four days since they'd picked the couple up from the side of the road? She'd had a niggling feeling, even then, that what they were facing was unprecedented.

They found a place to sit on the concrete steps

near Max's office. "Back in a few," Max said, and then he walked off toward a group of men standing by the mayor.

Shelby introduced herself to the man and woman on her left, people she'd never seen before. She wasn't sure if they were residents of Abney.

"I'm Maria Mendoza." The woman was shorter than Shelby, with long black hair cascading down her back. She was also in the last trimester of her pregnancy from the looks of things. "This is my husband, Alejandro."

Alejandro and Maria looked impossibly young. He nodded at Shelby and Bianca before reaching across to shake hands with Patrick.

"Are you new to town?" Patrick asked.

"Caught here when the flare hit." Alejandro placed a protective hand on his wife's back. "We were travelling from Dallas to San Antonio when our car died. It's lucky that we weren't out on the open road."

"Where are you staying?" Shelby couldn't imagine how terrified they must feel. They should be home, adding the finishing touches to their nursery and packing Maria's overnight bag for her hospital stay.

"Pastor Tony has found us a small garage apartment to stay in until we can make our way back to San Antonio."

They spoke for a few more minutes before Max returned.

"What is it? What's wrong?"

He shook his head once, and then he leaned closer and whispered, "Eugene forced an incompetence vote last night. The mayor won, but now Eugene's missing. Apparently he threw out some threats and then stormed out of the meeting. No one has seen him since."

Shelby wanted to ask more questions, but a hush had settled around them. Looking out across the square, she saw the crowd was as large as before, but folks seemed different— more wary, tired, expecting bad news.

Mayor Perkins stood up and thanked them all for coming. "The neighborhood watch groups are coming along well, our town is safe, and you all are working together. I appreciate that. The reason I called you here tonight is because we've received some reports from folks who have travelled outside of Abney. Although the news isn't good, I thought you had a right to know. Danny Vail will explain what we've learned, and then we'll both take questions."

Danny walked to the podium, which now seemed like command central for disaster updates.

Shelby felt herself leaning forward as Danny launched into his report. If anything, he looked more tired than the last time she had seen him. She wondered if he was sleeping enough or eating at all before remembering he wasn't her concern.

"We've had families travel to Killeen and Austin, to check on loved ones. This was done against the recommendation of Chief of Police Bob Bryant, but you all are free citizens. It's your decision to stay in Abney or not. It's also for you to decide if you want your children to stay and hear these details. Some of what I'm going to tell you is disturbing, to say the least."

His pronouncement caused some murmuring, but no one made a move to leave.

Fifty-Six

Did Shelby imagine Danny Vail looking her way? When Danny once again had the crowd's attention, he squared his shoulders and began.

"I'll start with some people who attempted to go to Killeen. The Travis family made it as far as their exit off 190, near the mall. There they were accosted by thieves, who stole what money they had. The Travis family was also held at gunpoint while the thieves siphoned their gasoline. Mr. and Mrs. Travis and their daughter were left stranded with no way to get home. Apparently, these types of attacks are happening at many of the exits. Think of the highway as a cattle chute. Once you're on one, it's difficult to escape."

Now the crowd was deadly quiet.

"Again, whether or not you choose to leave

town is your business, but we want you to understand that what you see in Abney may not be what you encounter elsewhere."

"Where were the authorities?" someone in the back shouted.

Shelby resisted the urge to turn around and glare at the man. The mayor had specifically asked folks to hold their questions until the end.

"That's a good question. Mr. Travis told me personally that he saw no evidence of a police presence, so we don't know what happened to their municipal structure. Perhaps they are simply overwhelmed at the moment."

"How did they get back?" someone else asked.

"That's the only positive news I have to give you. Some Good Samaritans showed up and gave them a gallon of gas, which was just enough to get them back to Abney."

Shelby noticed that Danny's face showed no emotion. He was holding it all in, the very picture of calm and authority. It didn't quite match with the man who had come to her home and suggested she get out of Dodge as fast as possible.

"Ted Gordon's experience is even more disturbing. I'm going to ask him to come forward and tell it himself."

Shelby had never met the man who joined Danny at the podium, but she'd read about him in the paper several times. He raised purebred horses —Missouri Fox Trotters, Tennessee walking horses, and Morgans. Ted Gordon was known nationally for being a superb breeder and a fair businessman. He looked like the typical small-town cowboy—sporting jeans, a button-down shirt, and a Stetson. She guessed him to be in his early fifties, and something in his quiet demeanor reminded her of George Strait— not that she knew him, either, but King George was a near legend in their area.

Ted gripped the podium and began to tell his story. "I went to Austin because one of my mares has developed a placental infection. We caught the condition early, but if it isn't treated— the foal won't survive. The mare needs three drugs that I don't keep at my place, so I decided to go purchase them."

He stopped and sipped from a bottle of water that Danny handed him. "If you know me at all, you understand how much those horses mean to me. I didn't want to risk losing the foal, and I couldn't let the mare suffer any more than I could let my own kin hurt. I'm not naive. I knew the trip would be difficult, but I thought it would be better to go now than later."

He pulled off his Stetson, wiped his brow, and resettled the hat.

"I saw the fires before I reached Cedar Park. I can't tell you if they were intentionally set or if they were accidents that had burned out of control, but a blanket of smoke covered from there down into Austin, as far as I could see. I made it almost to the toll road before the highway became impassable."

"How so?" someone called out.

"Cars—everywhere. Just abandoned on the freeways. I stopped, locked my vehicle, and walked through them for a quarter mile—trying to figure out what had happened. No one has attempted to move them or to create a path through."

Shelby felt Carter shift closer toward her. It broke her heart that her son was hearing these things, that he had to grow up in a world that was no longer safe.

Maria had begun to cry, and Alejandro put his arm around her—as if he could protect her from what Ted Gordon had left to share. On an impulse, Shelby reached over and squeezed the young woman's hand.

"I hurried back to my truck at that point and managed to back up until I could turn around. An hour after I first entered Cedar Park, I was headed back this way. I did stop at a vet clinic I'd used before. I knew they wouldn't have the antibiotics I needed, but I wanted more information on what had happened, in case I decided to try another trip. I had it in my mind that perhaps if I went a different way . . ."

He shook his head, staring down at the podium for a moment. When he looked up, Shelby thought she saw a layer of steely resolve laid over a deep and profound sadness.

"The veterinarian there told me that over a quarter of Austin has burned, is still burning. The Texas State Guard has set up a perimeter around a sixteen-block area, which includes the governor's mansion and the state government buildings."

"What about the university?" someone asked.

"Chaos. Some students are barricaded in their dorms. The main buildings have been looted."

"God help us." A woman near them began to weep.

"According to this vet, folks in the area were having their horses stolen. The thieves were also taking any old vehicles that still worked. Gasoline is becoming a primary method of trading, as is any type of food. Some people won't take cash anymore. They claim there's nothing left to buy with it. So primarily, it's become a matter of trade. All this in less than a week, which is truly difficult for me to believe."

"Any good news?" asked an older woman seated near the front.

"No, ma'am. I can't say there is, at least not from what I saw. However, I made it back, and I'm thankful for that. At least now I know that if I need something and it's not here, I'll have to find a way to live without it."

Ted had finished his story, and the mayor stood to take questions. There weren't many. What was there to ask? Leaving Abney wasn't an option at this point.

Alejandro helped Maria to her feet, and they passed through the crowd without saying goodbye. Shelby wanted to hurry after them, to offer some kind of help. But what could she give them? She barely had enough food for her and Carter.

As her small group made their way back toward home, she pondered Ted's words. The picture he painted pierced Shelby more sharply than a sword. She played his words over and again in her mind, but then she rejected them. Carter needed more medicine, and that medicine was in Austin. She would find a way to get it, regardless of what Ted Gordon said. She would not allow her son to die.

Fifty-Seven

The next day, Carter walked home with Kaitlyn after the meeting of the Brainiacs while Jason rode his skateboard in front of them. They'd had a productive morning at school working on Drop Appliances—Jason's name for anything that would help Abney citizens keep going until the lights came back on.

"Our solar oven is ready," Kaitlyn said. "All we need is something to cook in it."

"That shouldn't be a problem." Carter waved toward the trees they were walking under. "Lots of squirrel and dove."

"Ew." Kaitlyn scrunched her nose.

"Squirrel is pretty good," Jason declared.

"How would you know?" Carter asked.

"Read it online."

"So it has to be true."

"Yup. And my grandpa told me it tastes just like—"

"Chicken," they all three said at once, and then Kaitlyn was laughing and nudging her shoulder against his. Jason navigated a jump on his board, and Carter realized he was feeling almost normal.

Which stopped when they heard the faint echo of a rifle shot.

Jason pointed to their left. "Came from over there."

"Should we check it out?" Kaitlyn asked. "Maybe we should just—"

"Call someone?" Carter shook his head. He was about to suggest that she wait for them, when Kaitlyn slipped her hand into his.

Jason shrugged, picked up his skateboard, and they all walked in the direction of the shot. They didn't have to go far.

Deer had been a nuisance in Abney for years. Folks complained about how the animals ate the landscape plants, drank the water from the birdbaths, and even birthed their fawns in garages. Some people despised the deer because they'd caused so many car wrecks.

Others considered them to be pets and posted a constant barrage of pictures on social media.

Carter had never seen a person shoot one in the middle of town.

An old woman with long gray hair pulled back in a hair band was kneeling beside a good-sized doe and had already begun field dressing it. She held a skinning knife in her right hand and had made a cut from the groin to the breastbone. She didn't stop when they walked up.

As they watched, she sliced up to the throat, rolled the deer, and began removing the entrails.

"It's not exactly deer season," Jason said.

"No. It is not." She glanced up. "I could use your help harvesting the meat—need to hang and skin it."

"Hard work in this heat," Jason muttered.

"It is." She sat back on her heels and studied them. "We can get it quartered in no time, but I'll need your help loading the carcass onto this wagon."

"And do what with it?" Carter asked.

"Dump it in the field out behind the middle school. I'll give you each a portion of the meat for your labors."

Carter expected Kaitlyn to be sick. He'd hunted

with Max before, and Jason had hunted with his dad. They'd both helped to do what he'd just witnessed. Apparently Kaitlyn had too, because instead of looking horrified, she stepped closer to Carter. "We could cook it in our oven."

"Some of it." Carter rubbed at the muscles along his neck. It had already been a long day.

"That's all you're getting, but it's better than nothing." The old lady had brought along an ice cooler with wheels and a handle. "I need what's left of this deer removed before it starts attracting buzzards."

"Why did you kill it?"

"Folks on my street are hungry. A few are older than me, and they need some protein."

"It hasn't even been a week." Carter was still having trouble believing what he was seeing—an old lady harvesting a deer in the middle of town.

"Does that surprise you? We weren't exactly prepared for Armageddon."

The only thing Carter knew about Armageddon was how to play the video game. Come to think of it, people found all sorts of strange things to eat in the game.

"I'll go to the school and grab the oven," Kaitlyn said.

"You can't carry it alone," Jason said.

"There's a two-wheel dolly in the supply room, and Coach Parish said he'd be there all afternoon. The other team may still be there

351

working on their windmill. I'll get the oven, a bucket, and the dolly and meet you back here." Kaitlyn hurried back in the direction they'd come without waiting for an answer.

"Help me hoist this up." She'd wrapped a rope around the deer.

Jason and Carter pulled on the end of the rope until the deer was at a good height. The harvesting went faster than Carter expected. An hour later the woman pointed to a single-story A-frame house in need of painting.

"I live there. Come on over when you've disposed of the carcass, and I'll give you each enough for your family. It has to be cooked and eaten quickly or it'll spoil."

And then she was gone, pulling the cooler back toward her house.

"She's freakishly strong for someone that age," Jason said.

"I wish we had some gloves." Carter stood in the wagon, cut down what remained of the deer, and hopped back to the ground. Jason approached from the other side, and together they loaded it onto the wagon.

They dumped the carcass in a field where there were already two others, and then they stopped to clean their hands in the creek that ran beside the school. The water level was low, but it was still running.

Wiping their wet hands on their shorts, they

hurried back toward the woman's house. Not surprisingly, Kaitlyn had beaten them there.

"I think she's in the back," Kaitlyn said.

That was when Carter noticed the smell of wood smoke.

Walking toward the back of the house, they saw the woman had made a sort of spit over an open fire. The deer meat was already cooking.

"You came along when I needed you. Thank ya." She handed them three packages of meat wrapped in old newspaper. "Best get home and cook it up quick."

They thanked the woman, though Carter still felt as if he was in the middle of a video game. Any minute now, a mutant would jump out from behind a tree.

"Who's going to take the oven?" Jason asked.

"Max has a propane stove, and our gas stove still works." Carter shrugged. "We can use one of those."

"We have an old barbecue pit out back." Jason picked up his skateboard so he could walk beside them. "I have no idea how my mom will fix it up, but I'm sure she'll think of something."

"Sounds like you should take the oven, Kaitlyn." Carter knew she and her mom were on their own. She hadn't explained about her dad, but for whatever reason, he was out of the picture.

"Mom will love this. She's always saying we need to rise to meet a challenge." She raised her voice like a pastor at a pulpit and repeated, *"Rise to meet the challenge, Kaitlyn."*

They all laughed, and Carter felt better about this strange turn of events. Or maybe it was just that he didn't have digging duty today. They'd made it to nine feet, and the men had spent the morning building a shelter around the latrine. Since he didn't have a shift at the Market, he was free until four o'clock when he was to be at the roadblock.

They split to go their separate ways at the next intersection, where Jason lived two blocks over from Kaitlyn. Carter looked at her and said, "Don't do anything crazy with this," pointing at the dolly and the oven they had made.

"Tomorrow at nine," Kaitlyn called out.

Carter waved and turned toward home.

With any luck, he and his mom would have a hot meal sometime soon.

Fifty-Eight

On Wednesday evening, Max, Shelby, Carter, and Dr. Bhatti sat around Max's picnic table. For the first time since Friday, Max wasn't hungry. He didn't need a second bowl of the stew, but he reached for one anyway. It wasn't like they could refrigerate it, and Shelby had already delivered a couple of bowls to their older neighbors.

Surprisingly it was Farhan Bhatti who had sliced up the deer meat, sautéed it in onions, oil, and garlic, and added a gravy packet and more seasoning—all inside an old Dutch oven that was now suspended over Max's fire pit. "No need using up all your propane for something that will need to cook for hours," Bhatti had reasoned.

The smell had tortured him all afternoon as he worked in the house, dividing his possessions between things he would take with him and items he would attempt to trade. By the time Carter had returned from his shift at the roadblock and Shelby had returned from working at Green Acres, the stew was ready.

"Less than a week, and you'd think we hadn't had meat in a month." Shelby scooped up another spoonful of the deer stew. "Are you sure this won't kill us? Make us sick? I can't afford to spend an evening in the latrine vomiting."

"No worries. The meat was quite fresh when Carter showed up with it." Max popped another bite in his mouth.

"I wish you all could have seen her," Carter said. "This little old lady with a long gray braid hanging down her back. But she was strong, and she definitely knew what she was doing."

"Good thing the game warden didn't catch her," Shelby muttered.

"Our game warden hasn't made it back. He was working over by Lake Buchanan when the flare hit." Max considered licking his bowl, but in the end he placed it on the ground for the old stray tabby cat he used to feed. There wouldn't be any more cat food in the near future, so the least he could do was let her clean his bowl.

The cat began to purr as she daintily licked up every drop.

"The old lady was a little scary." Carter continued scooping stew from his bowl. "The entire thing was like something from a movie."

"The old ones have seen hard times before," Dr. Bhatti said. "They aren't quite as soft as the new generation."

"Speak for yourself," Carter said. "Dragging that deer carcass to the field was no picnic."

"True, but you've changed," Shelby pointed out. "A week ago you complained about having to vacuum your room."

"Guess I've toughened up nicely in only—" Carter paused, his eyes going up and to the left. "Six days. Wow. Only six days."

The same thought had been circling in Max's mind all afternoon. How could so much change so drastically in so little time? And what did that indicate about the future?

"Tell us about where you're from," Shelby said to Dr. Bhatti.

She'd been watching him since the meal had begun. Shelby clearly did not trust this man, and her instincts were usually good. Max needed to find out what he was hiding, not to mention what he had buried. He knew Bhatti was holding back something, but wasn't everyone? He hadn't told Shelby how frightened he was—how certain he was that things would get much worse before they had a chance of getting better.

And she was up to something. He didn't know what, but he'd known her too long to miss the signs—staring off into space, abruptly changing the conversation—and the look on her face after Ted Gordon had talked about Austin? Fear and desperation, followed by a hard, determined frown. Yes, Shelby was planning something she didn't want to tell him about.

Bhatti studied her with a somber expression, and Max thought he wouldn't answer—but he nodded once. Instead of jumping right into his personal story, he pushed back his bowl, tapped his pocket as if to find a pack of cigarettes there, and finally settled for folding his hands over his stomach.

Bhatti wasn't an old man—approximately Max's age if he had to guess. And yet many of his mannerisms were of an older man—like patting his pocket for something he had forgotten, resting his hands on his stomach, and thinking long and hard before he spoke. Perhaps it was because he was no longer hungry, or because of the peacefulness of night falling around them. Whatever the reason, the doctor seemed more relaxed than at any time since Max had met him—which admittedly hadn't been all that long.

"I'm from New York, which I'm sure you're quite familiar with."

"We went once," Carter said. "My mom had this writer conference thing."

Bhatti arched his eyebrows, but he didn't respond to that.

"Mostly we saw the touristy part of the city," Shelby explained.

"Which is not where I lived. But having grown up there, I feel comfortable in most areas—both touristy and otherwise. I must say, I wouldn't want to be there now."

"And your parents?" Max asked.

Bhatti shook his head, not bothering to explain.

"You don't sound like a New Yorker," Carter said. When his mother bumped his knee under the table—Max knew without having to actually see it—Carter said, "What? I'm sure he knows he has an accent."

"Indeed I am aware." Bhatti glanced at each of them. "My parents spoke both English and Urdu, the national language of Pakistan. Their accent was much heavier than mine. My grandparents, however, spoke only their native language."

"Urdu?" Carter asked.

"Yes. I visited my grandparents from June to August each year, so I became much more fluent than I otherwise would have. During those summer visits my accent would grow stronger. When I would return to New York, my accent would fade. What you hear now, I suppose it's a blend of the two."

"So you lived in Pakistan every summer?"

Max sat back and let Carter quiz the doctor. Teens had a natural interest in all things different, and Bhatti seemed much less defensive when speaking with Carter.

"Until I was in college. My grandparents lived —still live as far as I know—in Karachi, Pakistan's largest city."

"How big?" Carter asked.

"Over nine million."

Carter let out a whistle, and then he said, "Plenty bigger than Abney."

Max understood Carter's reaction to the idea of that many people. He had felt the same way when he'd moved to Austin—which was also plenty bigger than Abney. At first there had been an allure to that, but he quickly realized that he didn't fit into the hustle and bustle of a metropolitan area. Though he'd be the first to admit that the food was tastier, the parks were better, and the entertainment was far superior. The traffic? It was worse.

"Karachi is a big city, but there are still markets with fresh meat, where my grandmother—my nana—would go every day to purchase that evening's meal."

"Every day?"

"Many people in Pakistan have only a small refrigerator, so you purchase what you need for the next twenty-four hours. Anyway, that is how I learned to cook freshly harvested meat. It can have a gamey taste, but with the right spices . . ."

"The stew was delicious. Thank you, Farhan." Max felt strange using the man's first name, but he couldn't keep calling him Dr. Bhatti either.

"How did you end up in Texas?" Shelby asked, leaning forward, her arms crossed on the table. "And why did you leave Austin?"

"You are quite curious about my past."

"I am."

"And yet I know very little of yours."

"I didn't show up in your town, claiming to be a doctor."

"I have not claimed anything, although it is true that I am a doctor."

Checkmate.

Max had to give the guy credit for not backing down. But he had lived in a city with nine million people. Surely he could handle one suspicious Texas woman.

Instead of jousting with Shelby, Farhan stood and picked up his bowl and spoon. "I will just clean these up, and then I told Miss Connie I would look in on one of her patients. So if you'll excuse me . . ."

They sat in silence for a minute, then Max asked, "How's work, Carter?"

"It's over. Nothing left to sell at the Market. Graves said he'd get hold of us if anything comes in, but I'm not holding my breath."

His mom looked at him quizzically. "Where would he get more supplies?"

Carter doubted they'd approve of Graves's scheme to find the corporate supply trucks and take what was on them, but he told them anyway.

"I won't have you selling stolen goods," Shelby said. "We're desperate, but we're not criminals."

"Don't waste your energy worrying about that," Max said. "I imagine those trucks were looted the first night of the aurora."

"I'm pretty sure the stuff is gone," Carter said. "The last shift I worked, Graves was all out of sorts. Turns out someone took his list of trailers and routes. Whoever took the list probably already got their hands on the goods."

Max pulled off his baseball cap and stared at the rim. When he looked up, he was smiling. "Well, if anyone suddenly has a truckload of groceries that they're selling out of their front yard, we'll know who our culprit is."

Carter laughed and jumped up from the table. "I'm going to meet Kaitlyn."

"Now?" Shelby checked her watch. "Curfew is at—"

"Dark. I know." Carter picked up his own dishes,

and headed toward his house. "I'll be home in plenty of time," he hollered over his shoulder.

Shelby rolled her eyes, and then she pinned her gaze to Max.

"I didn't do anything."

"Exactly. I'm going home to do some work—" There it was again. She hesitated and backtracked. "Housework. But when Bhatti leaves, you come and get me. We're going back there to dig up whatever it was he buried."

And before Max could argue, she was gone.

Fifty-Nine

Carter could tell his mom didn't like Dr. Bhatti, but he seemed like an okay guy. And his cooking was better than his mom's, even on a good day when the power was on. He felt a tiny bit guilty thinking that, but even his mom joked about what a terrible cook she was.

He waved at Ed and Rhonda, who were sitting out on their front porch. Funny how suddenly he seemed to know everyone in their neighborhood. But when you dug a latrine with someone, you were instantly closer to them. For instance, he knew that Rhonda had recently had her knee replaced. She'd been putting it off, but the doctor had convinced her to do it before the heat of summer.

"Lucky thing I did too," she had explained to Carter. "I don't think anyone will be getting a new knee anytime soon."

Ed had chuckled at that. "You got in under the wire, dear."

At first Carter thought it was weird that they could joke around when everything was so bleak, but Ed had said, "Laugh while you can, son. Laugh while you can."

This conversation had taken place a few hours earlier when he'd stopped by to check on the progress they'd made on the latrine roof. He wasn't scheduled to work on it, but he was curious. The roof was at a slant, to allow rain to slide off. Carter glanced at the sky. No chance of rain now. He missed his weather app. Something could be to the west, heading toward them, and gone again before they had a chance to put out every bucket they owned.

Laugh while you can.

That idea had stuck in his head, and then Kaitlyn had crossed his mind. Jason had said that she lived two blocks over from him, and she had mentioned living on Sandstone Street. He knew where that was. Maybe he would just walk by.

Suddenly he was there, trying to look casual, and he spotted Kaitlyn and her mom sitting out on the front porch. Kaitlyn was reading a book, and her mom was making something with yarn and two big needles—knitting. Carter could remember Max's mom doing that.

Carter stopped in the middle of the sidewalk, and Mrs. Lowry looked up and nudged Kaitlyn. When she saw him, she slipped a bookmark into her book, set it on the table next to her, and said something to her mom. A smile lighting up her face, she ran out to meet him.

"Hey."

"Hey yourself." Her eyes crinkled into a smile. Her blue eyes reminded Carter of ocean water. He almost slapped his forehead at the idea. Why was he starting to think like he was inside a poem or something?

"What are you doing out?"

"I guess I wanted to stop over and see if the oven worked."

"It did! Dinner was actually good."

"You two come up here," Kaitlyn's mom called. She was bigger than Carter's mom, round, and the same height as her daughter. She had blond hair that must have once looked like Kaitlyn's, but now it was cut short and pulled back from her face with hair clips. Her voice was loud enough that no doubt the neighbors heard every word she said. "I made some lemonade, and there are still a few of those chocolate chip cookies left from last week."

"Lemonade?" Carter asked.

"It's sugar-free," she assured him.

He'd explained to her that he had diabetes the day before. She'd asked a few questions, but she had seemed completely cool about it.

"No ice," she added. "Still—it tastes pretty good."

He followed Kaitlyn up onto the porch. He thought it would be awkward, but it turned out her mom was a teacher and comfortable being around teens. "I accepted a job at the middle school. That's one of the reasons we moved here."

She stopped knitting and cocked her head to the side, same as he'd seen Kaitlyn do a dozen times. "I'm not sure that school will be in session, though. We might just have a longer summer break than we planned."

Her attitude was good, that was obvious enough. The fact that she was a teacher explained her loud voice—no doubt she was used to shouting to be heard in a classroom. What Carter remembered about middle school was not exactly calm and order, though there were a few teachers who managed to handle the preteens well. He suspected that Mrs. Lowry would be one of them.

Kaitlyn brought out a checkerboard, and they set it up on the floor of the porch.

"Can't remember the last time I played a board game," he confessed.

"We used to have game night once a week."

"And we still will," her mother interjected.

"It's every Thursday."

"Tomorrow?" asked Carter.

Kaitlyn looked at her mom. "Sure."

"You should join us, Carter. Can't say that we'll have pizza and Coke, but we'll rustle up something. By the way, I want to thank you for the venison. The little oven you kids made worked great. I was able to roast all of the meat, boil some potatoes on our gas grill, and make a fairly good meal."

"It fed us and our neighbors on both sides," Kaitlyn said. "I'm so psyched that it worked."

"You knew it would."

"I thought it would, but you never know until you try it on something real."

"Kaitlyn met the challenge," her mother declared.

Carter choked on his lemonade, nearly spewing it out all over the checkerboard. Kaitlyn patted his back, and Mrs. Lowry lowered her glasses and watched them both until she was sure he was all right.

They continued the game, and Mrs. Lowry resumed knitting. Then the quietness of the night was broken by the sound of music.

Carter looked up, glanced left and right. "Where is that coming from?"

"Mrs. Hastings, next door. She teaches piano lessons."

"Every night at this time she blesses us with her music." Mrs. Lowry nodded toward the house on the east side. "And she says thank you for the deer meat."

Carter hadn't realized how much he had missed music. Before the Drop, he constantly listened to iTunes—mostly country but some classic rock too. In the last week he'd become used to the silence. Now the melody that rang out through the night touched something deep inside him. The music was gentle, persistent, and stirring.

The next hour passed all too quickly. He lost five games straight. Who would have guessed Kaitlyn was a champion checker player? Then they walked through her newly planted vegetable garden, Kaitlyn pointing out where she had planted what, though very little had sprouted.

Mrs. Hastings switched from playing classical pieces to a ragtime tune that Carter had heard a thousand times coming from the ice-cream truck.

As they sat in the swing together, Kaitlyn told him about the book she was reading.

"I don't read much," Carter confessed.

"You're kidding, right?"

Carter shrugged, and because Mrs. Lowry had stepped inside, he took advantage of the moment and reached over to twine his fingers with Kaitlyn's.

She laughed and said, "Tell me you're not one of those video game geeks."

"Guilty."

"But not anymore."

"Nope. I haven't played a game in six days."

"Wow. It's like you've turned over a new leaf."

"Sort of."

"We need to find you a book!" She hopped up from the swing, and they wandered inside. They dropped to their knees in front of a bookcase in the Lowrys' living room—a room that didn't look so much different from Carter's.

"You'll love this one."

"*Alas, Babylon*?"

"It's great."

"What's it about?"

"Nuclear holocaust. Florida. Survival. That sort of thing."

"Sounds kind of heavy."

"Actually, it's kind of relevant," Mrs. Lowry said, walking into the room. "And the boys I teach always like it."

Carter started to point out that he had graduated and was a far cry from her middle school students, but instead he said thank you as he'd been taught.

"Kaitlyn, maybe you'd like to walk Carter to the end of the street. Wouldn't want him to be out past curfew."

Those words slammed Carter back into their reality. For a few minutes—playing checkers, eating cookies, and listening to Mrs. Hastings play the piano—he'd actually allowed himself to forget. As they walked back outside, he recognized the melody of "Amazing Grace."

"She always ends with that one," Kaitlyn said. "I like it because we used to sing it nearly every Sunday at my old church."

They talked about youth groups as they walked toward the end of the street. Most of the neighbors were picking up toys and hustling children inside. When they reached the corner, Carter stepped off the sidewalk and into the shade of a massive live oak tree. Then he did something that surprised him.

He pulled Kaitlyn closer and kissed her.

Carter had kissed girls before—plenty of times. But none of those kisses had been like this one. For a moment he thought they'd experienced some kind of minor earthquake. The ground seemed to shift under his feet. She kissed him back, snuggling into his arms, and Carter's heart felt like it flip-flopped in his chest. All too soon Kaitlyn was pulling away, a huge smile on her face.

"See you tomorrow?"

"Uh-huh."

"I'm going to check out a volunteer thing, so I'll meet you at the school. Say ten o'clock?"

Instead of answering, he simply waved, aware that a goofy grin had spread across his face and unable to do a thing about it.

He'd kissed her, and she seemed to have liked it.

She *must* have liked it because she was smiling.

Wow.

Suddenly he didn't care so much that the television didn't work or that he hadn't played a video game in a week, or that he had no idea if he'd be attending college in the fall.

Maybe his life was changing for the better.

That thought had just crossed his mind when he turned the corner onto his street. He glanced up and saw their house on the right. And suddenly to the south, the sky lit up and the ground shook.

Sixty

Shelby flew out of her house. She stopped only to snatch up the backpack and thread her arms through the straps. She heard a second explosion, ran to the middle of the street to stare up at the sky, and saw—nothing. Glancing around, she spotted Carter at the end of the street and ran toward him.

"What's happening?" he shouted.

"I don't know!" Shelby stood frozen, her heartbeat pounding in her veins. She motioned to Carter to hurry. "We need to get inside."

"It's not here," someone shouted. "Heard it over the CB. The fighting is to the south, in Croghan."

And suddenly Max was there, as he'd always been there—calm, steady, a haven in her storm.

"Are you all right?" Max asked Carter.

"I'm fine. I was walking home from Kaitlyn's and I heard—"

Another detonation rocked the air.

Max stepped closer as the street began to fill with people. "We can see better from the water tower."

"What do we want to see?"

"If they're headed this way."

"Why . . ." Shelby felt all the blood drain from her face, and suddenly the world swayed in front of her.

"Don't faint on me." Max reached out and steadied her. "I can go without you. I'll come back and—"

"I'm going." She wanted to tell Carter to stay home, but that would have been a waste of energy. He had already turned and was pushing his way through the crowd.

They ran down the street, passed the roadblocks, and made a right turn. Though it was nearly dark, nearly past curfew, no one stopped them or paid them any attention at all. They hurried on, and then they could see the water tower, the highest spot in Abney.

She could make no sense of what was happening. As they ran, a dozen images flitted through her mind.

Hiking at Bend and suddenly seeing the aurora.

Climbing the water tower with Max.

Fighting the downtown fire.

Max throwing her to the ground as she tried to reach Carter amid the gunfire.

The faces of Bianca and Patrick and Max and Carter.

And now the town to their south was being attacked? How could she protect her son from that?

But Carter hadn't needed her when the jeep had careened to a stop in front of him and the shooting had started. At some point in the last week he had become a man, shedding any last traces of the child he had been.

And Max? As they hurried up the hill, Shelby realized that Max had been and always would be a part of their family. It didn't matter if they lived next door to each other or not. It didn't even matter if society was crumbling around them. Max was the one person she could count on, no matter the situation.

A few folks had gathered around the tower, but no one had thought to climb it. Or maybe they were all afraid of heights.

"Stay here." Max squeezed her arm once before he hurried to the ladder on the water tower. Hand over hand, he began to climb.

"Guy's like a monkey," Carter muttered. He turned to Shelby. "Is someone actually bombing Croghan? Why? And how?"

"The women's prison is there," said a young

guy sporting a scraggly beard and holding a toddler in his arms. "Maybe they . . . maybe they overthrew the guards."

"They wouldn't have bombs, though."

Another explosion rocked the evening. Darkness had fallen, and Shelby glanced up, dazzled by millions of pinpricks of light. They reminded her of the past, of countless evenings she had spent camping with Carter when he was younger.

She was quickly brought back to the present by the smell of smoke drifting their way.

Max had made it to the ledge that encircled the water tower. Now a few teenagers were standing at the base, craning their necks, and staring up at Max.

"Definitely Croghan," Max called out. "Quite a few structures are burning."

"And the explosions?"

"I can't tell where they're coming from." Max had been staring toward the south, now he glanced down. "But someone is attacking them."

"Where is their police force?" The man switched his baby to his left shoulder. The child stared at Shelby with wide blue eyes and drooled on her dad's shoulder.

"Police aren't going to be able to help with this. Where's the state guard?" asked a woman about Shelby's age.

"By the time they get a message to Austin, the battle will be over." Max took one last look, and then he began to climb down. One of the teenagers pulled out a flashlight and shone it on the ladder's rungs.

Shelby glanced around for Bianca or Patrick, but she didn't see them. She was too short, and the crowd was too large. She was lucky to keep Carter in her sights. Her death grip on his arm helped.

Max had rejoined them when an Abney police cruiser pulled up. He left his headlights on, casting a beam out over the crowd. Shelby didn't know the officer who stepped out. He was probably fresh out of college—if he had gone to college.

"Chief Bryant is asking for help."

Everyone stopped talking at once.

"Croghan is under attack, and whoever is doing it might turn this direction next. We need shotguns, rifles, anything with a scope. If you don't have those, bring your handguns." He swiped at the sweat pouring down his face. "Though if they get that close, God help us."

"Where do we go?" an older man asked.

"Trucks will come by each of the checkpoints to pick you up. They'll take you out to the city limit line."

"We're not going to Croghan?" another man called out.

"No. Croghan's gone."

Shelby thought he looked more like a kid than

when he'd first stepped out of the cruiser. He seemed scared and uncertain. "We can't save them, but maybe we can save Abney," he said.

Some people stood around talking, asking more questions that no one could answer, and staring off toward the glow on the horizon— Croghan burning. Shelby realized with a start that Carter and Max were already pushing their way back through the crowd.

"Where are you going?"

"Home," Max said, not bothering to slow his long steps.

Shelby ran to catch up.

"I have an extra box of ammo," Carter was saying. "Should I take it?"

"Yes." Shelby matched their stride. "We need to take everything we can find."

"Whoa." Carter stopped in the middle of the street. "I'm not sure he meant for moms to come."

"We're all adults here," Max said. "Your mom's right. Gather your weapon, your ammo, and meet me outside in five minutes."

Sixty-One

The last thing Max wanted was Shelby standing guard, standing in harm's way.

But if she was with them, he'd be able to keep an eye on her.

He grabbed his rifle and a box of ammo, and

he wondered at the fact that he could be so calm. They were quite possibly under siege. How many had died in Croghan? Why the massive show of firepower? Had they resisted?

And who was the aggressor?

All good questions, but they probably wouldn't have answers for several hours. In the meantime, he wasn't going to stand by and let anyone burn up Abney. Not their town. Not his friends and neighbors.

By the time he stepped outside, Shelby and Carter were waiting for him.

"I can't believe we're doing this," Shelby muttered. Her hands didn't shake as she opened up the backpack, wrapped her Browning pistol in a towel, and slipped the entire thing inside.

Carter was carrying his granddad's Winchester rifle and an extra box of ammunition.

As they walked silently toward the end of the street, the occasional sound of explosions continued to reach them. Max wondered what the point was of the ongoing attack against Croghan. What was left to burn?

They reached the roadblock and found more than a dozen people milling around, waiting to defend Abney.

Max was surprised when Mayor Perkins showed up driving her pickup. She looked like she hadn't slept since the flare.

She got out of the pickup to address the

crowd, raising her voice to be heard above them. "This is a one-way trip, at least until sunrise. If you change your mind, you walk back—so be certain this is what you want to do."

No one hesitated. By the time Shelby and Carter climbed up into the truck bed, there was barely room for Max.

"You can ride up front with me, Max." Perkins hopped back behind the wheel without waiting for an answer.

As soon as she pulled out onto the road, Perkins started talking. "Our reports tell us that Croghan has major fires on two sides."

"Who's behind it?"

"Supposedly it started at the prison—you can imagine how miserable it's been in those cells."

"Do you believe that a group of women who are incarcerated for substance abuse started the fires? Carried out an assault on the town?"

"Desperate times, Max. Desperate times." She ground the gears from second to third.

Instead of arguing with her, he changed tactics. "Did the inmates take over the prison?"

"It's possible. It held more than six hundred inmates."

"There's at least a hundred guards—"

"Twenty-five showed up. All it took was one slip in protocol, which happened approximately three hours ago. Once the inmates had the keys, it was all over."

"Fatalities?"

"A skull fracture to the guard who turned her back on one of the prisoners. The rest escaped with cuts and scrapes." Perkins frowned as she hit fourth gear.

At the speed she was driving, they would be at the edge of town within a couple of minutes. Max needed to know what they were walking into.

"Where are the explosions coming from?"

"At the same time the inmates were fighting their way free on the west side, a different group hit the east side." A wave of uncertainty passed over Perkins's face. It made her look vulnerable. "The Croghan police responded with force."

"Which group did they shoot at?"

"The east group seemed the most dangerous. Someone had tipped the police off that they were led by a few die-hard survivalists. You can imagine how well equipped they are. A week ago you could purchase anything from a rocket launcher to a hand grenade on the Internet."

Max wasn't sure about that, but he didn't interrupt. Perkins was finally giving him useful information.

"Turned into an all-out battle. The police were pushed back, people panicked, next thing we knew the place was on fire. We heard their mayor put out a distress call to the governor—asking for state guard or anyone they could send."

"And?"

"And the response, supposedly from the governor's office, was that they would send help as soon as the situation in the capital was stabilized."

Max wasn't surprised in light of Ted Gordon's attempted trip to Austin. "The people attacking from the east, what were they after?"

"Can't say for sure. There's a tortilla factory on the south side of town. Maybe they wanted that. Maybe they wanted to see if there was any money left in the bank or medical supplies in the drugstore."

It was worse than Max had thought—an entire town wiped out in a matter of hours. But hadn't he just told Shelby that men would be willing to kill for ammo or medical supplies? The worst-case scenario he had tried to warn her about was happening, and the only thing they could do was to pray and fight back.

Perkins pulled up to what looked like a mobile staging area. Before she stopped, she glanced at Max and said, "I don't want to be right about this."

"I'm not sure you are."

"I care about the people of Abney, even though a fair number of them were willing to side with Eugene Stone."

"Not enough, though, Nadine. You're still mayor."

She shrugged as if those days were in the past now. "We need to do everything we can to keep our town safe."

As Max got out of the truck and rejoined Carter and Shelby, those words rang through his mind over and again. *Keep our town safe.* He wasn't sure that was something they could do. They could pray. But hadn't the citizens of Croghan prayed?

How many had been killed?

How many now had nowhere to live?

And for what? Some tortillas and Tylenol?

Beneath all of those questions was another, more profound one. Why did God allow such terrible things to happen?

He could maybe understand how a solar flare happened. Societies, even Christian societies, weren't immune to the forces of nature. Tornadoes, hurricanes, tsunamis, and more occurred every day. Their country had endured its fair share of natural disasters, along with a few terrorist attacks and the occasional stock market crisis.

But anarchy? Goons attacking their neighboring town?

On this side of the battle, men and women and yesterday's children—he glanced at Carter—were defending what little remained.

A string of trucks had been parked nose-to-tailgate across the road. As they lined up behind the barricade, Max's mind struggled with those questions. His thoughts drifted back to Pastor Tony's sermon.

His love will endure—forever.

He is good, and his love will last forever.

Your steadfast love, O Lord, endures forever.

Sixty-Two

For the first two hours, nothing happened.

The sound of explosions became less frequent, but smoke continued to drift toward them. People to the right and left of Max—including Carter and Shelby—checked and rechecked their weapons as the moon rose, casting shadows in front of them.

In the distance, Max heard the crackle of Bob Bryant's radio. Five minutes later, the man was pulling him away from his position.

"That was Stone."

"Eugene?"

"He's in Croghan." Bryant had opened the door to his police cruiser to snatch out a fluorescent vest. The dome light revealed that his face was flushed a bright red, and sweat beaded his fore-head.

"I don't understand."

"He has a message for Perkins, but he says he'll only give it to you."

"Me?" Max shifted his rifle to his left hand.

"He trusts you for some reason. Here, put this on so no one will shoot you by mistake."

"Eugene Stone doesn't even like me. And what is he doing in Croghan?"

"Apparently he's their new mayor."

Bryant gestured for him to put the vest on, but Max wasn't ready to take that step.

"Why doesn't he talk to Perkins on the radio?"

"In his own words, he wants this done in writing so it will all be legal."

"There's nothing legal about what Stone is doing, and if I get close enough to take a piece of paper from him, I might not be able to restrain myself from using this rifle."

Bryant slammed the door shut. The darkness masked his expression, but his tone left nothing to Max's imagination. "Perkins isn't going to agree to anything that Stone asks for, but this will buy us a little time. His directions are for you to walk straight down the middle of the highway for one mile—alone and unarmed. Take the paper he's drawn up and tell him you'll see what you can do. Try to stall."

"What good is stalling?"

"We're sending someone out to the Bar S Ranch."

"For?"

"Jake Cooper has some AK-47s and comm equipment. And Stanley Hamilton is bringing more ammo."

"And you're going to use the AKs?"

"If we have to—yes."

Max put on the vest and walked back to his position.

"Hold this for me." He thrust the rifle into Carter's hands.

Shelby moved to stop him, but he only shook his head. "I'll be right back," he whispered, and then he strode away from her. If he paused to think about what he was doing, he'd question his sanity.

Fortunately for Eugene Stone, he was not at the meeting place. Instead, he'd sent the city attorney for Croghan.

"You're involved in this?" asked Max.

"Doesn't mean I approve of it." Randall Black was in his fifties and had always struck Max as a stand-up guy.

"So why are you doing it?"

"Because my family is in Croghan. I've lived there all my life, Max. I'm not ready to run away and let the people attacking us take what we've built."

"That justifies siding with Stone?"

"I'm hardly doing that. You don't know what we've been going through in Croghan."

"I don't need to know."

"First the prison, then those thugs on the east side."

"We can help you."

"Eugene Stone stepped in and offered leadership when we had none. Our mayor wasn't even in town when this thing started—still hasn't returned. And the council has done nothing but bicker with one another." He shoved the piece of paper into Max's hands. "Take this. Take it to Nadine and talk some sense into her. She needs to agree to Stone's requests so we don't have another bloodbath. You've got two hours."

Before Max could argue, Randall turned and walked off into the darkness.

But he didn't need two hours. Bryant drove him to city hall, where Perkins had already convened the council. Calvin Green wasn't present, so Max assumed he would be standing in as city attorney. He read the note aloud before handing it to the mayor. "As your legal counsel, I strongly advise you to reject Eugene's demands. Respond firmly and with no question that you will not compromise."

"We're going to respond, but not with a note."

The vote was unanimous. The citizens of Abney would stand and defend their town.

By the time he made it back to his position, Bryant was handing out AK-47s with night scopes to every third man. "If they approach with spotlights, switch your night scopes off," he said.

Each man, woman, and teenager gathered around Bryant's cruiser. He reached into his glove box, pulled out a county map, and slapped it onto the hood of his cruiser. Someone fetched a flashlight and held it over the map. "We have a spotter in Stanford's barn—here, to the west of the highway."

"What about the east side?" Frank Kelton asked.

"I've put three men in the field. They have radio headsets. The spotter will let them know as soon as Stone makes his move, if he makes his move."

"Seems awful risky for the men on the ground." Mrs. Plumley squinted down at the map.

"They're ex-military, recently returned from the Middle East. They can handle whatever comes at them. Cooper equipped both groups with high-powered rifles."

"Do they have night scopes as well?" Max asked.

"Yes. If the town of Croghan makes a move, those men in the field will be our first line of defense."

Sixty-Three

After Chief Bryant outlined their plan, an hour passed with no action. Carter was terrified he'd freeze up when the shooting started. What he hadn't expected was to be fighting sleep from the battle line.

Max must have heard him yawn, because he

stepped closer and offered him a bottle of water. "How are you doing?"

"Okay. Bored."

"My dad fought in the Vietnam War. He once told me the only thing worse than being in battle was waiting on one."

"This is all so surreal." Carter stifled another yawn. "A week ago my biggest concern was who my college roommate was going to be."

"We make war that we may live in peace."

"Your dad said that?"

"Aristotle." Shelby crowded in next to them, still clutching Max's rifle.

Max had been given one of the high-powered rifles with a night vision scope. Carter was relieved to still be using his granddad's Winchester—it was the only thing he'd ever shot, the only thing he felt truly comfortable holding.

"I'm beginning to think this isn't going to happen." His mom rested her back against the pickup bed they were positioned behind. "Maybe Eugene has come to his senses."

Bryant's radio crackled, and a voice said, "Approximately twenty men moving toward Abney, a mile out."

His mom and Max hurried back to their positions. They were standing about six feet apart, and they'd been cautioned on when and when not to shoot.

The sound of gunfire echoed in the distance.

The moon hung high, like a lantern in the sky. Carter's heart rate accelerated as he made out three trucks speeding toward them, travelling side by side. They covered the width of the highway, and each had off-road lights mounted to the top of the cab. Suddenly Carter, his mom, Max—their entire line was bathed in the too-bright light.

Carter glanced at Max and saw him switch the night scope off.

Fitting the Winchester's stock tight against his shoulder, he pulled in a steadying breath and concentrated on what he was seeing through his own scope.

Gunfire burst from the trucks in a deafening rain of noise. To Carter's left was Frank, who stood, took aim at the truck on the left, and blew out the spotlights with three quick shots. The trucks in the middle and to the right suffered similar fates, and then the night scopes must have been flipped back on. Carter heard someone to his far left call out, "Half a dozen men approaching on foot."

He didn't hear much after that. His ears rang from the shots around him. Using the side of the truck as a stable rest, he peered through his scope and fired. His first shot went wide, but with the second and third he managed to shoot out the front tires of a truck. Max and his mom aimed at the men inside.

Their coordinated effort worked.

The truck swerved right, then left, and then sputtered to a halt. The driver slumped over the wheel. Two men spilled out the passenger door, but they didn't make it very far, falling to the ground only a few feet from the truck.

Carter scanned left to right—left to right. His job was to disable anyone who made it within a hundred yards. He couldn't see much farther than that.

Someone on the far side of his mom screamed, and his mom called out, "We need medical over here!"

He was glancing toward her, toward the sound of the man's groans, when he saw movement out of the corner of his eyes. One of the men from Croghan was barreling toward them, running toward his mom as she turned to help the injured man. He held a pistol in front of him and was firing as he ran.

Carter didn't have to think about it. He didn't need to debate the right or wrong of the thing. Every ounce of his being was flooded with adrenaline, and his only thought was of his mother. He raised his rifle, took aim, and fired at the same time that Max did. The man was lifted off his feet and thrown backward.

The battle lasted a few more minutes, but they were basically mopping up stragglers. A shout of victory rose as anyone who hadn't been killed or injured reversed directions and ran toward the south. What followed was an eerie silence as the moon continued to shine and the crickets resumed their chirping. Everything was the same as before, and everything had changed. Carter felt it like a weight on his chest.

"Will we go after them?" he asked Max.

"No. We won't." Max wiped at the sweat running down his face, and Carter saw blood dripping from a wound on his arm.

"You've been hit."

Max looked surprised. He craned his neck, staring at his left shoulder as if it wasn't attached to his left arm. "Didn't feel it happen. Must have grazed me."

"Sit down," Carter's mom commanded.

She pulled a roll of bandage out of her back-pack and began wrapping the wound—down around, over, repeat.

"Easy, Nurse Nightingale."

"Stop complaining." She tugged the wrap to make sure it would hold and tied off the bandage.

"You stopped the bleeding, but you also halted all circulation."

"I did not."

"My fingers are blue." Max held his hand up in front of his face.

She opened her mouth as if to argue with him, but no sound came out. Instead, her brave front crumpled and she dropped to her knees, weeping and covering her face with her hands.

"Hey, it's okay. It's over now." Max pulled her into his arms, glancing at Carter and shrugging.

"He's right, Mom." Carter clumsily patted his mother on the back. "We're fine. We did it. We defended Abney."

They stayed there a few moments, until Bryant walked down the line and thanked everyone. "Mayor Perkins is sending a fresh group to cover this roadblock. They had been providing extra support on the east side of town and are eager to do their part." His radio beeped and he hurried off toward his cruiser.

Carter's mind reeled with the memory of gunshots, the realization that dead men lay on the far side of their blockade, and the groans of those who had been injured on both sides.

Nodding toward the other side, he asked, "Will we help them?"

"We will," Max assured him. "Once we can confirm it's not a trap. Bryant's men are sweeping east to west." He stood and helped Carter's mom to her feet.

She wiped at her face and made a valiant attempt to pull herself together. "What now?"

"We're done here." Max motioned for Carter to pick up his mom's pack.

She squared her shoulders and pasted on a trembling smile. "Then let's go home."

Sixty-Four

"This is the longest night of my life." Shelby sank into a chair at her kitchen table.

Carter was already asleep. He hadn't bothered to eat, clean up, or change out of his filthy clothes, but she didn't hassle him about it. Her watch reminded her that it was hours past midnight.

"I can't believe . . . I can't believe what we just did."

"Only what we had to," said Max.

"I guess." She squeezed the bridge of her nose, shut her eyes, and forced back the tears. Crying was not helpful. She needed to be strong, especially now, but she was so tired.

"I'm a little afraid that if I sleep I'll see them."

"Maybe you should eat something."

She nodded and foraged around in the cabinets, coming away with two warm sodas and a can of peanuts.

"Don't you need to save these for Carter?"

"We all have to eat." She popped the top on her soda and asked, "Doesn't not eating bring on your migraines?"

Max shook his head and scooped up a handful of peanuts.

"No, it doesn't? Or no, you don't want to talk about it?"

"It's like insomnia—if you don't say the word, it might not happen to you."

"So if we don't say *migraine*—"

Max reached forward and placed two fingers on her lips, but Shelby batted his hand away.

"I saw you rubbing at your temples out there."

"I did not."

"You were standing next to me. Even in the darkness I could tell how tense your shoulders were."

They fell silent as they munched on the peanuts and drank the warm soda. Shelby wasn't sure she could keep any of it down, not as her mind combed over the events of the last twelve hours.

She stood, walked to a cabinet, reached in the back, and pulled out a metal tin. Setting the container on the table, she removed the lid and pushed it toward Max.

He peered inside, his eyebrows rising in surprise. "Shelby, I've never seen a candy bar in your house."

"That's because I hide them."

"You hide them?"

"I don't want to tempt Carter, but . . ."

"But what?" Now Max was grinning, even as he pawed through her secret stash.

"But a woman needs chocolate occasionally. I don't have diabetes. You can't expect me to give up sweets for a lifetime. Well, I would, you know, if that would help him."

Max pulled a chocolate kiss out of the tin, unwrapped it, and offered it to her. The minute the sugar and cocoa hit her taste buds, she groaned. He unwrapped a KitKat bar, broke it in half, and popped it into his mouth. Shelby chose a Snickers.

"How is Carter doing? Any major spikes or dips in his sugar levels?"

"Not that he's told me about."

"So he's adjusting to the change in his diet. And you've ensured that his future supply is safely refrigerated the majority of the time. You were smart to find a way to do that."

Shelby knew what Max was trying to do—help her see the bright side, focus on the good things, be thankful.

It wasn't working.

Her mood plummeted as she thought of the danger they'd been in, perhaps still were in. But it did nothing to dampen her appetite. She finished the candy bar and chased it with the soda. When the carbohydrates hit her system, she'd be full of energy—for about thirty minutes. After that, she would crash and enjoy the sleep of the innocent. At least it had always worked that way before.

Max grabbed her wrapper, wadded it up with his, and stuck the trash in his pocket.

So he would take care of the evidence. A man who would hide your chocolate wrappers and keep your secrets—even the silly ones—was a decent guy in Shelby's opinion.

The fatigue must be softening her attitude.

It would be better to get Max out of her house before she did something she would regret— like tell him how she truly felt, or admit her fears, or have yet another good cry on his shoulder.

She stood, faked a yawn, and waited for him to take the hint.

As he walked toward the door, he gestured toward the bins she'd arranged in front of the couch.

"Packing?"

"Not exactly." She looked toward the floor to avoid his eyes.

"Is that what you've been working on?"

"It's nothing."

"It doesn't look like nothing." He crossed his arms and frowned at her. "Why don't you tell me what you're up to?"

"Can't a girl de-clutter when she feels like it?"

"During a global crisis? I'm not buying it."

She opened the front door. "Do you think they'll attack again?"

He must have been tired, because he didn't fight her changing the subject. "Not during the daylight. Probably not at all."

Stepping out onto the front porch with him, it

surprised her to see the sun peeking over the horizon and a mockingbird lighting on her fence. Life went on.

"Why do you say that? Why wouldn't they attack again?"

"They weren't expecting an organized defense. When they drove up to our section, we aimed and took strategic shots, conserving our ammunition. We did not barrage them with a massive show of force—"

"Which we didn't actually have."

"We had enough. I think they understood that we were ready for them, and that we were not panicked. Jake's equipment was a big help."

Max reached up and brushed the mass of curls back away from her face.

"I'm a mess."

"You're beautiful."

Shelby shook her head, closed her eyes, and tried to think of something to say. "So we're safe?"

"As safe as we can be. Get some rest." He leaned forward and kissed her softly on the lips. Before she could protest, he turned and walked toward his house.

Sixty-Five

Shelby resisted the urge to slap her forehead.

Why had she let him kiss her? Getting romantically involved with Max would only complicate her life, especially now.

She walked back into her living room and stared at the three bins she'd been working on. There was a bin for what she hoped to trade with neighbors, and another for items she might be able to get cash for from a trade shop. Such trading posts had opened in the last few days. Finally there was the bin of items she would take with her to Austin.

After all, once she found the insulin that Carter needed, she didn't know if the seller would even accept cash. She would take her most valuable items with her.

She knelt on the floor in front of the third bin and fingered the box that held her wedding ring—a small diamond on a simple gold band. Setting it down, she picked up a slightly larger box. Inside it she had placed a velvet bag, which held her parents' wedding rings. Her mother's engagement ring—a single-carat diamond in the center with a small ruby inset on each side—was probably the most valuable thing she owned. Though she treasured that tenuous connection with her mom and dad, she also knew without any doubt what-soever that her parents would tell her to trade it.

They would have given up anything for their grandson. A diamond ring and two gold bands? She envisioned an old-fashioned balance scale—one used to weigh precious things. Were she to place the jewelry in her hand on one side of the scale, and her parents' love for Carter on the other, there would be no contest. From the day her son was born, their love had been both deep and wide, as it had been for her.

Thinking of them caused a heavy sorrow to stir deep in her chest, and she paused to rub her hand against her breastbone. Her parents had passed more than ten years ago in an auto accident that had killed them both instantly. She had no doubt she would be reunited with them one day. She'd long ago memorized the passage in Revelation that promised no more death or mourning or crying or pain. The future was certain. It was the present that sometimes gave her trouble. Just when she thought she'd learned to live with the loss of her parents, moments like this brought home how much she missed them.

"What would you think of Abney now?" She whispered the question, but expected no answer. Her parents had been plain, hard-working, faithful people. They would tell her to soldier on and keep the faith. They would tell her she was doing the right thing.

The last item in the bin was a nearly full gallon-sized Ziploc bag. More than any of the other items, she thought it might bring bartering power. She fingered the prescription bottles and peered down at the labels.

Tramadol from a minor day surgery the year before. She'd taken two, but hated the way it made her feel—the bottle was nearly full.

Ibuprofen, 600 milligrams. Her doctor had prescribed it when she'd developed tennis elbow from typing too much. Once she'd made her writing deadline, she hadn't needed the antiinflammatory drug. At least half of the pills remained.

Hydrocodone from when she'd had a gall bladder attack.

Tylenol with codeine prescribed for Carter the summer before when he'd had his wisdom teeth removed.

Celebrex from the one time she'd tried jogging and injured her knee.

The other medications didn't stand out in her memory. She couldn't remember their purpose or why they'd been prescribed—unfinished antibiotics mostly. Would she need them in the future? Maybe. But she needed them now more. Nine bottles in all. Why had she even kept them? She couldn't imagine, but they represented her biggest hope. She imagined her backpack becoming a little lighter each week as Carter used the insulin doses she'd been able to purchase.

Perhaps someone would be willing to trade one drug for another.

Was it illegal for her to do so?

She wasn't sure. It would be illegal to sell them, but she wasn't selling. She was trading, trading for something she desperately needed. Their pharmacy had officially closed the day before. The nurses and aides at Green Acres had been talking about it. Apparently there was a sign on the door stating they'd reopen when they had a delivery of medications.

Shelby sat back on her heels and studied the three bins. They represented the extent of what she could do for her son. And if they didn't work? She'd find another way. She would not give up on Carter.

She covered the bins with a blanket she kept across the back of the couch, and then she walked over and closed the curtains. No use tempting fate. As she had learned the last few hours, people were becoming increasingly desperate.

Sixty-Six

In Carter's dream, he raised his rifle as Max told him to, held the weapon steady, fired, and missed. Instead of coming to a stop, the vehicle accelerated, barreling into their barricade of trucks and running over his friends and family.

Killing those he loved.

Maiming his neighbors.

Destroying Abney like they had destroyed Croghan.

He sat straight up, reaching for the rifle, but his fingers touched only the quilt that had been on his bed for as long as he could remember. Sweat ran off his face and down his underarms, and his heart knocked against his chest like a jackhammer. He blinked once, twice, and then he sank back onto his pillow as he realized he was in his bedroom.

Morning sunlight peeked around the curtains, which he'd pulled shut. There was no breeze coming through anyway, and since they'd arrived home as the morning sky was lightening, he'd hoped to sleep until noon.

No such luck.

The watch he was wearing confirmed that it was twenty minutes after nine. He supposed three and a half hours was better than nothing.

The night before had been a nightmare. Yes, there had been a certain camaraderie—standing next to his mom, Max on her other side, men and women and other teens stretching to the right and left. But it had also been terrifying. The darkness thick around them, he worried that a rocket launcher would land in their midst before they realized it was headed their way.

He worried about hand grenades and snipers.

He worried about Kaitlyn and wondered whether she was at home with her mom.

Carter had always dreamed of the day when he could leave Abney, shake off the dust of his hometown, and walk into a future in a bigger town and a nicer place. But as he'd helped to hold the line around Abney, he had realized that *this* was his town. No matter where he travelled in the future, Abney would always be where he'd begun. He didn't want to see what he cared about destroyed by ruthless men with greed on their minds.

Kicking off his covers, he grabbed the cleanest set of clothes he could find and threw them on, not bothering to see if he'd put the shirt on right side out. He stumbled outside to the latrine. It was mercifully empty, though already the summer heat was warming the small space. Once he'd taken care of his bathroom needs, he wandered back into the house. Did they have anything left to eat? His stomach grumbled, and he vowed to devour the first thing he saw.

He needn't have worried.

His mom had set out a package of crackers and cheese—the kind she used to put in his lunch box. Long after he outgrew having his lunch packed, she'd kept eating them, saying they were full of protein and good for a quick lunch. In this case, they would be good for a quick breakfast—along with a bottle of water and some canned fruit cocktail in natural juice.

His mom had also left a note: *Wake me when you get up.*

She'd gone to bed after he had, so he took his time eating. He went to his room and separated his clothes into disgusting and less disgusting, and looked through his dresser drawers for something clean. By the time he was staring at the washer, realizing he couldn't use it, his mom had joined him.

"We'll find a way to wash them."

"Tell me I don't have to use a rock down by the river as you keep watch for bandits."

Instead of answering, she ruffled his hair and backtracked to the kitchen. When he caught up with her, she was staring mournfully at the coffeepot.

"Headache?" he asked.

"No."

"But—"

"But I could sure use a cup right now. I'd give my eyeteeth for one."

"Really? You'd let someone pull a tooth out of your head, just for a cup of coffee?"

"Maybe."

"You have a serious addiction."

"Had, Carter. I *had* a serious addiction."

By the time she'd found something to eat and changed into clean clothes, Frank was at their door.

"We need help down at the park if you two can spare the time."

"I'm supposed to be at Green Acres by noon."

"And I'm supposed to meet up with Coach Parish at the high school. We're . . . we're working on stuff." Carter didn't know how to explain their projects, and so far only the oven had actually been used. The windmill made of bicycle parts was still in the R&D phase.

"We've had a slew of refugees from Croghan."

"Refugees?" His mom motioned for Frank to come inside.

"They started showing up a couple hours after the shooting stopped."

"And we just let them in?" Carter asked. "No one thought that it might be a trick of some sort?"

"Most were women and children, hands raised and carrying little but the clothes on their backs. There were some men, but we checked them for weapons and then allowed them through the barricade."

"Where are they going to stay?" His mom sat down on the edge of the couch. She looked ready to jump into action.

"Local churches have joined together to find shelter for everyone, but they could use all the help they can get."

"I'll go to the park," Carter said.

"And I'll stop by after I'm done at Green Acres."

Thirty minutes later, Carter walked up to the makeshift processing center that had been set up at the city park. He was a little surprised to see all of the Brainiacs already working—Zane and Lila were handing out teddy bears to the small kids. Carter had no idea where so many stuffed bears had come from, but there seemed to be a lot of them. Quincy, Cooper, and Annabelle each carried a plastic bin that must have been full of snacks. They walked through the groups of people, stopping so folks could choose something from the bin. There were other kids as well, from his youth group and his high school. A few nodded hello when they saw him.

Someone had also set up a first aid area. Carter saw Dr. Bhatti using his stethoscope on an older man.

Residents of Croghan filled the park. They were homeless now, and the thought struck Carter deep in his stomach. How would it feel to have no home? No place to keep your stuff? No stuff to keep?

Carter saw Kaitlyn and her mom handing out bottles of water, and Jason was helping an old man and woman up into the back of a truck. Because he hadn't been assigned a task, Carter jogged over to him.

"Where are they going?"

"Different places. There's no single location big enough to handle all of these people."

As he and Jason walked into the shade, they both looked out at the people scattered around the park. There had to be a couple hundred, at least.

"What are we going to do with them all?"

"They have two options." Jason hopped onto a waist-high wall that bordered the creek that ran through town. Carter joined him.

"They can go to the FEMA camp."

"We have FEMA camps?"

"No, but someone sent word to the mayor that one has been set up in Hamilton."

"Why would they do that?"

"Skirmishes all over, I guess. A transport from Fort Hood is supposed to stop by this afternoon to take anyone who wants to go."

"Hamilton isn't much bigger than us."

"Smaller actually."

"So why is the FEMA camp there?"

Jason shrugged. He hollered out to Kaitlyn, who was slowly turning in a circle. When she saw them, she waved, a smile spreading across her face.

"I think she digs you, dude."

Carter didn't say anything, but his mind darted back to the kiss they'd shared the night before.

"The Drop has turned you into a babe magnet."

Carter chuckled. "One girl does not make me a babe magnet."

"Do you want more than one?"

"No. Of course not."

"A satisfied babe magnet. The Drop takes away some things, but it gives others."

Carter opened his mouth to argue with that, but he stopped when Kaitlyn walked up and offered them both a bottle of water.

"I haven't actually done anything yet," Carter said.

"That's all right. I heard about last night. Sounds like you earned a bottle of water."

She'd heard about last night?

Carter wanted to ask how she'd spent the evening—if she'd been at a barricade or huddled in her home. Instead he took the bottle of water, said thanks, and tried to ignore the way Jason was grinning at the two of them.

He sat on the wall, Jason on his right and Kaitlyn on his left, and the scene in front of him crystallized, as if he was viewing it on video. A tale about two communities locked in battle. There would be awesome music playing in the background as the camera panned out and each week's episode ended—with the required cliff-hanger, of course. It was a story straight out of Hollywood, and it was their life.

But they were together, and they were helping each other. Maybe everything was going to be all right.

The thought had barely crossed his mind when Max's truck skidded into the park. He was honking the horn as he headed straight for the first aid tent.

Carter, Jason, and Kaitlyn started running toward Max, as if there was something they could do. But Max didn't need three teenagers. He jumped out of the cab of the truck, and his next words carried across the now-silent crowd.

"I have Luis Castillo in here. He can't breathe."

Sixty-Seven

Max was afraid to move their fire chief. Luis Castillo was inside the truck, leaning against the door, his skin a sickly gray, and as far as Max could tell, he wasn't breathing.

"Give me some space," Bhatti grumbled, pushing through the crowd and climbing in the driver's side of the truck.

"Max, help me lay him down on the ground."

Two other men stepped forward. When Max opened the passenger door, they gently caught Castillo and lowered him to the ground.

"My medical bag is in the tent." Bhatti quickly tilted Castillo's head back and checked to see if his airway was clear. Confirming that it was, he formed a fist with his right hand and thumped Castillo in the middle of the chest. He checked the man's wrist for a pulse, shook his head, and performed mouth-to-mouth resuscitation.

As he moved back down to Castillo's chest, he said, "Tell me what happened."

"I was going out to the city limit—on the south side, to see if there were more folks from Croghan to pick up. Castillo wanted to ride along."

Bhatti had placed the heel of his left hand over Castillo's chest. The heel of his right hand went over his left, and he began compressions. He was pushing down harder than Max would have attempted, and the compressions were quick. It was something that Max had done with a dummy in a first aid class, but he'd never actually per-formed CPR on a person.

"And then?"

"He grabbed his left arm, couldn't catch his breath, and he started sweating."

"Classic signs." Bhatti's voice was calm, but each syllable came out in short bursts to the rhythm of his compressions so it sounded like he said "Class. Ic. Signs."

He'd been counting under his breath as Max talked. When he reached thirty, he stopped, gave Castillo two more breaths, and started com-pressions again. The doctor was already winded, though he'd only been working on Castillo a couple of minutes at the most. "How long ago?"

"Since he stopped breathing? I turned around when he grabbed his arm and grunted. He passed out as I pulled into the park. Maybe a minute before you started, two at the most."

"Do you feel comfortable taking over the compressions?"

"Yes."

"Get ready."

Max placed his hands one over the other. He was squatting on the left side of Castillo's body, while Bhatti was on the right. The doctor glanced up at him. "On three. One, two—"

As soon as Bhatti removed his hands, Max was pumping. Pain shot through his left arm, and he remembered his wound from the night before.

"Thirty compressions, after which I will give him two resuscitations. Harder and faster, my friend. Elbows straight and align your shoulders over your hands. You're doing a good job. Performing CPR is an arduous task."

Max was completely focused on Castillo now, aware that the man's life was literally in his hands. At the edge of his vision, he could see Bhatti pawing through his medical bag. He opened a bottle of baby aspirin, and set it next to the bag.

"Twenty-eight, twenty-nine, thirty."

"Stop." After he administered two breaths, he said, "Again."

Max's arms were beginning to tremble. Sweat poured down his face. As he counted, he prayed, "Please, Lord. Please, Lord. Please,

Lord." The words fell like a melody to the rhythm of his compressions.

Bhatti waited until he again reached thirty, gave Castillo two more breaths, and said, "Switch."

After resuming compressions, the doctor said, "Check for a pulse, please."

Max placed two fingertips on Castillo's wrist.

Someone had asked the crowd to step back, but Max was aware that they were watching. Hundreds of people stood by—and it was completely quiet as they all watched, as Castillo's life hung in the balance.

"Nothing."

"Try the carotid artery, side of the neck."

He studied Castillo's face as he focused on the artery, willing there to be a beat, praying that God would save this good man. "Yes! He has a pulse. It's very light, but yes."

"Good." Bhatti's face was red from the exertion.

Suddenly Castillo began to cough.

Bhatti rolled him on his side, grabbed the baby aspirin, and stuck one under Castillo's tongue. "I need you to chew this, Mr. Castillo. Can you hear me? Chew and swallow. That's very good."

When Bhatti looked up at him and smiled, perhaps the first time Max had ever seen the man smile, he knew they'd done it. They'd saved Luis Castillo's life.

Thirty minutes later, the paramedics had loaded Castillo into the ambulance.

"Want us to check your arm?" One of the men asked, nodding toward Max's left shoulder. The wound had reopened and blood once more stained his shirt.

"No, I'm good. I'll get someone here to rewrap it."

The paramedic nodded and hopped into the ambulance. A blip of the siren and they were pulling out of the park, headed toward the hospital.

"Is he going to make it?" Max asked.

"Possibly. If he rests, continues with the aspirin, and eventually gets the surgery or medication that he needs."

"And if he doesn't get the surgery or the medication?"

"That is out of our hands."

Max looked around them. Everyone had gone back to what they were doing before. Even Carter and his friends had walked away to help load refugees in a truck. There was a line of people at the first aid tent, waiting patiently on the doctor. He thought about what Shelby had said, about seeing Bhatti bury something in the backyard.

The man had a past he didn't want to talk about. Something he desperately did not want discovered. But that could probably be said of many people. What mattered, it seemed to Max, was how you dealt with the present. The past? It could be forgotten, or forgiven, or even buried. But the present was with you. It colored everything from how people interacted with you to whether you could sleep at night.

Max walked with Bhatti over to the tent. "What kind of injuries are you seeing?"

"A lot of heat exhaustion. Some cuts and bruises. Only one bullet wound so far."

Max had the distinct impression that he was about to say something comparing Abney to a third-world country. Their eyes met, though, and Bhatti only smiled and said, "Nice work today, Max. You helped to save a man's life."

"As did you."

"Feels good, doesn't it?"

"Yes. Yes, it does."

"If you pray, I suggest you get on your knees tonight and thank him for Mr. Castillo's strength, for his life which you brought back from the final journey."

It seemed a strange thing for the doctor to say. It occurred to Max that he hadn't really spoken to Dr. Bhatti about matters of faith. They'd been completely caught up with the necessities of this life—food and water and shelter and medicine.

But without faith, those other things were meaningless. Bhatti seemed to realize that, and in Max's mind, that raised the doctor even higher in his esteem.

"And now you should have your arm rewrapped."

He did as the doctor suggested. When the first aid worker was done, Max thanked her, waved at Carter, and climbed back into his truck to drive out to the checkpoint one last time.

Sixty-Eight

That evening, Shelby walked back from the Market empty-handed.

Carter had heard they'd found one of the trucks. It was supposed to arrive with extra supplies, and she'd wanted to be one of the first in line. She'd told herself she might actually be first because no one else knew about it yet. Carter only knew because Henry Graves had managed to get word to him, telling him to be at work at six p.m. But when they'd arrived, Henry had curtly informed them that no supplies were coming.

"What happened?" Shelby asked.

"I don't know what happened," he snapped. Running a hand over his face, he repeated, "I don't know."

He had swiftly turned back into the building and locked the door.

"Is he living there?" she asked her son.

"Looks like it."

"Huh."

"Yeah. He's never been a good boss, but since

the Drop—" He paused when Shelby glanced at him, her eyebrows raised. "The flare, I mean. Since that night, his attitude has changed from bad to terrible. And did you notice how awful he smells?"

"We need to tell somebody. Maybe Max can speak with him."

Carter hesitated a moment before he asked, "When is Max leaving for the ranch?"

"Day after tomorrow."

"Saturday?"

"Yeah."

"It's going to seem strange—not seeing him next door."

"We'll be okay, though."

"I know we will, but . . . well, it's none of my business, but it seems to me that he likes you."

"He likes me?"

"Don't tell me you haven't noticed."

Shelby willed her face not to blush. "Max and I have known each other—"

"Yeah. I know, but he does like you, Mom, *more* than like. You know what I mean, and he asked us to go with him."

They'd nearly reached Main Street. Shelby automatically stopped at the light, and then she realized there was no reason to—no cars were on the street. Everyone was saving their fuel for an emergency. "Is that what you want, Carter? To go with him?"

"I don't know. I wouldn't want to leave my friends."

"Or Kaitlyn, who I would like to meet sometime."

Carter grinned and resumed walking. "I guess we'll be fine staying in Abney."

"Of course we will be."

Their conversation was interrupted by a continuous, low rumble. Peering down the street, Shelby saw a military jeep pulling onto Main, followed by another and another after that. A long line of transports, medical aid vehicles, fuel supply trucks, and even a few tanks.

They stood there watching, mouths gaping, as others joined them.

"Maybe they're here to help," someone said.

"Nah. They're not even going to stop."

After that, no one said anything. They all stood there, a small group of Abney citizens, watching the long line of military vehicles roll past. Did it mean the federal government was once again in control? Did it mean help had arrived? Was there at least a plan for dealing with the effects of the flare?

As far as Shelby could tell, it didn't mean any of those things. The vehicles trundled out of sight. No doubt, the commander had told Perkins to open up the roadblocks to allow for their passage. And why wouldn't she? Who was going to stand up to a tank?

When the street was again empty, they resumed walking toward home. They were still a few blocks away, when Carter peeled off to the left. "Going to see Kaitlyn," he explained.

As Shelby continued toward home, she thought of Carter and Kaitlyn and groceries and Max. When she glanced up, she saw a man crouched in front of the front door at the corner house.

"Mr. Smitty?"

He looked her way and raised a hand in greeting.

Shelby hurried over to where he was working. "What are you doing here?"

He wiped a hand across his brow. "Didn't I tell you? I'm a master locksmith."

"You are?"

Had it been only a week ago that they had picked this man up off the side of the road? Now he and his wife were living in Abney, and he was working on locks. She thought her life had changed dramatically since the flare, but in that moment she realized that other people had endured more—had endured worse.

"I was. I retired a few years ago."

"But you're back on the job now?"

"I am. Fortunately, the hardware store still has a good supply of dead bolts, and since Mrs. Franklin here was robbed, she thought—"

"Robbed?" The word came out louder than she'd intended. She forced her voice lower and said, "When was she robbed? What did they take? Is she okay?"

He took off the baseball cap he was wearing, swiped at the perspiration beading on his forehead, and resettled the cap. "She's fine, wasn't even home when it happened. But she came back around noon, found the lock jimmied and her best silver gone."

"Silver?"

"I suppose it's good for trading."

"So she wants a dead bolt."

"She does. Because she already had a garden planted before this thing happened, she's willing to trade me a bag of tomatoes, squash, and green beans to install the lock. Joyce will be real happy with that. She makes the best vegetable stew—"

"Wait. I thought you were staying at the church?"

"We were. The pastor found us a place to stay with Maxine Welch. Do you know her?"

"I do."

"Nice lady. Widow. She had that big old house and was afraid to stay alone. She and Joyce are getting on nicely. Eases my mind, since I'm busy installing new locks for the folks who have been robbed."

"There's more than one?" Shelby reached a hand out to the porch railing.

"I'd say half a dozen in the last day or so."

"And you think locks will stop them?"

"I don't know about that. In my experience, if folks want in badly enough, they'll just break a window. Although, if they see a good sturdy lock, they might pass on to an easier target."

"How is this happening? The roads are blocked. Strangers can't even get into Abney."

"Which means it's not strangers." His expression softened, and he said, "I wouldn't worry. You live next door to Max. No one is going to mess with you."

Except that Max was leaving, and then she'd be alone with Carter.

What if someone had already broken into her house?

What if the three bins were gone?

She said goodbye and practically jogged home. She unlocked the door—a flimsy door handle lock, not a dead bolt like Dale Smitty had been installing for Mrs. Franklin. One look at her living room and she nearly melted in relief. The three bins were right where she had left them.

She stacked them near the front door and hurried to the storage room. Somewhere in there she had a collapsible two-wheel dolly cart. The thing was old and flimsy, but it might just work. Hurrying back to the living room, she fought the panic clawing at her throat. She had to hide the bins, put them somewhere no one would look.

She readjusted the backpack straps. It seemed she only took the thing off to eat. But she couldn't carry three bins' worth of goods on her back. Instead, she unfolded the dolly and stacked the bins on it, one on top of the other. She opened the front door and backed slowly out. When she reached forward to lock and shut the door, the dolly and the bins teetered.

Suddenly Max was beside her, steadying the load and looking down on her with something akin to pity.

"What are you doing?"

"I have to . . . have to take these somewhere."

"Why?"

"Because there are thieves, Max! Here in Abney." She glanced around him as if a cat burglar might be lurking in the bushes.

"Slow down." He placed one hand on each of her shoulders.

"I don't have time—"

"Just take a deep breath, Shelby. One more. Good. Now, tell me why you're doing this."

So she told him about Dale Smitty and Mrs. Franklin and the recent string of robberies.

"I heard something about that at City Hall today."

"You're leaving! It doesn't matter to you."

"Of course it matters." The change in his tone was like a slap in her face.

"I'm sorry. I didn't mean—"

"Yes, you did. But that's okay." Max pulled her over to the front porch rockers, dropped his cowboy hat on the table, and insisted she sit. "You're worried about whatever is in those bins. You're worried because—"

"Most of the day no one is here. And all we have is that flimsy lock!"

"Do you want a dead bolt? We might be able to trade—"

"No! I need anything I can trade."

"All right." They were both silent for a moment, studying the stack of bins. Finally, Max slapped the arm of his rocker and said, "What you need is to leave these with someone who is home all day. Right? These burglars, these cowardly thieves, they're hitting empty homes."

"I guess—"

"So who do we know that is home all the time?"

Shelby's panic had finally receded. Her head had begun to clear, and she knew in that moment who Max meant.

"Do you think she'll take them?"

"Of course. Has Bianca ever told you no?"

"And she's home all day—"

"To sit with her father." He stood, grabbed his cowboy hat off the table, and grinned. "Come on. I'll carry one, and you should be able to pull two on that contraption."

"It's a two-wheel dolly."

"Uh-huh."

"I paid a lot of money for it. Because it's collapsible."

He didn't respond to that, but he helped her stack two of the crates and fasten a bungee cord around them. He picked up the entire thing and carried it down the stairs, and then he went back for the third bin.

"Ready?"

"Yes."

She should have thought of Bianca herself. It was the perfect solution. She and Max walked side by side down the sidewalk, shadows lengthening in front of them.

"Max."

"Uh-huh?"

"Thank you."

He stopped, stared at her for a minute, and Shelby thought of what Carter had said. *He does like you*—more *than like.*

Max grinned as if he could read her thoughts. As they walked down the streets of Abney toward her best friend's house, he began to whistle.

Sixty-Nine

Shelby wasn't surprised when she stepped out the front door of Green Acres and saw Max standing outside waiting for her. It was a straight shot home—five blocks west on Fourth Street, followed by a left turn onto Kaufman. Several hours of daylight remained. She appreciated his concern, but she thought he was being a tad paranoid.

"You don't have to walk me home."

"So you want to deny me one of the few pleasures left in my life?"

"Pleasures, huh?"

"Video games—gone."

"You were terrible at video games."

"Television—a distant memory."

"You only watched sports."

"Pizza."

She shook her head in mock despair. "Why did you bring that up? Do you know what I'd give for a piece of stuffed pepperoni at this moment?"

"Which brings me back to the few remaining pleasures in my life."

"Oh good grief."

"Seeing your smiling face and the way your hair . . ." He cocked his head and walked around her slowly. "How does your hair do that?" he asked, coming to stop in front of her again. He reached out to touch it. "It's like a halo, like a wreath growing around your head. It's like—"

"That's quite enough." Shelby slapped his hand away, hitched the backpack up higher on her shoulders, and started down the sidewalk. "If we're going to talk about my hair, I'd rather we just walk in silence."

"I don't remember you ever being silent."

Instead of defending herself, Shelby changed the subject. "What has put you in such a fine mood today?"

"Am I?"

"You certainly seem to be."

They walked to the end of the parking area and turned right onto Fourth Street. Her watch said six thirty, and the homes they passed reflected that. Children played in front yards, from those barely toddling up through teenagers. Two middle school boys lay on the grass, a chessboard positioned between them. A teenage girl fed a bottle to an infant as she sat in a rocker on the front porch. In other yards, moms were setting dinner out on picnic tables or blankets. It was simply too hot to eat inside the house.

It all looked so picturesque, so 1950s American. A time traveler from the past might think it was the perfect life. Shelby could almost blot out recent memories and believe it herself.

If she hadn't lived in Abney the last week . . .

If she didn't know the people who had died . . .

If she hadn't fought fires or manned a barricade . . .

But she had, and Shelby understood it wasn't the perfect domestic scene she was walking past. It was just people, trying their best to get by. How would they survive July? And what of August when most days topped one hundred degrees? How many of her patients—and they were her patients now, though she was only a lowly orderly—were not physically strong enough to withstand the heat?

Max interrupted her morose thoughts with a bump of his shoulder against hers.

"Bhatti delivered a baby today."

"A baby?"

"One of the families staying at the hotel, the wife was pregnant with her first."

"I remember seeing them at the town meeting. Alejandro and Maria—"

"Mendoza. Alejandro and Maria Mendoza, and now there is an Eleanor Mendoza, named after Alejandro's mom. They're going to call her Ellie."

"She's . . . she's all right?"

"She's fine, Nurse Sparks. Has all her fingers and toes, and Farhan says she scored on the top of the Apgar scale."

"That is good news."

"Pastor Tony is trying to find them a home."

"There are at least twenty empty homes in this town."

"And more than twenty families who need them."

"Why don't we just move people in? If the homeowners return we can always move them back out."

"First of all, it's against the law."

"Those laws don't make sense anymore."

"I understand what you're saying, Shelby, but our laws are in place for a reason. We can't just operate in opposition to them because our feelings have changed."

"More has changed than our feelings, Max, and you know it. The truth is, your legalistic brain hasn't gibed with the new world we live in now."

"I won't deny that."

"Your house would be perfect for the Mendoza family. If you're . . . if you're still going."

"I'll leave at first light." Max hesitated.

Shelby knew that he was about to ask her again. He wanted her and Carter with him at High Fields because he wanted to protect them—but he didn't understand that she had to put Carter's needs first. Their future lay in the opposite direction. She hadn't shared that with Max, didn't dare bring it up. He would try to talk her out of it, and he would present reasonable points against her plan. She could always count on Max to be reasonable and persuasive.

He shrugged and bypassed their usual argument. "I would be happy to loan my house to the Mendozas, but Farhan is living there at the moment."

"One man versus a family."

"You still don't trust him?"

"No, I don't."

"He's done everything we've asked," Max reminded her. "We need him—Abney needs him. I'd hate for him to catch a ride on the next vehicle that's headed out of town."

"There are fewer and fewer of those."

Shelby was surprised to see they were nearly home. A vigorous argument with Max could do that to her—make time stand still and help her to forget how much her legs ached. Working as an orderly was certainly more physically demanding than hammering out ten to twenty pages of a romance novel on her computer.

As they turned the corner onto Kaufman, she saw Carter straddling his bike in the driveway of their house. He was talking to a pretty young woman wearing a Market T-shirt.

Shelby reached out and pulled Max to a stop. There was something about watching the scene unfold in front of them—something so natural and good and ordinary—that calmed her soul.

The girl laughed at whatever Carter said.

"Kaitlyn?" Shelby asked Max.

"I believe it is."

"I still haven't had the chance to meet her."

Carter saw them. He waved, and Kaitlyn looked up and smiled, pulling her straight blond hair back and away from her face. In that moment the two teenagers reminded her so much of herself and Max that regret resonated all the way to her bones.

She mourned the past that was between them

and all that might have been. She mourned the future and the things this new generation would never experience—a normal passage to adulthood, dating, college.

And underneath both of those thoughts was the pulse of her pain—the knowledge that Max was leaving.

Carter must have said goodbye. With a wave, he turned his bike toward them at the end of the street. Kaitlyn watched him for a few seconds, and then she crossed the street, picked up a bicycle, and turned away in the opposite direction, toward the south.

In the next breath, an explosion erupted from the house in front of Kaitlyn.

Shelby instinctively shielded her eyes against the blast. Fear swelled inside her, overwhelmed her, and then she was falling. The last thing she saw was the structure engulfed in flames, and the houses on either side collapsing, like dominoes falling one upon another.

Seventy

Max threw Shelby to the ground and covered her with his body, the backpack she always wore between them. From the corner of his eye, he saw Carter catapult off his bike, tumble toward them, and land in a heap in the middle of the street.

There might have been screams. There must have been. He could only hear ringing in his ears.

Shelby fought him wildly—her arms and legs pushing against him. He couldn't hear her cries as much as he felt them, deep inside his heart. When he was sure the explosions had ceased, he raised up, afraid he was crushing her.

"Are you okay?" he shouted.

But she wasn't listening. She was on her feet, running toward Carter, who now sat in the middle of the road, a dazed look on his face. Blood trickled from a cut above his eye. His legs were splayed out in front of him, and he swiveled his head left and right, as if he could make sense of the scene in front of him.

Someone ran up to Max, grabbing him by the shoulders and asking questions that he couldn't hear over the ringing in his ears.

"Gas line exploded!" Max shouted, though to himself it sounded as if his voice came from some distant cave. He began to jog toward the house that had collapsed when Carter jumped p, stumbled, pushed his mother away, and ran down the street.

When Carter dropped to the ground, Max understood and raced toward him. Shelby was only steps behind.

Kaitlyn lay on the sidewalk, broken and lifeless.

Carter had drawn the girl into his arms, tears streaming down his face.

Suddenly Max's ears popped, and he could easily make out Carter saying, "No, Kaitlyn, please. Please wake up. Please, Kaitlyn."

"Honey, she's gone." Shelby knelt beside him.

"I have to wake her up. Kaitlyn, wake up." Carter pushed her hair away from her face, cradled her head in the crook of his arm. He touched her cheeks and lips, and then ran his fingers down her arm.

Max checked for a pulse, though he already knew what he'd find. Her neck had been positioned at an unnatural angle, and her eyes stared up at the sky—unseeing, unknowing.

An explosion large enough to level three houses would have killed her instantaneously. "I'm sorry, Carter. I'm—"

"Don't say that! Do not say you're sorry. Do not say . . ." He dissolved in a river of tears, hovering over the girl, holding her hand, touching her face.

"Stay with him," Max said to Shelby. "I need to check for survivors before the fire spreads." He stood and canvassed the area, trying to figure out who and where he could help. The house that had exploded was completely engulfed in flames. The houses on either side had fallen flat and were heaps of rubble. Even across the street, houses had been damaged—including Shelby's and his own.

Max turned toward the house behind him,

which looked as if a giant hand had flattened it. There could be survivors under the rubble. They would need to get them out before the fire engulfed it as well. He wasn't worried about additional explosions because whatever had caused the rupture in the gas line had released all of the built-up pressure.

He ran toward the house, called out, stopped to listen, and then he moved a few feet and called out again. When no one responded, he went to the house on the south side of it. The northern wall had been pushed over, but the southern portion of the structure was still standing. Some part of his mind realized that people were streaming in from all directions. The crackle of the fire, smell of smoke, and shouts of dismay all seemed to come from a great distance, but this time it wasn't because of his hearing. His arms began to tremble, and it occurred to Max that he was probably in shock, his body and mind trying to catch up with the horrific event.

He needed to push forward, to look under the debris, to call out for survivors. Stumbling, he made his way around to the back of the house.

"Hello? Is anyone in there? Holler if you can hear me."

A trampoline sat in the corner of the lot, and the tire swing hanging from the live oak tree proclaimed that all was well. But it wasn't all well. The gas lines had ruptured, but why? Was it a result of the solar flare? Would they see the aurora again when the sky grew dark? He glanced up, saw only a deep blue sky.

He called again and again, stopping every few feet, looking for any sign of survivors. Was theirs the only neighborhood with damage? How many were injured? How many killed? Glancing toward the next house, he heard screams from the backyard. A woman was frantically clawing through the debris.

She looked up, saw Max, and screamed, "I can hear her. I hear my daughter!"

Max darted back out to the street. "We need help over here!"

He didn't stay to see if anyone heard him, or if they would come. There wasn't time.

When he reached the back of the house, the woman was still hysterically pulling at the wreckage. Smoke pushed toward them as the initial fire spread. People with blankets and buckets stood between this house and the one closer to the explosion, trying to create a firebreak.

Max realized he knew the woman. Of course he knew her—she was his neighbor. The family had been living there when he moved home seven years ago. Agnes Wright and her daughter Courtney. Mr. Wright had moved away five years ago.

Her home had fallen like a house of cards.

Bricks, wood, and other debris littered the yard. A lawn chair sat inexplicably on top of her roof, high atop the pile of rubble.

He reached for a board that Agnes was attempting to yank out and saw that her hands were bleeding. He wanted to tell her to stop, to let them handle it. Now there were a half-dozen men behind him accepting the boards, helping with the heavier pieces.

The air was filled with cries from the injured, the scream of an EMS vehicle, someone calling for a doctor. Max closed his eyes, shut out everything else, and listened.

He thought he heard—

"Everyone quiet." He moved closer and stepped on a dresser that shifted, nearly causing him to lose his balance. If they moved the wrong board, if they put weight on something with an air pocket under it, they might bury Courtney more deeply under the pile of debris. They might kill her.

The scene took on an otherworldly quality. A mockingbird sang. A dog barked. A slight breeze stirred the leaves of a tree—and then he heard it. A faint cry to the right.

Agnes leaned over as if in pain, crying over and over again, "Please, Jesus. Help us to save her. Please, help us."

"How old is your daughter, Agnes?"

When she looked up, her face had blanched

whiter than snow in winter. Max worried that she might be about to collapse, that the shock or the fear might be too much.

"She's fourteen. Courtney is fourteen."

"We're going to get her. Okay?" Max looked behind him and surveyed the group that had assembled. He turned back in the direction of the small cry he'd heard. "Courtney, we're going to get you out."

The group gathered around Max grew silent, and his throat was suddenly dry. He coughed once and tried again.

"Courtney, we need you to stay very still so nothing moves. When I call your name, just answer *here* so we'll know we're getting close."

There was no answer. Praying that God would save this one, that he would shower mercy on this young girl, Max said, "Courtney?"

"Here." The voice was small, weak even, and no doubt terribly frightened.

The men behind him began slapping one another on the back.

"Let's get her out."

"We can do this."

"Hang in there, Courtney."

Max knew there were others who needed their help, that they were working under a ticking clock. He was nearly overwhelmed when he allowed his mind to picture the block of homes now destroyed. How many people were buried alive? How many could they save?

One person at a time. That's how the world is changed, son.

His father's voice in his ear, clear and calm and steady.

"Ma'am, if you could move back and let . . . let Coach Parish stand up here with me." He hadn't realized who the man was until that moment. Parish nodded and took the mother's place.

"I just heard her, approximately two feet ahead. There must be a pocket. We're going to have to do this carefully."

"Like pickup sticks," Parish said. "Or Jenga."

"Exactly like Jenga." Very carefully, Max reached for the first board.

Seventy-One

Shelby tried to calm her son. Even as her heart broke over Kaitlyn and for her mother, for those with no home, for those still buried beneath the debris . . . as the sheer hopelessness of it all threatened to overwhelm her, she sought to comfort her son.

She tried to move him away to a safe distance, but he wouldn't leave Kaitlyn. He simply shook his head, held the girl whose life had been struck short, and wept.

Minutes passed as people from surrounding streets flocked in to help. Finally emergency workers arrived to begin triage, but few had yet been recovered from the affected homes. One of the paramedics walked up, crouched beside them, and said, "We should take her now, while we can."

Carter ignored them, or perhaps he couldn't hear them through his pain.

"You have to let her go now, son. Just . . . let her go."

Shelby didn't know how she could persuade him, how to reach him in the depth of his sorrow.

Patrick and Bianca appeared by her side.

"We'll follow them, Carter." Patrick gently pulled the boy to his feet and nodded for the emergency workers to load Kaitlyn onto the stretcher. "If you want to go with her, I'll take you."

Carter wiped a blood-covered hand across his face and nodded, though he was still watching Kaitlyn. When they covered her with a sheet, he literally fell into Shelby's arms, shaking and weeping.

Bianca rubbed his back, as Shelby had when he was an infant. Patrick placed his arms around them all, providing a protective barrier to this most intimate of families. They had shared birth and life and catastrophic changes together. They would accompany one another through this valley too. Shelby realized in that moment that it was only death. Yes, only. She understood, maybe for the first time, that it was a thin veil indeed that separated them from those who had gone ahead.

As sirens blared, people cried, and the assistant fire chief barked orders, Shelby felt, inexplicably, as if she was standing on holy ground.

The ambulance blipped its siren once. Shelby glanced up and noticed that one other corpse had been loaded into the bay. The EMS worker slammed the doors shut and climbed into the front next to the driver. Another ambulance remained to treat the injured.

Carter stared at the ambulance as it moved away with lights pulsing. There was no need to rush, no need to blare the siren while carrying the dead.

"I need to go with them. I need to . . . to be there when her mom comes."

"I'll go with you," Bianca said.

"We both will." Shelby had an almost irresistible urge to check the vials of insulin in her backpack. Had they burst? Had Max crushed them? What would they do if—

"Shelby, you need to stay here." Patrick nodded toward her damaged house, and Shelby saw that they hadn't escaped unscathed. Her legs began to shake, and she wondered if she had the strength to face what lay ahead.

As if he could read her mind, Patrick said, "We'll help you."

She looked at her son. Gratitude overwhelmed her that he was alive, that he hadn't been taken in this tragic accident, and immediately she felt ashamed for thinking such a thing. It was selfish. It was the cry of her heart, but what of Kaitlyn's mom? She would be devastated. It was all so unfair. She thought again of her earlier revelation —holy ground, divided by a thin veil.

"He needs . . ." She wiped at the tears streaming down her face. "He needs his eye looked at."

Carter reached up, wiped at the cut, and then he stared at the blood on his fingers.

"I'm okay."

"You'll need stitches, at least," said Shelby.

"I'll take him by the clinic," Bianca said. "Everyone here is going to have their hands full."

"Here, take my car." Patrick fished the Mustang's keys out of his pocket.

Carter looked at Shelby once before turning toward Bianca. The grief and confusion etched so vividly on his face tore at her heart as he walked away, Bianca's arm around his shoulders.

As soon as they were out of sight, she dropped the backpack on the ground and unzipped it. Pulling out the old blanket, she unwrapped the top box of insulin, opened it, and confirmed that they were unbroken.

"We're good?" Patrick asked.

She nodded and repacked the supplies. "Where do we start? With the rescue?"

"It looks to me like they have plenty of people doing that. We need to get to your house and see what can be salvaged."

"Why?"

But she knew why. Already people were trolling through the debris, pulling out what was useful, scurrying away.

"This is going to be a difficult site to contain, at least for the first few hours. If there's anything left in your house that you want, I suggest we get it now."

"All right, but I'll do it alone." When Patrick began to argue, she pushed on. "That's my one condition—that you go and check with the firemen before helping me. See if they need you to help look for people or fight the fire."

The blaze had diminished considerably, but did that mean they were safe? She'd felt safe walking home from work with Max an hour ago, and now her life was in shambles.

Patrick didn't look happy with her condition, but he nodded once, curtly, and strode in the opposite direction.

Shelby hurried over to the wreckage of her home.

Glass crunched beneath her feet as she made her way up the porch stairs. The windows had been blown out. There was no need to put her key in the lock. The front door had been thrown across the living room. And the inside of her house? It looked as if a tornado had passed through. The couch had been hurled against the opposite wall. Most of the pictures were gone, scattered, broken.

She remembered the bins that she had taken to Bianca's only the day before. They were safe. Was that a miracle? She didn't know. She felt numb as she walked into her office, and a cold acceptance crept over her. Resolve stiffened her spine, and she promised herself that she would not shed tears for this. Not while people were dying just past her doorstep.

The books that once lined her bookshelf were scattered around the room. The computer she hadn't been able to use since the solar flare lay on the floor. How much of her life had she spent in this room, spinning stories, living through her characters? She'd suspected that her old life was over—done and gone. She'd even mentally accepted it when she first saw the aurora, and again when the fire swept through the north side of the square. The first day she'd gone to work at Green Acres, she'd resolutely told herself that no one needed an author now. What they needed was a clean bedpan, fresh linens, a healthy meal. Her priorities had shifted and adjusted and readjusted to fit this thing they were living through.

And now, looking at her office, at the destruction of their home, her heart recognized that her previous life was over.

She was fortunate to be alive, to still have her son, to know a few people she could truly call friends. No family? That might be true, but God had provided others. He had provided.

As she moved through their rooms, making piles of clothes, pictures, even food, she heard a soft rain begin to tap against the roof.

"Thank you, God." The words slipped from her lips.

The rain would put out the fire. It would save what homes remained on their block. Never mind that it would also soak any items thrown out of the house. They were only possessions—only things.

As for her and Carter? They were now homeless. They'd joined the ranks of the people passing through Abney, the ones who hadn't been able to find a way back to their towns. They were no different from the men and women who had lost their apartments in the downtown fire. Their lives had taken on the same uncertainty as the Mendozas' and Dr. Bhatti's had.

Patrick returned and helped her pack items into pillowcases and laundry baskets. They covered everything with trash sacks and lugged it all to the curb where they waited for Bianca and Carter to return. Max had stopped by to tell them he was going to help in another neighborhood—another area where there had been a gas explosion.

The rain had stopped, but the street still

glistened in the last of the day's light. Not even dark yet. How had so much happened in so little time?

As they waited, several of her neighbors walked by—stopped and asked if there was anything they could do, anything that she needed.

Each time, Shelby thanked them and said she was fine.

She wasn't fine, but maybe she would be—eventually.

Until that day she would lean on the kindness of others.

Would they forget these days? In five years or twenty when life had taken on some sense of normalcy, would they push these memories from their minds? Or would they tell their children and grandchildren of the days of tragedy and how the town came together to help the injured and homeless and grieving?

"I need to go back inside," she said.

"I'll wait here with your things."

She walked back into her house, through the living room, and into her study. The plastic tubs that held her supplies had been thrown from the shelves, and some were burst open. Still it wasn't difficult to find the one she wanted. Opening it she pulled out first one tablet, and then another.

She might want to write—something. Not the romance stories of before, but maybe a chronicle of what was happening and how they were enduring. Possibly she could write an account not only of their sufferings but of their hope.

When would there be more paper? And what of pens? Were the pen factories still open? She doubted it.

Shelby dumped everything out of her promotional tub—bookmarks and postcards and key chains and business cards. She found a dust rag pinned underneath her printer, pulled it out, and used it to make sure the tub was completely dry. She put the tablets, all of them, inside. Then she searched for the boxes of pens and placed them with the tablets.

She walked out of the room. Slung across her shoulders she carried the backpack with Carter's insulin. Clutched to her heart was the bin of writing supplies.

Shelby didn't look back. She felt no need to study the house that she'd grown up in, the home where she'd raised her son. That was her past. The future, though it seemed heavy and dark, was in front of her.

She would face that direction instead.

Seventy-Two

Carter hated the way his mother stared at him, watched him, and checked on him constantly. He was fine. He had lived through the events of the last three days with only four stitches above his right eye to prove he'd even been on Kaufman Street the moment of the explosion.

Three days ago.

His world had tipped, turned, and changed completely.

"We struggle to understand." Pastor Tony stood in front of the place where Kaitlyn would be buried. He wore a white shirt, tie, and dress pants even though the heat threatened to consume them. Sweat streamed down his face, but he didn't notice. He seemed transported from their presence—his hands on the Bible, his gaze fixed on something Carter couldn't see, something in another place and time.

It was June in Texas, and after the brief rain the night of the explosion, the temperatures had soared to the high nineties. People were literally stroking out from the heat. He'd heard his mom tell Max that two more folks had died at Green Acres. They were succumbing to the harshness of this new life one by one.

That, and the line of open graves that extended to the left of the pastor presented a scene more horrific than anything that Carter had ever seen in a video game or on television. Life was turning out to be harsher than he had ever imagined.

"We weep and mourn, as we should. The Bible tells us to rejoice with those who rejoice; mourn with those who mourn."

Kaitlyn's mother began to cry.

Carter wanted to look away, to be anywhere but standing beside an open grave. He wanted to clap his hands over his ears and block out Pastor Tony's words.

"We do." Tony's voice cracked. "We mourn with you, for Kaitlyn, Mrs. Lowry."

Their pastor looked down the road, which ran the length of the cemetery. "For each of these, we mourn, and we will remember. We will remember their lives, their smiles, the way they touched our hearts. We will remember Christ's victory over the grave, God's promise of a circle unbroken, and the Holy Spirit's assurance that we will one day see him face-to-face and know—fully know."

They sang "Amazing Grace," the words coming to Carter even when he'd rather have forgotten them. His mother stood on his right, singing softly. Max, Bianca, and Patrick were on his left. His friend Jason was even there.

Each person in attendance had other things they needed to be doing—jobs, emergency preparations, endless meetings. Everyone had some-where else to be, except Carter. They stood with him, waited patiently, endured the heat, and joined the singing. A part of him realized that this was his family.

Another part felt as if he were watching the entire proceeding from a distance, as if this could not be his life.

The song mercifully ended, and Pastor Tony crouched in front of Kaitlyn's mother. Carter couldn't tell if he was talking to her or praying with her. Finally he stood and addressed the small group.

"In the second book of Kings we're told to pray for the remnant that survives." He turned a few pages in his Bible, searching, and then he looked up, concern etched across his face. "In Jeremiah 42:2, we read these words: 'Pray to the LORD your God for this entire remnant. For as you now see, though we were once many, now only a few are left.'"

He pulled a handkerchief from his pocket and mopped his face.

"Now only a few are left," he repeated. "Are we the remnant of Christ? I can't answer that, but I can assure each person here that you remain— even during your agony and despair—under the provision and care of your heavenly Father."

They prayed again, and Kaitlyn's body was lowered into the grave. At least she was buried in a proper casket. A total of eighteen people had been killed during the blast, and the local funeral parlor had run out of coffins. Carter's mom had explained all of this to him the night before. He hadn't wanted to hear, didn't think he needed to know, but she had insisted.

And now he was glad she had. Otherwise he wouldn't have been prepared for the line of graves, for the groups of mourners, for the pastors who made their way from one service to another, pausing in between only long enough to drink some water.

The service ended, and each person took their turn approaching Kaitlyn's mother. Carter followed the line toward her, determined that he wouldn't cry. He'd wept enough in the last three days to last a lifetime. He'd wept himself dry, or so he thought.

Kaitlyn's mother reached for his hand, pulled him into her arms, and whispered, "Thank you, Carter. Thank you for caring about my Kaitlyn . . . for being there with her when I wasn't."

He nodded, uncertain what to say.

Somehow it had weighed on his heart that she would blame him, that in fact it was his fault Kaitlyn was killed. If she hadn't been visiting him, she wouldn't have been near the blast.

He'd said as much to Patrick.

"I can assure you that she won't blame you," said Patrick.

"I had just talked to Kaitlyn, before . . ."

"Hey, look at me." Patrick had moved directly in front of him, waited until Carter met his gaze. "I spoke with her mother. She was delivering meals, Carter. She'd started volunteering earlier in the week. Kaitlyn was doing what her heart told her was important. She died doing it—and that's not a bad way to end this life and begin the next."

Coming from his mom or Max, Carter would have argued. But Patrick was different. Patrick had seen death up close, had even killed people while he was deployed overseas. He'd once said, "It's important to protect our country. If I'd died doing it—that's not a bad way to end this life and begin the next."

When he repeated those words standing next to Kaitlyn's grave, Carter knew that they came from deep within the man's heart. He understood that Patrick was not merely offering empty words of comfort. He was sharing his view of life—and death.

"Let's go," Shelby murmured.

The cemetery was only a mile from their neighborhood. It seemed everything in Abney was only a mile apart. But their way out led past the other grave sites.

In his mind he could hear the hammering of nails as volunteers crafted additional caskets from the lumber at the hardware store. He hadn't been there, of course. He'd barely left Bianca's house since the explosion, choosing to lie in bed huddled under the covers. There had been some argument about the caskets—he'd heard Max speaking to his mom and Bianca when they thought he was asleep. Some said the lumber should be saved, that it would be needed for other things.

Grief won, and the caskets were built.

Patrick had said about half of the lumber remained, but already the city council was making plans in case of another accident. He'd heard the words *grave diggers* and *shrouds,* and then he'd turned to the wall and refused to listen.

But try as he might, he couldn't ignore the life he was living. They had no home, few possessions, and no family.

Carter didn't even have a job, as there was nothing left at the Market to sell. How would he spend his hours? What would he do every day? And where would they live? They couldn't possibly stay with Bianca and her parents forever. The small home had been crowded with three. With five people, they literally tripped over one another. Where would they go? The questions circled through his mind, one after another— none of which had answers.

Seventy-Three

Max carried the last of his bags out to his truck. There wasn't that much aside from the supplies he had collected from his parents' list. The ranch was well-stocked, and his parents would have a lot of what they needed. His house had been damaged as badly as Shelby's, though at least it was still standing. He'd managed to salvage some clothes, but he'd left the remaining food and supplies there for Farhan.

"I'll lend him a hand," Patrick had promised.

"I know you will. He said he enjoys using a hammer after a day of attending sick folks."

"Bianca's not sure about him."

"Neither is Shelby. They both have a suspicious streak."

"As do I."

"Something you learned in the military, no doubt."

"No doubt."

Max made sure a blanket covered the bags of clothing, which were set on the backseat floorboard. The windows were tinted, so it wasn't likely that anyone would be able to see what was inside. They drove over to Patrick's apartment, he locked the doors, and then he pocketed his keys—pausing to see if his possessions could be seen from outside the truck.

"If they want in, they'll just break the windows," Patrick said.

"You're a fountain of comfort."

"That's my job, man." Patrick jammed a thumb in the direction of his apartment. "Want to grab a can of beans with me?"

"Actually . . ."

"Let me guess. You're going to walk Shelby home."

"My routines give me away."

Patrick leaned against the old truck, a pronounced frown on his face.

Max moved next to his friend, mimicked his position, and studied the street. The day's funeral had taken a toll on everyone. He'd been surprised when Shelby insisted on going back to work, but he shouldn't have been. She was a tough one, and she'd already taken off time to be with Carter. The boy seemed to want to be alone more than anything.

"Think you'll be able to talk her into going?" Patrick laughed and bumped his shoulder against Max's. "Don't look so surprised, Berkman. You're easier to read than a comic book."

"Shelby talked to you about it?"

"Yes. She asked me what I thought about your offer the night of the explosion, when we were waiting at the curb with all of her things."

"She did?"

"For what it's worth, I told her I thought it was a good idea." He crossed his arms, his tone serious. "Carter's never had an easy life, or at least not a normal one. But now?"

"Things have been bad since the flare."

"And we both know they're going to get worse."

Max turned and studied Patrick. "What have you heard?"

"Chatter. Most of it meaningless."

"But?"

Patrick didn't answer right away. When Max

thought he wouldn't, he cleared his throat and said, "Something I learned in the military— worry about what the enemy is saying, but worry more about what they're *not* saying."

"And in this case, the enemy is—"

"I don't even know, which makes it worse."

Max considered that for a moment. "You won't come to High Fields?"

"And leave Bianca? No."

"It's about time you tell her how you feel, bro."

"Now? With her dad dying and her mom frantically trying to keep him alive?"

Perhaps he was right. Max wasn't sure anymore. He only knew that he needed to get home to his parents, and he wanted Shelby and Carter to be with him.

"Go to your woman. Walk her home. Maybe the twilight will render you more charming."

Max thought about that as he walked toward Green Acres. He'd never been particularly charming, never even tried. He and Shelby had always been past that. They'd always known each other so well that any attempt to act in any way other than genuine had resulted in laughter and ribbing.

Sure, Max had suffered through the dating scene while he lived in Austin. He knew how to clean himself up, listen attentively, and say the right things. He knew how and when to bring flowers. But with Shelby? There had never been a need to impress her. She knew him down to the marrow, so he had no choice but to be himself.

She was coming out of the front door of the nursing home when he rounded the corner. Waving to acknowledge she'd seen him, she made her way across the front of the building and down the sidewalk.

"I'm going to miss this curbside service when you're gone." When he didn't respond, she asked, "All packed?"

"Yeah. I'll leave first thing tomorrow."

"I hope you find your parents are fine, Max."

"No doubt about it. They're tough and have probably lived through worse."

"Do you think so?" They turned left onto Fourth, in the opposite direction of their homes and toward Bianca's. "I vacillate between believing our parents and grandparents have seen worse times and thinking no generation in the history of America has dealt with these challenges."

They walked in silence the length of the next block, and then Shelby said, "Tell your mom and pop hello for me, and that I'm praying for them."

"Why don't you come tell them yourself?"

Shelby began shaking her head before he even presented his newest argument.

"Listen to me, Shelby."

They'd reached the Baptist church. For as long as Max could remember, there had been a garden to the south of the main sanctuary and benches situated along the walk. Flowers were quickly being replaced with vegetables, but the peaceful-ness of the place prevailed. He pulled her toward one of the benches. Instead of resisting, she sank onto it, leaned back, and tilted her face up to the sky. Though it wasn't yet completely dark, stars were beginning to appear and a slight breeze had picked up. Max could almost pretend it was a normal evening in June.

"Now isn't the time for your stubbornness," he said. He resisted the urge to rub at his temple, but the pressure there was increasing. It was a good thing he wasn't leaving until morning. Maybe this would pass. "I want you to seriously consider going with me, because . . . because this may be the last chance I have to take you there."

"What's that supposed to mean?" She still didn't look at him. Instead she seemed intent on studying the stars, as if she could find answers there.

"It means that once I get to High Fields, I don't know when I'll be back. I won't be able to check on you—"

"I'm a grown woman."

"I realize that. Don't you know that I fully realize that?" He stood and began pacing, fighting to banish the panic from his voice and pushing away the thought that time was running out. He turned to her and said the words that had been heavy on his heart for twenty years. "I am sorry you feel that I abandoned you—"

"You said you would come back!" When she finally looked at him, he saw tears in her eyes. " 'Three months, Shelby . . . and then we'll shed this town and find our place in the world.' "

"And I meant it, but—"

"Stop! Just stop."

There was no anger behind her words, only a deep tiredness. Max felt it as surely as he felt the pounding in his head.

"Shelby, I would do anything to go back twenty-six years."

"But you can't. And now we're different people—that's what you don't want to accept."

"We're the same people, it's only that we've travelled different paths. Do you regret the past so much? I know your marriage to Alex was terrible, but do you wish it hadn't happened? Would you do things differently?"

"You're asking me if I'd forgo having Carter, and of course the answer is no." Shelby ducked her head, her mass of black curls obscuring her expression.

Max had to step closer to hear her next words.

"That's not the real question, Max."

"What is?"

"The real question is, how can I trust you?"

"You doubt me because of something I did when I was little more than a child."

She ignored that and whispered, "You're asking me to put our lives in your hands."

"Maybe, but trust isn't what you're struggling with." Max had carried the guilt of his transgressions for too many years. Suddenly he was tired of it, tired of wanting something that he plainly could not have. "You're struggling with forgiveness. I'm beginning to doubt you will ever be able to forgive me for something I did when I was an eighteen-year-old kid."

Next Max did something that surprised even him. He turned and walked away, leaving Shelby to battle her own monsters, leaving her in the twilight dusk of a church garden.

Seventy-Four

Shelby and Bianca sat in the backyard. Shelby's eyes felt as if she'd rubbed sand into them.

Bianca had listened patiently as she'd poured out her heart. Now Bianca stood and paced back and forth in front of her mother's row of rosebushes. Stopping in front of Shelby, she crossed her arms.

"My *papá* probably isn't going to live through the summer."

"Bianca, don't say—"

"Stop." She held up her hand. "I've come to terms with this, and we both know it's true."

She returned to the rickety old lawn chair next to Shelby. "My *mamá* knows that too. We've spoken about it. We've prayed and we've cried. *Papá*, he slips away a little more each day."

Though her words were heavy with grief, she didn't cry. Perhaps she'd already shed all the tears she had. Perhaps, like Shelby, she felt numb.

"I'm telling you this"—she reached forward and claimed Shelby's hand in hers—"I'm telling you this because you are my best friend. The mistake you're making . . ."

Shelby attempted to pull her hand away, but Bianca refused to let go. Instead, she held it firmly in both of hers. "The mistake you're making is to think you'll have another chance. It's the worst kind of arrogance—to assume you'll have another day, another chance, another choice to make further down the road."

Shelby could only shake her head, any arguments lodged firmly in her throat.

"*Mamá* and I, we're grieving. Believe me, we are. But we're also grateful that we are able to spend *Papá*'s final days by his side. We're not counting on tomorrow, Shelby. Not on this earth. Our only real guarantee is in our salvation. In the promise that we'll be together again."

"So what are you telling me to do?" The words scratched at Shelby's throat and caused her eyes to burn even more.

"I'm not telling you what to do, *mi hermana*."

Bianca released her hand, reached up, and touched her face. "I'm only reminding you that everything can change—in an instant."

"I know that."

"So forgive him while you can."

"But—"

"And remember, you may not get another chance."

Three hours later, Shelby knocked on Patrick's door.

Patrick didn't look too surprised to see her. "Come on in."

"Thanks. Actually, I needed to talk to Max."

"I figured as much. He's sitting on the back patio."

Patrick walked her through the small upstairs apartment to the sliding glass doors. A gas lantern sat on the dining room table, which was only big enough for two. Across the table someone had spread a county map. The lantern cast its glow across the room, lending very little light to the patio, where Max was sitting, staring out at nothing. From what Shelby could see, the patio was decorated bachelor-style—two lawn chairs with an overturned crate between them.

"I'll just go inside and watch some TV," Patrick joked.

Max didn't say anything.

Shelby couldn't make out his expression in

the near darkness, but maybe that was better. This would be easier if she couldn't see him. His answer would be yes or no, and she didn't need or want the emotional baggage that went with either. She was too tired to make light conversation, so she plunged straight into the reason she was there.

"You were right about my needing to forgive. I'm sorry, Max. That isn't fair to you. The past needs to stay in the past. I'll try to do better." When he didn't answer, she pushed on. "Obviously our living at Bianca's isn't going to work as a long-term solution. I talked to Pastor Tony, and our other options aren't any better. There are members in our church who have a single room they will lend us indefinitely. While I appreciate their kindness, that doesn't seem like a good option either."

Instead of answering, Max leaned forward, his elbows on his knees, and waited.

"Carter's not doing well. His moods have been up and down since the flare, but at least when there was work and Kaitlyn I saw some light in his eyes. Now he just lies on the couch, barely eats, shuffles through his chores."

"Carter will bounce back."

"I think so. I pray so." She paused, forcing back the tears that threatened to consume her. Why did she feel so vulnerable when she had to accept kindness from someone else? Why couldn't she just be grateful? "What I'm saying is, if you'll still have us, and if you believe there's room at your parents' place—"

Max was on his feet before she could finish, drawing her into his arms and practically crushing her with his embrace. She pulled back, needing to say the rest, needing to say it all.

"A change of place, it will be good for Carter," he assured her.

She pulled away from him and stood with a small amount of space between them, yet it felt bigger than the West Texas prairie. "Your parents have always been like family to both me and Carter, but we don't want to be a burden. I've talked it over with him—as much as he will talk, which is mostly nodding and staring at the ground—and we're willing to work around the place and help in any way we can to earn our room and board."

Max backed up to the patio railing, and Shelby wondered if maybe he could see her in the light from the dining room. For some reason she felt exposed, as if he might be able to discern what she wasn't telling him. She walked to his side, and stared out at the live oak trees that shaded the apartment.

"There's more," she said.

"All right."

"There's something that I . . . that I have to do. After we get Carter settled."

"What?"

Instead of answering, she pressed on. "Promise me that you won't try to talk me out of it, and no, I'm not ready to share the details. That's my only condition, Max."

She turned toward him, her arms crossed around her middle, hugging herself tightly—trying to keep from touching his face, from walking back into his embrace, from begging him to take them to High Fields.

He didn't ask any questions. Didn't admonish her about foolish plans and dangers and their uncertain future. Instead he pulled her hand free, entwined his fingers with hers, and said, "We'll leave at six sharp."

When she walked back into the apartment, she hugged Patrick tightly and whispered, "Please take care of Bianca."

"Of course I will."

"And watch your back. Keep an eye on Bhatti. I know he doesn't seem like the devious type, but something about the man bothers me. You know he buried something in the backyard?"

"I do, and I'll get to the bottom of it."

Max insisted on accompanying her back to Bianca's parents' home. They didn't talk, didn't plan out the next day, didn't discuss the dangers. Whatever happened would happen, and all they could do was pray for God's protection and his wisdom. Twice he stumbled over something on the sidewalk. He was exhausted, that much was certain.

After Bianca opened the front door, he squeezed Shelby's hand and said, "See you in the morning."

She thought she wouldn't sleep, but she did—more soundly than she had since the explosion. She'd set the alarm on the old sports watch that Carter had given her, but she woke fifteen minutes before it was set to go off. Silencing the alarm, she folded her blanket, straightened the pillows on the couch, and stacked their belongings by the door. It was a pitifully small pile.

By the time Max arrived, she'd had her first cup of coffee. She sat in the kitchen with Bianca while Rosa attempted to feed Miguel a little oatmeal. Carter got up the first time she called him—another sign that things weren't quite normal.

If anything, Max looked more haggard than he had the night before. When she asked him about it, he waved her off, promising, "I'll be fine." Not I *am* fine, but I *will be* fine. Twice she noticed he turned his back to the morning sun, as if afraid it might burn him. He was acting odd. His Stetson was pulled so low that it tilted over his forehead. Something was off, but there was no time to quiz him about it.

After hugging Rosa and saying her goodbyes to Miguel, the four of them—Bianca, Carter,

Max, and herself—carried their pillowcases stuffed with items, the plastic container of writing supplies, and the three bins of valuables out to Max's truck. She was surprised to see that nothing was in the bed. Everything Max had packed was stuffed into the backseat, and he piled their goods on top of it. She only let go of the backpack when he insisted, "You can't wear it, and there won't be room up front with the three of us sitting there."

Carter allowed Bianca to hug him, and then he climbed into the truck. He sat near the window, a baseball cap pulled low over his eyes. The sun wasn't up yet, but the sky had begun to lighten. Pinks and purples spread across the sky suggesting this was any other normal day, but it wasn't. This was the day they were starting their life over.

"*Vaya con Dios*," Bianca whispered in her ear.

Shelby hugged her tightly. "I'll be praying for you and your parents."

Max pulled out a map and traced their path with his index finger. "We'll take the state highway north through Townsen Mills, past both of these farm roads, and turn here—across from the cemetery."

"That's the long way."

"Yes, but the roads are better. I don't want to get caught on either of these roads." He retraced back toward Townsen Mills. "They're not paved, and it would be a perfect place for someone to stage an ambush."

"Why are you showing me this? You're driving."

Max closed his eyes and pinched the bridge of his nose.

"Are you okay? Is there a problem? Maybe we should wait—"

"We're doing this today. Now. I wanted you to know, is all."

Then he motioned for her to climb into the truck. She sat squeezed between Max and Carter, and they drove out of Abney.

Seventy-Five

They hit the first snag leaving town.

They left Bianca's home, drove down Main Street, and were approaching the outskirts of town when Max spied several large diesel trucks parked across the road. To the left, and the right, and the left again. They made a sort of obstacle course. Max could navigate between them only if he drove slowly, and if someone removed the roadblock constructed of lumber and orange warning signs positioned in the middle.

He turned off the ignition to his own truck, murmured, "Wait here," and stepped out to talk to the folks manning the barricade.

"Could be an expensive place to park your vehicle," he said.

"Can't afford to drive them anymore," Josh Hunter explained, walking up and shaking his hand.

Max had handled a small misdemeanor matter for Josh several years ago, and the boy had cleaned up nicely. Now he was on patrol for the mayor—not bad for a kid who could have ended up in juvie for calling in a fake bomb threat when he was in middle school.

"Has anyone tried to breach it?" Shelby asked.

Max wasn't even a little surprised that she hadn't waited in the truck.

"Not yet. Our policy is to search folks for weapons before we allow them through, then someone escorts them to the south side of town. Once they're past the southern barrier, we return their weapons."

"So the road isn't closed." Shelby crossed her arms and tried to peer around the trucks to the road beyond.

"No. Being a direct route to Austin, Mayor Perkins doesn't want to stop legitimate folks from travelling if they have the means."

"If they have the gasoline," Max said.

"Exactly."

"So you let everyone through?" Max asked.

"Not everyone. They have to surrender their

weapons while they travel through town, otherwise they're turned away."

Max hadn't heard about this, but then he'd
missed the last city meeting. He'd decided
helping to bury folks was more important, and
besides—he wouldn't be in Abney for long, so
what they decided seemed irrelevant to him. But
confiscating weapons? Unless someone had
suspended the Second Amendment, that was
illegal.

Josh was yawning, having apparently pulled
the night shift. He resettled the ball cap he wore
and added, "We've had a few turn around and
say they would find another way."

"No altercations?"

Josh shrugged. "Two nights ago we had some
rough-looking guys threaten us."

"Bunch of drug addicts from the looks of
them," said Karen Schneider, who had walked
over to join them. She was also patrolling the
barricade. Max knew very little about her, only
that she'd been a corrections officer at the
women's prison in the town south of Abney.
"Couldn't stop scratching and had the most
awful smell."

"Bad time to try and go clean," Shelby said.

Karen shrugged. "Not much choice, I guess."

"Other than that, it's been quiet." Josh carried a
rifle, which he switched from his right hand to
his left. "The first few days, there were a lot of

people going through. Lately it's been maybe one or two cars a shift. Not many."

Max thought about the tank full of gas he'd managed to barter for. He'd traded most of the food left in his house because Farhan hadn't needed the canned goods. He was receiving rations from the city in exchange for his work at the nursing home and hospital.

More than anything else they carried, the gas in the truck made them vulnerable to thieves— but it was also their only way to get to High Fields. That worry was one of the reasons he'd wanted to leave early in the day.

"We're headed up to my parents' ranch."

"Good luck," Karen said. "I'll go tell the guys to move the barricades."

Shelby had begun walking toward the truck when Josh reached for Max's arm and pulled him back. "I don't want to seem like an alarmist."

"But—"

"There have been rumors about problems to the north of here."

"What kind of problems?"

"Thugs, gangs, whatever you want to call them. They hide off the road in the brush and pull out when you're too close to stop. They take whatever they want, leaving you barely enough gas to get away. Word is they've even killed a few."

"And you talked to someone who saw this with their own eyes?"

"Not exactly." Josh again shifted the rifle. "I have heard it from three different people now. Each of them heard it from someone else."

"Hearsay. Not exactly solid information."

"Solid enough."

"Wouldn't hold up in a court of law."

"Yeah, but the thing is, this isn't a courtroom. And these people who told us were terrified. You know what I mean? They rode in groups, left early in the morning, made sure they had someone armed and visible in the front or bed of the vehicle."

"All right." Max rubbed at the pulsing in his temple. He knew what the pain meant—what would overtake him soon—but he pushed the thought away. He would get Shelby and Carter to High Fields.

"Watch for red bandanas."

"Seriously?"

"I know. Sounds like something out of a B-rated Western, but apparently they cover up their faces so they can't be identified."

"I'll keep an eye out. Thanks for the heads-up."

"Sure thing. Y'all take care."

Josh again took up his position watching the road toward town, and Max jogged back to his truck. When he opened the door, the world tilted momentarily. He clutched the doorframe and waited for the sensation to pass. Fortunately, Shelby didn't notice. She was turned around and checking the backpack of medication. He pulled in a deep breath, climbed into the truck, and started the engine.

"What was that about?" Shelby asked. She nodded toward Josh.

Carter seemed to be asleep, but Max knew that could be an act. He shook his head, unwilling to add worry to what the boy had already endured, and drove forward.

Seventy-Six

It had been a couple of years since Carter had seen Max's parents, Georgia and Ted. When Max had first moved back to Abney, Carter had gone nearly every weekend to High Fields. Somewhere along the way life had become busy, and he always had to be somewhere else, doing something besides visiting them.

Not anymore. He had all the time in the world.

One part of his mind knew that he had to pull himself out of his pit of despair. He needed to be there for his mom.

Life wasn't fair.

He'd heard those words from every teacher he'd ever had, or so it seemed. Carter hadn't understood the truth of that statement until he'd held Kaitlyn's lifeless body in his arms.

Each time the memory passed through his

mind, a ball of grief burned in his gut. He wondered why she had died but he had lived, and he regretted that he hadn't been able to save her. His thoughts were caught in a loop, and the round and round exhausted him. The effort required to eat or work or even speak seemed too much.

He'd agreed they should move to High Fields because his mother thought it was a good idea. She wouldn't have brought it up otherwise. There was something else going on with her, though—something she wasn't talking about yet.

Carter settled against the truck door, now that they were finally moving. The barricade at the edge of town had seemed totally lame. Anyone with a big rig could have busted through it. And what were they protecting? There wasn't anything left in Abney—nothing in the grocery store, no money in the bank, no hope that things would improve. Abney was a great big zero, a total loss, something already in the past.

The lull of the engine helped Carter to relax, and he felt himself slipping into a light sleep. He could hear Max talking to his mom about red bandanas and bandits and danger and rumors. He heard it all, but the words reached him like static on a radio. He opened his eyes once to see Max rubbing at his neck, holding it stiffly at an odd angle. His mom was staring straight ahead when her eyes widened in alarm.

"This place looks like a ghost town."

Carter came fully awake, sat up, rubbed his eyes, and looked around.

She was right. Townsen Mills had been a true one-light town. But now there was nothing. Carter didn't see a single person.

As they drove slowly past the gas station, Max pointed toward the broken windows in the front.

The café was simply closed, boards nailed over windows.

"What happened here?" he asked.

"I suppose it's a hard spot to protect." Max gripped the steering wheel so tightly his knuckles turned white. "And there's no money to be made if you have no supplies to sell."

"No upside to staying open." His mom gawked out the window as they drove past the last building—an antique store that looked as if it had been emptied out.

Carter tried to process what he was seeing, attempting to understand how an entire town had disappeared. It was true that Townsen Mills wasn't much. Their kids came to school in Abney, but they were a town. Where had the people gone?

He was staring out his side window when he heard Max shout, "Hold on."

Carter's attention swiveled to the front, and in a split second he saw half a dozen jacked-up trucks pulling out of the brush. Sporting over-sized wheels, they belonged in a monster truck competition. Each had cranked up suspension for off-road driving. Hanging out the windows were guys wearing red bandanas and brandishing pistols.

Seventy-Seven

Max slammed the brakes to the floor, sending the truck into a spin and throwing everyone against their restraints.

"Get down!" Max pushed on Shelby's head, but she was buckled into the seat and it did no more than bend her over. Maybe that was what he was trying to do.

She fought against Max and clawed at Carter's seat belt, attempting to hit the release button. "Hurry. You need to—"

They were now facing the direction they had come. Max had jerked the wheel and stopped their spin, but before he could accelerate, something hit the side-view mirror and shattered it. Carter guessed it was a bullet. Hands shaking, he unbuckled his seat belt and attempted to crouch in between the seat and dashboard, but he didn't fit in the floor space. He only succeeded in falling off the bench seat and lodging the lower half of himself between the glove compartment and the seat. His mom was trying to lie across the top of him—smothering him, cutting off his air supply, and causing his legs to cramp.

"Get off me. Just get off!"

He exploded up out of the floorboard as Max accelerated. The force knocked his mom across the seat. Carter steadied her, pushed her back toward Max, and raised up to see out the back window.

"They're not giving up," he said.

"I see that." Max glanced into the rearview window.

If he crouched down he could be killed in a collision, which they were surely about to have. If he sat up and faced the front of the truck, he could be shot in the back of the head. Neither seemed like a good option.

His mom hollered at Max to be careful, as if he had a choice in the matter. They jostled left and right, Max driving like a crazy person intent on creating his own personal roller coaster. Carter tried to avoid the hail of gunfire that was sailing around them—popping like firecrackers on some nightmarish Independence Day celebration. A bullet popped against the top of the cab, ricocheting off it. Carter could hear pings on the tailgate, and then another bullet spidered the glass of his side-view mirror.

"They're either intentionally missing us or they're terrible shots," he said.

"They only have to get lucky once." Max was driving the truck so hard that the engine made a terrible, whining sound. "Find something to hold on to."

Carter still hadn't decided whether to stay crouched in front of the seat or try and get back up on it.

At that moment, Max made a hard right.

Carter careened into his mother, and she fell into Max—who was clenching his jaw and wrestling with the steering wheel. They barreled onto a caliche road. He knew this because the ride had been smooth, but now they rattled over the rock.

The truck hit a low spot in the road, bouncing them all up and against the roof of the truck. His mom faced the front, and she braced her palms against the dash, motioning for Carter to do the same. He pushed himself back up onto the seat and again fastened his seat belt.

When they tore through the first cattle guard, Carter thought it would jostle the fillings out of his teeth.

"Tell me what you see, Carter."

He couldn't see anything through the splintered glass of his side-view mirror, so he looked back over his shoulder. "Still coming. Three guys, or maybe four. Only two trucks now. Red bandanas and guns. Who are they?"

"Pad beople." Max didn't appear to notice his

speech was garbled. Instead, he grimaced and clutched the side of his head. The motion seemed painful, and his complexion had turned a ghastly white.

In that moment Carter understood. He remembered the time he was sixteen, when he and Max had gone to see a minor league baseball game over in Round Rock. He was looking at the same symptoms Max had exhibited on that trip, which had ended with Max lying in the backseat, groaning as Carter drove them home.

"Let me or my mom drive."

"No time thor fat." He gripped the wheel harder. "We're turning again. Ret geady."

It was like an awful game of pig latin.

Carter tightened the strap on his seat belt, then they sailed through another cattle guard and made an immediate right. His mom screamed as Max lost control of the truck. He overcorrected and they shot across the right side of the road into a cattle fence. Jerking the wheel back to the left, Max once more tromped on the accelerator.

Turning in his seat, Carter saw their pursuers had stopped at the cattle guard. "We lost them. They didn't even try—"

The words died on his lips as Max slumped against the door and his mother grabbed the wheel. She pushed his foot out of the way and slowly, gently applied the brakes with her left foot. It wasn't until they came to a stop that Carter thought to look up and out of the front windshield.

They'd risen at the crack of dawn and travelled through barricades and a deserted town. They'd nearly been killed running away from bad guys who were probably still back there. Turning around wasn't an option. Through the front windshield, Carter could barely process what he was seeing. In front of them was supposed to be safety and a place of refuge. Instead, he found himself staring at yet another barricade. It stretched from fence to fence and was manned by at least four people with rifles. Rifles that had been raised and were pointed directly at them.

Seventy-Eight

Shelby's first concern was Max and Carter.

"Are you okay?"

"Yes," said Carter.

"You're sure?" She was turned in her seat, running her hands up and down his arms—checking for broken bones or bullet wounds.

"I'm sure."

"They didn't—"

"I'm fine, Mom. But who are those people? What are we going to do about Max? Are we going to die here? Why did we even come?"

Instead of answering, she said, "Help me move him over."

They both got out of the truck. She didn't know if the people tending the roadblock would shoot, but she didn't think so. She'd stopped the truck a good thirty yards back, and she posed no threat. Plus, she had no other option. She needed to get in the driver's seat.

Shelby ran around to Max's side of the truck and carefully opened the door. He nearly fell out when she did, his eyes fluttering open for a moment before closing again.

"Pull him over, Carter."

"I'm trying, but he's deadweight." Carter froze, his eyes finding his mom's.

"He's not dead. It's only a migraine. A very bad one. You remember."

"Yeah. I do."

Once they had him in the middle of the seat, his head resting back in an awkward position, Shelby climbed back into the truck and buckled him in. She pulled Max's hand into her lap and felt for a pulse—one of the few medical skills she'd acquired while working at Green Acres. It seemed erratic, but strong, the beats from his heart tapping a rhythm against her fingertips.

"He's okay?"

"He will be. We need to get him to the ranch, find his medication, and get him into a dark room." She started the truck and drove slowly toward the barricade.

"Are you sure this is a good idea?" Carter asked.

"No."

"But—"

"But where we're going is down this road." She glanced at Carter and attempted a smile. "Have faith, son. We've made it this far."

She stopped ten yards from the collection of farm equipment, vehicles, and armed men.

"Are they going to shoot us?"

"I don't know. I don't . . . I don't think so."

No one moved, so Shelby switched off the vehicle.

"I'll do it."

"No!" Turning to Carter, she said, "I'll do this. You stay in the truck."

"But I could—"

"Stay here. Promise me."

He nodded once, and she knew the odds were even that he would follow her out anyway. She added, "Watch after Max."

She stepped out of the truck, her hands up in the air, palms facing toward the armed men. Crossing those thirty feet felt like the longest walk of her life, but what choice did she have? They couldn't drive back the way they had come, and this was the only way forward.

Her eyes scanned left to right—four boys

477

between the ages of fifteen and twenty if she were to guess. The oldest of the group, greasy black hair flopping in his eyes, straightened up and pointed his rifle at her. He wore a dirty T-shirt and had the tanned outdoor look of a kid   raised on a farm. "You need to turn around."

"We can't do that."

"Ma'am, no one goes down this road who doesn't live down this road."

Her heart was pounding so hard she could hear its rhythm in her ears. She swallowed, closed her eyes, and prayed for courage and strength and wisdom.

"Ma'am, I need you to turn around. We don't want to hurt y'all."

"We do live here."

"Say again?"

"We live here. What I mean is, we will be living here. On the High Fields Ranch—Georgia and Roy Berkman's place."

The teenager consulted another boy—this one chubby with a shock of red hair. Both stood in the beds of two separate trucks, peering over the cabs. The other two stood at the ends of the barricades. They didn't speak or move, but kept their rifles pointed at Shelby. Whoever had trained them had done a good job. She doubted anyone would get down this road without permission or a gunfight.

"Berkmans don't have no daughters," the black-haired boy said. He seemed to be the spokesman for the group.

"No. They don't, but they have a son. We're here with Max, and he's . . ." Her tears started to fall, but she didn't dare brush them away. "Max is hurt, and he's in the truck." Her arms began to shake, but she didn't dare drop them to her side.

The redheaded boy had been crouched down, resting his rifle over the cab of the truck. He reached for something next to him and pulled up a pair of binoculars. One hand still on the rifle, he studied the truck through the binoculars.

"It's him."

Shelby heard crickets, the *cheer, cheer, cheer* of a cardinal, and the ticking of the truck's engine.

"He doesn't look so good." Dropping his rifle and binoculars on the cab of the truck, he jumped out of it with surprising agility.

All four boys ran toward her, past her, and to Max.

Shelby's legs finally gave out. She dropped to her knees on the caliche road, barely noticing the dust and rocks. Hands on the ground, she bowed her head, and she thanked God that his protection and guidance had brought them home.

Seventy-Nine

Max woke to complete darkness. He didn't need to see to know that he was in his old bedroom at High Fields. The smell of cedar had pervaded the place since they'd built it when he was just a scrawny kid. Though his family had continued to live in Abney during the week, they'd spent nearly every weekend at the ranch.

He swung his legs to the floor and sat up. His head felt like a giant ball of cotton, but the horrific pulsing in his right temple had ceased.

Lurching to his feet, he crossed the room and opened the blackout curtains. The sky was barely tinted with light—sunset or sunrise? Pulling on a pair of shorts and a T-shirt, he walked across the hall to the bathroom, where everything seemed to be working. He raised the back of the toilet tank and noticed someone had added a few bricks to it, converting it to lower water usage. Washing his hands, he ignored the image in the mirror and instead hurried to the kitchen, where he stopped short in the kitchen doorway.

"Sleepyhead is out of bed." His mother smiled as she came over and stood on her tiptoes to kiss his cheek. "I hope you're feeling better."

"I am. Thanks."

His mom wore jeans and a T-shirt that said My Superpower Is Quilting. What's Yours? Her hair was slightly grayer than he remembered—which didn't seem possible in just three weeks' time. She looked healthy, though, and didn't seem particularly disturbed by the turn of events.

Shelby studied him over the rim of her coffee cup, a smile playing on her lips. Black curls spilled in every direction, but she looked rested. She looked better than she had in the truck, as she'd been trying to cover Carter's body with her own.

The memories rushed back at him with the power of a freight train. He pulled a chair out from the dining room table and dropped into it.

"How's the migraine?" His father held up the pot of coffee, and Max nodded gratefully.

All of his life Max had been told he was the spitting image of his father, and he supposed that was true. Many times looking at the man felt like looking into a mirror.

"Better. It's much better."

His mom bustled around the stove. "You were in some terrible shape yesterday."

So it was sunrise. He'd slept nearly twenty-four hours.

"Good thing you had Shelby with you." His dad carried two steaming coffee mugs to the table, placed one at Max's spot, and sat down across from him.

How many times had they eaten in this room, the four of them? His mom and dad on one side of the table, he and Shelby on the other? It was as if the pieces of a puzzle had clicked together and he could finally see the picture clearly.

"Shelby's been telling us all the news from Abney." His mom set a loaf of uncut bread on the table, along with a tub of butter and a jar of fresh preserves.

"How did you manage to cook the bread?" Max asked.

"The oven still works, but it heats up the kitchen too much. Your father is quite the mechanical engineer. He made me an old-fashioned oven out of some spare barbecue grill parts."

"She has to go outside to use it."

"But I don't mind. Cooking outside, it feels almost natural."

"It will be interesting to see if you feel that way in August." His father winked and passed Max a small pitcher of cream.

Max sipped the coffee and listened to his parents discuss the chickens and cow and general details of farm life at High Fields.

"We're using the generator to keep a few things cold," his mother said. "Including Carter's medicine."

When he'd downed half the cup and the migraine cloud had begun to fade, Max asked, "Carter is okay?"

"Sleeping in. No surprise there," Shelby said.

Max could tell she was still concerned about Carter. He understood the reasons for the frown lines between her eyes, but at least she wasn't carrying that backpack with her everywhere. No one needed that type of burden. You couldn't carry life and death on your back like some sort of tortoise shell. Somewhere, sometime, you had to lay that burden down. It seemed, for the moment, that she had.

"How did we get here? When did I pass out?"

"You were doing a pretty good imitation of Jeff Gordon before it happened."

"I remember pulling onto the county road with the monster trucks in hot pursuit."

"We had heard about them," his father said. "It's part of the reason we set up the blockade at the county roads. Once those hoodlums found out we would fight back, they moved on to easier targets."

"That's the last thing I remember seeing. Logan Hunter manning the roadblock."

"I wasn't sure he was going to let us through." Shelby attempted to laugh, but Max could tell from the way she stared down into her coffee cup that she was still shaken by the events of the previous day.

"Shelby talked them down. After they realized who you were, they radioed ahead and we met her at the gate."

"Radioed?"

"CBs and such. It's funny what people have found in their barns and sheds that have proven useful since the flare."

So they knew. Of course they did—Jerry Lambert had told him as much. But hearing it from someone else, and seeing it for himself were two different things. His parents knew about the flare, about the extent of the damage, and they were handling it as they handled everything— by moving forward one step at a time.

His father mentioned the flare so simply, like another aberration of nature that they would somehow work their way through. In the same way that they'd survived floods and droughts, harsh winters, and record-high summers. His father's quiet confidence did more to ease the anxiety in Max's heart than a hundred govern-ment bulletins.

Suddenly Max realized he was famished.

He ate two pieces of the bread while his mother scrambled eggs. They'd never switched over to an electric stove and kept the large propane tank outside well-maintained and full. It wouldn't last them through the winter, though. His parents, more than anyone else, would understand the importance of saving resources for the coming days. Max was surprised she was using it to cook breakfast when they could have made do with the bread. No doubt, she was celebrating the return of her son.

Eighty

As they ate they discussed the aurora, the notices from the federal and state government, and how things were deteriorating in Abney. His father asked specifics about what the council and police and emergency personnel had done.

After Max had explained as best he could, his father grunted.

"I don't know, Dad. On one hand, they're pulling together and doing well." Max sat back, his stomach full for the first time in several days. "But each time they're hit with another tragedy—"

"Like the gas explosion." Shelby met his gaze.

He took another drink of his coffee. "Each new emergency seems to surprise them, as if they half-expect an emergency response team to appear out of nowhere. I'm not sure they've grasped that no one is coming to help, that this is their life now."

"I suspect it will take some people longer than others to come to terms with that." His father placed the lid on the jar of preserves.

"We've had our share of losses," his mother said. "Howard Johnson died of a heart attack. His wife, Millie, had to move in with some neighbors. No one felt it was safe for her to live alone."

They were silent for a moment. Max guessed they were each thinking of the people who had died already from this cataclysmic event. How many more? His mind shied away from the thought. The important thing was that Shelby and Carter were here. They were safe. His parents were fine. Even if the situation grew worse, they had each other.

"The Johnson land will still be farmed," his father said. "And perhaps some of Millie's boys will show up—though how they'll get here from the city I can't imagine."

His dad stood, picked his cowboy hat up off the counter, and placed it on his head. He wore a long-sleeved cotton shirt and overalls. Max marveled that he'd ever worried about his parents. They seemed to be adapting amazingly well.

"We're glad you're home, son." His father placed one hand on the back of his chair and the other on the back of Shelby's. "And glad you brought Shelby and Carter with you. We prayed, you know. Prayed each and every night that God would bring the three of you here. Together, we'll find a way through this thing."

He walked out into the June heat. No doubt he would work outside until dinner, as he had done most every day since retiring from his job twenty-four years earlier. Max's mother rose to clear away the dishes, and Shelby stood to help.

"I'll change my clothes and go work with Dad."

"You'll do no such thing." His mother turned to face him, a spatula in her hand and a determined expression on her face. "Physical exertion is a trigger, young man. The day they diagnosed you with basilar migraines I promised the Lord that I'd do my best to help you through it." She waved the spatula in his direction. "There is no need provoking another one of those episodes. Take it easy today. Stay out of the sun."

"But he needs—"

"He does need your help, but the work will wait. It will still be there tomorrow. If you absolutely must be busy, I have some green beans to snap and purple hull peas to shell. Electricity may be out, but the vegetable garden is doing just fine."

Max realized it was futile to argue with his mom. So instead he spent the morning helping to move Shelby's things into his grandparents' one-bedroom house, which was only a few feet from the main house.

"You don't have to do this," he said. "There's room in the main house."

"I think it will be better."

So they dusted shelves and made the bed with fresh linen.

Max's mom reminded him there was an old cot out in the barn, so he found it and set it up on the screened-in back porch. It would give Carter a measure of privacy, at least until the weather grew cold.

Shelby was making up the bed when Max pulled a chair close to the cot and insisted that she sit down. He sat on the bed, causing the springs to creak, close enough that their knees were touching. "I want to apologize," he said.

"You don't need to do that."

"I do. I made mistakes—a lot of them since the flare."

Max stared down at his hands, remembered holding the rifle and killing the man barreling toward them in the truck. "I thought that I could keep things going the way they always had. That's why I tried to reason with the teenager who staged the car wreck that first night."

"You couldn't have known—"

"I should have." He looked up at her. "I should have realized sooner that everything had changed. If I'd accepted that, maybe Mr. Evans would still be alive."

"That wasn't your fault, either."

"No. But I might have prevented it." He rubbed both hands up and down his jawline. Finally he leaned forward, waited until she was looking at him, and said, "I won't make that mistake again. I'll do whatever I have to do in order to keep you and Carter safe."

Carter showed up at lunchtime, with dark circles under his eyes and his hair jutting out in a dozen different directions. Before Shelby could ask, he assured her that his blood sugar was fine and proceeded to devour everything Max's mom put in front of him.

After they'd eaten, Max's mom showed all of them how to use the old wringer washer. "We didn't have one," she explained. "But Millie Johnson did, and she was happy to exchange it for a promise of fish once a week throughout the summer. That will be one of your chores, Carter."

Carter shrugged, but Max didn't think he'd actually mind walking down to the creek and spending an afternoon each week with a fishing pole in his hand.

"Why can't I have that chore?" Max pretended to sulk as they filled the old tub with water from the cistern, added a small amount of soap powder, and proceeded to wash their clothes.

By late afternoon Max had joined Shelby on the back porch, which stretched across the length of his parents' home. The view was toward the south, toward Abney. They sat facing one another, a small table between them, two metal bowls on the table. Beside Shelby was a large box of purple hull peas that were waiting to be shelled. Max held the box of green beans.

"My mom always did plant too much."

"It's a good thing she did."

They spoke of the drive from Abney, the dangers they'd faced, and their worries for friends back in town.

"But you're good here, right?" Max sat back and watched as she split open another pod, dumped the peas into the pan, and dropped the shell into a bucket. It would be used for slop for the pig that his father had recently traded half a dozen chickens for.

"We're grateful, Max. This has always been a peaceful, healing place for me. I'd forgotten that. It's . . . well, it's been awhile since I've been out to visit."

"We're safe here, Shelby. As safe as we can be, and I think the work will be good for Carter. It will give him less time to dwell on what has happened. Not that he should forget."

"No. I don't suppose he'll ever forget Kaitlyn or the last few weeks, but maybe . . ." She stopped shelling and gazed out over the Texas countryside.

It was scrubby land, marked by a few hills and too many cedar trees. But families had carved out a living on it before, and Max was sure they could again.

"Maybe here he can have the time and space to heal. That's what I pray for."

They didn't speak of their last night in Abney, when Max had asked her forgiveness or how she'd shown up at his door and admitted that she needed him. That was the past. Everything that came before the solar flare was the past. As deep shadows crept across the vista, Max understood that they would have to turn all their attention toward the present and the future if they were going to survive.

For the moment, his family—all of his family—was safe. He would be on his knees before bed to thank God for that. As for tomorrow, he would have to trust that the grace and protection that had helped them reach High Fields would also see them through the days to come.

Epilogue

One week later

Shelby waited until the sun was a giant ball of red touching the horizon before she began preparing for her journey. After dinner, while Georgia did the dishes and Carter and Roy played a game of checkers, she walked over to their little house and pulled out the three boxes of supplies she'd carefully packed and repacked the last four nights.

Food, first aid kit, blanket, money, and valuables for bartering. Her hand paused over the handgun and ammunition, which she would rather not carry with her. But what if she needed them? What if she had to protect herself? She stacked the three boxes one on top of the other and picked them up. Not that heavy—

considering they carried any hope for her son's future.

When she stepped outside, Max was waiting. At his feet were three five-gallon jugs of water—the kind that some people once took to the grocery store to refill.

"Thought you might need these."

"What are you doing?" she asked.

"Helping."

Instead of arguing, she tightened her grip on the boxes and followed him to the side of the house where she'd parked the Dodge Ramcharger earlier that afternoon.

"Where did your parents get the water jugs?"

"When they lived in town, Mom went through a spell of digestion problems. She read online that bottled water might help."

"What happened?"

"She was better in six months, and Pop had accumulated quite a few empty jugs."

"Waste not—"

"Want not. I filled them with water from the spring out back. It's fresh."

Max set the jugs on the ground and raised the back hatch of the Dodge.

"I don't need this much water, Max."

"We do."

She dropped her stack of boxes on the ground, half-hoping one would land on his foot. "We've been through this before."

"And there's no need to go through it again."

"You're not going with me."

"Yes, I am."

She pushed each box into the back of the Dodge. Max added the jugs of water and closed the hatch. Instead of walking away, as her heart told her she should, Shelby turned and leaned against the old SUV. The mileage would be terrible, but she wasn't going that far. A tank of gas, which she had, should be enough. It wasn't the distance that was the problem, it was what she might encounter in Austin that worried her.

Max moved beside her so that they were both staring out at the Texas landscape—the Hill Country, where people travelled to vacation and experience the good life. Only that life had been ripped apart, and now they were picking up the pieces.

"I can't believe your dad is loaning me this car."

"Are you kidding? With a V-8 engine, four-wheel drive, and storage that you can access from inside the vehicle, it's the perfect urban disaster machine."

Shelby laughed. She wanted to cry, but she laughed. That might have been her exhaustion peeking through.

"You're not going without me, Shelby. Accept that, and we can move forward."

"You don't think I can do this alone."

"I don't think you *should* do it alone. God put

us together for a reason. We grew up as best friends for a reason."

"Our past is—"

"Irrelevant? It's not, because you can trust me."

She heard the frustration in his voice, but she didn't yield.

"You've heard the same reports I have," he said. "Austin isn't going to be easy."

"It's a two-hour drive."

"It was. It isn't anymore. Two days down, two days to find what you need, and two days back—if things go well."

She'd done the same math in her head, but she hadn't wanted to admit it—not out loud. Six days alone in a world gone dark, a world filled with increasingly desperate people.

"I'm going with you."

"And if you're killed?"

"If I'm killed I'll be dead, so it won't bother me much. If you're killed and I'm here enjoying the easy life . . ." He nudged her shoulder with his. "I couldn't live with that."

She closed her eyes, willing her tears away. When she opened them, the last of the sun's colors had faded from the sky. "Carter will barely talk to me."

"He's a teenager. He'll get over it."

"Your mother thinks I should wait to see if supplies show up in Abney."

"She worries about you."

Shelby turned so that her knee was propped up on the bumper of the vehicle and she was facing Max. She needed to see him, look directly at him, when she said this. It didn't matter that darkness had almost fallen. She knew Max well enough to read his reactions, even in the dark.

"What if you have another migraine?"

"That's a risk, but there's a bigger risk that you'll be attacked by marauders, or that you'll find a situation in Austin that is untenable. Together? Yeah, we'll get there and get back with Carter's medicine and a small propane refrigerator."

"Your parents have a refrigerator that works. Georgia said—"

"The gas won't last through the winter. We need something smaller. Something just for the meds."

She considered that and nodded. "I have to find it, Max. I have to. I can't watch my son die before my eyes when there's something I can do to prevent it—even if that something is a long shot." Her voice dropped to a whisper. "We have a little more than a month's supply left. That's it."

She didn't realize she was crying until he reached forward, cupped her face, and rubbed away the tears with his thumbs.

"God won't give us more than we can handle, Shelby. You can count on that."

She pulled away and swiped at her nose. "Sounds like something you'd stitch onto a pillow."

"Well, I wouldn't. I'm no good with a needle."

Shelby tried to still the fear that caused her heart to hammer. She knew she was doing the right thing. She had cried and worried and prayed since that first night when they'd seen the aurora as they hiked the trail from Gorman Falls. She'd known, even then, that Carter's insulin would be the biggest problem they would face.

She and Max stood there, shoulder to shoulder, as the stars made their appearance—right on time, every night, regardless of the state of man.

Finally, Shelby turned to him and said, "We leave at first light."

Discussion Questions

1. Even before Shelby fully understands their situation, her first instinct is to check on her child. Our parental instincts are strong, and often they supersede everything else. But as they drive home, she understands the need to stop and get information as well as help others. She has to go against her deepest instincts. The Bible speaks about helping others in the story of the Good Samaritan (Luke 10:25-37). Does this apply even in times of emergency, or should we have a "family first" mentality? Why or why not?

2. Max convinces the grocery store manager to go against company policy, open the store, and sell what supplies he has. Was this a good or bad decision? What might have happened if he hadn't opened the store?

3. When the downtown fire breaks out, the townspeople fight it the old-fashioned way—with blankets and a bucket brigade. Though they are faced with an increasingly grim situation, the people of Abney don't give up. One theme of this story is that there is much we can learn from the older generation.

Name three practical things we could learn from our elders.

4. Pastor Tony reminds his congregation that God's love *endures forever.* The world is crumbling around them, but God's love is unchangeable. How does this help us when we are facing tragic situations?

5. This story takes place in a small town, and most of the people attend one of the local churches. The churches, in return, naturally respond to needs within their community. Name some outreach programs your church participates in. What are some needs that aren't being met or planned for?

6. Shelby misses her parents, but she knows she will be reunited with them one day. What things can we be certain about as far as the future? How can those promises help us through any present trouble?

7. Throughout the story we see that some people rise to the occasion—they become stronger, more helpful, and more faithful. For others, though, the emergency is a reason to turn against their neighbor, to put their own needs first, and to step away from their faith. What can we do to ensure that we stay in the first category? Another way to ask that

question—how can we be the hands and feet of Christ to others during a tragic situation?

8. As Pastor Tony preaches at the funeral service, he draws their attention to Scripture in Kings and Jeremiah. Actually there are 67 references in the Bible to a remnant. This word simply means "remaining," so the remnant of Christ would be those remaining in him. Read the following verses: 2 Kings 19:4, 2 Kings 19:31, Ezra 9:8, Isaiah 10:21, Isaiah 37:31, and Jeremiah 42:2. Discuss your reaction to these verses.

9. Carter's faith is shaky at best. Before the flare, he went to church because his mother went. It's also a comfortable, safe place for him. He hasn't quite worked out what he believes yet. After witnessing some horrific events, his beliefs are shaken to the core. What can a parent do to help guide a child—even a grown child—into the faith?

10. The story ends the way it began—with Shelby worried about her son. The parent/child relationship is one of the most precious gifts we receive from God, and it defines every decision we make. It's a burden and it's a blessing. Share verses of Scripture that help us know how to navigate our family relationships.

Author's Note

Massive solar flares are not fiction. The Carrington Event occurred September 1, 1859. Aurorae were seen as far south as the Caribbean, and telegraph systems throughout Europe and North America failed. More recently, large solar storms were recorded in 2003, 2011, 2012, 2013, and 2015. Research by NASA scientists indicates there is a 12 percent chance a large storm will happen in the next 10 years. This report stresses that while a CME is not physically harmful, it could blow out transformers in power grids and disrupt satellite/GPS systems. A recent assessment by the Department of Homeland Security reported to Congress that a massive electromagnetic pulse event caused by a solar flare could leave more than 130 million Americans without power for years.

In 2014, an explosion in the East Harlem neighborhood of Manhattan in New York City leveled two five-story apartment buildings, killed eight people, and injured at least 70 others. According to city officials, the blast was caused by a gas leak.

Basilar migraines occur in 1 of 400 migraine sufferers. They are a disturbance in the brain stem. Symptoms include dizziness, double vision, slurred speech, temporary blindness, loss of balance, and loss of consciousness. Migraine specific medications are avoided for these types of migraines because they may constrict the basilar artery and lead to stroke.

Emergency Preparation Lists

Foods with a Long Shelf Life
- Maple syrup
- Honey
- Salt
- Rice
- Corn starch
- Sugar
- Vanilla extract
- Vinegar

Medicinal Herbs to Be Added to Tea or Other Drinks
- For a cough, add rosemary
- For stomach cramps, add mint
- For menstrual cramps, add oregano
- For achy joints, add curry powder

What to Pack in an Emergency Kit*
- Water—one gallon per person, per day
- Food—easy-to-make and won't spoil
- Manual can opener
- Flashlight
- Battery-powered, solar, or hand-crank radio

*per the Center for Disease Control

- Cell phone with chargers
- Extra batteries
- Health and safety supplies, including a first aid kit
- Medicine (7-day supply), other medical supplies, and paperwork about any serious or ongoing medical conditions
- Emergency blankets
- Soap, toothbrush, and other personal care items
- Family and emergency contact information
- Multipurpose tool
- Copies of important documents such as insurance cards, immunization records, etc.
- Extra cash
- Map(s) of the area
- Extra set of car keys and house keys

Basic 3-Month Emergency Food Stash*

- 50 lbs. white flour, or 100 lbs. if you can't grind the 50 lbs. of wheat berries listed below
- 50 lbs. wheat berries (to grind into flour)
- 10 lbs. dried corn (popcorn works great) to be ground into cornmeal as needed, or 10 lbs. cornmeal

---

*Used with permission from Georgia Varozza's blog. More details at http://georgiaplainandsimple .blogspot.com/p/expect-unexpected-emergency.html

- 25 lbs. oatmeal
- 20 lbs. white rice (brown rice turns rancid sooner than white)
- 15 lbs. pasta noodles (or 15 lbs. durum wheat berries to grind and make homemade noodles)
- 25 lbs. mixed dry beans and legumes (such as pintos, white navy, red kidney, lentils, and split peas)
- 20 lbs. sugar
- 5 lbs. salt
- 3 lbs. dehydrated whole eggs if you don't raise chickens
- 5 lbs. butter powder
- 1 gal. cooking oil (olive or vegetable, or a combination)
- 2 large jars peanut butter
- 12 lbs. powdered milk (comes in 4-lb. boxes)
- 1 lb. baking powder
- 1 lb. baking soda
- 5 lbs. yeast
- 1 gal. vinegar
- 1 lb. sprouting seeds (alfalfa and broccoli seeds are small, tasty, and easy to sprout)
- 1 gallon water per person, per day minimum (More is better, especially if you live in a hot climate. Also think about storing additional water for washing up.)

Homemade Laundry Detergent

1 bar soap
1 c. baking soda
⅓ c. salt
2 c. water

Grate the bar of soap. Mix soap, baking soda, and salt. Add the water and mix in a large bucket.

Homemade Toothpaste

⅔ c. baking soda
1 tsp. sea salt (optional)
1–2 tsp. peppermint extract or peppermint oil (see How to Grow a Victory Garden)
water

Mix first three ingredients, then add water until you reach the desired consistency

How to Grow
a Victory Garden

- Choose a place to plant your garden. Consider your backyard, side yard or front yard. Pick a sunny spot with soil that drains well. Window boxes, containers, and even roof-tops are good places. Most plants need at least six hours of sunlight, so plan accordingly.

- Determine what plants grow well in your area to increase your chance of success. Remember to include herbs and medicinal plants.

- Create compost using grass clippings, produce scraps, layers of newspaper, etc.

- Prepare your soil with homemade compost.

- Choose healthy plants or start seeds indoors. Make sure the room is warm (such as a bathroom) and well-lit. If possible, choose a room with a south-facing window.

- No space? Ask your local city offices if there are any community gardens, or help a neighbor who has growing space in exchange for a portion of the harvest.

- Tend your garden every day. Remove pests and dead leaves. Water as needed.

How to Perform CPR

How to Perform CPR on an Adult*
1. Place the heel of one hand on the breastbone.
2. Place the heel of your other hand on top of the first hand.
3. Position your body directly over your hands.
4. Give 30 chest compressions. These compressions should be fast and hard. Press down about 2 inches into the chest.

Note: It is not recommended that you try mouth-to-mouth breathing unless you are a trained professional.

How to Perform CPR on a Child*
1. Place the heel of one hand on the breastbone.
2. Keep your other hand on the child's forehead, keeping the head tilted back.
3. Press down on the child's chest so that it compresses about ⅓ to ½ the depth of the chest.
4. Give 30 chest compressions.

---

*from the National Library of Medicine

About the Author

Vannetta Chapman writes inspirational fiction full of grace. She is the author of several novels, including the *Pebble Creek Amish* series and *Anna's Healing*. Vannetta is a Carol Award winner, and she has also received more than two dozen awards from Romance Writers of America chapter groups. She was a teacher for 15 years and currently resides in the Texas hill country.

For more information, visit her at
www.VannettaChapman.com.

Center Point Large Print
600 Brooks Road / PO Box 1
Thorndike, ME 04986-0001 USA

(207) 568-3717

US & Canada:
1 800 929-9108
www.centerpointlargeprint.com